ISBN: 978-1-7360728-0-6

Independently Published

First edition

"If there's a book that you want to read, but it hasn't been written yet, then you must write it"

Toni Morrison

To my husband Chris and my children Estelle and Cael, without whom this book would have been completed 21 years earlier.

ONE IN THE BUSH

By K. G. Cooper

DISCLAIMER

In my opinion, "One In The Bush" is extremely childish, vulgar, coarse, has colourful language and at times possibly controversial. Now, if that is something that interests or intrigues you, then read on Macduff. If you feel that you may have a mild sensitivity to some or any of the above statements of facts, then may I be bold enough to suggest that this book is not for you. This is not a judgment call, you understand, it's a warning of sorts. You know yourself better than I to make the decision as to whether to continue reading or not. Please also keep in mind that it is incredibly poorly written.

It is a tongue-in-cheek romp that follows the exploits and adventures of three girls as they travel Down Under during a gap year. Ultimately, it is a tale of redemption, growth and friendship.

The intention behind writing this book is and has always been to hear, evoke and create laughter in whatever form that takes. When we laugh, we give ourselves over to the immediacy of the present moment which in turn gives us permission to let go of any tension. Laughter can help open our eyes to previously unnoticed absurdities that can make life seem less serious - the Platypus is the perfect example of this.

I believe that in that moment of pure, unadulterated release there is only joy which in itself can be immensely liberating and healing. For this reason, I make no apologies to the reader who finds it offensive - you take responsibility for how you wish to respond or react to One in The Bush. Don't shoot the messenger, or the writer for that matter. If, however, you feel drawn to "One In The Bush" in some way, or you feel the need for some witty banter, light-hearted entertainment and, in my humble opinion, some laugh-out-loud moments, then "Keep Clam and Carry on Reading".

I have changed the names of some people in this book as I would like to maintain their anonymity and privacy. I have also changed the names of some of the more challenging characters as I have accepted their apologies, forgiven them of any wrongdoing and am no longer as pissed off with them as I once was, nor do I want to embarrass them or their descendants. They may also be stronger than me and might want to beat me to a bloody pulp. The names of the horrible characters have not been changed, so if you recognise yourself in this category then you need to change, not me. All other characters, stories and events in this book, even those based on real people, places and bad behaviours, are entirely fictional. The secret to this creation is knowing exactly how to hide my sources…. hopefully.

Life is supposed to be fun. It's not a job or an occupation. We're here only once and we should have a bit of a laugh.

-Billy Connolly-

Lights, Camera, Action

BRRRIING, BRIING ......BRRRIING, BRIING.....
BRRRIING, BRIING.....BRRRIING BRIING...

JULES

Somewhere in my dream I am rudely interrupted by the constant ringing in my ears, just before George (as in Michael), leans in to kiss my already pouting, waiting, plump, wet lips. It's MY dream after all and a girl can dream, can't she? As the incessant ringing continues, it dawns on me that it's an external ring and not an internal one. It's actually a phone ringing, maybe it's Lesley.

I leap out of bed, catching sight of myself in the mirror as I pass, and see my reflection as a lolling, lumbering carthorse, dragging a white beanbag of all things, between my legs. Not quite the agile young Giselle I imagine myself to be. I answer.

"Lesley?"

"No, it's me."

"S'mee who?"

"Not Smee...ME."

"Me who?"

It's beginning to sound like a bad knock-knock joke.

"Mikey."

"Mikey who?"

"MY key doesn't work so help me out here will you? Phnarr, phnarr."

I'm right, a bad knock-knock joke.

"Mikey????........ As in Mikey???.... MIKEY??"

"The one and only, tall, dark and handsome… ha ha ha."
Silence.

"Okay, not so handsome, but tall. Lesley's boyfriend, Mikey. Ha ha."

Some more silence.

The laugh is undeniable, unmistakable.

"Omg, Nursie's, oops, I mean, of course, LESLEY'S boyfriend. Sorry, yes...MIKEY..."

I run through to Ange's room and start to shake her awake.

"MIKEY!" Pointing to the receiver.

"Everything okay Jules? Does my voice sound that different already? You've only been in Sydney a few months. Am I that easily obliterated from your memory?"

"Yes, sorry, I'm still half asleep. Jeez, is it really you? What time is it in Aberdeen? Why are you calling ME? Has something happened?"

"No, no, all good here. It's early evening but I wanted to make sure I caught you before you head out for the day."

"I'm afraid Nursie's, oops, I mean Lesley's not here anymore."

"Anymore?"

"Did I say anymore? I mean, anyway. She's on an early shift and not here."

"That's ok, it's actually you I want to speak to anyway."

"Really??"

Still gesticulating. Ange is feigning boredom, pretending to stifle a yawn and cutting her wrists.

"Yeah, I'm thinking I'm going to take some time off work and come over to surprise Lesley."

"What...Really? You're thinking of coming HERE to surprise her?"

Ange puts her fingers down her throat.

"Is that a problem?"

"Ehh...YES... I mean, what did you just say? It's a bad line, I thought you said you were taking time off work and coming here. Do you mean HERE as in Sydney here?"

This repetition is all for Ange's benefit, who has put the pillow over her head and gone back to sleep, not in the slightest bit fazed or interested by this turn-up for the books.

"YES, I'M THINKING OF TAKING SOME TIME OFF WORK AND COMING OUT TOOOO SURPRISE LESLEY DOWN UNDER. SOUNDS LIKE SOMETHING FROM 'DEBBIE DOES DALLAS'. BUT NOT. Phnar, Phnar."

"NOOOOOO. I'm not deaf you know, you don't need to shout, I hear you just fine."

"Sorry, I was trying to help you out as you said it was a bad line."

"Oh right. Yeah, she'll love that."

Ange's muffled laugh can be heard from under the pillow.

"I'm going to need you and Ange to help me make this secret operation work."

"Suuuure! We'd LOVE to help, wouldn't we Ange?"

Ange comes out from the confines of duck feathers and shakes her head.

"Not me. I'm having nothing to do with it."

"What did Ange just say?"

"She said she can't think of anything better she'd rather be doing."

"It would be a kind of covert operation of sorts."

"More than you know. I ... sure ... WHEN?"

"Probably not until December, which gives me two months to work my notice and come up with a wicked, cunning plan. She'll be happy, right?"

"Happy? I can't think of any of the other dwarves she'd rather be. She'll be cock-a-hoop. Over the moon. Thrilled. Ecstatic. We just have to locate her."

"What do you mean "locate"?"

"Did I say locate?"

Ange is nodding....

"Yes, I did say LOCATE. We'll need to find the perfect LOCATION is what I meant."

She breathes a huge sigh of relief.

"How exciting Mikey, why wouldn't she be Happy?"

"What did Ange say?"

"Oh, just ignore her, she's as excited as I am and is shaking, oh for feck sake. Nodding. Yes, NODDING her head as we speak. She's overjoyed."

"Everything ok? You sound a bit strange."

"Yeah, I've still got ….eh…. jet lag."

OMG…. why in the hell did I say that? We've been here for months. I do wish Ange would stop rolling all over her bed holding her sides, pretending they're splitting with laughter.

"I know we've been here a while already, but I have a chemical imbalance."

"Is alcohol and marijuana considered a contributory factor towards your 'chemical imbalance' Jules?"

I wish Ange would shut the feck up.

"It takes me longer than the average human bean to get over it."

It's all so cringey. I want to punch the lights out of Ange's smug face.

"I know we promised to give all communications a break until we were reunited, but I'm miserable without her and I'm really going to need you and Ange to help me make this secret squirrel plan work. Will you help?"

"You're happy to break your promise to her? She might be raging."

"I'll take that chance Jules. Being without her is like having a limb chopped off, you know like Tom without Jerry, Laurel without Hardy."

"Lesley without friends."

"What did Ange say?"

"Sonny without Cher, toast without butter, sex without a condom."

 Cringe.

"Yes, well, I'm sure we could go on all day Jules, but I need to get some work done here. It won't work without you. You in?

"Suuuure! I'm 110 % in and Ange is too. Whether she likes it or not."

Ange is shaking her head and heads off through to the kitchen.

 "Kind of a secret though, so no blabbing. It won't work if she knows."

"Rest assured, she won't be able to find out from us."

"Can you keep it to yourself without letting her know?"

 "You better believe it. When did you say you're coming out again? I mean out here, not OUT OUT."

Why did I say that?

"I think that's her coming back though Mikey. Better go before she catches us. I'll mark it in my diary."

"Yeah, right, like that'll be happening Jules. Have you suddenly started to channel Miss Marple?"

 "Shhhhhhhh, shut the feck up. NOT you Mikey, I don't want Lesley, yes Lesley, to hear us."

"You'd have to have a pretty loud voice for her to hear you Jules. Fat chance of that happening, unless you have a voice like a foghorn."

"Ignore her Mikey."

"I can't make out what Ange keeps saying, but I'll keep in touch through email nearer the time and we can plan the specifics, or pacifics as Lesley calls them. HA HA…...Jules? JULES??? We must have been cut off."

SHIT... SHIT …. SHIT…. SHITTETY SHIT. That's it, we're done for now. Ok, ok, deep breath. What do we do now? Where do we start? How do we start? Should we even start? Maybe I should call him back and tell him. No, no, that wouldn't be right.

"Hi Mikey, Jules again, I should have mentioned earlier, but Lesley is missing. She's been gone for a week already. No, no, we haven't tried to look for her yet. No idea where she is. Well we kinda think she's heading to The Bush, not her bush you understand, THE Bush, The Outback, Northern Territory. Yeah, no idea why she took off."

Nope that is NOT going to happen. We can't tell him that. Maybe tell him she's travelling.

"Yes, on her own. No, we didn't stick together."

That's not going to happen either, and I am definitely, definitely not going to tell him the truth about her disappearance. We'd come out of this looking really, really bad. There's only one thing for it, we're going to have to go find her and bring her back in time for the Bondi Beach reunion date. Yup, that's what we'll do, we'll find her and bring her back. Sorted, sounds like the perfect plan. What could possibly go wrong?

ANGE

HA, HA, HA, HA, Jules is having a complete meltdown, a total paddy, maybe even a mild panic attack. She's had a call from Mikey who's supposedly, allegedly, coming out to surprise Lezzers''. Well more like the surprise will be on him. She's NOT here, surprise, surprise, you've travelled 30,000 miles to see your girlfriend who's not actually here. She's disappeared without a trace. The look on his face will be priceless, especially when we tell him that we've not even bovvered' to go look for her. She just took off, no idea why. The letter she left was somewhat vague, even though it was as clear as that she wanted to get away from us. And I emphasize the word "US". Jules is ranting on now about leaving Sydney, buying a car and heading out of town to find her. That all seems a bit of a knee jerk reaction to me if you want my opinion. She'll be fine. Does she really think we'll be able to find her? What are the benefits to calling it a day here, buying a car, going on a road trip, finding her and bringing her back? Hmm, maybe experience some more of Australia, meet some new boys and have some fun escapades. Bob's your uncle, Fanny's your aunt and it's all smelling of roses in the garden of Lezzers'' and Mikey. When I put it like that, a road trip does sound like an exciting adventure, it actually doesn't sound like too bad an idea. She's probably got over despising us by now anyway, is lonely and ready for us to come get her, even though her last words to us were: "You two go together like Drunk and Disorderly. You're positively pitiful. Shame, SHAME on BOTH of you."

Perhaps I misheard her and she really said: "It's been an absolute pleasure travelling with you both this far, but time to move on, you take care now."

Close enough.

If truth be known, I'm bored and so ready to get out of Sydney for a while, maybe being on the road will help my liver deflate. Every cloud and all that.

"I've got the perfect solution Ange. Let's buy a car, follow her trail."

"And how do we follow her trail exactly? This isn't Hansel and Gretal - she won't have left us breadcrumbs you know."

"It's Nursie we're talking about here, she's bound to have left one. It's so simple, we follow her trail, find her and bring her back. When we do catch up with her, we'll apologise for any wrongdoings, she'll accept because that's her nature and we'll all travel back to Sydney for a Jolly Happy Christmas. No wucking furries mate."

"No wucking furries indeed. Do you really believe it's going to be that simple Jules? We're just going to buy a car, set off on a road trip halfway across Australia, find her and bring her back in time for Mikey's big reunion?"

"Look, Ange, there is always a solution to everything and this seems to be the perfect one. All we have to do is buy a car, find her and get her back before Christmas Eve."

"Have you heard yourself? BUY a fucking car, find Lezzers'' somewhere in The Bush and get back here for Christmas Eve? Have you lost your mind? Don't answer that, I already know what you're going to say. We have absolutely no idea where she is. Besides, we haven't a "Scooby Doo" whether or not she's even made it to The Northern Territory. Besides it's only, I reckon, oh let me think, 349,129 sq kilometres away! The only thing we know for sure is that she's got a job on an Aboriginal Reserve."

"It's a start, isn't it? Besides, I miss her. You must miss her on some small level?"

"Yes, about as much as an old man's urine stream misses the toilet."

Three months earlier, Edinburgh International Airport

ANGE

Cheesy peeps, my head is about to explode. We're taking the kangaroo route to Australia, hopping here, hopping there, stopping in Singapore for a night or two then on to Sydney. My head is pounding and thumping at the mere thought of it all. I'm too scared to open my eyes in case they burst, spewing out some soft, grey aqueous humour mixed with brain and tequila all over the floor of the concourse. It feels like I have the entire entourage of a building site wearing their heaviest tackety boots and a few extras thrown in for good measure, hammering happily away in my mental playground. Banging and stomping on steel girders against steel girders, all taking place on the main stage in my head. The bones of my skull are brittle, breaking and rattling around. My entire headspace has swollen to the size of a hot air balloon, and is on the verge of imminent explosion, spreading matter over the check-in trolley dolly and desk at Edinburgh International Airport.

"AGGGHHHH. The pain."

LESLEY

What a hullabaloo Ange is making. She drank far too much last night, in my opinion, and is now suffering the consequences. She's moaning, groaning and complaining that she has a tumour in her head, when we all know it's a self-induced hangover. My offers of pure unadulterated Vitamin C have been met with a wave of her hands and barrage of abuse.

"Leave me, Nurse Nancy, to crawl into a corner and die quietly."

Hm, if only. I've just recently met her, but my guess is this drama queen doesn't do anything quietly. I'm offering to help her tie her designer scarf around her head. And all I get is:

"Leave my fucking Steve McQueen" - I think that's what she called it -" scarf alone."

Could have been Alexander though... whatever it was, it ended with some kind of Queen. She ties the scarf around her head, covering her eyes as if she's scared they're going to fall out. Truth be told, I'd prefer if she ties it around her mouth. I'm a nurse and I know for a fact that her eyes are not going to fall out like she keeps insisting. I can't help shaking my head and tutting as she's her own worst enemy. A few effervescent tablets in some water will fix the dehydration. But no, she prefers to make a scene in public and wallow in her self-inflicted misery while imposing it on us and everyone else at the airport. I try to smarten her up a bit as she looks quite skuzzy lying on the floor. I brush her matted hair, gently I might add, and for a nanosecond I seriously think she is going to hit me.

" If you look better Ange, then you might feel better. Take a deep breath and breathe deeply. See if that helps?"

"Is that the advice you'd give someone who is having a stroke Nursie?"

Well I never heard the like - 'A' she calls me Nursie, knowing full well that's not my name but my vocation and 'B', well, 'B', she might even be right about the stroke as she's talking out of the left side of her mouth and there's a constant flow of saliva making its way to a stagnant pool on the airport floor where she's sprawled out very unladylike I might add.

It's only the third time I've met her and although the other two times were bad, they were mild in comparison to this. She must have really tied one on last night. So glad I left early as, with my sensible head on, I knew today was going to be a long day with a 16-hour flight ahead of us to Singapore. Neither funny nor clever, that's what I say. All that's missing is a crown over her curly, auburn locks to accentuate this Diva behaviour. It's only a self-induced blinding hangover she has, not going blind like she believes. I feel for her though, it can't be pleasant being in this much discomfort. She's actually treating me as if all this is MY doing. She's even refusing the pain medication I have offered. More fool her, it's only prolonging her suffering. If she wants to wallow in her own misery, then so be it. I'm so over Ms S Elfish. I'm only trying to help.

JULES

I've never seen a brawl at an airport before, but I think if Lesley offers Ange one more pain tablet, Vitamin C pill, cucumber eye mask, ice pack, or comes at her again with a hairbrush, shakes her head, lifts her eyebrows any higher or tuts one more time, Ange will lose it completely and rip her throat out. I've seen Ange raging before and it's not a pretty sight - think of a tormented bull with it's gonads tethered, being taunted by a wee blonde Barbara Windsor-type person bustling and fussing about in a garish outfit waving a red flag. It's what she gets like I'm afraid. Not the most patient patient, that's all I'm saying. Not a very good or willing one either. I know Lesley means well, but she hasn't gauged her audience here. Every man and their dog has heard Ange telling her to leave her be, for the umpteenth time. All this "I'm a nurse, I know what needs to be done here" stuff is all very well, but she's been bleating on for over an hour now. At least she's not focussing on me, or Mikey for that matter, who got up at 4am, I might add, to take us all here. He's waiting patiently for her attention so he can say goodbye to his girlfriend of three years. If I had a boyfriend and I wasn't going to see him for 12 months, then I'd be making sure I gave him a parting gift he wouldn't EVER forget in a hurry. She's very lucky to have someone totally besotted with her, a constant figure, there all the time, waiting on her hand and foot and not just on Friday or Saturday night. A big, burly, dark-haired Orkadian galah of a bloke. I swear she could even drive Mother Theresa to binge drink. She looks so sweet, demure, innocent and immaculate. Not a blonde hair out of place, not a crease in any of her clothes, even her modest makeup is perfect. She looks so together. Ange and I, on the other hand, look like bags of shite in comparison. Admittedly, Ange is worse right now, her long, curly red, voluminous hair is matted with goodness knows what. Her makeup from last night is merging with tears and is coursing its way like a lazy river down her face, dripping in coloured pools on the floor. She even has one of her false eyelashes stuck to her chin, giving her the Hercule Poirot look. She can't be told though, that she looks like an extra from The Three Billy Goats Gruff book series. Lesley, on the other hand, looks fresh, clean, together and ready for every occasion. Even a long-haul flight. She must have been up for hours in preparation. So have Ange and I mind, although we haven't gone to bed yet. Plenty time for that when we're dead.

LESLEY

Mortified, that's what I am, MORTIFIED. What was he thinking? Which part of all this does he think is quite so funny? Honestly, if I wasn't leaving him for 12 months, I'd swing for him, so I would. It's embarrassing and bad enough crying in front of the customs ociffer as we say our final goodbyes, weeping and blubbering into my hanky as he rummages through my carry-on. I do have an entire dispensary, so it is taking him a while to line up all my necessary medicines on the table in front of him, which incidentally are lifesavers in my opinion as you just never know what types of bacteria and viruses these foreign countries have. Totally different strains from the ones we have here you know. You can never be too unprepared, that's what I say. In fact, I was a Girl Guide for many years and their motto is "be prepared" which is exactly the example I live by. Maybe he thinks I'm a drug ass. That doesn't sound right. Donkey? Horse? I'm sure I'm on the right track though. Anyhoo, you know what I mean? Some kind of carrier thingamajig. I'm sure it's something to do with a donkey. Never mind, not important.

If it isn't bad enough him tossing my vials on the counter, completely ruining the alphabetical sequence they are in, I might add, there's a rather large queue beginning to form behind me which is making me feel rather tense. People are beginning to fidget. I can tell by their constant shuffling that they are becoming increasingly frustrated with the hold up, as am I. It does indeed seem to be taking a laboriously long time. The man looks into my bag and without breaking eye contact he pulls out a box wrapped in brown paper.

"What's this?"

"I'm terribly sorry Ociffer, I have absolutely no idea."

"It's Officer, Nursie."

"That is precisely what I said Ange."

"Did you pack your suitcase yourself Miss?"

"YES!"

"Would you mind opening it?"

I really have absolutely no clue what it is or how it got in my bag. I am as surprised as he is. Maybe some drug pin smuggled it in there while I was attending to Ange. You do hear about these stories you know. You can't trust a sausage these days, that's what I say. I open the parcel very slowly, listening for a ticking noise, not knowing whether it's going to be a bomb, powder or that green stuff that students like to smoke. In fact, now I come to think about it, why have they not deployed a squad to open it if they are this concerned?

"Mule, that's the word I was looking for, a drug MULE."

Did I just say that out loud? Nevertheless, I take the package from him and I gingerly peel back a corner of the beautifully wrapped parcel, only to expose a box of Milk Tray chocolates. My favourite. awwww, bless his cotton socks, Mikey must have slipped it in there when I was on nurse duties with Ange. What am I thinking about leaving him for a year? He really is a good man. Possibly even marriage material. The custom ociffer is still rummaging in my bag and, again without breaking eye contact, he stops, looks into the bag and looks at me.

"WHAT NOW?"

Truth be told I am beginning to feel a slight tremor of excitement, I'm not going to lie. Perhaps he's come across a small, wee blue jewellery box, you know the ones you get from Tiff Fannies or my absolute favourite jewellers, MacIntyres of Edinburgh on Frederick Street. Mikey has always been the romantic type, his final parting gift to keep me in check, not that I need that you understand, I have no intentions or desire of straying.

He deserves my complete undying loyalty and that is exactly what he's going to get. Without removing his hands from my bag, Agent Jack Mehoff beckons two of his colleagues to come join him. He looks even deeper into my eyes. I detect some slight amusement. He raises his eyebrows and without blinking says to me in an unnecessarily LOUD voice:

"Miss, I have to ask you once again, did you pack your bags yourself?"

"Yes."

Maybe too abruptly, but I really, really want my hands on the wee blue box. I can barely contain my excitement and I am tingling all over. I turn towards the girls. I can feel it in my groin girls, Mikey has put something very, very special in the bag for me. Something for me to remember him by when I'm travelling Down Under. There's some giggling going on behind the desk, but I'm eager to have it.

"Please take me out of my misery and just give it to me."

I close my eyes tight shut in anticipation and put my hands out, Oliver Twist style, to receive it. I feel something cool, long and oblong-shaped being placed in my palms, not the small cube box shape I am expecting. It has a smooth, silky, gliding feel to it, not unpleasant, not quite wet but not dry either. The texture is ribbed and has a glossy texture, somewhere between lip gloss and lipstick. What the hell? I open my eyes when the hysterical laughter almost bursts my eardrums. I look down with a mixture of dread, trepidation and excitement to see the largest, longest cucumber I have ever seen in my entire life with a condom on the tip nestled in MY hands. I can feel my cheeks burning.

"Miss, you're not allowed to take vegetables out of the country, you'll need to dispose of it any way you see fit."

"Something to remember him by, eh? Who needs a man when you have that gigantic gourd to satisfy yourself with Lezzers''?"

"I'm going to ignore that remark Ange."

"Being a nurse you must be used to seeing unusual situations with vegetables. Maybe when we get to Sydney you should consider starting your very own vegetable patch."

"You know I may very well do that, Ange, as I'm told I have green fingers."

"That leaves me in no doubt if you carry on playing with cucumbers."

There are peels of laughter from Jules, my fellow passengers and the ociffers. I look the customs chap squarely in the eyes, lift the offending article up high and drop it from a great height - well, not that great I must admit, I'm only 5ft - but great for me nonetheless, into the bin beside the table. It makes a resounding thump as it lands in the empty metal container and continues to vibrate there for ages. Is it a real vegetable or is it, in fact, one of those new fandangled' Ann Summers vibrators? I believe they even have one that looks like a rabbit, of all things. Not sure why a rabbit over any other animal. Regardless, I'm not going to be sticking my hand back in there to find out. What was Mikey thinking? So not funny. But possibly very useful on those lonely nights when I'm going to be loyal and faithful to him though. Too late now. I'm sure they sell cucumbers in Australia. I almost fall backwards over Ange who's back on the ground, still holding her head, ears and eyes, only now laughing so ridiculously loud. A tad over the top and put on if you ask me. It's really not that funny. I wonder if she's laughing at me or at the cucumber. I'm not sure.

ANGE

That has to be one of the funniest things I think I have ever seen in my entire life. It takes her a while to work out what the fuck she's holding. She isn't in the slightest bit amused. I'm not sure which plant-based giggle tickles me more, the cucumber or her beetroot face. It makes such a clatter going in the bin that I think maybe it is, in actual fact, a real vibrator. I'm now wondering if anyone will notice if I sneak it into my bag. I'm laughing so hard that I'm on the verge of throwing up again. Lezzers'' just got roasted by the custom officers for having a womb broom. She is protesting too much, in my humble opinion, to anyone who will listen that it must have been her boyfriend.

"Yeah, right that's what they all say you saucy, saucy thing. We've all seen "Carry on Nursie".

Good on Mikey, didn't realise he had it in him, let alone a sense of humour. Not sure Lezzers' sees it that way. Taking it waaaay too personally and oh so seriously. Puts a whole new definition to the word INTENSE. She's not even sure how to hold the damn thing. She's a nurse, for fuck sake, I'm sure she's held many a gourd before - even the pickled, old, shrivelled wrinkly ones. Shame she's not able to take it with her though, she's going to need it on those hot summer nights, when the beaches are burning and the fog's crawling over the sand and she's feeling like a Bat out of Hell. Either that or she may want to consider loaning it out to us at the very least. I'm okay with double dipping. Won't be the first and I'm quite sure it's not going to be the last.

JULES

That has certainly perked me up no end, but then the same custom's officer stops me and searches my bag. I'm sure there's no cucumber lurking there, so I have no idea why.

"No liquids allowed. You're going to have to dispose of this bottle."

"Eh, what? I don't think so. Do you know what this is? This is Irn Bru.[1] you know? Pure unadulterated liquid gold of the gods, that's what."

"I don't care if it's the piss of kings and queens, it's not going beyond customs."

"This is sacrilege. There's no way it's joining that phallic symbol disguised as a cucumber."

I open the bottle and slowly, deliberately, drink all 1.5 litres of the stuff. He stands there with his hands on his snakey hips and watches me drink every drop. I'm taking my time, trying to savour every last mouthful. Not an easy task, but totally manageable. I even manage a resounding, elongated belch when I'm done.

"Satisfied?"

"Not quite Miss, TSA has a 3-1-1 rule. We cap the size of any liquids, gels, creams, pastes or aerosols..."

"I'll show you airsehole."

"...that you carry on at just over 3 ounces: 3.4 ounces or 100 milliliters for each container, to be exact. This perfume is over that."

"Whaaat? NO, that's my favourite Opium, by YSL. I might not be able to get it over there. Besides, there's not much left, it's just in a big bottle."

"Sorry, rules are rules."

Maybe childish, but I start to spray every inch of me until it's all done, even my foof [2] gets a blast. I give him a wee puff as my finale. PRICK. I know I now smell like a brothel on opening night, but it gives me a huge amount of satisfaction to see his hairy nostrils flare out.

"Satisfied?"

"Not quite Miss, your foundation is also over."

"Whaaaaat? That's my very expensive 'Bitch face' foundation."

I grab it from him and start to smear it all over my face. There's much more than I realise, so I have to put it on my neck, arms and legs. No time for blending baby. I'm sure I must look like Pocahontas.

"Satisfied now?"

"Almost but not quite. Your toothpaste..."

Before I can stop myself, I grab the tube from him and begin to squeeze it down my throat like squeezy cheese. What kind of toothpaste is this anyway? It's revolting. It's got a silky, sleek, smooth finish to it and smells of roses. Roses?? I look at him and see he's still holding the toothpaste, twirling it round his fingers. Then what the feck is in my mouth pressing my cheeks to full capacity and dribbling out and down my top? Nooooooo, it's my very expensive face cream. Keeping my dignity and without swallowing, unusually, I might add, I take the toothpaste from him and put it in the bin, followed by my empty tube of face cream.

"Thaaatisfyd?"

"You're free to go Miss, have a safe flight."

I do try to say, "thank you", but with a mouthful of moisturiser, it comes out more like "Fack you".

Honestly your Honour.

ANGE

How in the hell are we going to sit in these tiny seats squished together like sardines? Well, smelling marginally better, thanks to Jules's overkill with her perfume. She has so much of it plastered over her fizzog[3] I'm surprised that through osmosis she's not pissed as a fart. We have to sit like this for hours and hours. The seats only recline back by an inch and every time I open my tray table I brush my breasts, which is very annoying, but to be perfectly honest, mildly satisfying. I'm glad I have the window seat, at least I can lean my head against the cool plastic, tremoring Perspex. Actually no, I'm not comfy at all. Perhaps the hair of the dog is exactly what I need. I have to pass the time somehow in this flying tin, so it may as well be inebriated.

JULES

Not really my first choice to sit in the middle of these two, as I can already feel the frostiness vibrating from Nursie. Her mouth is pursed like a cat's arse and she is as tense as feck.

"My mum used to tell me that if the wind changes, your face will stick like that."

She looks at me, pulls her Minnie Mouse eye mask down over her eyes and goes to sleep. Unusually, she hasn't smiled at anyone, let alone spoken since Cucumbergate. It was Mikey's doing, nothing to do with us, but she seems to be taking it out on us. All we did was laugh. She could have laughed at me with a full bladder of Irn Bru fit to burst, glistening lips, smelling like a hooker and resembling a Katie Hopkins lookalike. It's really tight in the middle. What's going to happen if I get claustrophobic and start hyperventilating? Ange has her arm over my arm and Nursie's elbow is digging more than three inches into my ribs. I give up, I'm going to join Ange in drinking enough so that I pass out, which is the only solution I see to being contained in this metal straitjacket.

LESLEY

If Ange's not careful she's going to give herself alcohol poisoning. She's already drinking again and the plane hasn't even taken off. Consuming this much on an empty stomach is not good for her or anyone else for that matter. I've decided not to waste my breath and say something I might regret, but the mini bottles are spilling over to my tray now. It looks like I'm the biggest culprit in their happy 16-hour binge, which I certainly am not, and I'm making sure the hostess knows that all the empties belong to these two lushes.

I'm trying to decide whether they're helping her out by putting them closer to her so she doesn't have to stretch or whether they're winding me up. Surely, they wouldn't do that, would they? Especially after the trauma I've just experienced. I'm beginning to think that Ange may also have an addiction, as now that I think about it, I've never seen her sober, ever. Or at least without some kind of alcoholic beverage in her hand to be pacific, even if it is only wine gums. Drinking at 30,000 feet is going to dehydrate her more.

"Perhaps you girls should consider the golden rule of one wine, one water to keep your hydration levels up."

Ange puts her fingers in her ears every time I begin to open my mouth.

"La di da, la di da, la di da di da."

"How rude. Everyone on the plane can hear you."

"Di da di da."

Maybe she has blocked ears and is trying to clear them.

ANGE

I swear if fuckin Nurse Nancy Loose Lips Lezzers' tutts once more in my direction, she'll develop blisters on her tongue. Bet she has some cream or magic potion for that as well. Well, I have my own wee magic potion right in front of me, it begins Char and ends in Donnay. It does amuse me no end to wind her up though by loading her tray with empty bottles. How easily I am entertained.

JULES

When we finally land in Singapore, we check in to the hostel and go to Bouquet Too Much outdoor food market which is recommended by The Lonely Planet Guide Book. It's a short walk thankfully, as it's humid, sticky, hot and it's 8pm for feck sake. Stifling really, I can barely get enough oxygen in my lungs and I'm struggling to breathe. I, for one, am starving and so ready to eat something decent after all that plane food. When we get there, I see not just one rat, but five, and we're not even at our table.

"This is not a good idea eating here. Perhaps we should go somewhere else."

"It's recommended, Lesley. Besides, rats are clean apparently and it's all part of the adventure and experience."

"That's all very well Jules, but I'm not sure what I have in my Mary Poppins medicine bag for food poisoning."

"Och get over yourself Lezzers', it's not like these furry vermin are pooping and peeing all over the food, the bottles and the tables."

"How exactly do you know that Ange? How do they know not to spray their toxic waste liberally and everywhere? It's disgusting and there's absolutely no way in hell I'm eating anything here."

"Suit yourself, it suits me fine."

"And me."

"It's like a bubonic plague playground waiting to happen."

I keep telling them both till I'm blue in the face that the state of the hygiene here is failing miserably, which is so surprising really, because the rest of Singers is shiny and clean. It must be a front to lure tourists in and what lies behind the facade of the Universal set design is the true underbelly of the city. The servers aren't very clean looking either. Their aprons are manky' with what looks like blood, excrement and chicken giblets smeared all over. I wouldn't be surprised if they've been scratching at their testicles then handling everything - and that's just the ladyboys. oh my Gawd', there are people, old and young, blowing their noses everywhere. They're closing alternate nostrils and projecting whatever contents they have from their nasal passage. Wherever it lands seems to be totally acceptable. Oh, my goodness, they're even spitting. I have seen my fair share of all things revolting, but this takes the biscuit. I have the constitution of a cow, but even my stomach is turning. There is not a fat chance in hell that I'm eating or drinking anything here unless it's sealed, and even then... I'm so glad I took a couple of antibiotics and a wee sup of Imodium before coming here. Purely as a precaution you understand, you just never know when travelling in these underdeveloped countries. Be prepared, that's what I say. I think Ange, just to spite me, is deliberately overindulging in the all-you-can-eat $5.00 buffet.

"You'd better ca' canny[4] on that tiger beer, I hear it's really strong."

My warning falls on deaf ears as they order another round.

JULES

Really? Who is she to tell us what we should and shouldn't do. Don't drink that, don't eat that, take this, take that, walk here, walk there, watch this, watch that. For feck sake, I'm beginning to lose the will to live with her. She's already gone through at least three travel-sized bottles of sanitizer, wiped down our table so much that she's practically removed the varnish. Won't make a jot of difference - it's Asia, what does she expect? She's not even tempted with the sticky rice as she thinks the water may be contaminated.

"How do you know that's even chicken? How do you know that's beef? Just because they tell you, doesn't mean it is. For all you know it could be monkey gonads. They eat monkeys here you know and dogs and rats. Plenty of them to pick from in this food market. Smells like horsemeat to me. The beer could genuinely be tiger piss, or rat piss."

YADA', YADA', FECKIN', YADA'.

"Lezzers', shut the fuck up. If you don't want to eat, then fine, don't, but let us eat and drink whatever we fucking well want. We're big girls now and don't need the food hygiene police on at us."

"No need to be like that Ange, I'm only trying to help."

"Well don't. Ange is right Lesley, it's not helping."

I know I'm rolling my eyes, but I can't stop myself. Ange seems to be handling it better than me, though annoying her by emphasising the amount she's shovelling in her gob, washed down by the bottles of beer she's inhaling. It is mildly entertaining though and has become an eye-battle standoff at the Not Ok corral. Ange is beginning to look like she might be struggling as she's actually straining to swallow. Her eyebrows are knitted together highlighting the number 11 between them. However, she is continuing to put food in her gullet, forcing down every bite. The white part surrounding her hazel/green eyes is turning pink. Nursie has folded her arms, sat back and is watching with those beady blue eyes and pursed duck lips. Her head is tilted in "I told you so" fashion.

Ange is definitely struggling with the backload of food and drink, but give her, her due, she's persistent if nothing else. I can almost see the last 'pork' dumpling fighting to squeeze past her reluctant tongue. She's doing this entire charade just to annoy. This non-verbal confrontation appears to have no strategy whatsoever and I don't think it will allow Ange to come out victorious. If she carries on like this, I fear it will be ten points to Nursie.

ANGE

Boy this is a busy wee place, lots of people, dogs, cats, chickens, ok, and a few rats, not that we'd have been able to mistake them for anything other than what they are as Lezzers' keeps pointing them out. It's an open-air food market in Singapore, FFS, rats are a given. May well be their national animal for all I know. It is very humid though. My usually buoyant curly, auburn locks are feeling less jubilant and limp, but as Jules says:

"Fa's looking at you onyway quine".[5]

I agree, no-one knows me here and no one is paying the slightest bit of attention. They seem to be more interested in swatting the three flies per person giving everyone the Pig Pen from Snoopy look.

Lezzers' has one of those bamboo fans and is waving it manically about like a windmill. She's even speaking with a blocked nose as she says the smells are burning her nostril hairs. Relax Princess Perfect Polly, nothing is coming over you. The more she bats, swipes, squeals and swats them, the more the flies and mosquitoes seem to multiply. Serves her right, silly cow.

In the meantime, I've managed to find the quickest, nimblest route to the hot bar, looking nothing short of a majestic gazelle on the plains of the Savannah. Weaving here, dodging there, it's not that hard to navigate the quickest route to the buffet display once you know how. Time and time again I navigate the maze of people, small children and animals, more to annoy her than anything else.

She's now an authority on all things Asian. Bleating on about spices, hygiene, and how to acclimatise gently and safely into new cultures. Three times now, to be precise, I've been able to duck and dive through the crowds and be back at my seat in record time. I should be in the Guinness Book of Records. I don't know what she's bumping her gums about anyway, she's not even eating - just yapping on and on, making the whole experience wholly unpleasant for us to sit and enjoy our dinner. Speaking of bleating, it probably is goat, but what does she expect, organic, grass-fed, plump chicken? Either way, it's really, really good. I have to say though, that it is unexpectedly filling. It does creep up on you all of a sudden and I do feel rather stappit[6] - perhaps the speed I'm consuming it isn't helping either. Not that I'm going to let on and see the smarmy satisfaction on her chubby face. I can feel all the monosodium glutamate pudding at the back of my throat as it gently trickles its way back up, moving like a slow-moving glacier, coating my tongue, laminating it with a fine, white, sticky finish. It's testing every muscle of my ever-increasing swollen belly. Och well, never mind, I've got the constitution of an ox. I think I've eaten a whole one of those tonight as well. I'll be fine, but oh me, my belly is now bigger than hers for sure, and that's really saying something. My determination to prove her wrong is possibly a mistake, it seems that it's going to backfire on me and be my downfall. Not that I'm going to let her know. Actually, I think I'm in a bit of trouble here, but by hook or by crook I'm not going to let it show. I know exactly the way to the toilet, having passed it on my previous food trots, so I'm going to calmly get up, without drawing any attention to myself and make my way over there. There is considerable pressure on my diaphragm and I'm beginning to find it hard to breathe. The rate of my swallowing has increased and it all seems to be building up to a downward pressure. I'm sure no one has noticed. Fa's clocking[7] me anyway? Actually, only one pair, the beady eyes of Lezzers' haven't left mine. She surely has no clue if I nonchalantly get up and remove myself. After all, it's not my first rodeo.

LESLEY

Ange isn't looking well at all. She has beads of sweat on her upper lip and her breath is coming out in short snorts through her nostrils. I've seen this defensive posture before in bulls. They usually grunt, snort and make low bellow noises when feeling threatened. All that's missing here is her pawing the ground, head shaking before she enters the fight or flight state. I do hope it's the latter as I'm not ready to be bowled and gored by a mad cow. She's almost opaque in colour and very clammy looking. I've seen this before on the wards, the lull before the storm. I am in absolutely no doubt that she is about to chuck up. I'm directing the slight breeze from my hand-held fanny towards her to see if that helps.

ANGE

I know the suspicious eye of Lezzers' has latched on to me, but I can't say anything as I'm afraid there will be a whole lot more than words come out. It might be easier if I just pass little puffs of wind from my backside, like a tiny dray horse in fun-sized batches as inconspicuous as I can, again, nonchalantly so as not to attract any attention. I can feel the slight breeze from her fan which does seem to be helping, again not that I'm going to admit that one.

JULES

Cheesey creeps, either a small rodent has died under our table, which wouldn't be a huge surprise given the state of the market, or someone is farting like a dray horse. It smells of something or someone hideously decomposing and rotting from the inside out. I glance at Ange as I can hear a slow, steady stream of hissing like steam coming from her direction. What is that? It's like air being released from a balloon. It's absolutely repulsive. Nursie is staring suspiciously at her also.

Ange's eyebrows are raised to her auburn hairline, the skin puckered and folded in. Never have I seen anything quite like this, they're almost in a perfect V-shape. She looks like Widow Twanky from some amateur dramatic pantomime. What's going on? There's definitely something dead lurking close by, much closer than what's on the buffet table that's for sure.

ANGE

I'm resolved, this is something far more serious than gas and it is most certainly potentially explosive. I'll be damned if I let Lezzers' see this.

LESLEY

She looks like she's slipping into a state of shock. She has absolutely no idea how quickly even a small amount of grease, fat, fur and gnat's piss can make its way through one's intestine at breakneck speed. Can't say I didn't warn her. I close my fan and use it to point in the direction of the toilet. I know where it is as I had to pay a wee visitation there earlier. There is no point in warning her what she is about to experience.

ANGE

I know exactly where the toilets are and do not need her patronizing directional handheld "fanny" cues. She must think I'm a fucking kid. It isn't too hard to get there, but not sure if it is the actual toilet or a piss take. Same thing at the end of the day, so in for a penny in for a pound, put your best foot forward and all that. I think Lezzers' is taking the piss but I'll deal with that later. There's a time and a place for that, I have other more pressing things to deal with right now. It's neither funny or clever, as she says on a regular basis. Well, she is neither funny or clever, and it's nor, and not "or " for the record. I brace myself, take as deep a breath as I can, which isn't that deep due to the backload in my mouth, and head into the dark, dank, musty latrines, going where no man has been before. There's a hole the size of a large dinner plate, smaller than my arsehole for sure, in the ground with a filmy layer of water in a bucket and a stained, cracked jug beside it. Surely not. Please no, let this all be some hideous nighthorse, a cruel and mocking mirage of my imagination and not even a pleasant one at that either. To think that the local sanitation inspectors, or whatever they're called here - in fact, there very likely isn't such a title, in fact, there clearly isn't such a job. You'd never get away with this in a proper restaurant and I use that word loosely. No way you'd want to "rest" here, maybe "rant" for sure in this restroom, as Americans call it.

At least I'm here with the contents of my bowels still intact, only just, mind you. I do feel slightly relieved that at least I'm here, small hole or not. In a few moments, this will all be behind me, s'cuse the pun, soon I will be completely relieved, literally and physically from this nightmare. I think that the smaller, safer-looking stall at the farthest end looks like the best choice. It's far enough away from the door just in case there's some noise accompanying the removal. Wouldn't want to disrupt anyone's dining experience, now would I? The pressure on my anus is at biblical proportions and I know that evacuation is imminent. My eyes are smarting - sweat, or it could even be Tiger Beer, is literally trickling down my nose and dripping from the tip. Like a gentle stream of sorts but it's certainly picking up the pace, more like a torrent river than anything else. Everything is clenched so tight that nothing can slip through, thanks to my extreme yoga practice and my teacher yogi Nos Mo King.

I'm very conscious that threatening my very existence is a menacing forthcoming sequence of physiological events that are going to take place and be entirely involuntary. I'm also aware that, when that moment arrives, there is absolutely not a fucking thing that man nor beast can do to avoid it. There are no brakes on this high-speed train Baby. I have to be smart and quick, very quick, in fact, if I'm going to prevent any more collateral damage than is necessary. I need to make the shift from it all being internal to the expelling of whatever needs to leave externally. Make it like Britain and exit the EU as smoothly and effortlessly as possible. Well, that turned out to be a shit show, so not going with that one.

Thankfully I bought a pair of those backpacker harem pants with the chevron pattern on them from Bugis Street. They're very trendy, cheap, comfy and oh so handy at this particular moment as they have an elastic waistband. Thank you Hezus. Ever so slowly, I slip my thumbs under the elastic, move numero uno, tick. Gently, smoothly, easily done. At the same time, I do need to bend slightly forward to direct my derriere towards the miniscule hole. I slide them down over my hips oh so steadily, with ease and grace, hooking my slippery, sweaty, sausage-shaped fingers gingerly further into the waistband of my knickers at the same time. I pull them together in one swift, systematic, collaborative, awe-inspiring action. This is an Oscar Worthy performance right here. This is where it all aligns perfectly in a flawless expulsion of waste matter, courageously evicted with dexterity, poise and speed.

Timing is paramount here, and if I do it properly, then I can empty my full, expanded bladder at the same time. It is the ultimate move in confidence, coordination and finesse and will rival that of a Bolshoi ballet dancer, or if I'm not careful, a lumbering cart horse. Nonetheless it will be a spectacular sight that I can eventually share with my grandchildren. Just as I'm about to set off the chain of events, I hear Lezzer's scratchy, squeaky, Glaswegian, irritating, Minnie Mouse voice at the stall door.

"Whatever you do Ange, do not under any circumstances look down at the floor. Keep your eyes straight ahead, in fact, close them if you can."

Now, what does any normal human bean do when someone says that? When they tell you not to do something, hmm, hmm, exactly, you do it. I make the regrettable mistake of looking down at the floor and tucked away in the corner, near her pink croc-clad foot is a massive pile of steaming puke. How did she know that was there? Maybe because the only thing missing from it is all the Milk Tray wrappers. Already there are cockroaches, leggy, winged, unidentifiable beasties, bathing and munching in, on and around it.

LESLEY

Oh no, she's clocked my vomit. I couldn't help it, I had to make myself sick as there was no way I could sit in the food court with anything in my stomach, it had to be completely empty. I thought it would help me feel better. She'll never know it was me.

ANGE

In normal circumstances, vomit doesn't really bother me, all it requires is a bit of mouth breathing, no wucking furries, sorted. However, I am now in physical pain from the tremendous weight on my abdomen and the tight clenching of my buttocks is now sooo intense that I hit a rarely experienced gag reflex.

LESLEY

OH NO!!! I've seen this before, once the gag reflex starts, there's no going back or holding back. I sidle away from the open stall before all hell breaks loose.

ANGE

Where is she going in my hour of need? Calls herself a nurse? Retreats at the first sign of a wee[8] bit of diarrhea. The combination of events are all proving too much for me.

LESLEY

I recognise the moment of doomed projectile vomiting immediately, however, my attention is diverted to the going-ons at her other end.

"OH, NO"

Her anti-aging provocative underwear are only as far as her knees. The last time I felt like this was when I watched Murder On The Orient Express - you just know you're watching a train wreck about to happen. She doesn't know this, I'm sure, but sickness always takes precedence over bowel movements, no matter what rocket is being launched from the booty. Something I learned and have always remembered from my nurse training. Maybe it's only taught in nursing school and you have to be an actual nurse like I am to know it. Apparently, it's an evolutionary thing since defecating yourself won't kill you, but being sick takes presence of mind to accomplish so that you don't choke and asphyxiate yourself. Who knew? Ange certainly doesn't and no point telling her all the facts right now, just the basics. I'll leave it for another time so she knows in the future. It won't help her now anyway, but it is a very interesting fact of nature.

She looks eerily like a deer caught in headlights. I can just picture the headlines now: Astronomical tidal waves of human excrement drowns 1,000 diners at the popular open-air food market in Singers. I'm well out of the way as the enormous plug of foul, rotten masticated vermin, embedded with pockets of tepid liquid, comes barreling from her backside. I have never seen anything quite like it in my entire life, and being a nurse, I have seen plenty. I'm still worried she's bending over so much that her head is lower than her backside and she's only halfway down towards the hole.

"SQUAT CLOSER TO THE HOLE. LOWER YOUR BUTTOCKS, THEY'RE TOO HIGH!"

ANGE

Florence Fucking Nightingale has been twittering on about something to do with choking, then starts shouting at me to squat, when all hell breaks loose from my bum-hole. I feel the very heavy doors of my sealed vault explode from the internal combustion. Thankfully I believe I am not going to be sick like she has predicted, as I've managed to swallow it all back and hopefully channel it out the other end.

The evacuation tsunami is of such force and precision to the back curve of the toilet hole that it slams high into the wall behind me instead, missing the intended hole completely. I can feel the sweat on my neck and I feel really, really dizzy and light-headed. I think I'm going to faint.

"NOOOOOOOO!!!! STAND UP Ange!!!!"

Lezzers' is yelling at me to stand up, but I know that I've reached the point of no return. I'm not sure whether this is relevant right now, but I have always considered myself to be relatively stable gravitationally wise. Well, not always on a Friday or Saturday night, but then they have extenuating circumstances usually. I am going down, no matter who is yelling at me. Somebody try to stop me.

LESLEY

I have never witnessed such a force of nature either in a ward, YouTube video or a David Atomborough documentary. The only thing that comes close to this is watching firemen on a training exercise practice with an industrial power hose on a large, deep pool of mud, water and sand, even that isn't really close to what I'm witnessing now with my own beady blue eyes.

There is a significant amount of the putrid stuff on the rim of the hole though, and she is planning to sit on it. Lordie Lordie. It's like being an extra on a horror movie set - you know you have no lines and are just an observer. While all this self-deprecating is going on, I notice that, in actual fact, she's going to be sick after all. By the time she collapses over the gaping void, her cheeks are being pumped up like an overinflated helium balloon.

ANGE

My mouth is filling up with a goodly portion of the "rat" dumplings which is the last thing I remember consuming. I'm trying to sit up and place my head slightly above my opened, bent legs, aiming for the hole which I know is there somewhere. My head is now positioned between my knees, directly above the waistband of my trousers, which are midway between my knees and ankles, but, call it a gut feeling, something isn't right with this picture. I remember with horror that I'm not wearing my skinny jeans but I'm sporting the local attire which identifies and differentiates me as a backpacker, and god forbid, not a tourist. I was so pleased with them at the time, drawstring waist, elasticated ankle, crotch down to my knees, but there's so much material and it doesn't seem quite that straightforward. With very little warning, and with one almighty barf,[9] kinda' how I imagine childbirth but from the other end, some 20lbs of rancid, pureed, all-you-can-eat Asian buffet mixed with beer and what looks like pubic hair, and two thirds of undigested and indigestible yeast rolls, leave my body and are deposited and cradled in the crotch of my non-tourist Harem pants. It all comes to a steady, sloshy stop, resting in the hammock of my patterned groin.

LESLEY

In the space of several seconds, I hear some leaking gas, some more gagging and retching and then, as quickly as it starts, it stops. Very surreal. I can't believe what I have just seen. Here I am staring at Ange, in the smallest toilet on the planet, with her new trousers full of puke and her back smattered in excrement, which is also at least 5ft high and covering 90% of the stall. At exactly the same time, in some delusional, hopeful fashion, we both instinctively look for the toilet roll in the desperate hope that someway, somehow, they have a roll a mile long made of industrial strength, highly absorbent paper, preferably attached to a showerhead at the very least.

Nada Nothing. Mịmī xarị as my phrase book says.

ANGE

FUCK FUCK FUCKETY FUCK!!!! This is one of those FUCKING countries that uses their hands to clean themselves, isn't it?? I would need to have Lady Liberty's hands to clean this shit up. Lezzer's eyes are the same size as her gaping mouth. She's a nurse for fuck sake, surely seeing this is second nature to her.

LESLEY

I have never ever, in all my life, seen anything like this before, EVER. It's completely out of this world. So surreal.

ANGE

Before you can say "Jack Shit", she is suddenly back in her Nurse Nancy mode.

She disappears out the door twittering: "That's another fine mess you've got us in, or yourself at least. Don't go anywhere."

"Ha di bloody ha."

LESLEY

I know exactly what needs to be done here. I order Jules back to the hostel to get towels, clean clothes and room spray.

JULES

What the hell? Nursie suddenly appears like the slappers, oops I mean clappers, bustling her way through the crowded market, ordering people around. I'm commanded to go to the backpackers for a change of clothes while others are instructed to bring buckets, and BUCKETS and BUCKETS of water to the loos.[10] Noone is questioning her authoritative manner. Must be important. She's very direct, matter of fact and no one is doubting her mastery or what she needs.

ANGE

It all seems a tad OTT and unnecessary, more like an exercise in military precision. Lezzers' has taken control of the extremely hazardous, toxic situation, has delegated, directed and managed the troops. There is no questioning or misrepresenting the tone of her voice. It is a calm, no fuss, no nonsense, no complaints, determined approach. Who knew? Still sounds very bossy.

LESLEY

The water pressure on the water hose isn't as powerful as I'd hoped, but considering how precious a commodity water is here, she's lucky to have it at all. The crap mixed with puke is still dribbling down her body in slow motion, trickling under the door and escaping into the drains of the open-air food market to join all the other shite of the day. Lovely.

JULES

Ahhhh, that's why she wants room spray. She's optimistic. I'm not sure which is the worst smell, the two bottles of vanilla room spray or the fetid, foosty[11] air mixed with Ange's discharge. I do, however, know it will take a whole lot longer for everyone's singed nasal hair to grow back.

ANGE

Lest I ever forget, please let someone remind me that nurses are worth their weight in gold. Lezzer's is worth quite a bit it seems, maybe platinum. She's still very annoying though.

"Thanks, Lezzers', I'm not sure I could ever have done what you just did."

It's Lesley, and och, don't mention it, that's what I'm trained for after all."

"Okay, it's a deal, let's never ever mention this again - ever. Beer anyone?"

JULES

Not quite sure of the full, nitty gritty details as to the horrors that took place in the Singapore latrine, but when the girls emerge, Ange is wearing the Hawaiin shirt and board shorts I'd bagged from the lost property box. It should be called the please lose it property box. She doesn't seem too bothered by the whole thing, seems happy enough wandering about looking like a giant pineapple, especially with a bottle of Tiger Beer in her hand.

"Better ca' canny Ange, your body has been through some trauma, mild, but trauma nonetheless."

"Don't sweat the small stuff, Lezzers', I've got it all under control now. The only side effect I see here, is that I'm totally exhaustipated."

"Exhaustipated? You mean exhausted?"

"No, exhaustipated. I don't give a shit."

"Is that meant to be funny?"

"Maybe, but not as funny as renaming this place The Suppository."

"The Suppository?"

"Yeah, because it's a complete dump."

LESLEY

While I was visiting Jurong Bird Park the following day, literally watching a big, fat black rat drag a heron by its squawking neck down into the depths of its burrow, Drunk and Disorderly were necking Singapore Slings at Raffles Hotel. Thankfully, it rendered them unconscious by 5pm, so a relatively peaceful evening was had by all.

It is so lovely getting to know my fellow Trackers, a hybrid of travellers and backpackers. I'm learning how to play backgammon, a few card tricks and I'm able to give back by sharing a few first aid tips I've learned from my travelling so far. I'm well aware it only takes a minute or 15 to share, but it may save someone's life in the future. They seem far more open to listening than Jules or Ange. I tell them that when feeling nauseous after a trip to a foreign food market, they should eat ginger in some form, sniff peppermint essential oil and control their breath. They seem so appreciative of my informative advice. I tried to share this free guidance to the other two, but all Ange could say was:

"The only ginger I want to eat is Prince Harry."

Australia

LESLEY

We fly to Sydney the next day without any of the debacle, humiliation and drunkenness of the last airport adventure or flight. Sydney is simply one of the most beautiful, amazing, cosmopolitan cities I have ever had the good fortune to see, let alone I'm getting to live here for a while. How lucky am I? It offers nearly 150 miles of breathtaking shoreline with natural beauty and dazzling iconic architecture.

It already feels so much more like home. We fly in over the harbour, lucky enough to see the opera house and the bridge from above. The sprawling natural harbour is also home to the famous Bondi Beach, apparently the core of an alluring beach lifestyle and thriving surf culture. One of the most magnificent and best patches of sand that I have ever seen in my life. The water is to die for which I believe happens regularly with rip tides, drownings and a handful of shark attacks. I'm told there are signs and warning flags posted everywhere it's unsafe to swim, so it's neither funny or clever to ignore them, that's what I say.

The locals here seem so much more like us than the Singaporeans, they even speak the same language, just a whole lot easier. The food is fresh, divine, delicious and gourmet worthy - not a drop of grease or animal hair or faeces in sight thankfully. I have already managed to secure a job through a nursing agency at Bondi Junction before we even set foot on this originally Aboriginal land, so feel truly blessed and grateful when we find a lovely flat at 19, Hastings Parade, within walking distance of the sea.

Jules and Ange are in no hurry to find work, but I need to. Jules's parents are divorced and they each send her a monthly guilt-allowance cheque. I believe Ange is almost estranged from her alcoholic mother, far be it from me to judge, but they do say alcoholism runs in the family. Her dad is dead and left her a considerable inheritance, I understand, so neither of them are in a great rush to secure any work.

I believe that getting familiar with the locals is, in my opinion, important to understanding and getting to know a culture. Ange believes she can get the same results by drinking at local bars, watching and getting to know the lifeguards, surfies and nubiles at the beach, which is a stone's throw from the flat. Just beautiful. I wish my Mikey was here with me to be part of it.

It's only a two-bedroomed duplex but it is plenty big enough for us. I'm more than happy to take the sitting room, the sofa is also a pulldown bed and is comfy with a snuggly duvet and a couple of fluffy cushions. It will be fine, no need for anything more… other than Mikey that is. Besides, it's the only room with a TV, and, as I am addicted to Neighbours, it will be even better than fine. I am looking forward to living in the same country as Harold Bishop, Madge, Mike Young, Scott and Charlene and the rest of the family. I feel closer to them already.

Jules and Ange toss a coin to see who gets the biggest bedroom. Another reason for me getting the sitting/bedroom is that they're the ones 'entertaining' the other sex and need more privacy, not me. I'm staying loyal to my Mikey. I wonder what's he doing right now? He'd love this garden - it's south-facing and walled, a shared space with the other three flats. So far, no sign of any of our own neighbours, which is a shame as you need to know and get on with them as you never quite know when the poo poo is going to fit the shan and go all cattywampus.[12] I'm going to bake a batch of cookies and drop them in with a card to introduce ourselves. A bush in the hand catches the early bird and all that. It's the right thing to do.

It's literally a five-minute walk to Bondage Beach, oops I mean Bondi, but that's what Ange is calling it and it's stuck. I personally prefer not to think before speaking, so it just comes out the way it does, and more often than not, I'm just as surprised as everyone else to what I say. Och, I don't pet the sweaty things anyway, I just get on with it. I'm loving my superduper wee jobby[13] at the local hospital in Bondage, tch, there I go again, Bondi Junction. The shifts are long and the pay is not great, but where in the world do they pay nurses their worth? Hmm?? Exactly. That's only my humbug opinion, you understand. Luckily, I'm not in it for the money, I see it as a calling. I like to make sure the girls know where I'm coming from.

"This is my mission in life girls. I feel it in my waters."

"You're the one always harping on about cures, so perhaps I can offer one here. One or two electrolyte tablets in some water will help."

"Och you are a silly billy, Ange, I meant that nursing is my true and inherent passion and vacation."

"No shit, Sherlock."

"A stab in the dark here, Ange, but yours and mine may well be drinking, taking narcotics, shagging and dancing like Beyonce - that may well be our pure unadulterated vocation."

"I resemble those remarks Jules, but fairy snuff, I surrender to all things debauched and hedonistic."

Who am I to judge? There's a big, bright yellow circle in the sky most days which makes a huge difference to one's mood and wellbeing. Makes me want to hum a merry tune and whistle while I work. I really, really hope that pair of barflies settle down soon, find a job and stop behaving as if they're teenagers on holiday in Shagaluf. It's so warring having them being in full-on party mode all the time. They don't even try to be quiet when they come in at 2, 3, 4 in the morning with their dates, and I'm not talking about the fruit of the palm tree here, but a voluntary coupling of two, or sometimes three or more unsuspecting, usually Australian surfies, for some hanky panky. They know I'm probably in bed after a 14-hour plus shift but that isn't stopping them stomping around like a herd of eleflumps, laughing like hyenas and screeching like crows. They can be such retrobates at times. Make that most of the time. It's exhausting, and more often than that, I know I have to get up in two hours for my next shift. I can hear them in the kitchen making a mess, cooking, baking goodness knows what.

Experience has taught me that they'll run out of juice just before I have to get up, crash out in their respectable rooms with whomever they have brought back, leaving the entire shambles for me to clean up when I get home. They do know I am on early shifts.

JULES

I know it's only 4 in the morning, but I can't sleep, I can't sleep, I can't sleep. It must be jet lag…or something, even though we've been here a few weeks now. Maybe it's all those Red Bulls and vodkas I had at The Tram on Bondage Beach, either way I can't sleep. A cheese toastie washed down with a sleeping tablet might do the trick. I'm sure Nursie has something for this in her first aid stash that I can borrow. I try to shake her awake, and after a bit of tutting, she hands me some melatonin. I take at least five because they're herbal, so I should be okay. She isn't particularly chatty which is unusual as she's usually keen for a twitter. She's often got something to say about how lovely the weather is and how sitting in the garden drinking tea is almost perfection personified. I do wonder how she can sleep so easily and naturally though. It would drive me mad everyone coming in at all times and making such a hullabaloo. It must be the sleep mask, wax earbuds and constant buzz from her white noise machine beside her bed that does the trick. She should have held out for one of the bedrooms, but she insisted, so was met with no resistance from either of us. Ange and I had to play rock, paper, scissors. Can you cheat at that game? If you can, then that's how I reckon she ended up with the biggest room. It's actually fine by me anyway as she has more visitors, or hagbackers as she calls them, than I do.

At least Nursie isn't entertaining, well at least not men, that is. She's proving to be very entertaining and fodder for us. Her malapropisms are a gift. I'm quite sure I'll be doing my fair share of making merry though, so having our own rooms is perfect for that purpose. Nursie, in true nursie style, had already lined up a job before we even got here, which makes me feel marginally guilty, and I do mean marginally. Okay, I don't feel at all guilty that she needs to work and we don't. She worked a few jobs to pay for this trip. She's an adult orphan as she keeps reminding us both and has to make her own way in this world, unlike us who had a "privileged upbringing".

She bought a small flat in the west end of Glasgow and makes no money from it really, just covers her costs, so she has to work - as she keeps reminding us on a daily basis. She knows full well that my parents are divorced, are in other relationships and find it easier to throw money at the problem - which is me, it seems, rather than love, acceptance and guidance. It's not my fault. Who needs them anyway? I can do this all on my own.

I have some money that I saved from my part-time job, where I actually met Lesley as we were both waitresses while she was at nursing school. I was studying psychology at uni. If push comes to shove, I know I can call either or both the parents again to get a bung[14] if needed. They do send the occasional cheque to cover any costs. Sometimes it works, as they're in direct competition to see who can better the other and be the most loving, yeah right, parent.

Ange is in a slightly different situation as her beloved dad died a few years ago, leaving her a shitload of dosh. She's estranged from her alcoholic mother, and has little to no contact with her older brother, whom I have only met a handful of times in all the years I've known her. They do seem like two peas in a pod, hence the conflict I guess. Ange and I went to an all-girl's private primary and secondary school together, and although we were friends, we never really ran in the same circles. I occasionally saw her at the same uni where she studied, and I use that term loosely, English. I was surprised she even found out I was going to Australia for a gap year, but even more surprised when she said two weeks before we left that she was "Gracing us with her presence".

In hindsight, I never ran it by Lesley, not that I think either of us had a choice in the matter. She was coming and that was that. Anyhoo, my point is that neither Ange or I had to get work, but I feel obliged to try at least so I don't come across as some entitled, private school yahoo. I applied for a receptionist job at The Sydney

Herald last week, and low and behold, they're giving me an interview tomorrow, actually, TODAY. The melatonin pills are doing diddly squat and I know Nursie has some more goodies in her Spongebob toilet bag, so I'm going to score a few sleeping pills while she's out for the count pretending to be awake. She doesn't even hear me, let alone stir, as I nab a couple and scarper before being caught red-handed. I can at least get a couple of hours' kip before I need to get ready.

I've not had very much, in fact any reception experience, but how hard can it be to answer a phone? I studied psychology, can string a joined-up sentence together, well, Monday through Friday, 8am to 5pm at least. Weekends I have more difficulties with the joined-up speaking than usual. I look good, so it's a bit of a slam dunk really. First impressions for the clients and all that.

I heard Nursie tell Ange that if she took a tablet at 9 pm, then she'd sleep straight through till the next morning, so if I take half, well quarter then, I should get a few hours at least, better than none. Can't be arriving with Gucci bags under my eyes. The tiny, wee torpedo-shaped, white feckers are far too small for my sausage fingers to half, let alone quarter, so I think I'm going to make the executive decision by taking a whole one. Nothing is happening so I'm going to pop another one. I head through to the kitchen to finish my toastie before going back to bed and, just as I'm putting it in my mouth and about to swallow, I'm startled by an apparition of a small blonde pocket rocket wearing a nurse's uniform, hands on hips and mumbling something I can't quite make out. Her lips are moving, but the volume is turned down, or it could be that my hearing is muffled somehow. She shakes me. Aggh, to my horror I realise I must have bobbed off with my head on the kitchen table and my right cheek and ear are nestled comfortably in my half-eaten cheese toastie. What's happening? I can still feel one of the tablets at the back of my throat. What time is it?

LESLEY

I'm sure Jules has an interview at 8am, so not sure why she's sleeping in the kitchen with her head in her cheese toastie. I spy the packet of sleeping tablets and the melatonin.

"Did you take these? BOTH? TOGETHER? You'll be like a working zombie all day Jules."

"Walking, Lesley. It's a walking zombie."

"That's what I said, didn't I? Regardless, if you don't try and flush them out of you immediately, then you won't be working or walking. I'm telling you right now, missy, and that's a fact. Neither funny nor clever to go mixing your drugs."

"Okay mum, now I have to dash or I'll be late and so will YOU."

JULES

How can I flush them out? Drink loads of water, that'll do the trick. Jeez. Let me backtrack and get some kind of semblance here. Right. Started with the sleeping pills I stole, oops I mean borrowed from Nursie, which are the size of tic tacs and my stumpy fingers were never going to be able to half them, let alone quarter them, so I remember taking one, then thinking it wasn't working, so I took another, which I can still feel at the back of my tongue. FECK. If I flush it out by drinking some water, then it might slip down my throat and I'll never make the interview. I'm going to try to cough it out instead. Cough, cough. This is exhausting and I can feel my ribs threatening to break under the constant hacking. It's still lodged there, not budging.

I look in the mirror and can see the tip of the pill at the back of my throat like the top of Casper the ghost popping up to say boo. Cough, cough. The obstructive wee blighter's not dislodging, that's for sure. This is not going to happen on my watch. By hook or by crook, it's coming out. That's it. Hook. I can see it there and try to hook my fingernail round it and flick it up and out, but it's making me gag involuntarily instead. Surely it won't make too much difference if I swallow the whole thing. I can go to my interview and then come home and sleep. Or I could go to sleep now and get another job. No, no, quitting is for snoozers, I mean losers. My financials are depreciating quicker than Bono signing up for a Humanitarian convention in Dublin, and I refuse to call mum and dad again to wire me some money over before the end of the month. It's all very well getting money from them, but really, how will I grow and learn as a person by doing that all the time? Hmm, I sound grown up and quite mature already. Who knew?

Lesley has a nursie job banking or something like that, she said, I wasn't really listening. I'm assuming that it has something to do with hospitals otherwise there's some cruel bastard not telling her she doesn't need to be wearing a nurse's uniform to work in the bank. Mind you, someone's needs might be being met there. She seems happy enough, judging by the constant, never-ending warbling and whistling that comes from her general direction though. I think she must be working 48 hours a day as she's not coming out at night to play with us. Her loss. Grrrr, it's still there but appears to be dissolving at a rapid pace, given the white paste covering my tongue.

It'll take a wee while to get to the interview, which gives me no time to change my clothes from last night. Och, they'll be fine. I feel like I'm daydreaming, in a dwam. I'll walk there, a nice brisk walk will blow the cobwebs away, and I probably won't even notice the effects of the tablets.

ANGE

Where the hell is she going in her nightie, high heels, bed head, handbag, crud on her cheek and an umbrella? It's not even raining. Well, maybe she's afraid she'll get sunstroke. She's in a complete stupor and hasn't brushed her hair. Clearly Lezzers' isn't around or she'd have been all over that dishevelled dag like white on rice and done it for her.

"Good luck with the interview. Bring back some milk and a pizza will you. Pertty pleeeze."

JULES

Everything seems to be happening in slow motion. People are staring at me as I walk by them. Maybe I'm being too paranoid, but to be perfectly honest, I'm not even sure now whether I took sleeping pills, birth control tablets or laxatives. Only time will tell I guess. It's still hard to swallow and I can feel it, whatever 'it' may be, teasing the edge of my tonsils, on the verge of slipping down, past the point of no return. Cough, cough, cough. How is it possible that it's taking this long to remove the feckin' thing? I'm still unable to retrieve it as it seems to be quickly dissolving into a thick mush. Maybe if I wipe my tongue with a hankie I'll at least get some of it off. Or maybe I should hold my breath then cough without opening my mouth and get it out when it least expects it. That'll do the trick. I feel as fresh as a dozy, oops I mean daisy. It doesn't take too long at all to get to the place, and although I do feel my eyelids drooping slightly, I manage to hold them open as I lean on the reception desk, soon to be my desk, I might add.

Not quite sure why I brought my umbrella, it's glorious out there. Why is it open? I'm inside. Bizarre. What am I going to do with it now? When the receptionist isn't looking, I hook it onto the leaves of the fern beside the desk. She'll never notice. My actual eyeballs are drying out, which is helping keep the lids open thankfully. Not sure why the receptionist, eh excuse me, the TEMPORARY receptionist keeps staring at me – surely she's seen people doing facial exercises before. Tempted to ask her if she'd like my photo, rude cow. I'm not in the slightest bit surprised they're replacing her, she's so unpleasant.

I'm trying desperately not to blink any faster than I think I am. It feels like I'm watching everything in high speed stills to the tune of yakety sax. I really need to take my attention off my eyes and focus on something else. There are many, many, many framed photographs on the back wall behind Moodonna, the grumpy receptionist. There are awards, framed newspaper headlines and photographs adorning the entire surface of the wall. A rogues' gallery for sure. The same old geezer appears to be in almost every photo, print and poster. He's standing in all his glory with David Beckham, the Queen, Kylie Minogue, Huge Jackman, Bob Hawke, Kerry Packer, Russell Crowe, a real rogues gallery if ever I've seen one. Oddly enough, in some of the pics, not all, Dame Edna Everage is also there. I think it's her anyway, could be Elton John. Maybe even Fozzie Bear from The Muppets. My focus is a tad blurred, but I'm pretty sure there's no mistaking that fine, almost balding, purple hair doo and those ridiculous oversized coloured eye glasses, defo Dame Edna. How does she manage to get in all of them? Especially the one with the Queen. I'm still tittering away at the ridiculousness of it all, when MooDonna calls me through for my interview. I'm slightly taken aback to see that the gentleman in all the photos, not Edna, but the other one, is the one

with the ginger hair greeting me. Large, bordering on rotund, with
a combover of at least 12 strawberry blonde hairs, and the most
orange face I have ever seen. Think Oompa loompa and you're on
the right track. Now that I'm closer, it might even be that
Uhmerikan twat from The Apprentice. Could be. I swear he looks
me up and down at least twice. I know I'm cute, but there's no
need to make it quite so obvious. Probably fancies me, and it's
definitely that insidious, egotistical lech from The Apprentice.
There are a few other indistinguishable men sitting around the
board table also.

"Sorry for the wait..."

"No wucking furries. You'll get it off when you're ready. A
bit more exercise, less pavlova and you'll be hunkydory. You don't
look too bad by the way."

"Pardon?"

"In all the photos at reception, you look, well, not too bad,
you know, happy with all those celebrities. Not quite sure how
Dame Edna got her ugly mug in so many though - photobombed
most of them, no doubt, the complete Prima Donna that she is.
How do you know her anyway?"

'I don't know her."

"Did I say Dame Edna? Silly me, I meant Elton John."

" I don't know him either."

"Divine??"

"No."

"Fozzie Bear with a frock? Phyllis Diller?"

I'm beginning to detect a slight irritation creeping into his voice. I am being too paranoid, perhaps it's curiosity.

"I do not know and have never met Elton John, Dame Edna Everage, Divine or even Fozzie Bear, let alone had my photo taken with any of them."

"It's just that I was admiring your photo gallery, like I said, at reception, and in a considerable amount of them, you have your arm round, well, I'm going out on a limb here, but some kind of drag queen lookalike. Not even a great one at that."

I know I should have stopped there, but I have him hook, line and sinker interested. The three other blokes sitting at the table are fidgeting for some reason and they all have their heads down and are rubbing their brows. If I'm not mistaken, they look like they're stifling laughter. How many men does it take to interview a receptionist in the first place? That's a rhetorical question, but it does beg an answer, why so many men to interview one receptionist? I have heard that Australian men are chauvinists, but surely not this blatant. Did I say that out loud? I can't tell the difference at the moment between my inner world and what's being heard in my outer world. Very surreal.

They're still all twitching slightly, not the head gaucho, but the rest are. No doubt jealous they hadn't noticed the photos before. They can't even lift their heads to make eye contact with each other, let alone me. That's how good I am. Slam dunk. No eye feckin on my watch boys.

"You're mistaken."

"Come again?"

My blinking seems to be ramping up and it's getting harder to keep my eyes open. I'm sure it must look like I'm flirting my Betty Boo eyelashes at them.

"YOU ARE MISTAKEN YOUNG LADY."

"I'm NOT. Come, come with me and I'll prove it, come, all of you come."

Off I march, confidently, out of the room and down the corridor with them eagerly trailing behind.

"Look!"

I point to the closest one.

"There's the one where she's looking incredibly butch, and if I may be so bold, slightly obese and ruddy-faced. In this one, her makeup looks like a small child has been set loose with a pack of colouring pens, either that or she's auditioning for the role of Witchy Woo.... look.

"That one, ha, she's tried to backcomb her receding, balding hair to give it a fuller look. More like a fool's look. Ha, ha, she's even trying to cover the fact that her lips look like a dog's anus with ruby red lipstick. You can put makeup and a frock on a pig, but it's still a pig at the end of the day. Her jowls are in a different time zone from the rest of her body. Wouldn't you agree?"

Everything begins to move in an even slower, dream-like motion, like the Cornish Pixies from Harry Potter after receiving The Immobulus Charm from Hermione. The pill is definitely beginning to take effect after all. I swear there is tumbleweed drifting through the reception. It's suddenly very chilly and I involuntarily shake and my head starts to bob up and down as if dooking for apples.

There's something about the way MooDonna hides behind her hands and the three other blokes stand there with tears in their eyes, mouths gaping open like a toad that's been stepped on, tells me that I am somehow mistaken.

I can feel myself begin to tremble uncontrollably, blinking rapidly, and at that very moment, the urge to cough comes over me and the tic tac frees itself from the depths of my oesophagus, shoots across the room at breakneck speed and lands on the lapel of Donald's Saville Row suit. I'm hoping it happens quickly enough not to be noticed. It blends in quite well with the other tiny specs after all. His face has turned from a mild orange shade to, well, more like a bright red angry shade.

"That's not Elton John, Dame Edna, Divine, Phyllis Diller, Fozzie Bear or some drag queen. That young lady happens to be my WIFE. You're fired. Interview over."

ANGE

OMG, that has to be one of the funniest things I've ever heard. I'm not able to keep my face straight as she tells me about what she remembers about her interview. She comes back looking like a bag lady in her nightie with her umbrella attached to a plant tucked under one arm, a bottle of milk under the other, and holding a pizza. How she got back in one piece is a miracle, as she still looks like she's sleepwalking.

I'm laughing so hard when she tells me, and to add insult to injury, she fell asleep in a chair at the reception and only woke up much later when the paramedics were shining light in her eyes. They had to give her the once over, which I'm sure perked her up immensely, then kindly dropped her off at The Flying Pie, our local pizza and sausage roll place around the corner. She even managed to snag a double date with them for tonight. Yippee. Winner winner chook[15] dinner. Well, maybe not quite, she didn't get the job. But someone might get a job later if they're lucky, a hand job that is.

"Plenty more jobs in the classifieds as they say."

"Why didn't you stop me going out in my nightie?"

"Didn't think it looked too bad. Besides, you'd still have said what you said to Donaldo, even if you'd been dressed to the nines and all suited and booted. You don't want to be working for a company like that anyway if they can't see the funny side to that. On the plus side, you must have got the job, because he couldn't have fired you if you hadn't."

"I feel sick."

"Hand the pizza over here then."

I open the box and there is no fucking topping on the bloody thing. Jules swears blind she asked for a cheese pizza with olives, artichokes, anchovies and pineapple, but it's a blank circle of dough. What a cheek they have exploiting a vulnerable bag lady. I don't have the time to walk around there, so I'm going to call them, give them a piece of my mind and demand a replacement immediately.

"G'day, Flying Pie here, how can we help?"

"Yes, my very fragile, vulnerable friend picked up a pizza from you an hour ago and you gave her a box with a frisbee bread."

"A frisbee bread?"

"Yes, just a bread circle with no toppings."

"Sorry to hear that, if you'd like to bring it back, we'll be happy to replace it for you."

"We live around the corner; would you be kind enough to drop one off. Pretty please, we're getting ready to go out and only in our underwear. Our flatmate is a regular customer, spends almost all her wages in your shop eating you out of sausage rolls and pickled eggs."

"Ahh yes, you must be talking about Lesley, I recognize the similar Scottish accent."
"Similar, but not, I'm an Aberdonian and she's a Weegie.[16]"

"Not sure what that means, but she's lovely regardless. Always smiling, always has a kind word to say to whomever is working or even a customer. Because it's for her, I'll gladly make an exception."

No need to tell him that Lezzers' isn't here, she might get the crust if she's lucky.

"You'd better start choppin those pineapples, she'll be expecting extra."

Now that's what I call service, not even 20 minutes later the bell goes. I open the door, holding the offending open box, displaying the blank pizza dough base. There is a boy, or perhaps a Wee Jimmy Krankie impersonator, at the door in his Flying Pie uniform which is much too big for his munchkin frame.

"See? You must have been preoccupied with your schoolwork or something, but you totally forgot to put any toppings on the pizza, not even a cheeky wee olive to be seen."

He takes the box from me, closes the lid, turns it over, opens it again and shows me the pizza with the mish mash of toppings scrambled over the now top. In her adulled state, the silly cow must have walked home with an upside-down pizza box. Now who looks the fool?

"I can only apologise, Jimmy, but I am one of Jules's carers, Lezzers' being the other. She's part of the care in the community programme and sometimes makes these ridiculous mistakes that most normal people, like you and I, wouldn't make. Certainly not me anyway."

"No worries, have this one on the house."

He says this in his squeaky pre-pubescent voice as he hands me the box the correct way round. I may have slammed the door in his face, but who cares. Unlikely I'll see him again unless I'm passing the primary school playground anytime soon.

"Come on Jules, I'm getting cabin fever, let's go to The Bondi Tram for a hair of the dog before we meet our hot dates. It'll cheer you up, besides they're having a $1 tequila shot night. How could it possibly go wrong? Would you mind changing before you go? I don't want to be mistaken for nursie doing her bit for society by voluntarily taking out one of her care in the community patients down to the beach for an ice cream. Whose needs are being met there begs the question?"

She comes through to my room 30 minutes later wearing a two-piece suit, a bralette and a mini skirt, edged along the hem and top with shells.

"Nice shell suit."

"It's not a shell suit."

"Is it a two-piece suit?"

"Yea. Where is this going?"

"Does it have a gazillion shells attached to it? Yes. Nice shell suit."

"What the shell are you on Ms. Shellfish? Now, shell we go out drinking and dancing?"

"Speaking of shells, Nursie says she doesn't care for eating crabs or any other crushed Asians for that matter."

"She also doesn't care to think before bumping her gums."

"Cruel, but fair. Now, call me old-fashioned, but I do think your skirt needs to be longer than your vagina. You take a slight bend forward and everyone will be able to see the remnants of the sleeping pill at the back of your throat. Just saying."

"Ah well, as Nursie would say, jealousy gets you everywhere. Now let's go party."

LESLEY

Got back to Hasting's Parade after a 14-hour shift to a lovely peaceful, quiet house. Pure adulterated bliss. I stopped in at The Flying Pie to pick up some sausage rolls for us all, but as there is no-one here, I can have them all to myself. Wee Jimmy, who works at The Flying Pie, was a tad strange tonight, if truth be told, and kept saying how he admired and respected everything I do and all I have to put up with. Not sure what he was on about, but told him the feeling was neutral nonetheless.

I took my rolls and a few cheeky pickled eggs and trotted home as I'm eager to get back and watch Neighbours. It's at a really exciting part where, if I'm right, Scott is going to ask Charlene to move in with him. Doesn't get much better than this, well, if Mikey was here watching it with me, that would make it perfect. We could snuggle on the sofa bed watching it together while eating the sausage rolls. How much better does it get than that?

It's fabulous being here in Australia, it feels like I'm so close to all these characters. In fact, Jimmy, at the Flying Pie, also watches it. I think maybe everyone who is anyone watches it here, so I do like to go in and have a blether about what's happening. He even gave me a free roll tonight as he said I deserved it after 'pizzagate', whatever that means, possibly a new show I need to look out for. He told me it had amused him and his colleagues no end. Regardless of what he meant, it was unnecessary, but very kind and thoughtful. There is never a reason not to be kind in my opinion.

It's actually lovely to have a regular place you can go to and be recognized immediately, other than a drinking establishment, that is. Just saying.

Jules and Ange feel the same way and do boast that everyone knows them also, but again, that's the pubs, the nightclubs and their seedy hangouts. I'm sure I know exactly what they're known for, but it's their reputations, not mine. Just saying. Not for me though - I would much rather they know me at the pizza parlour, the shops and the hospital. Jules and Ange aren't in the slightest bit interested in what I have to say, think or feel anyway. Last week when I was telling them the storyline of only the most watched soap in the world, Ange, who had only been half listening anyway, or not listening at all, actually thought I was telling a real story, about real people, bless her.

"Silly billy that you are, I'm talking about Neighbours. It's not real, but only based on real stories, people and events."

"Good to know, not. It's also good for you to know that's 30 minutes of my life I will never get back. You need to get a life, Lezzers'."

"It's all based on true stories, you know, and there's always a lesson to be learned in each and every episode."

"The only lesson I need to learn is where the off-switch is and for the telly also."
I'm going to rise above it. It's not worth getting into it with her. I'm going to focus on tonight's episode instead, which is going to be incredibly good as Scott is going to ask Charlene to move in with him. Have I already said that? Perhaps that's why Mikey's nickname for me is "Dory." You only have a 10-second window with me and then, poof, just like that, it's gone. I can't wait though. If the theme tune isn't the national anthem here, then I don't know what is. It certainly should be.

JULES

We leave Nursie a note telling her we're at The Tram on Campbell Parade, Bondage Beach. She'll no doubt want to curl up on the sofa eating sausage rolls and watching her beloved soaps rather than come out to play with us. The place is packed to the gunwales. Everywhere I look there seems to be folk taking full advantage of $1 night. Tequila is being slammed, snorted or spewed all around us. The waitresses have the bottles in their gun holsters and are certainly working for their money. I'm not sure whether I'm going to get pissed, stoned or pregnant just by walking on the positively sticky, tacky carpet. I'm sure there are cultures, viruses and bacteria hibernating in the threads just waiting to be absorbed through the soles of my flip flops. Ange is wasting no time snorting, chasing and chugging down the liquid gold, which isn't actually gold in colour, but some clear cheap shite probably made by squeezing the secretion from the carpet every night. Yuck. She reminds me of one of those baby birds with gaping mouths waiting for its next sustenance. She's quaffing[17] the stuff as if it's going out of fashion and is in every position imaginable, upside down, backwards, forwards, inside out as the alcohol is poured down her throat. Only the door jamb swing restraint is missing from the drink line up. At one point, I look over and see her being held upside down by her ankles as her mouth is being filled with 'tequila' by the shot waitresses. The gauchos in their chaps grab her hands and feet and start to swing her. The first time is a tad violent and as she's propelled forward and backwards swiftly, the regurgitated liquor is projected in a spectacular spray over anyone and everyone that is within close proximity. Thankfully it isn't anything worse than spirits and it'll dry soon enough. Some extra 'je ne sais quoi' to the carpet pond.

"What's wrong with your face?"

I notice as she's dumped unceremoniously to the fetid ground.

ANGE

As soon as Jules mentions my face, I notice that I haven't got my complete vision and everyone and everything looks kinda droopy. This is possibly what a stroke looks and feels like. The gauchos have clearly dislodged my eyeballs from their sockets. What's happening? Why does my entire face feel like it's dissolving?

JULES

WTF! Her left eye is almost closed and her right one is the size of a saucer. Quasimodo eat your heart out. I'm not sure if she's salivating or it's a stream of tequila dribbling out of her swollen lips. I mean seriously WTF? Maybe all the drugs I took earlier are indeed having an effect of sorts and I'm hallucinating. If Nursie had been here rather than eating pastry-encased sausages, watching back-to-back episodes of Neighbours, then she may have been able to tell if Ange is having a stroke or something. She's obviously having a complete reaction to the tequila, which is probably sperm, piss, saliva and blue agave all mixed together… Well, I know that she's not allergic to the former as she can easily be a vessel for the world's sperm banks.

"I think you should go to the toilets and take a look for yourself."

I would have gone with her, you understand, but I'm not sure my own legs are stable and they still feel fragile and wobbly after Tic Tac Gate. They still feel decidedly hollow, and earlier on I actually involuntarily won the dance competition just by crossing the floor, not even trying to gyrate. NOT that I'm complaining you understand, it's a $100 prize money and a bottle of tequila. The sleeping pills are still coursing through my bloodstream, mixing with tequila, beer and pizza. Strange really as I've only spent $20, so not sure why I feel unsteady on my pins. I can only stand, fixed or glued to the same spot, and watch as she ironically tootles across the dance floor to the beat of Razolight's Stumble and Fall. She'll never win Dancing with the Stars at this rate, although she's staggering uncontrollably, she still appears to be keeping the rhythm. What is she doing now? Is she doing what I think she's doing? Shirley not. Very odd behaviour.

ANGE

I ever so casually cross the dance floor, trying to get to the dunnys[18] to inspect the damage, but I'm not actually sure I know where they are, so I pretend to boogie as I look around for them. I think I maybe spin a wee bit too much, as my head continues to spin well after I believe I have stopped. I pretend that it's completely deliberate and that I'm rocking my inner John Travolta disco dance move. Ah, ah, ah ah, Staying Alive. Even if it's just to hold myself steady. Hips swivel, feet shuffle, back and fore, hand to the ceiling to the floor, back to the ceiling again. Thanks to Mrs Cruickshank for the lessons I didn't fully appreciate at the time when I was in fourth year at secondary school. I hope I don't suddenly get it mixed up with The Gay Gordons that she also taught.

Who's looking at me anyway? I certainly hope not that cute gaucho I plan to take home later. That's what I'm trying to convince myself nonetheless. Fellow gyraters do seem to be giving me the body swerve though. I need help. I'm aware that my face feels somewhat tight and swollen. When I look down from my open eye, I can see my cheek in very close proximity. It's BRIGHT red, taut and throbbing. On the plus side, a balloon has no wrinkles, so I look much younger than my 23 years. I spot a good-looking girl standing at the back of the nightclub staring at me. She looks very approachable and somewhat familiar. Have we met before? I know what I'm going to do, I'm going to ask her where the bogs are. I glance over my shoulder to see where Jules is. She's staring back at me, shaking her head and pointing frantically in another direction for some reason. Yeah right, you might fool others, but not me. Trying to pay me back for the "shell suit" and "vagina" comment no doubt. Sorry Love, no flies on me, well maybe a few coming from the rancid carpet, but I'm not going to fall for it.

JULES

I can see Ange contemplating her next move and there is nothing I can do about it, as not only am I stuck to the floor, I can feel some warm liquid swilling about in my mouth, KNOWING without a shadow of a doubt that if I swallow, it'll come back with a vengeance. I try to windmill my arms about to get her attention and tell her she's heading in absolutely the wrong direction.

ANGE

The pixelated, blurry girl is still there, looking in my direction. Even with my temporary fuzzy vision, I can tell she's very friendly, call it instinct if you like. She's wearing a very pretty top, tight fitting, emphasising her big tits. It has small flowers, I believe, adorning the strapless ensemble emphasising her ample cleavage. She still looks vaguely familiar but I can't quite put my finger on it. I can tell that she's one sexy, smokin' hot mama though. Not many people have the confidence to get away with a boob tube like that. The closer I get, I can see why she's hanging at the back against the wall. She looks like she's had some facial trauma, maybe a burn, maybe surgery, maybe both. Good idea showing off lots of bosom to divert attention from her somewhat grotesque profile. Not quite the Adonia I initially thought. Hence why she's by herself I guess, like Norman No Mates. I focus on her as much as I can and step confidently towards her, trying to show that her distorted facial features aren't in the slightest bit disturbing to me.

"Scuusse ne? Dew ooo naw whey da toyles a?"

It's hard for me to speak as my face feels so tight, it feels like it's about to burst.

It's getting a bit awkward as she appears to be mimicking me. The cheek of it, in fact, two very large bulging ones at that. She keeps staring at me with her gaping mouth, eye half shut in a Hunchback of Notre Dame sort of way. She literally looks a real train wreck close up, like someone has slapped her with a raw piece of meat. A well slapped farmer's arse[19] if you ask me. I've started, so I may as well finish. I'm going to have to raise the volume level somewhat to a shout as she may possibly be deaf as well.

"WHEY A DATOYlEH A?"

English might be her second language, so I give her the benefit of the doubt by using my best charade acting. I tap two fingers to my upper arm giving her the two syllables clue, one finger now. The word toy, as in the first syllable of the word toilets, is too hard to act out so I decide to go with the "sounds like the word boy" instead. I point to my genitalia and dramatize someone small with a tiny penis. Most people would get it for sure from my enactment, but all she does is imitate me. She's the freak of nature, not me. I wonder how she got past the bouncers and allowed in to this exclusive discotheque in the first place? It's rather pathetic actually. I'm tempted to just punch her balloon face and be done with it. I begin to swear loudly at her, certainly loud enough for everyone there to hear what I'm having to deal with here. She remains looking at me, parroting every little thing I'm doing. Who in the hell does she think she fucking is, Jennifer Saunders? I ignore the gentle tap on my shoulder.

"TELL me where the FUCKING toilets are bitch?"

I see that Jules has come up behind her and they're both looking at me. She's laughing and putting a comforting arm around HER shoulder. It almost feels like she's putting it around mine as well. How the hell does she know her? I'm the one almost in hysterics after all. I'm slowly turned around to face her. WTF is going on?

JULES

I see Ange bellowing at a mirror fixed against the back wall. She seems very distressed and apoplectic. Everyone is giving her an understandably wide berth. I manage to get myself unstuck and sludge my way across the dregs towards her. If there was a prize for the best Frankenstein walk tonight, I'd bag that prize also. I gently put my arm around her, turn her towards me and guide her to the toilets. I'm not sure she realises she is berating her reflection, but that wee gem can wait until tomorrow to be shared. Ange tries to knead her face like Playdoh into some kind of normal state. I decide to take a well-deserved seat on the pot while she finishes up manipulating her face like the vintage squishy rubber finger puppets. There's no way she can be seen in public like that. It just goes to show that monsters can indeed live among us and periodically show themselves. She's unquestionably showing that side of her personality tonight. I know I need to sober up as the music is still pumping loud and furiously in my ears, and the tequila, beer and pizza are lurking like the crest of a wave somewhere in my gullet, undulating over my uvula. The remnants of the sleeping pills still coating my tongue are only adding to it. I'm going to stay in the cubicle, riding the Mexican blue agave waves, until it all settles down. If I close my eyes, perhaps it'll ease up. I suddenly come to, rather abruptly. I know I'm on a mission of sorts, for what I'm not sure, but I need to get out of here quickly.

Ange is nowhere in sight. I wash my hands and try to dry them under the broken hand machine. A very helpful, eh not, girl tells me that I have my hands under the condom appliance and not the dryer.

"I know that, I'm only testing your observation skills. Besides, I'm actually going to buy some as I feel it's someone's lucky night."

She isn't in a hurry to leave, so I'm forced to buy some rubber johnnies so I don't look completely stupid. I buy a packet of apple-flavoured ribbed ones, two packets of the Glowing Pleasures and three edible ones. I'm sure they won't go to waste. I find Ange back on the dance floor, jigging about with a couple of cute boys who look very much like the paramedics from earlier. We all seem to be stuck on the carpet - who has a carpet as a dancefloor anyway? Swaying our bodies to and fro to Tina Turner's Private Dancer as she belts out "All the men COME in these places, and the men are all the same, you don't look at their faces, and you don't ask their names, you don't think of them as human, you don't think of them at all, you keep your mind on the money, keeping your eyes on the wall". Hearing the word "COME" reminds me of my recently acquired purchases weighing heavily in my pocket so I suggest we take the party back to our pad.

"They are even dishier without their uniforms on. Hopefully, if all goes according to plan, we will see them in the uniform they were born in. I wouldn't kick either of them out of the bed for eating crackers, so we may have to flip a coin. Very dishy indeed. My first real Aussie bloke, well almost, but no need to count the others as they weren't actually in Australia.

LESLEY

What time do you call this? All of a sudden, I'm rudely awakened from a very passionate kiss with Scott Robinson by an almighty crashing and banging. Oh no, I think our flat is being burgled as I hear glass being broken and thuds. It does sound like half of Sydney, along with some heffalumps, are through the house. With a huge sigh of relief, I can now hear Ange's booming voice. Within two seconds the place has turned into a scene from Mamma Mia and Dancing Queen comes on, accompanied by a few screeches, lots of laughter and random words that are in no way associated with any song I know of. Perhaps it's the rapper M and M's, but certainly nothing from my playlist. I can hear male voices, so decide to put my eye mask back on, secure my soundproof earmuffs and be thankful they have decided not to come into my bed/sitting room to party. Every cloud has a sliver of a lining.

Somehow, I manage to doze off to the beats that are still penetrating my head and vibrating my bed. I awake some time later, it feels like 30 mins but when I look at my bedside clock, I see that three hours have passed already. There is an eerie sense of stillness in the air. Has everyone left and/or gone to bed? Just like that? Have they quietly gone to their respectable rooms with their respective men? I'm straining for any clues, but can't tell. I watch the light from under my door for a minute or two. Nada. I get up, slowly open it and inch my way out to the hallway. The lights are all blazing, but nothing. Actually, I can now detect something. It's very, very faint, almost like a lapping sound, like a dog drinking water. Have they brought a dog back with them? The noise is definitely coming from the direction of the kitchen, so I gingerly tiptoe along the corridor towards the supping noise. The closer I get, the more I hear the guzzling noise. Surely a very big dog drinking something. With my back against the wall, I pass their two closed bedroom doors, creeping closer to the sound. I can see the lights are on in the kitchen and the ceiling fan is whirring gently.

The back door to the flat is wide open and the porch light at the top of the stairs leading down to the garden is off. I move carefully through the kitchen towards the back door, and in the dim light of the moon, I can just about make out a mass lying at the bottom of the steps, a mass of auburn frizz cascades over the bottom step while the rest of the form is sprawled on the grass. There are two bodies entwined. Absolutely no question who one of them is, but what are they doing? Have they fallen down the stairs and are unconscious? Are they hurt? Maybe it's better that I don't want to know what they're doing. Her head is nestled snugly in the arm of another body who is half lying on the bottom step with his lower extremities on the ground. He appears to be lying on his back with his arm around her. Why are they at the bottom of the cold garden steps when there is a perfectly good bedroom in the house? That is why she got the room after all, no need for all this el fresco stuff. I squint some more, trying to take it all in, but I'm still not able to tell from where I'm standing if they are alive or dead. My instincts tell me to be cautious. I don't want to turn the light on, just in case there's something going on that I'd rather not cast under a beaming spotlight. I can detect the gentle snoring sounds of Ange, and the louder heavy breathing of her armour are mixed with the lapping, sucking and licking sounds which is strangely compelling, erotic and has definitely piqued my curiosity. I cautiously take the steps one at a time, careful not to disturb them. I'm a nurse and it's against my Nightingale pledge to go back to bed without making sure they're okay. It's been raining and the

steps are slippery, so I need to take my time. The noise gets louder
and louder the closer I get.

"Ange? Ange? Is that you? Are you okay? You know
you're sleeping at the bottom of the communal stairs, don't you?"

I can hear the flies, moths and mosquitoes being zapped by
the electric bug killer which is mounted above the door. It casts a
sinister blue glow into the darkness. I stop about three steps down
and stand still, trying to glean the entire situation before moving on
any further. The noise is getting louder the closer I get and
is definitely coming from down there beside them.

"Ange? Jules? Hello down there, wakey wakey."

I venture onto the next step. Still can't see what's going on.
I tiptoe down another, then the next, hoping for a better view, and
focussing using the blue light and the moon which is softly
illuminating the two mangled figures.

"OMG!!!!"

I'm horrified at what I see before my eyes, and then all of
a sudden, BLACK. I waken at the bottom of the stairs with Jules
looming over me.

JULES

I awake with my mouth superglued to the roof of my mouth
and sadly not down the throat of the hunky paramedic p/t surfie
Aussie dude who is snoring loudly beside me. It is the singularly
most chilling scream I have ever heard. It takes me a few moments
to gather my thoughts and realise where I am. I bolt out of bed,
expecting a bloodbath run through to the kitchen and out the back
door. Nursie is lying at the bottom of the stairs and is practically on
top of Ange and her bloke in some peculiar menage-a-trois. She's

splayed out in a crumpled horizontal yoga warrior pose, but on her belly. Quite frankly, I have never seen anything like this before. She must have fainted. She begins to come round as I get to her. Ange and her bloke are sitting up, totally disoriented and are blinking themselves awake.

"LOOK!"

We all look to where her finger is pointing, which is directly at the guy's groin area. It all comes back to me in a series of still, black and white snapshots. Plain as day, hanging out of his spaver is the biggest sausage roll, without the puff pastry. It has tiny little bite marks out of it and I can see the neighbour's tabby cat sitting nonchalantly beside him, licking her lips, paws and cleaning her whiskers, not in the slightest bit fazed by all the stuff and nonsense going on. The paramedic looks down and removes the chewed banger, I'm sure he did bang her into the bargain, from his zip and chucks it at the cat, who gladly takes it and scampers off. Nursie looks like she's in shock. I think I know what happened here.

"Lesley? It's not how it seems. What you saw wasn't his larger-than-the-average-Aussie-sized penis, but a sausage from the Flying Pie. You hadn't eaten it so we were having a bit of fun with it. We all had the munchies and took it in turns to share the pastry with each other. Ange took the sausage and put it in his spaver to make it look like his donger[20] was hanging out. It was terribly amusing at the time, but maybe you had to be there. Not long after that, I went to bed, leaving that pair slow dancing with only the sausage separating them."

She is a nurse for feck sake, does she not know the difference between a sausage and a penis? With a few discrepancies, they're all pretty much the same. Once you've seen one, you've seen them all. Unless, of course, you've been lucky enough to have been with some freak of nature that's hung like a donkey. It's the sausages that have more diversity to them. Flat, fat, skinny, chipolata, even square. The more I try to reassure her, the more my tongue sticks like a pillow to the roof of my mouth and I think I end up sounding like I'm clicking and spraying her with putrid, warm tequila residue.

Ange is still somewhat comatose but she's managed to sit up slightly, looking like a zombie, legs splayed along the grass. She's still in that boozy half-awake stupor. She was totally oblivious to Nursie's shrieking, clattering down the stairs and the cat munching at the bloke's genitals. I shake her shoulder gently and attempt to describe what has just happened. Ange and her bloke have ruby red lipstick smeared over their faces, giving them a ceremonial war paint warrior look. I take my hankie out and begin to wipe it off. Suddenly, without warning, with a Queenie wave and a

"G'day ladies", the bloke jumps up, zips up his spaver and disappears over the fence at the back of the garden. Just disappears into the night, never to be seen again, with any luck that is. A real shite in Kninning armour.

"Wait, wait. Kiss me. Kiss me as if it were the last time. No prizes for guessing Jules? "

"Casablanca,1942? "

"Correct."

"No wucking furries mate, every good girl needs a man to ruin her lipstick and not her mascara."

So funny, he went quicker than Nursie can get a sausage roll down her throat and that's really saying something.

Ange is alert all of a sudden and appears none the worse for wear after her night on the tiles, or stairs in this case. Nursie looks a tad more battered than Ange does after her tumble. Why they were lying there in the first place is a mystery and perhaps another story for Ange to recant if she recalls it at all at a later date. Even though she may never truly know, as I doubt she will remember any of the previous night's antics as we really tied one on, I'm having trouble myself. The only winner, winner, sausage dinner out of all this is the Pussy. Nursie is sitting on the bottom step rubbing her leg and elbow. Thankfully she didn't break a bone or knock her teeth out - that would have sucked and been far more serious than a slight bruise. I'm trying my best non-verbal communications with the thumbs up, but she sits there, shaking her head, massaging herself.

"I'm not happy Ange, I thought you were dead."

"Which one of the seven dwarves are you then?"

Why did she have to go say that? I can feel the one-sided friction in the air. I am going to have to say something to keep the peace.

"Ith awliite Lethle, Ith wath onay a thothage."

I can tell, I can just tell that this could be the straw that breaks the camel's, or the pussy's back. She looks resigned and sad. She looks up at me, her silk sleep mask still propped on her forehead, her pale blue eyes matching the light of the insect zapper, are filled with tears, one escapes and trickles down her face. I don't know what to say or do.

LESLEY

Jules stares at me as I rub my bruised leg and elbow. I don't usually sweat the petty things, but didn't she realise that she attended to Ange's smeared makeup before checking to see whether I was okay and hadn't broken anything? I know this sounds really catty, but if they both ate more makeup than they wear, then maybe, just maybe, they'd be more attractive on the inside. I try to make some kind of sense as to what has happened here. It all happened so quickly. It was apparently only a pussy I'd heard, then I saw the cute wee tabby cat eating something between the guy's legs. That's a fact. How was I to know? An easy mistake I say. I had assumed he must have been dead before he'd allow that to happen to his penis. I genuinely thought it was midnight snacking on his appendage which was clearly hanging from his zip in his jeans. Considering I was at the top of the stairs, it was night and I couldn't quite see, it was an easy mistake to make. Jules can only communicate like a ventriloquist dummy, but I know by her thumbs up that everyone is alive at least. All she does is repeat.

"Thauthageth. Thauthegeth. Thauthegeth"

How the hell could I have known it was a sausage? I'm not sure how much more my nerves can handle this. I am not their keeper. I'll have to clean the kitchen before going back to bed as there's nothing worse than getting up to a pigsty.

ANGE

Jules tells me what happened in the House of Horizontal Happiness. Seriously? This is the funniest thing ever. Lezzers' fainted, fell down the stairs, scraped her finger and all because of what she thought she saw. The definition of animal porn for sure. How I larff. She picks up the knocked over wine bottle from the step that has the unused tampon as a stopper. Genius idea if I might say so myself. I wonder whether you could make some money selling them in liquor stores? I do manage to hold it somewhat together as she hobbles back up to the kitchen. She's muttering and mumbling under her breath something about having bruises on bruises. Thou protesteth too much methinks. However, something gets the better of me and I find myself being the unflinching wall of courtesy, and as a way of apologising, I offer to take them out for Sunday supper when she gets back from work - besides the hair of the cat won't go amiss.

"Hope you're feline better by then. Perhaps we should go out for some Mexican Purritos. I'm kitten you Lezzers', wherever we go will be purrfect."

"Let's just nip this all in the butt, Ange, and move on."

"Furry one Ange, very furry."

"Right ladies, it's a date. After Lezzers' has finished work, we'll all go out for a lovely evening at one of the cafes on Bondage beach, that's sure to do the trick. Let's all be pawsitive about all this, now I'm off for a shower and a cat nap. Lezzers', remember to change out of your pawjamas before heading to work. Night, night, see you later."

I hope Lezzers' see's that I'm only joking here, having a bit of a larff, at her expense right enough, but a laugh nonetheless. They do say laughter is the best medicine and she's a nurse, as if we could ever forget. I do hope that Jules puts her thinking cat on for this evening's entertainment and is ready with some more catisms. It certainly entertains me with this somewhat unnecessary apology of taking her out tonight as a way of apologising, after all I wasn't the one to fall down the stairs.

Silly cow.

LESLEY

I'm not sure how truly sorry Ange is but I'm tired and too stiff not to accept the lovely offer of a Sunday evening supper. I could do without being the butt of her jokes though. Blowing out someone else's flame in order for theirs to glow brighter is not the right direction in my opinion. Neither funny nor clever, that's what I say. Work isn't too busy, so I get back in plenty of time to have a shower and change before heading to the open-air Lamrock Cafe on Campbell Parade with its panoramic views of Bondi Beach.

Ange and Jules have already got some kind of joke going between them. I do try to join in with "Ho ho I get it, you almost had a mange tout last night," which cracks them both up.

"Think you mean menage-a-trois Lezzers'."

"That's what I said, Ange, mange tout. And it's Lesley as you fully well know. I do actually know what I'm talking about."

"Hmm, you hide it well. And I'm pretty sure that's what I called you. Now come on, let's make like hockey players and get the puck out of here. There's a large glass of Sauve out there calling my name."

The cafe is beautiful, little tables with white linen tablecloths, wicker chairs and an amazing view of the surfies all dotted on the horizon, their silhouettes highlighted magnificently by the sunset. Truly breathtaking. There is something very calming and peaceful about listening to the ebb and flow of each wave as it comes towards you, then recedes. I close my eyes to capture the moment, take a full, deep, fulfilling breath, and as I do, I suddenly get an overwhelming smell of vomit. I'm a nurse you know and there's no mistaking that smell.

"I hope I'm not alarming or disturbing anyone, but I have an incredibly strong sense of smell, some may think of it as a gift, and I can experience aromas, such as gas, bouquets of heady flowers etc, more strongly than the average person, and right now I can smell vomit."

"Ahhh, you have hyperosmia, but to be fair Lezzers', you're not able to tell the difference in smell between a cock and a sausage, so I am somewhat surprised that you have this gift as you say."

"There is absolutely no need for you to be quite so vulgar Ange, just call it a penis."

"Really? Why use penis when there are so many other choices."

It's so unnecessary and frankly, crude."

"How about a womb broom? More to your taste? Trouser Snake? I know, I know, a weapon of ass destruction."

"You're being unnecessarily childish now."

"Oh, I can go on all night. Sex Pistol, Russell The One-Eyed Muscle, or how about Rumpleforeskin? That's a good one and my personal favourite. You got any Jules?"

"Have I??"

"You do not have to partake in this Jules, it's all so childishly simple."

"It's actually Simply Childish, Lezzers'."

"I know what I said, Ange, and it's Lesley for the record and the final time."

"That's what I said, didn't I?"

"It's a bit of fun that's all, no harm done. How about Long Dong Silver and Knob Goblin, or knob gobbling as the cat was doing."

"Were you sick last night Jules? I know that smell distinctly."

It's definitely wafting from her direction.

"No, but I'll always be twice as sick as you are. OMG, I can smell it, maybe I was. I still smell ripe."

Ange notices the obvious aroma and starts gagging.

"You must have been sick Jules, that's why your tongue was stuck to the roof of your mouth this morning - it was all those congealed, sticky carrots, msg and tequila binding it together in a neat little package. Did you not have a shower today?"

This is not very helpful of her to point that out. People sitting at tables close to us have begun to notice all the commotion and as I'm watching them put their napkins over their mouth and nose, my guess is they've noticed the smell also.

JULES

Nursie asks me if I'd been sick last night almost at the same time as I inhale the unmistakable smell of puke. It does seem to be seeping from my very pores. I'm wearing one of the paramedics' sweaters he left behind in his haste to vacate the premises. I had intended for it to be added to my ever-increasing collection of trophies, as some may call it, but now I can smell sick on it, it's going to have to be thrown out. Bastard, it must be his vomit. The dirty son of a bitch, that's why he probably left it. I peel it off and throw it down onto the pavement but the scent still seems to be clinging to me. Maybe I had been sick on myself after all. I take off my shirt and lob it on top of the sweater as it must have been that I chucked up on. The smell still permeates my nostrils. The girls are both pinching their nostrils and feigning gagging noises. I realise to my dismay and horror that it's coming from my jeans. Oh no, disgusting. Perhaps someone was sick beside me and sprays of their vomit had hit my legs. There's only one thing for it, I take them off.

LESLEY

Jules is oblivious to the fact that she is making quite a scene. Folks are starting to stop on the promenade to watch as she is literally stripping down to her underwear. She is standing there, deliberating her next article removal, when the waiter comes over to our table.

"Excuse me Ms. but before you go on any further, I believe it's the bowl of parmesan cheese in the centre of your table giving off the aroma that you're smelling and not the chunder you believe it to be. I'll remove it from the table shall I before you remove anything else?"

I have to say it does make me laugh out loud as it could have been any one of us that reacted like that. Thankfully, it wasn't me though. I'd have been mortified, but Jules laughs it off, and in her underwear, she bows to her sidewalk audience who give her a resounding clap. The evening meal is super, sans parmesan. At least two bottles of wine have been ordered and consumed as I sip on my coke. I innocently drop it into the conversation without being too judgy. See, coke. I can easily say that word. I'm not as prudish as they think.

"I believe that's at least a week's worth of your five-a-day in all those bottles of wine you're drinking. That should keep you topped up for a while."

"Congratulations Lezzers', a full sentence, and if truth be known, one has to have a belief in something. And right now, I believe, I'll have another bottle of wine. Garcon???"

Their drinking seems to be getting out of hand, their bad behaviour and foul language are escalating. Everyone is staring at us. I make a point to hold my coke bottle in my hand in case anyone mistakes me for this headsonastic conduct. It's not who I am and deep down I know that. Ange told me last week that "Deep down you're a good person," which I initially thanked her for before she added: "Yeah, 6 ft deep down."

So hurtful, unnecessary and unkind. This is not what I want from this incredible experience and opportunity. I'm going to have a long, hard think with myself. I saw some adverts in the local rag looking for nurses in The Outback. That sounds interesting enough, I'll take a closer look at it when I get back to Hastings. Do you know that the nickname for The Outback is The Bush which means to live off the land by means of hunting or fishing? Apparently to live in The Bush is a preferable means of lifestyle. I think it sounds quite vulgar myself.

JULES

Lesley has become very quiet and I think it's got something to do with Ange who does enjoy baiting her - sees it all as a bit of sport. I have to say, although some of it can be close to the bone, it can also be very funny also and she most certainly does lend herself to it sometimes. All her little ways, quirks and malapropisms are fodder for sure. She does look sad, though, which isn't good. I'm going to try really, really hard not to use my wisecracks against her. But oh boy, she doesn't make it easy on herself. I'll have to be more aware that I need a gagging order before I respond to her ways. Not sure even a speeding train can stop Ange on her tracks when she's in full diatribe flow though. Och, she's not that bad, and she does have a good, kind heart. I really do value our friendship but I am not the booze-swilling, drug-taking, shagging machine she thinks I am - well, maybe just a little bit of all of them, but I think I mean well also. Moderation and all that, one has to have balance in life. I can only speak for myself here as Ange has to own and take responsibility for her own behaviours as we all do. Easy to always lay the blame at someone else's feet, but at the end of the day, when push comes to shove, it's up to each individual to be aware of the impact of their behaviours and actions. As of tomorrow I'm going to detox, yes that's it, a detox and maybe join a local gym, Bondi Beach Express seems to fit ..fit? That's what I'll be, FIT.

My dad used to say, "I'll be so fit it's not even funny."

My days of beer guzzling, head-banging, bar fleeing, shagging and dancing-on-tables days are finally going to be behind me. My liver will thank me for sure. Stand and deLIVER. I'm going to sign up first thing in the morning before tonight's alcohol leaves my bloodstream and I change my mind. It's not over until the fat lady sings… tra laaaa!!!!

LESLEY

I leave the girls hellbent on their self-destructive path and head home. I pass The Flying Pie, but I am completely full, having filled up with my fair share of horse's doovers to start with. My belly is definitely bigger than my eyes. I pop my head in the door to say a quick "Hello" and give Wee Jimmy a wave. Perhaps I'm trying to show them that I do have friends and not the "saddo" they think I am.

"G'day Sheila, fancy a roll or two?"

"Och Jimmy, I've just eaten and am fair stappit, I couldn't even manage the tiniest of sausages, not even one given from you. But thank you."

"Wait a minute, I've got something else for you in the car."

He comes back with a lovely, bushy green plant that has serrated-edged leaves and small flowery buds that radiate up from the base.

"For me? Och you shouldn't have you wee sweetie pie. Thank you so much. I love plants and am told that I'm a plant whisperer. I will cherish, love and nurture it. It smells delightful and the foliage will certainly bring some much-needed cheer to the flat."

"You're welcome. Enjoy."

Not sure why the wink, so I wink back. We go back and forth winking at each other until it gets a tad awkward.

"I'm known for my green fingers, you know, and I promise to report back regularly on her growth and progress."

How kind. A random act of kindness goes a long way. I'm chuffed to bits.

ANGE

Lezzer' decides to throw the towel in and call it a night. I, however, have a second wind, and in need of some more pelvic service, I see it as my pubic duty. There are a number of cute boys hanging around here, so thankfully plenty to choose from. As I begin to scan the place, I suddenly spot RUSSELL CROWE, and I do mean THE Russell as in Crowe, sitting with a wee pal, tucked away in the corner. OMG! OMG! I'm only the BIGGEST most adoring fan of this Aussie Adonis. He may well have a baseball cap and glasses on to disguise himself, but there's no mistaking this pure, unadulterated muscular beefcake. Must be a tad intimidating for his scrawny pal to have a Herculean chum whose muscles strain against the fabric of his white linen shirt at the forearms, biceps and chest. His shirt is unbuttoned to his sumptuous pecs, exposing a glistening, tanned, sculpted, well-defined chest. Be still my beating vagina. How I'd like to run my tongue over them. I am a mahoosive fan of this burly god and see this as my opportunity to snag a good one for my collection Down Under.

"Settle petal, you're behaving like an uncool chick, which we both know we're not. Treat 'em mean, keep 'em keen and all that."

"I don't care about playing it cool, he is not, absolutely not slipping through my fingers. The only thing those fingers are going to slip through is the elastic on my silk Agent Provocateur knickers. This is a chance in a lifetime. I'd hate to be telling this story in years to come but ending it by saying I regret not going over to chat to him."

"I hear you, but he's clearly having a quiet dinner as he's in the corner and has undeniably gone to great lengths to disguise himself."

"I disagree, anyone who wears their shades in a restaurant at night deserves to be recognized. I think he secretly wants to be noticed and adored."

"I still think it's lame. But you do you."

"He's in the corner of none of your business and go fuck yourself. I'm going over and that's final. Besides, I have to be me, everyone else is taken."

"Instead of bowling over like some scary obsessed fan, why not wait till he goes to the loos at least and then run it by his mate."

"Good idea Batman. I'll ask his gawky looking chum if Russ will take a photo with me. That should be enough to break the ice. Better take a good look at his pal as he's going to be yours."

"You'll be right, I'd rather be poked in the eye with a didgeridoo than have a fumble with that. He looks a few stubbies short of a six-pack, but thanks for the offer."

"I'm going to give it a fair suck of the sauce bottle, so to speak, and do it. He might even invite us to join them. The evening will evolve into a soiree of easy conversation and laughter that soars with buoyant banter, fun and frivolity. We'll then take a romantic walk along the beach and I'll invite him back to my place where I'll fuck his brains out."

I wait and watch avidly, not even blinking or engaging in Jules's witty wisecracks. I'm sure she's warming to the idea of having his Norman Wisdom lookalike pal. Russ eventually gets up and heads to the toilets. This is my time, the moment I have been waiting for my entire life. I wait patiently until he is out of sight, then race over to Stormin Norman.

"Excuse me Sir, but I am only Russell's biggest fan and I'm willing, ready and able to do anything, and I do mean anything, for an introduction and a cheeky wee photo with him."

"Really?"

"Well, I'll tell you what. I'll run it by him and if he's up for it, I'll call you over."

"Bonza, ya beaut, thank you. I'll be waiting, just over there with my cute, single pal. I love Americans, couldn't eat a whole one, but love them nonetheless."

I'm not long back in my seat when Russell returns. I see them having a tete-a-tete and looking over towards our table. I can see Russell's smile from here as he beckons me over. I am beyond ecstatic. I leap out of my seat, dragging Jules with me. I need a wingman; besides she can have the pal. My gift to her. I try to be cool, but I'm fawning all over him, so is Jules I might add.

"What's your favourite colour, Blue??"

I offer as an ice breaker.

"Would you prefer, what's your favourite pastime, sport?"

Not sure he gets the subtle nuances, but he smiles. I snatch the camera from Jules and hand it to Norman.

"Here, would you mind taking this?"

After the photoshoot is over, he thanks us and gently, but firmly, dismisses us. No walk on the beach, no rumpy pumpy back at Hastings Parade. No wrapping my laughing gear around his didgeridoo. Fairy snuff, I get it. Och well, why limit yourself to one particular fish when there are so many more in the ocean to be sampled, that's what I say. Not long after that, they leave.

"Garcon, cheque please."

"Your bill has already been taken care of by the gentleman in the corner of the restaurant."

"What? Are you fucking kidding me? Russell Crowe paid our colossal bill?"

"No Ms, his friend Tom Cruise did."

JULES

I could kick myself for not recognizing Tom, what a numptie[21] I am. I'm sure if I'd played my cards right, I could have had his jumper to add to my Australian experience. No point in crying over spilt milk, although I think it takes Ange a few hours to stop her crying. I decide to cheer myself up the next day by sticking to my plan, even though I have a blinding hangover. I call the gym before I chicken out and make an appointment with my very own personal trainer. His name is Terry and apparently comes free with the first six sessions. Crikey, it could have been Tom and Terry for me had I been paying more attention. I only plan on doing six gym sessions anyway, unless he's juicy, then it'll be Terry and Jules. I check out his profile and he is, of course, a strapping 12 stone of lush yumminess. He's the real Aussie deal to boot, 26, tanned, enjoys surfing, I'll give him something to surf, enjoys barbecuing and even has a part-time job modelling for a swimwear company. Ya Beauty, the beagle has landed. Somebody try and stop me. I see Wee Jimmy gave Nursie a rather established marijuana plant which she has given pride of place in her bed/sitting room. She doesn't have a clue what it is and is proudly showing off the "luscious ferns" and waxing lyrical.

"One of my lovely friends has been kind enough to give me this plant as a gift. How thoughtful. I love all these acts of random kindness."

If she gushes any more than she is right now, she'll combust with all that cheesy gratitude and appreciation for someone who has enabled her development as a part-time cannabis grower. I'm not so sure that Wee Jimmy, the local drug dealer, deserves that high, lofty praise or what his true intentions are with our very own nurse.

"He probably fancies the pants off you and it's his way of getting into your Hello Kitty knickers."

"Och away with you. He's young enough to be someone's son so he is. It's an innocent wee gift between friends."

"Not quite so innocent Lezzers'."

"We'll be laughing about all this soon enough that's for sure."

"Exactly Jules, laughter is good for the mind, body and soul."

"I think we need to have you tested again Lezzers'. If nothing else, an eye test will suffice."

This only gets a few clucks from her. This should be so much fun. Let's sit back and see how this all develops. She's excited, but not as much as us to see how many plants she can cultivate with her green fingers from this one. It'll be no time till they're ready for personal distribution. Ange and I wink at each other, knowing that we're the ones that are going to reap the benefits of her "green fingers".

If she tells us that once, she tells it a thousand times. Not that green, maybe muddy brown, as she clearly can't tell the difference between a fern plant and a cannabis one. She is super animated though and is twittering on that "a bush in the hand catches the early bird girls".

"You'd better believe it Lezzers'!"

I'm hoping Our Terry agrees with Nursie on that particular point.

ANGE

I'm very suspicious as she seems very enthusiastic about this fitness malarkey. There's something she's not sharing with me and it's for sure more than gaining "strength and flexibility".

Huh, I'll give her a week. Can't put my finger on it but she's up to something. I don't quite know what it is yet, but believe me, I will find out. There must be a boy involved some way, somehow, as it's not like her to be this enthusiastic over a gym - well maybe a Jim, but certainly not a gym.

JULES

The alarm goes off at some outrageous hour. Who in their right mind would choose to get up at 10 in the morning? It's tough getting out of bed, but the thought of Mr. T waiting for me in tight spandex is a very appealing incentive to say the least. And I'm correct, he's waiting for me at reception and does not disappoint. Long, wavy golden hair, twinkling flirty McGertie sapphire-blue eyes and a large, and I do mean LARGE, suckable pair of very snoggable lips. He has dazzling pearly white teeth, maybe a tad too white, possibly veneers, but I can overlook that. I don't care what anyone says, I'm not that shallow. I can feel a stirring and a longing vibrating from my cotton gusset just by standing in reception. Be still my hammering honeypot. Damn I now wish I had paid a bit more attention to my attire. Terry must think I'm a complete dag[22], wearing Ange's baggy shirt that says "Bad as I wanna be", no makeup, pajama bottom shorts and unbrushed hair. If Nursie had seen me leave the flat in this state, she'd have chased me down with her Mason Pearson handy bristle, nylon hairbrush, and fuss over me until she was satisfied I didn't look like a dog's dinner.

Her preference would always be to do it for me with her absurdly expensive boar bristle tool of less destruction. Oh Gawd, I haven't even cleaned my teeth, which he's bound to notice if he gets too close as he's clearly obsessed with fangs. Do horses have fangs? He can't be too particular given the choppers he's chosen for himself. A mere thought to file somewhere in my mental playground for future reference. Speaking of file, perhaps he'd benefit from a wee file of his gnashers himself. Another mental note to self, dress as a hot babe tomorrow. My instincts are usually spot on and I still feel it in my loins that we have an immediate connection. Groin connection more like. The very delicious Terry gives me a tour and shows me some stuff like big black machines, ropes (hmmm, they might COME in handy), a sauna (even handier), and a massage room. Is this the setting for 50 Shades Of Gym or what?

"Is it a red room?"

 Snorkel, snortle.

"What did you say Sheila?"

"Nothing Bruce, oops I mean Terry."

Is he that stupid and/or chauvinistic to address a female with the slang name "Sheila"?

Is he that unaware it's derogatory and rarely used these days. All he's doing is highlighting his chauvinism and thick-as-mince characteristics. Without doubt, we are two countries separated by the same language. If I'm to get anywhere with him, I need to pretend that I am a shallow, narrow-minded, superficial, ditzy broad. He needs to see me as a kindred spirit if this relationship is to progress. I laugh out loud, perhaps a tad too loud as he puts his finger to his mouth.

"Shush. There are people here, Sheila, who take their workout very seriously and prefer not to have hysterical interruptions."

"Nooo? Shirley you can't be serious?"

"Fair dinkum[23], not a word of a lie."

He is very serious and doesn't detect my sarcasm in the slightest. Seems over the top and very dramatic if you ask me, so I'm going to ignore his last comment and not attend his minor performance. Instead, I am going to focus on his body and enjoy watching the skillful way his muscles ripple, twitch, tighten, shine and glisten as he demonstrates each station. Folk pay a great deal of dollarydoos to watch this kind of entertainment and I have a front row seat. Now, there's a concept and a half. Charge the punters to visit a performance at a gym just to watch the natives' gym junkies in their natural babe-magnet habitat. Unless of course they look like the Neanderthal cart horse on the rowing machine. No one would want to spend good money watching that grunting monstrosity, they'd all be demanding a full refund and compensation for post-stress visual workout disorder.

Terry, on the other hand, is truly inspiring. I've found my perfect workout right here, eyeballing him and the other groaning, flexing stud muffins. I know by my beating heart and throbbing raspberry cave that I am burning a minimum of a 100 if not 1000 calories by using my imagination alone. Meg Ryan eat your heart out, anything you can do, I can do silently better. I think. The only difference being that I don't have to fake my fanny flutters. He shows me how to do sit-ups which I tell him would be much easier if I have a fixed stick or something between my legs. Having brain cells and a sense of humour must be above his pay grade, as he smiles blankly and continues to encourage me, especially when I lie down on the mat and tell him to

"Watch and sweep" while I demonstrate what I can do with my very flexible hip thrusts. Sans hands I might add.

"Keep your hips down Sheila and focus on lifting only your head and shoulders up and down."

"Said the bishop to the bishop."

It's more challenging than I thought it would be, to be fair, but I do manage to lift my head off the mat. I can already feel my abominable muscles firing. It probably helps that I'm sucking and holding in everything on a cellular level in that area. What a fantastic week this is going to be. I am positively buoyant.

"Au revoir Cherry."

"G'day Sheila. Catch ya later!"

I skip all the way back to Hastings Parade.

LESLEY

Jules seems very pleased with herself when she arrives back home, as high as a kite and not the usual high she has a pension for, if you know what I mean. I'm not a gym/exercise rabbit, so credit where credit's due, at least she's doing it which is more than either Ange or I. Ange considers her extracurricular nightly activities enough exercise. Given the number of sessions she's had she should be as fit as a butcher's block. I give Jules lots of praise for even starting, she deserves it. I get plenty of exercise on the wards though, but I feel I'm putting on weight. The other day, as I was heading to The Flying Pie, it was raining outside for the first time in ages and I had to hold my jacket together with a bungee cord. People are beginning to notice. I walked by one of those automatic barrier arms that regulates traffic and it lifted as I passed. There wasn't a car in sight so it must have thought I was the car. How embarrassing. Thankfully the girls weren't with me as I'd never have lived that down. I'm too ashamed to tell them.

ANGE

One day down, watch this space. She does seem very proud of herself and is wandering around in her sports bra and shorts showing us the difference in her six-pack...only one six-pack for me... cheers!

JULES

The minute Nursie heads to work I enjoy assisting Ange in finishing the six-pack - well, it would be terribly rude not to and there is no point in starting seriously until I start properly tomorrow. After the six-pack, which disappears quickly, like I mean really quickly, like it evaporates quickly, we head to the pub for a few cocktails. I am definitely in the mood and have the taste for a Screaming Orgasm, which is vodka, coffee liquor, amaretto, baileys, cream and milk. You wrap your lips around the rim of the glass and, using no hands, skull it. They go down easily and smoothly without touching the sides, almost like throwing a sausage up an alley. The next day I wake up surprisingly early, early enough to shower, get my war paint on and dress in my most revealing provocative gym bunny ensemble. I feel like crappe diem but I am optimistic about my session today as opposed to last night's session. I ask the bartender from last night, Pistol Pete or something like that, to leave the minute he opens his eyes as I have work to do. Not a complete lie. I drink an entire cafetiere of fully loaded caffeine to fully perk me up for my much-anticipated, impending date, finally making it out the door, only marginally late. Terry is still as gorge the 2nd day and doesn't seem too bothered that I'm running a bit late. He makes me lie on my back, I had enough of that last night to be honest, and asks me to push a very heavy iron bar.

"I'd much prefer an Irn Bru, made by girders, over an iron bar."

That disappears into the air. Wooosh, there it goes, right over his head. Not sure if it's out of spite or not, but he adds more weights to the already heavy dumb bells. WTF? Seriously? Why is he doing this to me? Can he not see that I am but a mere delicate little flower? I have even put on some extra special glossy lippy, only for him, which I can now feel sliding out of the corners of my mouth. I can feel beads of sweat, I'm assuming it's sweat, I've never actually experienced it before, on my top lip of all places. My legs are wobbly, mainly due to the detoxing from last night's binge. If they wobble any more in the hot pink Daisy Dukes I wore specially for him, I'll create an earthquake, a tremor at the very least. I also get a whiff of the distinctive leftover smell from Pistol Pete trapped but slowly making its escape and leaking into my gusset. I finish my exercise and am ready to call it a day when he points me to the treadmill. Did his mother not teach him that it's rude to point? Somewhat blunt, but masterful at the same time. Hmmmm, a double session today it seems. My guess is he isn't ready to have me leave him just yet. He seems happy enough when I finish the 1/10 mile. I manage a slight sashay as the machine ramps up to almost 2mph. His rewarding smile makes it all worthwhile. I feel great. I'd buy at least three bottles of this gym endorphin stuff if I could possibly add a smidgen of some vodka. I might suggest it and advise them to advertise it as a probiotic with alcohol. I'm going to be so fit and healthy.

I thank him for a perfect date and butterfly my eyelashes at him, okay so maybe it's a bit of eye fucking, but he doesn't shy away so no harm done. In fact, he eye fucks me back.

"Au devour Mr T, see you tomorrow."

"Fair dinkum Sheila."

JULES

For feck's sake, the only way I can brush my teeth is by moving my mouth back and forth on the brush as it lies on the vanity counter. My arms are paralysed and are hanging by the side of my body. How is this even possible? All I did was pick up a small pole and lift it over my head a few times, with a few bicep curls thrown in for good measure. Surely that can't paralyze you, unless I've trapped the nerves to both my arms.

LESLEY

Jules asks me to take a look at her arms and chest as she thinks she may have "herniated" her biceps, pectorals and triceps. She's walking around like one of the ensemble from River Dance.

"Don't worry, it's only muscle fatigue. You must have overdone it at the gym. Here, let me rub in some tiger's balm I bought in Singapore, that should help."

ANGE

Two down...

JULES

I manage to walk to the gym but am more than aware of the stares I'm getting from Joe Public. Have they never seen Lurch from The Adams Family? I can almost feel the knuckles of both my hands dragging on the pavement at least 2 ft behind my body. I'd be staring too if it wasn't me. There is no way I can do anything more at the gym today, but my guess is that he'll want to see me anyway. See the damage and trauma he has inflicted on my poor defenseless body. When he sees my predicament, and that I won't be able to do this session, hunky Mr. T is going to ask me out on a real date. However, he seems a tad impatient as I shuffle towards him. He is tapping his watch face as I come through the doors trailing my elongated arms behind me.

"Time is money."

"But my arms aren't working!"

"It's perfectly natural to feel that way after a session, especially as you're a gym virgin."

"Virgin on the ridiculous more like."

"The best thing for you to do is to get back on the horse's saddle..."

Like his teeth...

"and stretch it all out."

Stretching doesn't sound too awful, so I give in and follow him past the smelly, hairy ogre lumbering on the dreadmill, spraying chest hair mixed with sweaty mildew in every direction. It's quite disgusting, vile and repugnant, like a gross scene from Animal House or Blue Peter. What were they thinking when they called it a dreadmill anyway? He snaps his fingers, seriously, he snaps his fingers at me, trying desperately to get my attention.

"It usually takes a whole lot more than a snapping of fingers to make me come."

"Never mind that, grab this."

"Here's hoping..."

He wastes no time giving me some really heavy dumberdarnbells.

Agggh, what are you trying to do to me? These are too heavy for my weak arms."

"1lb is not heavy."

I beg to differ, Mr. Know it all T. He is a tad snappy, and not of the finger variety, and is more than a little testy with me.

"Sheila? Your high-pitched squeals are beginning to disturb some of the serious members."

"I say that's slightly anal of them, wouldn't you?"

If he had given me a feckin glass of water in a lead crystal glass instead, perhaps with a splash of voddy, then I wouldn't have had any need to feckin project my inner squeals. I hadn't really noticed it before but his voice is very nasally and far too perky this early in the day. And another thing, he's actually reprimanding me in this whiny, shrill tone that's now getting on my tits. He's even whistling his "s's" through the gap in his ill-fitting nag's teeth. I have never heard sentences finishing on such a high note before in my entire life. Do all Australians finish their sentences with a question? I hadn't noticed until now. I'm now thinking that his balls haven't even dropped, 26 my arse, 16 more like, and since when have sentences ever finished in the word

"BUT?"

I'd like to butt his feckin beaky nose, that's for sure, and knock those domino gnashers clean down his galling throat. My chest is really, really aching when he points, yet again, rude bastard, towards the dreadmill. I tell him I think I might be having a hearter and that my boobs will bounce uncomfortably and end up in a different time zone to the rest of me as I had forgotten to wear my sports bra today. He doesn't argue, he puts me on the stair monster instead. I do tell him that I don't need this particular machine as I never really climb that many stairs on a regular basis given the choice. These days it's so much easier and energy efficient to use the lift, conveyor belt or an escalator, so I can't really see the need for this particular exercise. He says it will help me enjoy life more, make me feel happier, jump-start my endorphins and some other shite like that, but I stop listening as his voice is beginning to scratch and score the hairs in my eardrums. I'm outta here.

"Au revolting Mr. T from now on, you'll find me hiding from all forms of exercise. If you need to find me, I'll be in the fitness protection programme."

LESLEY

Silence is golden. However, the anger in the air is palatable and I might even get my head to play with if I say something. She looks fit, fit to burst that is. She's moaning and groaning that every muscle in her body hurts and that she doesn't think she'll ever be able to walk, eat, drink or have sex again.

"I've pulled every chakra known to mankind from my root to my crown and all the sneaky ones in between."

"You can still talk though which is an absolute delight for all of us."

"You're so right Ange, every cloud has a sliver of a lining."

"Silver. It's silver lining, and not sliver."

"You know full well that's what I said."

Not to take the attention from her, I notice that my fern has small red spider mites, so tell her I'm heading down to the garden centre for some pesticide that won't kill the plant. They're doing fantastically well. I've had to separate them as they are growing so much and the wee buds are multiplying by the day. I now have ten altogether. They're growing like little weeds. That's what I'm going to call them, Audrey Two, from the plant in Little Shop of Horrors.

ANGE

Ha, Lezzers' is amazed that all her loving care and attention to detail is being rewarded by her plants multiplying and growing like "weeds". If only she knew that she is now formally classified as an illegal drug grower. Tempting as it is to tell her, I think I'll sit back and enjoy watching it organically unfold, there'd be no fun or enjoyment if I told her now what kind of plants she's nurturing. Besides, that would ultimately spoil the crop she's growing and I know that I will bear the fruits of her labour soon. My ears are beginning to bleed listening to her drone on and fussing all over Jules like a clucky, clicky fat hen. She's twittering around, sponging her down, giving her smoothies through straws, rubbing her all over with deep heat.

"You need to try and be a bit more sympathetic here Ange as she's in pain."

"Yeah, Ange, be more sympathetic towards me."

"Just because you're in pain Jules, doesn't mean you have to be one."

It's definitely getting on my tits and making me feel ill just watching the pair of them. It's like observing some terribly sad, poorly cast lesbian porn movie. I wink at Jules and hand her an apple.

"I think you need to work on your core some more. Or if that's not to your taste, perhaps you'd prefer an avo cardio instead. I know, let's open a bar called The Gym, then we can brag about going there every day. The only machine we'll ever really need is the ATM or condom machine."

At least she laughs, groans and whimpers at the same time as holding her sore abs. Lezzers' tutts and shakes her head.

"You have zero to no compassion Ange and one day you'll see that these cheap putdowns will leave you very unpopular."

"And??? Your point is? Speaking of popular, do you know that if you spent more time putting dicks in your mouth over sausage rolls then I'm sure you'd beat me at the popularity contest?"

"You know without having to ask, that I deeply resemble those remarks."

JULES

I leave them to it and head to bed, as in the morning, by hook or by crook, I'm going to slip into the gym surreptitiously, cancel my card so I don't get charged and slip back out again before being seen. I wake up early the next day, almost as fresh as a Waratah flower, the emblem of New South Wales. I awake the next day bright and early and stiff as an old board, but I'm determined to carry out my cunning plan, which fails miserably as Mr Not Your Average Purebred T, is actually waiting for me at the main desk, tapping his limp, floppy foot, arms crossed, his thin, cruel lips pulled back in a very unattractive frothing sneer exposing his large porcelain Clydesdale gob. He has the audacity to point his watch on his wrist. Why do people do that, but don't point to their bum when they ask where the toilets are?

He's trying, and almost succeeding, in making me feel intimidated, preying on me like a rabid vampire, ready to pounce. To suck me dry, but not in the biblical sense anymore you understand. That ship has well and truly sailed, leaving him a castaway. I feel pure relief at this realisation, I am now pleasantly happy to report. We all know that vampires are make-believe, like elves, gremlins, eskimos and the G-spot. He does look very convincing though and I'm genuinely scared for my life and shaking in my Uggs. It really isn't even my fault I'm 30 mins late - it took me that long to button my feckin shirt. He orders me through to the gym and demands I lift some dumbbells, yes one would need to be DUMB to keep lifting them for no real reason. When he turns his back on me, I leg it to the loos, well I try anyway, but end up crossing the floor like a gimpy Galen from the Planet of The Apes who's just pissed their pants. He catches me by shirt tails. I manage to wriggle free, leaving him holding my blouse, and bolt for the ladies. What a relief, he won't get me in here. At some stage, he's going to have to go get some pony nuts for himself, then I can make my escape. Alas, he actually has the audacity to send in some minus-size-0 Sheila to retrieve me. He's standing waiting for me when I reappear and forces me on to the growling machine beside Fred Flintstone. The sick, sadistic knob that he is.

"Look, I didn't mean to bolt like that, but I literally just started my period."

That usually stops most men in their stride, but not Trigger here.

"Super, by tomorrow you'll be back firing on a ¼ of your cylinders."

"Au re feckin voir."

LESLEY

And breathe, I'll ignore the swearing, the threats to discombobulate and the accusations that she's making against this poor lad Terry.

"Look here Jules, there are two things that can occur in our interactions with others and they're usually a form of reflection and projection."
"I'm not sure I'm up for one of your lessons Lesley."

"It's important. Reflection is when experiences reflect back to us from others that show us aspects of ourselves, and projection is where we externalise aspects of ourselves onto others that aren't actually them. See what I'm saying?"

"Truly fascinating. Did you get all this information from a Christmas cracker?"

"No silly billy, but it's true, projection can be anything that we avoid seeing in ourselves and instead only see in others, good or bad, whereas reflection is always occurring, even if we are too busy projecting out to notice the underlying messages that are reflecting back to us, about us. Get it?"

"Projection reflection, mumbo jumbo. Are you saying I look like a horse?"

"I personally think that's exactly what she's saying."

"Och Ange, behave yourself, that's not what I'm saying at all. When we become more emotionally mature, awake and alert then we can stop projecting our baggage out onto others. Only then can we invest our time in working through what life is reflecting back to us."

"Reminds me of the story about the problem they were having at a private secondary school. Some of the girls had been going into the boys' toilets and kissing the mirrors with their red lipstick. It was taking the janitor ages to clean the red imprints every day. Eventually, the head teacher pulls the girls she believed to be the culprits into the toilets and tells them she knows it's all done in jest and looks aesthetically pleasing to see their lips reflected all over the boys' mirrors, but it is a chore-and-a-half for the janitor to clean them. She then asks the janitor to show them exactly what is required every time he cleans them. The jannie proceeds to take his rag, rinse it out in a toilet bowl, gives a quick wipe of the urinals, then begins to wipe the mirrors. The girls begin to gag and wipe their mouths at the mere thought of what they must have been kissing every time they plastered their lippy lips on the mirrors. The school never had the problem again."

"I remember that story. In fact, YOU were one of the main culprits Ange. It was you, wasn't it?"

"That's my story of reflection. Does it count? It stopped me kissing mirrors forever. I projected my teen lust on the lovely boys' lips behind the bike shelter instead."

"Good story Ange, when the teacher is ready the student appears."

"Isn't it the other way around?"

"If you'd have let me finish, I was about to say and vice versa."

"These are great anecdotes, but I'm still feckin sore!"

"Tell you what. Let me draw you a lovely warm bath with bubbles, lavender and Epsom salts. You'll be fine and dandy by the morning. Trust me I'm a nurse."

ANGE

I draw Jules a bath with a lead pencil when Lezzers' leaves the room which makes her laugh and cry at the same time as she holds her cramping belly. She really has started her period and it hasn't been an excuse after all. Lezzers' may have spotted my piece of art when she comes back in and she may well have noticed me rubbing my hands together with glee that I almost have my barfly buddy back, but she doesn't bat an eyelid and keeps completely schtum, so much so that I can't see any semblance whatsoever of any lips on her face, puckered or otherwise. She has completely sucked them in until they have all but disappeared. Now, that's a skill she should be honing if you get my drift. I'd better get out of her way, she's in full-Nursie mode duty, so I head to the liquor store before it closes. I feel an imminent session coming on and not of the gym variety.

JULES

I am so grateful to Nursie for the fabulous bath, massage and chicken noodle soup. She even tucks me in bed after. I feel like I'm at a spa resort and I'm not in the slightest bit tempted by the night cap Ange keeps trying to ply me with. I just want to curl up and sleep. I awake the next day bright eyed and bushy tailed, full of beans and ready to take on the world. I'm going to begin by taking on Mr. T, if only to prove a point, not sure what that point is yet, but I know there must be one. I hate him more than I've ever hated any other human bean in the history of hate. The girls tell me I'm wasting my time, but against my better judgment I go nonetheless. When I get there, with good intentions I might add, he complains that what I'm wearing isn't gym etiquette. Feck him, I'd feckin turned up, hadn't I? "It's not cool or company policy to wear pyjamas to work out in, even if you are wearing your trainers."

"How can you even tell these are my PJ's? Everyone else looks exactly the same as me."

"Not everyone is wearing a matching two-piece garment cotton attire with sheep on them."

"Feck sake, minor details!"

"And it's a big no, no to swear out loud."

"Look Lester Piggott, if I'd have been able to undress out of my nightwear and redress in gym attire, that would have been exactly what I would have done, but my limbs are actually paralyzed, and it's all thanks to you that I'm in this mess in the first place. So don't go throwing, or should I say projecting the blame on me. Besides, take a Captain Cook matey at some of the other sights here? For instance, the very large, follicly challenged caveman snorting in the corner is wearing a pair of tiny children's-sized lycra blue, spandex shorts, 100 sizes too small for his gargantuan figure. That bloke over there, also flabby, has a striped unitard. I mean, who wears striped unitards these days. Other than bananas in pyjamas that is. The stripes are at least going in the right direction, all the way up his arse. Has no one informed him that the Jane Fonda days of looking like that finished in the 1930's and has not, in fact, and will never make a revival. I can also tell every one of their religions just by glancing at the steroid-induced disproportionate outline of their throbbing manhoods through the shiny, clingy fabric. There are women over there, flicking their hair, rimming their lips with their acrylic fingernails, wearing nothing but a thong, and I do not mean on their feet, it looks like dental floss between the cheeks of their derriere. Tell me what that is about? Whose needs are being met there I wonder. At what point do they see their reflection and think

"Yup, this is a good look". We're not talking Olivia Neutron Bomb here, let's get physical. Physical. We're talking more like heifer hips. My sheep pj's are tame in comparison. There's some serious spandex chub rub going on that's more suited to lighting a barbie[24]. I swear I can see sparks flying from all the spandex being chafed together from the dreadmill and stair monster."

"Let's not waste any more time shall we, let's get straight down to business and do some work on your triceps and lats today, we haven't done those yet."

After all that, he still wants me.

"I'm a freak of nature and don't really need lats as I've never really found an occasion to use them. Giving them a miss would be an advantage and less time-consuming for you in particular. Perhaps I'm jumping the gun here, the triceps-look is so passe and old-fashioned these days so it isn't really necessary for me to look like a pre-hysterical dinosaur in this day and age. I think you're teasing me here and pretending they're part of the human anatomy and not a primitive creature. Either way, it is certainly not needed to be part of my physique."

He takes no heed of what I'm saying and lays me down on a bench, telling me it might be easier to lie down and he'll hand me the hand weights to do chest presses with instead.

"If you give me anything that is even an ounce heavier than a rainbow-sprinkled doughring then I'll be out the door before you can say, the horses break from the starting gate."

He gives in and puts me back on the walking machine.

"Walk it off Darlene."

I fly past him, accompanied by the entire flock of Lamb Chops I'm sporting at 90mph, crash landing into the skeleton in the corner. Only when the skeleton moans from underneath me do I realise that it's the teacher's pet Sheila from the other day, the one that retrieved me from the latrines. How the hell my face manages to land in her bright yellow elastic, synthetic camel-toed fabric, beggars belief, but I do. Why couldn't it have been a softer, more comfortable landing? Like a regular cheeseburger from Mickey D's. I look up from my muff-munching position and see Mr T looming over the top of me, his nasty little wrinkled giblety gonads hanging out the side of his baggy jersey shorts. I feel some upchuck in my mouth. It's his bloody fault in the first place for not telling me what the up-arrow on the machine is used for. I'm outta here.

"Au revoir Red Rum."

ANGE

She's almost back, Hallelujah.

JULES

The next day, he obviously feels compelled to leave me a voicemail in his grating, shrilly Aussie accent, daring to ask me why I hadn't shown up for our workout? OUR workout? All he does is bark orders through his muzzle. What the feck does he really do there I ask myself? He minces around, bullying poor defenseless babes, handing objects over, checking out his reflection and projection in the floor-to-ceiling mirrors constantly and pressing various buttons on various machines. Aye, mainly my buttons I might add. Workout? Out of work if he carries on treating people like that. Just hearing his mean little voice makes me want to kick something with my trainers, but I lack the strength to even lift the TV remote control and end up watching almost four hours of Jeremy Kyle because I can't change the channel. I resolve myself to wait until Nursie is back from work as I know Ange is in her room totally ignoring my cries for help as she has someone of the male species there with her.

I'm beginning to lose the will to live when she eventually surfaces and redeems herself by coming through with a case of cava and a bag of grass to commiserate or celebrate my return. Nothing speeds up a recovery quite like the care package of a family-sized bag of cheese and onion crisps, a box of Maltesers and a mahoosive spliff. Nursie can keep her baths. This is all the exercise I need, drinking, eating and smoking Marie Ju Wanna. The only gym you will ever see me in from now on will be in Jim's bed, the rather attractive, nubile, blonde, blue-eyed lifeguard at Bondage Beach. And not the Krankie kid at the Flying Pie in case you were mistaken. Remind me in the future that I'm allergic to gyms and exercise. Never to make that mistake again or ever to be repeated.

ANGE

When I get rid of the overnight lodger and come through the house, I find Jules watching some mind numbingly dull programme which destroys brain cells by the second. She perks up immensely when I show her the survival provisions I purchased yesterday.

"It has all been so traumatic, thankfully the saga of Terrygate is well and truly behind me."

"If God or anyone else had wanted you, or any other unspecified person, even a cave dweller, to lift weights, squat, sweat unattractively in unitards wearing an unattractive dental floss thong, then they'd have sprinkled diamonds or cocaine at the very least on the ground. You get more than enough exercise just by pushing your luck young lady. Let this be a learning lesson to you that if it makes you swell, your cheeks red and sweat uncontrollably, then you're having an allergic reaction to it. Now, which would you prefer first? A frontal lobotomy or a bottle in front of me?"

"You should be a politician Ange. Let the fun and frolics begin."

LESLEY

I come home after a 12-hour shift in the ER only to find we've been burgled. My bedroom/sitting room is completely trashed and Jules's lifeless body is lying in the centre of the room with what I think is a gun, yes, it is definitely a gun and a smoking one at that, beside her. There is a distinct smell of bananas bizarrely enough in the air. I hear a loud scream and realise it's coming from me. My heart is racing. Come on Lesley, hold it together and do what needs to be done here.

ANGE

It did seem like a good idea at the time and it was positively encouraged by Survival 101 in the Backpackers magazine.

"Let's get Hitched."

I'd bought it purely for safety reasons, you understand, and had no intentions of actually using it. It was as cheap as chips and it had only one "careful" owner - only used once apparently.

I admit it now, I know nothing about taser pocket guns, but it came with instructions and I can read. It's pocket-sized and has only 230 million volts, whatever that means. No stronger than one of those pen mozzie zappers I'm sure. No doubt similar to a bright light bulb. So, I think it's perfect protection really. It states that the effects of the taser are short-lived with no real long-term effect on the assailants, allowing the user, yours truly in this case, adequate time to retreat to safety. Cool beans. One can never be too careful or prepared these days. Fuck, I'm beginning to sound like Lezzers'. As long as I don't start looking like her, then we're all good in the land of Top Gun.

I won't lie, I'm excited to try it out as I've always seen myself as some badass assassin, like Black Mamba in Kill Bill. Jules is equally excited when I show it to her. It's fully charged and ready to go. I point it at the sofa first, pull the trigger. Nada. Rien. Nothing. Not so much as a miniscule spark. Fuck, I'd bought a duff one from Toys Guns R Us. I press the nozzle against the metal table and squeeze the trigger slowly. A faint blue current of electricity can be seen darting between the points.

AWESOME!!

JULES

After a couple of drinks, Ange decides to show me her new purchase. It's intriguing, I wonder what it feels like to be shot with it? Maybe like a heavy, full-on tickle? Anyway, I'm game to have her try it out on me. Can't be that bad, it isn't as if it's a real gun after all, just a mild sting.

ANGE

Jules offers to role play with me and pretends to be a pyjama-clad, dangerous, homicidal, axe- wielding, sexually deviant intruder. It's fully returnable if it doesn't work, so win win. We decide to reenact the scene in Lezzer's bedroom/sitting room as it's the largest and has a sofa and chair for Jules to hide behind. Jules goes through to the kitchen to get ready for her heroic part while I skim the rest of the instructions. Blaaa, blaaa, blaaa shock...blaa, disorientate ...spasms...bodily fluid...yada, yada yada...doesn't seem that bad.

Even my Rampant Rabbit has more power. There is no way this tiny, cigarette-sized device can do all the things it's saying it can. Bloody sales pitch, marketing racketeers, I say.

HOWEVER. What happens next is almost beyond description and it happens so quickly that all the facts may well get in the way of this, a good story.

"May the fourth be with you."

Out of the blue and to my left, I see and hear a black-clad figure jumping over the sofa, lunging at me with a serious-looking weapon in hand wearing a Lone Ranger mask and a bikini of all things. Fuck me sideways, a real fucking intruder. I jump up and run round the back of the couch, trying to catch my breath, my heart racing. I pop up, take a shooting stance and with a one second, I swear yer Honor, pull lightly on the trigger.

JULES

Holy mother of Michael Hutchence slip-ons of mass destruction. What the feck is happening?

It feels like I've been attached to an electric bungee cord and am being slammed against the carpet over and over again. It all goes black.

ANGE

Oh, oh, I try to grab Jules as she flails around the room about 3 ft off the floor but can feel the blue current attach itself to me also. It's throbbing and pulsing through my entire body, even my teeth are lit up. I come to a fetal position, tears in my eyes, body soaking wet, possibly body fluid, nipples on fire, shorts nowhere to be seen. My legs are tingling and smoke is coming from the top of my head. I see Jules draped over the sofa with smoke coming from her head also, her mask appears to have melted to her forehead and, I believe, baked banana is smattered over her chest. Ah, so a banana was her weapon of choice and not the lead pipe I imagined her holding. Easy mistake.

At that very moment, I notice Lezzers' come through the door. She briefly takes in what is unfolding before her disbelieving eyes and screams like a wild Banshee[25]. It should be us screaming really, not her.

LESLEY

It is beyond all comprehension what is lying before me. I try to ascertain what has taken place, but can't for the life of me phantom it out. Ange has got up from her foetal position on the floor and is sitting in the armchair that now finds itself tilted against the wall in the far corner of the room, about 8 ft from its usual place. She is holding a gun in her hand which I realize very quickly must be a taser as it still has sparks coming from the nozzle. Her shorts are hanging from the mantelpiece and Jules is draped face-up on the sofa with a Lone Ranger, seriously? A Lone Ranger mask melting, yes melting, onto her forehead. Her bottom lip is swollen and looks the same size as a 10 lb kettlebell. A real trout pout if ever I've seen one. Eat your heart out Kim Kardashian. There is a steady stream of drool cascading from what I believe to be every one of her orifices on to the floor. She appears to have a blowtorch burn on her thigh the size of the Sydney Opera House and there is banana puree over her chest and midriff.

There's a foul, unmistakable odor of burning skin, hair mingled with banana and that's when I see that Jules has shat herself. She is so out of it that she doesn't seem to notice let alone care.

Who's going to have to clean all this mess up? Yes, of course, ME!!

ANGE

Lezzers' goes ballistic and I mean really apoplectic, ape shit, like I've never seen the likes before. I mean I know she can go pure dead mental but this takes it to a whole new level.

It crosses my mind to zap her just to calm her down, but it's all out of juice unfortunately. She's like the Seven Hormonal Dwarves rolled into one. You know, Itchy, Bitchy, Bossy, Bloaty, Teary, Sweaty and…. etc and PSYCHO. She is literally screeching at us and I mean fuckin ragin[26].

"This is quite frankly the final match in the powder barrel. You pair are inconsiderate, self-absorbed, selfish and egotesticle. Not a considered thought for anyone else. This might be the straw that breaks the camel's bawbag[27] for me"

"Don't hold back here Lezzers', get it off your chest and tell us how you really feel?"

"This is no laughing matter Ange, and certainly no time for jokes especially as you've almost incinerated your bestie over there. Get out of my sight while I clean Jules and this place up. Leave the gun with me. I'll dispose of it later. I clearly give you more credit than you deserve as I thought you'd know better than to play with guns."

"If I did get a penny for your thoughts, how much change would I get back?"

"Out. NOW"

JULES

Lesley finally calms down, cleans me and puts me back together. She puts the room back together with military-style efficiency and in lickety-split time, hey presto, the room is back to its usual immaculate state. She gives me a glass of water and hands me back my contraceptive diaphragm which had been ejected from my lady tunnel at great speed during the shoot-off and had landed on the coffee table. I only have it as a preventative as I'm nowhere near as sexually active as I usually am. Ange has suggested that since I'm not using it for its intended purpose I should put it to some extra use by offering it out as a shammy, that way I can at least make some extra money cleaning cars and windows when it isn't being employed.

Nursie is scarily quiet and, after making sure I'm okay, she checks out her beloved plants. All 30 of her Audrey Two plants have been knocked over, so she lovingly and gently puts them back together, takes them outside and plants them in the garden as they're multiplying at an incredible pace and have all but taken over her bedroom/sitting room/greenhouse.

She's a good, kind soul and I don't know how she puts up with us, I really don't. I need to make it up to her somehow. I feel so much better after all her TLC that I mention there's a fancy dress party at the Bondi Tram on Friday night. That might be what we need, all of us, out together having fun. She's on a late shift Saturday, so is game for a night out and an opportunity to bring us all back together. Ange is always game on for anything, mainly to hunt it down for its meat, either in the male form or for mere sport. I'm going to go as Dame Edna Average as a nod to feckin' up my job prospects, Ange is going as Crocodile Dundee and Nursie has decided to go as Freddie Mercury and not the nurse we thought she'd be going as.

Now, there's an ongoing hooha over this as Ange thinks that she needs to go as an Australian, even a Koala Bear would be better than Freddie in her opinion. There's prize money involved and Ange believes she only has her best interests at heart. Never mind the fancy dress competition, this stubborn battle of wills seems to be the contest of choice. Neither seem willing to back down and concede. You've seriously never heard the like. I'm away outside to prune the cannabis plants.

LESLEY

Who does she think she is? The fancy dress competition at The Tram is exactly that, fancy dress. Doesn't say "Australian Dress" or have anything in the title even remotely related to anything Down Under. Who does she think she is, trying to impose her will on me and my choices?

If I want to dress as Freddie Mercury, then that is precisely what I'm going to do. I've already bought a wig, large handlebar instantly identifiable moustache and a white jumpsuit, so Freddie is exactly what I'm going to go as.

"Alright already, I give in, any way the wind blows, doesn't really matter to me. The show must go on, the show must go on, inside my heart is breaking! My makeup is flaking but my smile stays on. Easy come, easy go, a little high, little low, any way the wind blows doesn't really matter to me. You know you can be fairly determined when you're Adam Ant about something, in fact, very scary moose, scary moose, now off you go, get ready to do the fancy dress dangle."

"I get it. Those are all lyrics from Queen. Well two can play at that game Ange. You can dance, you can jive, having the time of your life."

"Here we go again. Close but no cigar Lezzers'."

"The feeling is neutral Ange."

ANGE

She may think that she has won this battle, but she hasn't won the war. Watch this space. By hook or by crook, I will.

JULES

What a hullabaloo Nursie is making. She can't find her Freddie moustache anywhere and thinks that it's the one accessory that will be instantly recognizable as her being Freddie.

"No harm done here, I watched Blue Peter as an ankle biter and have made scores of moustaches for men, ladies, rugrats, dogs and cats in my time. Give me 15 minutes to cockle something together for you. Everything will be okay in the end and if it's not okay, then it's not the end."

"Awww, thank you, thank you Ange. That's so unusually kind of you. I don't care what they say about you, you're not nearly as bad as you look. You're a lifesaver. Freddie won't work without it, you rock."

"Ach, don't mention it, it's the least I can do. We should call this place the Hokey Cokey House, where anything can be turned around."

I don't like this one little bit. Ange is being unnaturally helpful and accommodating. Nursie doesn't look the slightest bit suspicious, but I for one smell a rat.

LESLEY

I've gone and lost my moustache which must have fallen out of the bag somewhere, but Ange very kindly offers to make me another one, pacifically for me. I didn't even ask, she offers to do it out of the kindness of her heart. Here's me thinking she is entirely selfish, only out for herself and never considers others. Shame on me. There's my lesson of the day. It's easy to jump to conclusions about people by the way they behave, but you can never tell who someone really is behind their sarcastic put downs. She disappears through to her bedroom with scissors, glue and double-sided sticky tape.

"I'm an old pro and can knock anything up in no time."

True to her word, in no time at all she is back with the most wondrous, silky bushy moush moush. It's not quite perfect as it has a ginger tinge to it, is curly and somewhat coarse in texture, but it'll absolutely work. She flicks her head upside down, side to side.

"I've got loads of hair, no one will ever notice that I'm minus a few."

Bless, she cut some hair from the back of her head.

JULES

Ange comes back into the room with a real-hair moustache, cut from her own hair. Wow, even I didn't see that coming. Cutting her most treasured locks for Nursie, highly unusual and very suspicious. She keeps winking at me, but I put it down to the fact that she may have trapped a few rogue hairs under her eyelid.

ANGE

The Tram is busy, full of nuns, priests, a few Crocodile Dundees, a shedload of Ednas, but not one single, solitary Freddie.

"Look Ange, I was right, not one Great Pretender."

She's fair chuffed[28] with herself over this one.

"Look how original I am. I'm surprised no-one else thought of coming as Freddie, aren't you?"

"Yes, very original indeed, and more than even you know you Great Pretender, you."

She enters herself in the contest, just to be fair here, I do try and persuade her not to, but she can be very stubborn at times. I'm sure if she only knew the full truth, the whole truth, then she wouldn't have, but she doesn't, so I don't stop her. Neither she, the judges, the audience or the other contestants will be any the wiser.

LESLEY

I'm over the moon, tickled pink. I am the only Freddie here and with white sequined jumpsuit, glasses and my bushy moustache, I am practically a dead ringer for him. I am so chuffed. I decide to enter the competition, nothing gained, nothing ventured and all that. I get up on stage and take my place beside a mediocre koala bear. I know that's going to be popular, but there are colonies of them here tonight. On the other side of me, there's an Aborigine in what I believe to be national attire, an outfit decorated with coloured dyes and an intricate weaving pattern. Not sure if they're actually in fancy dress costume or just their usual clobber. There's a girl dressed in black with a vegemite sticker on her tummy, a guy with a hat with corks on it. The Crocodile Hunter with a fake, well, I sincerely hope it is, crocodile. There's a giant inflatable kangaroo with a girl in its pouch. Now, that's clever. A guy in his surfie gear with a plaque round his neck that says

"Shark Biscuit".

I'm sure I'm in with a shout.

ANGE

She doesn't seem to notice that everyone around her is dressed in some kind of AUSTRALIAN attire, like I said. When she catches my eye, I dig into my pocket and pull out the Freddie moustache that she'd bought. I stick it on, return her smile and wait to see her reaction when the penny drops.

LESLEY

I spot the girls at the front of the stage and catch sight of Ange's face. She looks, if I'm not mistaken to be wearing a moustache with her Crocodile Dundee outfit. I don't remember her wearing that to begin with and don't actually remember Peter Hogan having one. She smiles at me, nodding and stroking it. The other hand is pointing and scratching her groin. I'm not quite sure what she is trying to convey to me. I've never been that good at chairaids, so I'm slightly puzzled. In no time, the judge is beside me, remarking how good my costume is, especially that my moustache which looks like "pubic hair, and very typically Freddie".

The lightbulb goes on and it dawns on me EXACTLY what she has done. Shirley not! She wouldn't. Would she? I look over and she's nodding as if to say. You're right, I did.

I glue my legs together, bend at the waist, and with a swish of my arm, I bow and exit stage left, my honour still intact. The minute I am in the wings, I rip it off immediately, which takes the top layer of skin off my upper lip. Although I am mortified, nobody other than Ange seems to notice and I can leave with my head held high. The audience is clapping, thinking my stage left exit is all part of the act and that it was my intention all along to bow and take this gesture as part of my performance as a final curtain call. Shame on her. How could she? I can tolerate a fair amount, but this really crosses the line.

JULES

I see Nursie take her final bow and exit stage left. Great dramatic performance. Then I see her as she rips her facial hair off all of a sudden. There's a turn-up for the book, a very typical gesture of Freddie. It goes down a storm. Not sure where she's gone, but I give her a resounding clap and wolf whistle.

"ENCORE! ENCORE!"

Ange is roaring with laughter beside me and I see now that she's wearing the original moustache. She shouts in my ear over the applause that she'd snipped her pubic hairs, which were long overdue for a trim, and glued them on to a pantie liner, then cut it out in the shape of Freddie's moustache. I'm shocked and aghast at this revelation. I sincerely hope it wasn't a used panty liner to add insult to injury.

"What a beeitch."

"Well, I'll be itching for a while that's for sure. Did you see her face? Priceless."

"You have stooped to even lower levels with that one Ange. How could you be so callous?"

"Settle Petal, it's only a joke and I mean no harm by it. Besides, the audience likes it. See it as a form of payback."

"Payback?? For what exactly? Disagreeing with you? Challenging your opinion? Get a feckin' grip. You really need to take a long hard look at yourself Ange."

"Lighten up will ya. You've got to admit, it's quite funny."

"Somehow, I don't think you'd be saying that if it were you up there sporting someone else's pubic hair on your upper lip."

I'm about to go find Nursie, when they announce the winner.

"G'DAY fellow Aussies, Pommy bastards, seppos, drongos and dags. THE WINNER OF OUR CONTEST TONIGHT IS…. DRUM ROLL PLEASE ROGER TAYLOR……. FREDDIE MERCURY!"

She is nowhere to be seen so I go up on stage to collect her prize money and trophy for "MOST ORIGINAL" contestant of the evening.

LESLEY

I can't believe she actually did that. Who in their right mind would even THINK of doing that? I am horrified to think I'd been wearing her pubic hair most of the night, and in public to add injury to insult. I may even have licked my lips. GADZOOKS. There is no way I am staying here a moment longer just to be humiliated by her "jolly japes" as she sees them.

When I get home, I scrub my teeth, scrape my tongue and put aloe vera on my throbbing upper lip. They look bee-stung, flared, red and swollen. I barricade myself in my bedroom in case she tries to come in later to say sorry. I am not ready for her disingenuous apologies and regrets.

In the morning, I almost trip over a trophy etched with

"MOST ORIGINAL"

which is sitting outside my bedroom/sitting room door along with an envelope containing $200.

Well now, there's a turn up for the books. I had won. I turn it over in my hands and am actually quite delighted. I'd won something. I never win anything. How Ange behaves is totally out of my control, but how I respond as opposed to react to this is well within my control. I choose not to react, but rather to respond to it so I take the furry panty liner out of the bin, attach it to my winning golden chalice and put it on the shelf, pride of place in the bedroom/sitting room, not only as a mark of my own sense of humour, but also to remind me what kind of person I am dealing with. Let's see how she likes having her g-hinger bush on display for all to see. I am happy to forgive her, but I'll remember it always as I have one of those photogenic mammaries.

ANGE

Well, well, well, Lezzers' does have a sense of humour after all, good on her. I initially thought perhaps I'd gone a step too far and blown our friendship clean out the door. Not sure how I feel about seeing my pubes on the mantelpiece for everyone to see though. My own doing, I guess, so I have to roll with the punches. However, I wasn't aware that they are quite as g-hinger as they are. Gadz. Time for an overhaul down under methinks. Snipping bits of pubes for her moustache has left some very clear divots in my bush. I'm going to head to the local salon "Pretty Kitty" for some much-needed attention.

An absolutely stunning, leggy, blonde - and I use the latter term loosely - greets me with a "G'day. Need some attention Down Under?"

I'm not as original as I clearly think I am as I've been referring to my muff as Down Under for months. You know as in Wanted Down Under if you get my drift. No?? Okay, can I see your minge menu please?"

The menu has the full list of services offered. Let's see how many different ways there are to make your "pudendum" more appealing to the general pubelick. What the fuck is a "Pudendum" anyway? Sounds like the inner workings of a grandfather clock.

Glancing at the highly graphic colourful illustrations, I am under no illusion as to what "Pudendum" is. All I really need is it manicured and a cheeky wee dye, maybe purple for fun, and perhaps a bikini wax as The Barbary Apes are creating mayhem on my inner thighs. There is nothing on this menu quite as basic as that. But, if I'm up for it, I can have:

1. The Brazilian - A landing strip (for easier take-off and landing for all the lovely Aussie surfer boys is my guess).

2. The Hollywood, Sphinx or American Eagle - All the hair is removed - the front, the middle, all the way to the backside, leaving you entirely bare. This service requires three therapists and three hours (whose needs are being met there I wonder).

3. Las Vegas - A Hollywood with added accessories: Bejewelled or Vajazzled on your Mound of Venus. This service requires 4 therapists and 3 1/2 hours, which includes drying time (I can only assume the extra therapist is there to hold the video recorder).

4. A New Yorker - The pubic tuft is shaped into an apple symbol, dyed red or green. Choose between a Golden Delicious, a Honeycrisp or a Fuji (or in years to come a Granny Smith).

5. A Down Under - Six stars placed strategically for all six states (I have enough room down there to put the star-spangled banner, all 50 states and the stripes).

No, no, I'm losing the will to live just by reading all this and it's waaay too painful methinks. Besides, the price is outrageously astronomical. I actually find it hard to believe that someone would be willing to pay to have all this done to their foof when all they need to do is go to the chemist and get one of those easypeasy, peel-off, pain-free wax strips for a fraction of the price. How hard can that be?

The only "Down Under" I need is a willing, able and highly talented participant with macroglossia. I head to Ropers Seaside Pharmacy to pick up a cheap kit. Fluff Be Gone looks as good as any. I'm optimistic that it has to be less painful than the "vajazzling". I choose one with the cold pressed thingymajigs with "soothing aloe. No melting lumps of burning wax". Just rub the strips together, create friction, kinda like chub rub I guess, and when it feels warm to the touch, peel apart and press on unwanted bush. Wait 30 seconds and gently peel. No Muss, no fuss, no fuzz. Bob's yer uncle and Fanny's your bald aunt. Sorted. I head home with my purr-chase and take myself off to the bathroom for my very own spa afternoon. The two pieces of cloth feel fairly hard and I know it will take ages for me to get them to be even lukewarm, so I use Lezzer's hairdryer to speed the process up a bit. It takes less than five minutes and they peel apart beautifully, like a succulent clementine skin. I lay the top one on the side of the bath and place the other very carefully across my fuzzy inner thigh. I see where all those therapists come in to play, I could certainly use Jules, or even better Lezzers', to be my lovely assistant. I take a deep inhale and…yank it off…it works…yahoo! It isn't the best feeling in the world but it isn't the worst either. I can feel a slight tingling sensation, but tots doable… I got this…slam dunk. I feel ferocious, empowered, fighter of all wayward unwanted pubic hair.

Goddess of the smooth, hairless body parts, smoother than the smoothest of smoothies.

I decide there and then that I can create my own visual art with the second strip. The Picasso of Pubiscus, Leonardo De Vagio, Remnants, Rusty Crowe. Forget the latter, I'm so over him. I prefer Top Crotch now. I put my foot on the loo seat, and I do EXACTLY as I have just done before, no deviation, no embellishment, no differentiation, no variation whatsoever. I place the strip to the right of my hooha and press it down firmly till it almost reaches my anus. It is an exceedingly long strip Mr Kipling, I notice. I inhale deeply, brace myself…RRRRRR…(1, 2 , 3…4…5)… IIIIIII… (6…7…8….9…..10…..) PPPPPPPP…….

"FUCK!!!!!!"

I'm blind!!! Blinded by excruciating pain. Oh, my giddy balding aunt…. this is fucking agonising. Stars and blinking lights are machine-gunning from my peepers and when they begin to ease up, my vision slowly starts to return. I wish I hadn't really looked down towards the damage, I see I've only managed to pull off a mere slither, and I'm talking 2 cm of the loathsome strip.

"SHITE!!"

And breathe...very fast...very fast…pull it QUICKLY…. RRIIPPPP. The whole room begins to spin and my vision is a blur of spots, colour and fireworks. I think I might even pass out. I can hear steel drums playing somewhere in headspace. The increasing expansion in my head is practically at bursting point.

BREATHE...

BREATHE….

I brace myself to glance at my delicate, throbbing honey-pot. A wax-covered strip stares back at me. I want to gloat in the glory of seeing my hairy pelt stuck to the perpetrator of my discomfort. I lift it gently within blurry reach of my eyesight and focus on the cloth I'm now holding 4cm from my face.

No Hair!!

Where's the hair??

Shitty shite, fuckety fuck. Where's the wax??

The product must be faulty.

I slowly look to my nether regions, my foot is still propped on the loo seat and I still see hair, the hair that should be on the cloth.

 I tentatively touch my pulsating groin.

"NOOOOOOO…"

"WAX!!!"

I run my fingers over the most sensitive part of my body, which is mildly erotic if I care to admit, but not only is it still covered in hair, but it includes big clumps of hardening wax. I straighten up as my back is beginning to hurt, but as soon as I have both feet terre ferme, I realise to my absolute horror the huge, catastrophic mistake I have just made.

Sealed shut.

My furry fanny is SEALED SHUT, leaving the inner vaults in consummate darkness.

"SHUT SHIT SHUT."

I penguin walk around the bathroom, muttering, sputtering, spluttering, spitting, cursing like a rabid hairy beast. What can I do? What can I fucking do? Mary, Mother of Lezzers'. WWLC? What Would Lezzers' Chew? Here's another fine mess I've gotten myself into.

"Open Sesame!"

Hoping against all odds that the mouth of the cave will miraculously yield, open up and reveal its hidden treasures in all its glory. I feel a stinging sensation in my bladder. That only means one thing, right? I will myself not to pee, please, please, no peeing. Then it comes to me, maybe peeing is the very thing to wash away the waxy build-up. At the very least, it might soften the unwanted sucker. Will it work? Hmmm, perhaps not. What else do I have to hand? Not the hairdryer, I'm not that stupid. What about a hot bath? That should do it. Hot water melts wax, yeah? I pour a lovely HOT bath. You know, the kind where your skin goes bright red, waxy looking and resembling minker's tartan. Well, it's already crimson and glistening, so nothing ventured, nothing gained. I slip in gently and as gracefully as Little Mermaid. Once sitting, I look to see if the wax is dissolving, alas…. NOT! I didn't notice until I got in that the water is hotter than the rolling boil used to cook lobsters. My legs turn from a rather unusual shade of pinky red to somewhere between the colour of corned beef and roadkill. They look like two suckling pigs rolling around in a clear plastic bag.

Is there anything worse than having your panty hamster stuck together? Oh yes, being glued to the bathtub, in scalding water, which incidentally doesn't melt wax. Complete fallacy. Whoever started that particular urban myth needs to be hung, drawn and quartered, left to rot in a pot of scalding wax. Another disclaimer here. Not to be tried at home kids.

I begin to holler for some assistance. I'm able to use my big toe to drain the water at the same time, multitasker extraordinaire.

Lezzers' would definitely be able to fix this, then I remember that she's doing a double shift today. And in my hour of need as well, how terribly inconsiderate of her. I need her NOW, not in a few hours' time. I could kick myself if my legs weren't stuck firmly together. Bloody hell, Jules will have to do for the time being.

JULES

I hear a high-pitched screech coming from the bathroom. The voice is loud and demanding.

"Jules?? Where are you?"

"Ange?"

"Of course, it's me, who else do you know that would be shouting for you in the middle of the afternoon from OUR bathroom?"

I go to the door and she informs me that she's stuck in the bathtub and that her legs are glued together. That's a first. Well, I think that's what she's saying at least. How is that even possible? What has she done? It's all punctuated with expletives, which I choose to ignore.

"I have company at the moment Ange, so if you give me 10, I'll get rid of him."

"Make it 5. I need you NOW!"

I had been enjoying a rather lovely afternoon date with a very attractive German boy, Franz, or something like that, I'd met at the fancy dress party the other night. Seems a shame to cut it a tad shorter than I'd anticipated, but truthfully, I'm done. Takes me a bit longer than I meant to hustle him out the flat, as I wasn't actually done as I previously thought. When I see him out the door, I promise we'll do it again soon... NOT. His faux leather lederhosen dungarees are such a turn-off. I'm back to Ange in virtually no time at all. I knock on the door.

"Hello, hello, cooee, anyone here?"

I slowly open the bathroom door to reveal Ange, true to her word, stuck firmly in the bathtub, naked from the waist down, like a flailing whale without the flipper. One of those froggy bath mitts hiding her genitalia. She's sound asleep. I gently wake her up and she looks up at me with those sad, hazel doe-like eyes.

"I'm stuck. What took you so long? Shirley you could hear in my voice that I needed you?"

"Sorry, it took longer to get rid of Hans than I realised."

She explains what's happened and I try, without much success, not to laugh, but I just can't hold it in. I laugh so hard that the tears are streaming down my inner thighs. I have to sit on the pot beside her as I am actually peeing myself silly. She doesn't join in, just glowers at me, waiting for me to literally and physically get it out of my system.

"Sorry Ange, Schadenfreude should be my middle name, other people's misfortunes are my gain. You'd be the first to say that if the strip had been on the other person's leg, then you'd have found this entire scenario highly amusing. If the strip had been on the other thigh, namely mine, then you'd have been merciless."

We go through various solutions and decide that scraping it off carefully with a razor might be the best plan. Personally, I like the idea of calling the fire brigade, but she tells me that's me showing my selfish side again.

"Forget the razor, this calls for more extreme measures. Let me see if I can find the number to hire a bulldozer."

While she painfully dry-scrapes her wombat wig, I sit watching from the cheap seat adding dialogue to the unfolding event.

"Don't worry Ange, I'll stick with you. What are friends for after all if they don't STICK together? Stick it out, you're doing great. Reminds me of the visits our family used to make to Mme Tussaud's wax museum when I was younger."

LESLEY

I come home to some shenanigans going on in the bathroom. I poke my head round the door to see what's happening. I'm exhausted after a fairly traumatic double shift, but can't resist a wee peek.

ANGE

Jules is warbling in my ear about wax, sticky stuff and some other shit in her usual fashion when I notice Lezzers' blonde noggin pop round the door. YIPPEE, she'll know exactly what to do.

LESLEY

In unison, Jules and Ange are trying to tell me what's going on and how they've been trying to fix it. I pick up the box it had come in and notice the lotion that came with it to "gently remove excess wax". I put a liberal amount on the froggy mitt and her inner thighs. Dear Lord, how much wax had she used? The wax gently dissolves.

ANGE

"HALLELUJAH!"

Lezzers' is very calm and professional. She applies a liberal amount of the lotion to my inner sanctum.

"OH, MY GAWD!!"

My scream is probably heard in The Outback, and certainly puts an end to Jules's wittering. I ALMOST laugh out loud seeing the look on her face. I scare the bejesus out of her. It is soooo painful but I'm becoming numb to any sensations in my nether regions. It subsides fairly quickly though. Lezzers' carefully wipes off the remainder of the wax, but to my dismay I see that there is still a colony of hamsters snuggled up down there. I am too impatient, I push her hand out of the way and grab the razor which I know will annihilate the furry creatures. I feel nothing anyway. One could have amputated my left arm and I wouldn't feel a thing. The lotion that comes with the kit has removed all the excess wax immediately which makes the shaving effortless. FFS. Why doesn't the box tell you that FIRST? Seriously, what do they have to lose? Aside from hair that is. I tell Lezzers' that I owe her one and that if she ever wants a change of career then there is a place called

Pretty Kitty begging for her talents. She pats my sticky hamster.

"There you go Ange, all done."

I won't lie, there are more than a few fanny flutters before I remember whose hand is down there.

JULES

The bells are still ringing in my ears from Ange's joyous shrieks. I try to congratulate her and add that if she is still thinking about dying her pubes, then I think she would make an excellent suicide blonde, dyed by her own FURR hands. I can't help but notice that she has more than her fair share of pubic hair down below, under her arms and on her top lip. Must be a genetic disorder.

I, for one, am NOT going to be the one to point that out though. She pays no attention to us and continues to go on about the swell gel in the water as her legs look like "skinned porkers".

I have to agree. She grabs the towel from Lesley and gets out of the bath, claiming that I had been about as useful as a chocolate teapot. Lesley and I shrug our shoulders. Lesley then cleans the bathroom of the copious cotton strips, wax, and pubic hair. Good on her. I'd throw up if I had to touch any of it. Goodness knows how many different samples she'd come across intertwined with the original ones.

LESLEY

I can barely keep my eyes open, I am exhausted. I know that if I want to soak in a lovely warm, bubble bath later then I'm going to have to be the one to clean this mess up. I always have disposable gloves somewhere close by which I'm going to need here as one can never be too sure what you're being exposed to and most certainly in this case. No offence or judgement towards Ange, you understand, but one can never be too careful these days.

I detect various different colours of rogue pubes in the bath and around the sink that Ange must have cast. I would prefer not to think about her extracurricular activities, but it's hard not to miss, given the evidence. I might suggest she take a few days of antibionics as a preventative measure. It's her wellbeing at stake after all.

Once I've finished cleaning I go outside to cut some aloe vera leaves and leave it on a plate at her door. That should calm the redness down.

JULES

Ange comes out of her bedroom and into mine. She is walking like John Wayne and has green slime oozing through her toes. She must have stepped on the aloe that Nursie kindly left for her. She's muttering: "How careless of her to leave this green pus stuff on my door threshold. She might have told me first as I've just come out of my bedroom and stepped straight into it."

The swelling is on her inner thighs and fanny, not her toes, so what harm is done? I return her glare.

"Be grateful and more appreciative of the fact that she actually came to your rescue."

"Not soon enough though, was it? I'm scarred for life."

As I sit there watching her wallowing around in her own self-pity, I notice that someone must have slipped a rubber ring around my midriff when I wasn't looking. Where did that jelly belly come from? It's surely not part of me? Since when did I have a colossal 3D gut? Being overweight runs in my family. Actually, NO-ONE runs in my family, maybe that's why we are all built for comfort, not speed. We are all of the comfier build. There are ways around this that might make it easier for me to wrap my head round - for instance, if I stand on stilts and weigh myself, I'd be the perfect weight for my height. I shout through the bedroom door to Lesley and ask if she has anything in her nurse's Mary Poppins bag that dissolves fat overnight?

"Write a food diary and I'll take a look at it."

Sounds simple enough and if that helps me lose weight then I'll scribble in a journal till my heart's content and my spare tyre will disappear. I sit at the kitchen table and ponder what I eat on a daily basis. I have some crisps and dip in front of me. Eh, no judgments here, it helps me think. I haven't started yet have I? I'll start properly tomorrow.

Great start to the next day, I feel buoyant and ready to begin my new regime. The next day I am raring to go. For breakfast I start with; A grapefruit, of the very pink variety, less calories I assume as why would they make calories vibrant colours? A slice of wholegrain toast, sans butter, a cup of cereal with unsweetened coconut milk. I have to dip the toast in the milk to make it less bland and more chewable. I pour myself a large mug of black coffee which tastes very bitter and turns my tongue brown. It is a great start though and I already feel myself shrinking. I'm on a roll, as opposed to being one. Why does everything have to be food-related I ask you? Now for lunch. I know it's only 8 am, but I'm still hungry so I fry myself a fist-sized portion of Snapper fish with a cup of raw spinach. You gotta love Popeye the Sailorman. Full of goodness and builds muscle and strength. I've seen how eating it affects him. Hopefully my biceps will pop out like his. Followed by a smattering of blanched almond slivers, accompanied by five strawberries, a drizzle of balsamic glaze, a cup of fennel tea and an organic blueberry muffin, which is at least two of my daily fruit and veggie intakes. My inflatable midriff ring is positively melting away before my eyes.

I'm rather peckish by mid-morning, so have the remainder of the muffins from the bumper value pack of 25 for $6. A bargain not to be overlooked when I spotted them in Aldis. Each one is the size of an individual blueberry so it counts for all my daily fruit intake. Sorted. I'm STILL hungry, so I have a tub of Baskin Robbins, only 4 oz, low fat I might add, ice cream, homemade vanilla with a smidgen of hot fudge and a dusting of crushed pecans. Ya beauty, extra fruit portion for the day. Are nuts fruits or vegetables? Hmmm, no matter. To be sure, I'll add a cheeky wee maraschino cherry. My day is getting better and better.

By the time dinner comes around at 4.30pm, I'm famished and parched. Ange brings home a six-pack of beer, and as it would be rude not to join her, I have one as they're only little stubby-sized ones, they don't really count. One bottle doesn't even hold one full glass, well not the usual size I drink. She also has 8 bottles of pick-and-mix wine, so I have to try the red, white, rose, and fizz, hell, even that Riesling shit will do. I haven't been drinking enough water so punctuate each glass of wine with a glass of water for balance. When you drink wine, you also have to have something to soak up the alcohol, so I have four garlic dough balls, shared with Ange I might add, one extra thick crust stuffed with cheese pizza, again shared with Ange, and to be brutally honest here, she does eat the lion's share. We manage to prune some of the Audrey Two's, skin up one or three doobies, followed by a small bucket of buffalo wings - tastes like chicken to me... oh well. Ange is still eating more than me, so I can probably take two-thirds of the calories off for my portions. We smoke some more contributions from Nursie's cannabis plants, which are now like a forest in the back garden. Ange has been sneaking out there unnoticed and snipping some cuttings, drying them and rolling them into some very moreish homemade, homegrown spliffs. We name all the plants "Audrey. 1-50"

There are at least 50 Audrey clones out there now. Nursie is totally oblivious, none the wiser and continues to innocently nurture and cultivate our supply, unaware of the fact she is likely the number one weed grower in the nation. In fact, she continues she is keeping us in the state that we have now become accustomed to. By late evening, and after having smoked a copious amount of reefers, I am STARVING again, and I mean really, really ravenous, so I have three party-sized snickers, the full size would just have been pure greed, you understand, and a portion of buttered popcorn, which is definitely vegetable. Trick must be to eat a variety of meals regularly throughout the day. There must be at least 20 "TO GO" puddings and sweet things in the boxes in the fridge that Nursie brings home on a regular basis.

She has more or less deserted us, with all the hours she works. She must be stressed, but if you arrange those letters slightly, we benefit by having her desserts in the contents of the very full fridge. Literally, all we're eating is just desserts. She has stopped making the home cooked meals unfortunately as she says she has no time - so no lentil vegetable soup, no shepherd's pie, no lasagne, no mince and tatties, no fish pie or beef stews, only choices are from doughrings to cheesecake, pavlova to key lime pies and ice cream to mouldy berries. It looks like there's even a marinated kangaroo meat burger lurking under a foosty cabbage.

There is so much stuff in here, most of it beyond all recognition. It wouldn't surprise me if there's a flock of dodos hiding out in the produce drawer. Noone thinks to look in there for anything after all. There's also a whitish spongy-looking thing which is either a floury bap or Ange's contraception cap. She said it was missing. I'm definitely not about to take a bite to check. It's probably been fermenting on the shelves for weeks. That's meant to be good for you right? Some folk drink this fermented kombucha shit, don't they?

Not the same looking at all these boxes and deciding what to eat, it's so much easier when it's put down in front of you. I might tell her she's working too much and that it's not good for her health…. or mine for that matter. Although I do think it's helping my waistline as I can't be bothered cooking or eating really. I do miss not having her bumbling about the kitchen so much though, fussing over me in her overly attentive way. She is still managing to stack the dishwasher and keep the place clean though, which is a blessing in disguise.

There's enough grass left over for another two wee numbers. I'm only up for one more tonight, so Ange decides to use all of it in one spliff, which turns out to be the most monstrous thing you have ever seen. I'm surprised it doesn't need scaffolding reinforcement. It's the size of an extra-large, super-duper, fully absorbent tampon on steroids. That's going to count as my exercise for the day as it is much heavier than it looks. Lifting it to my lips is similar to a bicep curl with a 3lb dumbbell. We are famished, so we share the last slice of the New York style cheesecake. That's my dairy taken care of today at least. I can hardly open my eyes, let alone my mouth, but can't stop myself from ladling it in. I have so much going in there, it may even be seeping from my ears along with my mouth, only to be witnessed by Nursie who opens the door and walks in from her shift.

LESLEY

I'm so looking forward to putting my feet up, catching up on Neighbours and having the last of the cheesecake I'd bought. I'm not going to lie but I'm hoping The Girls are out for the night, leaving me as usual with some much-needed peace and quiet. I can hear them in the kitchen.

"Coo Coo"

I pop my head round the door. OMG! Jules looks like she's choking, her eyes are bloodshot and rolling around in her head. She's frothing at the mouth and something is clearly stuck. Ange is sitting back, staring at her, not doing anything. Lucky for her that I have walked in at this exact moment. I go into full nurse service mode and yank her up out of her seat, turn her back to me, place one foot slightly in front of the other for balance, make a fist with the hand which is holding her around her waist, grasp my fist with my other hand and perform between six to ten abdominal thrusts until the blockage begins to dislodge. All kinds of things come up and out over the kitchen table. I can't quite tell which offending thing actually was the perpetrator of her choking, but there is a particularly large piece of undigested grapefruit of all things. Ange is in absolute fits of giggles.

"She's not choking Lezzers', she's got a mouthful of cheesecake that's all."

"MY cheesecake?"

"No need to show off your very admirable skills here. You remind us regularly of them."

If I'd known it was only cheesecake she was choking on, I might have been a little less enthusiastic, that would eventually turn to liquid and pour out.

"Show off? Show off? I thought I was saving her life."

JULES

What the hell? One minute I'm enjoying my pudding, the next minute I'm being manhandled, turned practically upside down and assaulted to the point I lose most of my day's intake. Hmmmm, every cloud and all that.

LESLEY

It's an honest mistake and most anyone I know coming from my profession would have done exactly the same. I apologize, help clean her up and the kitchen table, which is strewn with a smorgasbord of EVERYTHING. You name it, it's there in front of me, aside from the kitchen sink, that is, because it's overflowing with dishes. Surprisingly there isn't a cuddly toy thrown into the mix. It saps one's energy living with these two, not sure how much more I can handle.

ANGE

Jules is delusional as she tucks into yet another Tim Tam. She's now decided it isn't her diet that's making her put on weight, but that she has water retention. Yeah, like an entire body of water retention. It's happened by snackccident is my guess.

JULES

The next day, I tell Ange that I'm totally fed up with all this diet malarkey, so we decide to pull an all-dayer and go to the pub. Sitting at the bar later, I am aware of the fact that my belly area is making hissing and bubbling noises. One of those peanut butter Tim Tams from last night must have been off. I feel a well dodgy tummy coming on. There is something way too familiar about this scenario for my liking as I goosestep my way to the loo, just in case. I don't want a repeat of Ange in Singers. My attention is momentarily diverted to the condom machine, and not the hand dryer. I've learned that mistake. It advertises "Smart inventions to decrease the population". So does halitosis, but there's no mention of that here. The face of it has all sorts of slogans to encourage customers to buy. Like "Don't be a ding dong, cover your shling-shlong". My personal favourite is "If you're going to banger with a franger, then cover yer wanger".

I never knew there were so many different types. There's "The night-light condom, non-toxic, glows for 30 seconds when activated by light."

Not specific about the type of light, could be a street light, car light, sun light, neighbour's torchlight, back light and/or stage light. Some of the other condoms are shaped, textured, coloured and come, 'scuse the pun, in various flavours.

"Baked Beans."

Seriously? Hmmm...

"Cadburys."

Does sound rather more appetising than beans.

"Tastes like it feels."

"Vegemite."

The national food of Australia. There's a ditty I hear played often on the radio for

"Castlemaine xxxx beer. Got the taste for it, just can't wait for it, I can feel a xxxx coming on."

And "Australians wouldn't give a XXXX for anything else."

These double entendres will blow most Uhmerikans away as "XXXX" is a brand of condom in the good ole Us of A. That type of supposed, alleged marketing is up there with Brewdog marketing slogans. Even the ditty has absolutely nothing to do with the xxxx condom, but it would spoil the fun to tell The Americans that. There's even "Lambskin condoms which are made from the intestinal membrane of a lamb. These condoms are truly a natural animal product, not suitable for vegans or vegetarians who may prefer to use latex sleeves which is produced from the Hevea Brasiliensis rubber tree and is the protective fluid contained beneath the bark."

Who knew? You learn something new every day.

"Lambskin condoms are apparently the oldest type of all condoms. There are records of men using lambskin condoms during the early part of the Roman Empire."

Haggis is also encased in said product. So, the moral of the story goes that if you don't have a prophylactic handy, use a haggis skin, or vice versa. Anyway, I have some more pressing business to take care of first before choosing my condom. My selection will have to wait temporarily until I'm done with my ablutions. I sit down on the pot and make myself comfortable. My guess is I'm here for the long haul. Suddenly a voice from the adjoining stall pipes up.

"Hey, you. How's it going?"

Now, I'm no shrinking violet, but I do feel that my purifications are a sacrilegious event and not the time for striking up a conversation with a complete stranger. Very likely a cultural thing as Aussies are known to be rather forward and overly familiar. Being the friendly chick I am though, I decide to reply.

"Not too bad thanks. Just hanging in there, well, bits of me are, other bits falling out."

Short and sweet, to the point, not unfriendly, and not too open-ended either.

The Voice comes back.

"What are you doing?"

I rack my brain to hear whether the voice is familiar, but no, can't retrieve anything about it that sounds even close to anyone I know. This is a really stupid feckin question considering the circumstances of our conversation. Regardless, I still find myself engaging.

"Och you know, I'm catching up with some friends for Happy Hour. Ha ha, ha..not in HERE you understand, but through in the bar. What are you doing?"

DOH!!! Didn't mean to ask a question.

"Ohhh right!"

The voice replies abruptly.

"I'm almost done here, can I come over?"

Bloody hell, my first encounter with an Australian lesbian lunatic. However, even in that awkward moment, I find myself being my usual polite, British self and decide to put an end to all this nonsense once and for all.

"I'm flattered and all that, that you want to come over here, and I have nothing against muff munchers, but this stall is way too small, even for little old me, and I'm not quite finished."

The Voice shouts…

"Listen, I'll have to call you back as there's some freak of nature in the next stall who's taking the piss out of me and joining in on my conversation with YOU."

FECK FECK FECK. I despise mobile phones and think they should be banned from toilets. How embarrassing. I wait for at least 10 mins before skulking out from the safety of my stall. I keep looking at everyone's feet in the bar though to see if I can spot the instantly recognizable bright yellow crocs she is wearing. Come to think of it, she might recognize MY silver-embellished flip flops or thongs as they're called here. Thankfully she'll never get the chance to see my real thong, but that's one for another day.

ANGE

Jules is way too embarrassed to stay at the bar, as every time she sees a flash of yellow, she thinks it's her stall buddy. She points out every yellow-clad foot that passes by. There does appear to be an unusually high demand for yellow foam clogs. It's becoming rather tedious so I suggest going back to the flat to partake in some of Lezzers'' Audreys. I have snipped, dried and bagged more of the homegrown delicacies that are still coming along nicely in the back garden. She has absolutely no idea that she is the biggest cannabis grower and now dealer in the hood. When the time is right I'm going to tell her that she'll get life in some dodgy correctional facility in Parramatta where ex nurses are always the flavour of the day. That should put the wind up her sails.

On the way, back we decide to go a different route as Jules doesn't want to be seen on the main esplanade as she might be recognized. Maybe from the peculiar dance moves she displays on the dance floor at The Tram, or the fact that she has slept with half of Bondi, but certainly not from having a conversation with someone in the next toilet cubicle, whom she didn't even see, aside from the yellow feet. We pass a hamburger joint called, wait for it, "HEART ATTACK GRILL".

HAG for short. Like the hag in the next toilet to Jules no doubt. Eat too many of these burgers and we'll certainly look more like one that's for sure. Is it just me, or is there more than a passing coincidence that Lezzers' also likes her burgers? Jules says she's so hungry she could eat a surfie's arm, so we decide that it's worth the risk and swan through the giant burger doors to see what's on the menu.

There's a flashing red "WARNING" light above the counter.

"Our burgers taste great, but may be hazardous to one's health, however, the management, which changes frequently due to unfortunate circumstances, believes it's an experience for every victim dying for a taste."

How can we resist it? We settle into a booth and check out the "Cardiac Arrest" menu. Maybe this is why Lezzers' likes it as it has a medical element to it. Interestingly, one can order a single, double or triple bypass burger with unlimited amounts of cheese, full fat of course. It comes with double deep-fried french fries in goose fat, not dissimilar to the contents of Lezzers''s buttocks I imagine. If that doesn't give you an immediate hearter, then their serving staff might. They are young, very young, even younger than us, fit-looking, much fitter-looking than us. Doesn't mean that they are though and their insides are very possibly like scrambled eggs. Their 'girls', if you know what I mean, have been surgically enhanced and there's more plastic in their faces than at an

International Tupperware party - and that's just the men. Some of their ample assets are still in UK time. For a laugh, I ask what the time actually is there at this moment. We do appear to be the only normal-looking people in the place which should also be called the Redneck Riviera. Plenty of singlets, tattoos and dental work opportunities to be had. The staff are wearing nurse outfits. This is definitely why Lezzers' comes here, so she can wear her uniform and feel even more at home. I am sure she points out at every conceivable opportunity that she is a bona fide nurse, a REAL one as opposed to the fake ones here alongside their burgers and boob jobs. I'm pretty sure there's no one left on the planet that she hasn't had the chance to tell. The difference though is that the hemlines of the waitresses here are more like NHS fanny pelmets and barely, and I do mean barely, covering their punani. Lezzers'' one comes down to her mid-shins, almost meeting her sensible, flat, comfy shoes - and I am talking about her hem here, although, who knows these days with all the crossbreeding that goes on in the west of Scotland what she's hiding under all that pressed, starched cloth. Reminds me of The Diddymen.

This place makes Hooters, Twin Peaks and Sweeter Meat Down Under look more like an organic coffee shop. Kids welcome, which in itself is interesting as that's all they seem to employ. Hiring from monasteries and nunneries only…..not! We decide to save our cash and burn it another day. Head to "The Flying Pie" for a $5, metre-long sausage roll instead. Why get the whole pig, when all you really want is the sausage right?

JULES

We end up meeting some of our chums at The Flying Pie and invite them back to the house for a wee sesh. Six lovely young himbos at our cervix…...hopefully. The afternoon has certainly taken a turn for the better. We sit in the garden among the illegal foliage drinking beer and rolling joints the size of rolled-up socks. It's like The Ghan's carriages, long and in quick succession. It seems to be going so well. Ange decides that a game of tangles is exactly what the Dr ordered. Now for those of you that don't know, tangles involves one of the participants turning their back on the others while the players take the hand of each of the other individuals standing beside them so that they are now in a linked circle. The group then has to tangle themselves together without letting go of each other's hands. The challenge is then for the untangler to turn around and get everyone untangled by giving instructions, like so- and- so go through so- and-so's legs, so-and-so go under so-and-so's arms etc. The idea is to have the participants arrive back in the original untangled standing state, again without ever letting go of each other'□™s hands. This game requires clear communication and cooperation from every player. Therein lies the problem. Easier said than done after a few beers and a 101 spliffs. I am upside down, hands between my legs, looking like I'm giving birth to a head of one of the nubile delights. Ange is literally sitting on the face of another one and we are rolling around, trying to get our balance, when we realise we've actually forgotten to put one person out to untangle us. It looks like some semi-clothed gangbang, or at the very least, an illustration from a bad version of the karma sutra. When through the dense herbage comes the call of a shrill birdie.

"Get OFF my plants. You're flattening them, get off NOW!"

LESLEY

When I hear all the noises from the back garden, I pop my head out and see to my horror all these complete strangers, punctuated with Jules and Ange flailing around all over all my plants. I can see they've broken the stakes I spent HOURS and hours of my time off lovingly putting together. They are now all broken, horizontal and as flat as pancakes. Not the majestic, lofty 5 ft, almost as tall as the greenery I had left before my 6 am shift. All have been trampled. Jules and Ange are bent, twisted, literally and physically and contorted in a sea of gyrating, undulating bodies. It's alright for some. They look like they may even be superglued together. Apparently, they are playing some silly childish game, but my lovely plants. I could cry.

ANGE

What's her issue? It's only a bit of harmless playful fun with a few friends. Besides if you're clever, you can design it to be sitting almost entirely on some hottie's face. I was doing precisely that when she rudely interrupts us. She should really take a chill pill, let down her permanently coiffed peroxide hair and lighten up a bit.

"Keep your hair on, Matron, I'll help you fix them by cutting them back and smoking them."

"Pardon?"

"I said, I'll help by cultivating them and re-staking the seedlings for you. You'll never notice the difference."

"Don't touch another thing, Ange, I'll do it as you can't be trusted. Now get out of my sight, ALL of you."

Most of them are practically ready to be cut down, dried and bagged for human consumption anyway. I can get round to that at a later date. I'll let her wallow in her weeds for a bit longer.

JULES

Ooops, I apologise, pat the blanket of crushed cannabis plants and head back inside to leave her to weep and repair the damage. It shouldn't take too long if she's the female version of the David Bellamy world she professes to be. They'll soon be back bushier, bigger and brighter than ever, not unlike Ange's hair. We leave her to reconstruct the collateral destruction and decide to take the party elsewhere. We know when we're not wanted. It's a bit of fun, no harm meant. If she knew what the plants really are, she'd be sure to be happy they'd almost been destroyed. Instead, she continues, albeit obliviously, of reestablishing herself as the Drug Queen pin-up she now is. She hasn't noticed the amount of pruning, drying and smoking that has been going on.

"You can leave this till later you know and come with us, let your hair down a bit."

"Thank you, but I'm way too tired. Tired of all your shenanigans, that is."

"We're not intentionally meaning to upset you. If you change your mind, we'll be down at The Tram. Please join us if you can and we'll try to make it up to you. Honest."

I think our social hand grenade behaviours are getting to her a bit. I guess it's safer knowing that Ange is with me as opposed to against me. Wouldn't want to be on the receiving end of her brutal barbs. Lesley should be thanking me that I'm taking her with me and not leaving her here. No matter how hard we try to have a normal night, we always end up, well, compromised in some way. We manage to ditch the six lads and are sitting at the bar minding our own business when two guys selling knock-off Aboriginal art come and join us.

LESLEY

I put the stakes back up, and although they don't look as perky as they had been in the morning, they aren't too bad from the squishing they'd had. I decide to let it go and join the girls at the bar. I haven't been out in a while, other than work, and could quite happily go to a wee glass of sauv or two to relax me. Besides I still believe that forgiveness is key and that our relationship is worth saving - Jules more than Ange - but I'm working on her. It makes it unpleasant to live together and have any ill-feeling between us.

They're sitting at the bar with some local, indigenous men when I arrive. This is great, maybe I can find out some interesting facts about their culture, their art, their ways of life and their plights living in Australia.

ANGE

Lezzers' appears and starts to ask all these very dull questions about their Aboriginal work, their origins and their art. How she even knows they are the actual artists, let alone Aborigines is beyond me. Och I don't even care. I'm losing the will to live listening to all of it. Thank goodness for the wine, which is excellent by the way, hits all the right spots. The wine is called "19 Crimes". The label states that there were "Nineteen crimes that turned convicts into colonists back in the day. Upon conviction, British rogues guilty of at least one of the 19 crimes were sentenced to live in Australia, rather than death. This punishment began in 1787 and many of the lawless died at sea. For the rough and ready prisoners who made it to shore, a New World awaited them. As pioneers in a frontier penal colony, they forged a new country and new lives, brick by brick. This wine celebrates the rules they broke and the culture they built".

How cool is that? It even has a downloadable app "Living wine labels" so that when you scan each label, you can hear the historical stories from The Infamous. It's not quite so easy to get into Australia these days, and stealing fish from a pond or river, which happens regularly in Scotland, won't get you deported, unfortunately. You're more likely to get in with an application through appearing in "Wanted Down Under" on television.

She hardly pauses for breath, gibbering on, totally oblivious to the fact that everyone is bored stiff with her mundane diatribe of dull facts, which aren't really facts at all. She does, however, punctuate her one-way conversation to reprimand me when I begin to sneeze.

"I'm a nurse you know, so do know it's good to cover up when you sneeze. But some ways are better than others, so sneeze into your elbow, Ange, not your hand. Please."

All this is more for the benefit of the artists and not us you understand.

"Of course, mum, I'll keep that in mind the next time"

LESLEY

I'm sure Ange is deliberately trying to be disruptive here by sneezing every two minutes. She's spreading her germs everywhere, so I have to keep reminding her what precautions she needs to take. I stand closer to her to protect the boys from her sprays. I have an institution the size of an ox and am up-to-date on my inoculations so am happy to take one for the team. I'm impressed how well the boys speak English and tell them so. Credit where credit is due, given that English is their second language.

ANGE

Very good English indeed.

"They were only just telling us they'd picked it up from 'The Fair Dinkum Possum's Guide to Learning Aussie in Six Weeks'."

She takes it in like soup.

"Now that's impressive, six weeks? Good on you mates."

"I'm joking Lezzers', English IS their native tongue."

"Och I knew that you Silly Billy. I can tell by their accents that they're Australian."

"Actually, they're Maori."

"Easy mistake Ange and if I may repeat myself, use your elbow when you sneeze. Next you'll be telling me they're not even artists."

"Oh they are, they're the genuine article, the real deal artists… piss artists that is."

"ANGE! I can't believe you just said that, it's so poetically incorrect."

"Politically, Lezzers', politically incorrect."

"That's what I said, you don't need to put words in my mouth. And for the umpteenth time, it's Lesley!"

"That's what I said, didn't I?"

"Ahhhh, ahhhhhh, ahhh…..."

Her eyes begin to smart and I see she is on the verge of yet another sneeze and remind her for the umpteenth time the protocol for sneezing in public.

ANGE

I feel a sneeze coming on so get ready...

"ELBOW, ANGE, ELBOW!"

Sure enough, the sneeze comes and as I bring my inner elbow to my face. I realise a second too late that I am still holding a full glass of red cabernet in my right hand which propels its contents at the speed of lightning straight into Lezzer's face who is standing way too close to my left. She stands there blinking rapidly as the red liquid drips from her brows, tip of her nose and chin. It's too hard for all of us not to laugh. Her white t-shirt is wet and clinging to her pert large buswams.

"OOOPS, sorry, it was a complete accident!"

"I'm sure that even you wouldn't do anything this deliberate, Ange. I'd better go home and change."

"Either that or stay for the wet t-shirt which is coming up later. You're bound to win... get another trophy for your collection."

"I'll pass thank you. I was about to call it a night anyway as I have work in the morning."

JULES

It is funny, but I do hope that it wasn't deliberate. She insists it wasn't, but one can never be too sure where she's concerned. Nursie leaves us at the bar and Ange continues her eye-fucking with the two boys. It almost feels like we're all playing winking murder without actually playing the game. They tell us they have to continue going round the bars selling their art, but offer to meet us at the nightclub The Flesh Exchange later. If they play their cards right, then that is exactly what is going to happen.

We get there after midnight and find that they have a reserved booth in the club with the best ogling position ever and are clearly waiting for us as they beckon us over to join their table. The place is packed, and hopping with half-clad men and women. The dance floor is positively undulating, groaning and throbbing under the palpable sexual energy and tension of the hot dancers. One of the guys produces a lump of blow the size of Ayers Rock and I know by Ange's expression that it is Goodnight Vienna. Tatties. Instinctively I know we should bail now, but something always stops me. Some might call it stupidity.

ANGE

They happily hand it all over to me.

"Feel yer boots Sheila!"

Or something like that. I don't care what or how they say it, all I know is where I'm heading with the blow. Somebody try and stop me.

JULES

Oh, my giddy aunt. Give me strength, Ange appears back at the table with what I believe to be a blind man's walking stick, but it turns out to be the biggest spliff I have ever clapped eyes on. Cheech and Chong eat your heart out. They'd be very proud of this exquisite piece of art. I'm afraid, very, very afraid.

ANGE

You can't look a gift horse in the face and refuse the challenge. I surprise myself with the unique piece of art that I produce. It is clean, straight, plump and worthy of any top art prize. It may even take the best place in the Guiness Book of Records for being the biggest, baddest joint known to mankind. Maybe not, Woody Harelson or Willie Nelson probably still hold that record. The one called Barry tells me it's skunk or something like that and that perhaps I should go easy.

"Don't teach your granny how to suck eggs Bazzer."

PAH! Stuff and nonsense, what does he know?

JULES

I suddenly become aware of some high-pitched howling and as I arrive in the present moment, I realize it is unmistakingly Nursie's voice. When did she arrive at the club? As she comes in to focus, I can see she is wearing her Sleeping Beauty nightie. Why would she wear that to the club? Doesn't make sense. She is shouting something I can't quite make out yet and it's LOUD. We are in Ange's bedroom and I can now see she is grabbing armfuls of clothing from the floor, the bed and the chairs. She's throwing them at the two naked 'artists' standing in the middle of the room.

"PUT THEM ON NOW. The police are banging on the front door."

Where did they come from anyway? How did we get here? So many questions racing through my head. Ange's bedroom walls and ceiling are flashing rotating blue lights which is very strange, almost like Doctor Who's Tardis has just landed in the centre of the room.

Barry and his friend are standing buck naked in front of me. WTF? I look around to see where the tardis is. What on earth is happening here? I thought we were in the club smoking…....OH OH…smoking!

"The police are outside. I need you to grab Ange and take her and the drugs to the bathroom. NOW!"

There is no mistaking the urgency and authoritative tone in her voice. I scoop up the drug paraphernalia, the hash, grab Ange, and shove her into the loo.

"Get rid of it Ange!"

Shit, this might be serious. I stand in the hallway as Lesley opens the door to the police at the same time as escorting the two half-clad boys out.

LESLEY

"Good evening Ociffers."

Did she just say "Ociffers?"

"Is there a problem here? I'm just seeing my guests out. I'm a nurse you see and these two are my anatomy grinny pigs."

"There have been complaints of loud noises Ms."

"I do apologise, these two upstanding citizens of the world are starving artists and moonlight as still-life models in their spare time. It was only a harmless study session and a very productive menage-a-trois if I'm really honest. I've been so engrossed in the learning of the naked male anatomy tonight that I got carried away and hadn't realised the time. It won't happen again…. EVER. You have my absolute word on that."

"There have been several complaints tonight Ms, so pipe the music down."

I am so tempted to tell them that I am one of the complainants. For the past few hours I've been coming through to the bedroom at least a dozen times to turn the music off, and each time I turn my back, the music goes back on. In addition, there always appears to be another article of clothing in the accumulating pile in the middle of the room. They must be playing strip poke her or something. When I heard the distant sirens, I knew without a shadow of a doubt that I had to sort it out as there are enough drugs in here to sink a battling ship. I'm absolutely not going to go down for this pair of fools. I'm mortified, compounded by the fact that the policeman is winking at me. They're all openly giggling now. Thankfully the two boys have slipped through their nets and are streaking their way down towards the Parade. This is singularly the most embarrassing, affronting thing that has ever happened to me, even worse than Freddie-Gate. They clearly think that I have been partaking in flagrante delicto. I'm not sure I'll ever forgive them for putting me in this position. Thankfully, Ange has been instructed to flush all the drugs away so at the very least there's no evidence to pin on us. Hopefully she stays in there until they are well and truly gone. My nerves can't cope with her thinking the police might be strippers coming to join the party. The lead ociffer tweaks my cheeks between his thumbs.

"Hope you had fun Little Lady, now take Sleeping Beauty back to her bed where she belongs at this time of night. I'm sure it's been fun, but now it is over."

ME... ME??? THEM. That pair of goons through the house? NOT me, I wanted to scream. He doesn't really think...I...surely...he doesn't...does he? The shame of it all. I can feel my cheeks burning. However, I just have to smile and suck it up Darlene. I take it. Whatever it takes to get rid of them I guess, rather than the alternative.

I can see the bare bottoms of the artists under the street lights, laughing and dressing themselves as they disappear around the corner. I close the door and breathe a huge sigh of relief. That was close, the closest I've ever come to being arrested and going to jail. I go back to the bedroom. Both of them are lying on the carpet like the number 11, fast asleep. I'd like to give them a piece of my mind but I am at a loss for words. I have just saved their lives, taken the blame for their drunken orgy. Nothing, no acknowledgement, no thanks, nothing. I get a blanket from the bed, place it over them and put two very large glasses of water beside them. I don't want them to catch a cold or get dehydrated in the middle of the night. This is the final end. No more games. I'm done. I can't and won't take anymore. The tears come gently and in a steady stream as I look on at this pitiful sight. I wish my Mikey was here to comfort me. I turn the stereo and the lights off and clear the mess. I still couldn't have them stepping on some of the broken glass and hurting themselves now, could I? I make the decision there and then that I'm going to leave first thing in the morning. I'm heading to nurse in The Outback where I know my skills are needed, beneficial and of value. My worth will not be dismissed by the tirade of abuse and a dismissive wave of a hand. I applied a while back to work with the indigenous tribes in an Aboriginal reserve in The Outback and had heard only yesterday that they not only wanted me, but actually needed me.

"Needed" - that's the word they used. This seems like the perfect time. My very own hero's journey. I don't need them or their drama anymore. I'm going to pack and write them a letter. I'm well and truly done here.

JULES

Warm sunlight streams brightly through the gap in the curtains, penetrating my retina. I can feel its laser-sharp light aim a direct hit on my pupil which is blinding my vision. I try to jump up, or at the very least move, to avoid being its unwavering, relenting shaft. I blink, trying to bring the room into some kind of focus and semblance. I see the light dust fairies twinkling, floating and drifting all around me. Moving gracefully, easily, gently mingling with the somewhat stagnant air.

Ange and I are lying on the floor facing each other with a blanket over us. There is a palpable eerie stillness and silence in the atmosphere. What's happening here? I stare at the dust fairies, willing them to spill their secrets and knowledge of the night, or maybe the last two nights...or...? Who knows? I have little to no recollection as to how long we've been lying here like this or why. If they could, would those magical fine pixie particles spill the truth, the whole truth and nothing but the truth. I know in my gut that whatever has happened here isn't good. Guilty as charged yer Honor.

I listen to the silent room, is it a mere coincidence that listen and silent contain the same letters. There is a feeling of peace and inactivity in the flat, only punctuated by the occasional squawks of the cockatoos outside. I say the cockatoos outside, but in all honesty, it could be the smoke alarms going off in my cerebral jungle gym. The light is burning my eyes and my tongue is plastered to the roof of my mouth. I try to drag my awareness back to my surroundings and focus ahead of me. I am almost eyeball to eyeball with Ange's lifeless-looking, open, dull, bloodshot blank eyes. The only way I know she isn't actually dead is because there is a pulse under her right eye that keeps flickering at me. A cross between communicating something in morse code and a life support machine.

In the silence, I listen to the gravelly, throaty rhythm of her breath. At least she is breathing. For a moment, she stares back, her left eye half-closed. Every 40 seconds or so, in slow motion, cautiously as if avoiding as much pain as possible, her cracked, dry lips move like a goldfish. Her mouth moves between puckering tight and gaping open, then closed again. In other circumstances, she may well win a prize for the great impression of a floundering guppy, or a blubbering whale out of water. I stare back into the dark chasm of her soul, aware of the drool seeping from the chasmic void hidden from deep inside. It trickles out in a constant stream onto the carpet nestled beneath her ear and between us. Her curls are matted, frizzy and wild, bound together with some unidentifiable, sticky substance. Her lips are like a dry pig trough with a messy surround. No Man's Land…certainly not if man or beast ever saw her like this anyway. A whimper escapes from between the abyss. The other noises come in fast and furious and in quick succession, like a pneumatic drill right behind my eyeballs. The rat-a-tat searing pain and agony occurring every 10 seconds or so.

What have we done to cause this inexplicable trauma? My memory floats in and out of existence like ether suspended just out of reach in the expansion of time and space. This is what a blackout must feel like, either that or selective memory. Fine line. My eyeballs are throbbing, pulsing harmoniously and steadily with every galloping heartbeat. I'm thankful there is even a heartbeat.

Without deviating, they match and hold the beat of my hammering ego which is repeating the me, I , am loop. I sense my swollen engorged lids among other body parts.

We remain fixated on each other until the rays of light dim and fade gradually to a dark, ominous shadow. The dingy streetlight casts its haze over the steadily darkening room. Night. How many hours have we been immobile? Where's Nursie? Why has she not appeared to check in on us? We both seem to have suffered from transitory, involuntary rigor. I try to move at periodic intervals, alas to no avail.

Out of the blue, I notice a slight sensation, a tingling of sorts in my fingers, which progresses slowly up my arm then sporadically throughout my body, creating a mild vibration all over. I tentatively inch my hand towards Ange. A grunt-like noise escapes the cave. I even manage a slight grunt back. She moans again…

"EH…OH…I…MA …EA."

"EH?" I manage to reply…progress.

"EH…SOH…TING…IN ….MA EA."

"THe Son IN YO EA."?

"… I TINK I DEF … I CA HEA."

Ange is beginning to horizontally panic. I can hear the rise of hysteria in her cry. I can almost decipher what she is saying. I think she's telling me she's deaf and there is something in her ear as she is now gesticulating towards her right ear. It takes me at least ten minutes to pull myself on to my hands and knees and another ten just to raise my head one centimetre off the floor. I crawl towards her, knowing that I am scraping, dragging my knees and cheek along the carpet receiving a well-earned carpet burn for my efforts in the process. Not a great distance between us, but it's laborious, strained and hard. I can almost see sparks from the friction of the weight of my head and lower limbs chafing the nylon carpet. My head trails reluctantly behind the rest of my body.

I manage to lift it up and over her body until I am eyeballing her right ear. I gently move the mass of curls with my nose from the area that I believe her ear to be. I'm so shocked when I come within millimeters of the monstrosity that is spewing from her that I fall backwards. What looks like larvae has erupted from her volcanic inner sanctum and come to a dried halt around her lobe.

"FECK…There IS something in your ear. I think it might be a BAT."

"AGGGHHH…. GEH IH OW!"

She begins to cry softly, still not really able to move. Tears cascading continually merging with the saliva snail trail.

"THEY IH SOHIN IH MA EA, they ih sohin ih ma ea."

Slowly, repetitively, steadily, creating a beautiful melody that comes together, merging her words, timbre and inflections with the stillness and ambience of the room. Almost hypnotic.

I FECKIN KNOW there is something in her ear, I can see it loud and clear. I'm not quite sure what I can do about it really. I mean, should I be calling a vet or the bird protection society. Is a bat a bird? What if it's a rabid?

"I think there's a rabid bat in yer ear."

"EHHHHHH, GEH IH OW!"

I haul myself fully to my hands and knees so I look like I'm almost doing a modified down-dog of sorts over her stiff form. I casually approach the bird or bat which has now retreated back to the false security of its lair behind the flock of unruly curls, hiding from the bloodshot gaze. I carefully untangle the knotted bulk of auburn shambles to reveal and expose it to the light.

"IS IT ALIVE?"

I see the undulating of the living breathing being as it moves rhythmically with every one of Ange's pulsating breaths. I can just about make out the black beast using my blurred double vision. I lean in closer to inspect it. I know without a shadow of a doubt that I am likely going to either wet or shit myself, possibly both, if it leaps out and latches itself to the tip of my nose. Noooooooo, surely not! C'est non possible. My eyes, which are now wider than humanly possible stare into the dank orifice. I sniff…. FOR SURE…. no shadow of a doubt…

Ange seems to be paralysed from the neck down.

"It's ok Ange, relax, I've got this."

I start to laugh, even though the pain continues to ripple through my body. It's actually quite funny. In fact, downright hilarious. I gently prise, tease and eventually pluck out the bat. It's only made of a hard, dark, foreign resin like matter and pops out relatively easily from her ear canal. The misshapen plug is like one of those wax plugs you use to block out sound. I believe the French call it a boule quies. The monstrosity nestles in the palm of my hand and I wave it in front of her eyes.

"Not a bat. Well maybe a bat, a bat-shit load of BLOW. You were meant to flush it down the loo not wedge it in your ear canal."

Got to admit, pretty darn smart if you ask me. Upstairs for thinking, downstairs for dancing. Who would even think to look in her ear? We make eye contact over the magnificent mound. Now there's a sentence I never thought I'd be using in my lifetime. We both start to laugh and within minutes are in convulsions, rolling around the floor, tears streaming down our faces. Even though we are both in agony, we alternate between clutching our heads and our bellies, roaring with laughter. With a sense of relief and total abandonment of control over every orifice, we let go of all the tension, anxiety and rigor that holds us in place.

ANGE

Maybe three to four hours have passed since I first became aware that I'm even alive. The daylight has long but disappeared. I only know this because the room is now in darkness and only a street light can be seen poking through the curtains, illuminating our forms. I must have kept passing out and coming to. I thought I was deaf, but Jules has removed the offending creature and is holding it in the palm of her hand. I can just about make out a large jobby of all things nestled amongst the creases of her palm. Why is she holding a jobby? Surely it hadn't been in my ear? Why would I have a jobby in my ear? And HOW had it got there? Those dirty fucking artists must have shat in my ear. Fuckers.

It doesn't smell like a jobby though. All these images start to flash through my memory projector. Boys, spliff, more spliffs, dancing, drinking, music, clothes flying, hash, sirens, police, Lezzers', toilet, ear, blow. It's all coming back to me in a series of very colourful stills.

It takes at least another hour or two after hashgate to finally come round and enter the world as we currently know it. How come Lezzers' hasn't come to our rescue? Where is she in our hour of need? Our pleas for help have gone unanswered. Calls herself a friend? We manage to eventually get up on all fours and staying that way, we make our way through to her bed/sitting room. There is absolutely nothing of her own personal possessions in sight, here, in the kitchen or the bathroom. She must have done a moonlight flit.

JULES

There are two very large glasses of water beside us and when we are somewhat hydrated, we alternate between shuffling Toulouse-Lautrec on our knees style and on all fours back through to the sofa in Lesley's rather empty bed/sitting room. I hold up Ange's ear accessory with pride, reenacting Rafiki's part as he holds Simba aloft in the Circle of Life. The king has arrived.

How we are even in this state is beyond me. How come we've been like this all day? How come Ange's room was trashed last night and immaculate today? Where did the blanket and water come from? Where is Lesley? And all her stuff?

"I can't quite put my finger on it, but we're missing something pretty important here in my opinion Ange."

"Where is she?" we say in unison.

We find a letter rolled up and placed as a cork stopper in an empty bottle of prosecco on the kitchen table. This does not bode well. A feeling of doom and gloom settles deep within me.

LESLEY

I read the letter out loud.

"Dear Jules and Ange, or should it be Drunk and Disorderly, Cheech and Chong, or even Bad and Badass? Sad and Sadass seem more appropriate I feel. I could go on indefinitely here, but I'm sure you get my rift. As you constantly like to remind me, I prefer not to think before speaking, which is why I have had to resort to writing this letter. It's taken time and some very careful consideration to reach this point. It has required a fair amount of effort, thought and soul-searching to decide what I need to say and do here. Looking at the pair of you as you lie stoned, drunk and completely out of it, I reckon I'll be well and truly gone by the time you're fully conscious.

Last night was the final ice on the cake, the straw that broke the camel's toe. There have been way too many others to document, but this is not the correct place to go off in a tandem. However, I am not, categorically not, risking being associated, let alone accused of being a drug dealer and living in your House of Hash. It doesn't take a rocket surgeon to see that all that dried lavender hanging in your bedroom Ange is in fact ganja, any fool can see that.

I know you think I take most things in like soup, but I know a cannabis plantation when I see one. Everyone's a cricket and you definitely take the price for that one. I have tried my darndest to get you to see it all from my point of view and have worked hard to pursue our friendship. It's not easy being in my shoes as my dyspraxia, OCD tendencies and malapropisms can be a challenge. Some of your responses to me and my ways show a distinct lack of compassion, empathy and quite frankly a lack of respect from one human being to another.

For instance, "Do you ever wonder what your life would have been like if you'd been given some oxygen at birth?" OR "You have something on your chin, no, the 3rd one down" OR "I was hoping for a battle of wits, but I see you are unarmed" OR "Quick, check your face..I just found it in my business" OR EVEN "No need to worry about a few lines on your face as balloons have no wrinkles". AND FINALLY, "Have you joined the magic circle? I notice that all the chocolate and sausage rolls have disappeared."

These are only some samples of the many, MANY put downs, innuendos and insults that I have endured over the past few months, and quite frankly my dears, I'm done.

I have a bus to catch in a few hours, but suffice to say that the abuse you directed at me hit me directly in the core of my being, whether it was intended or not. It's taken me awhile to get to this place where I can now see that all this has absolutely nothing to do with me and not to take any of it personally as it's a mere reflection of you. It's obvious that me being part of your mangetout is no longer serving me any purpose, so for that reason, I set you both free to go ahead on your self-destructive paths.

I'm taking a wee adventure of my own before heading to my final destination in The Outback. I'm nipping this whole journey thing in the butt and am going to help the indigenous people here in Australia, who not only need me, but actually want me around. I'm thrilled that I've been offered a nurse position in the Northern Territory alongside The Flying Doctor's team. I'm sure it will come as a huge relief for you both not to have me "nagging" or "fussing" or "worrying".

The feeling, believe me, is completely neutral and I feel a weight has been lifted from my shoulders and the tension and stress I must have been carrying has been let go. What a relief.

If, however, you do find yourself in the unlikely event of needing me, you can find me in a reservation close to Alice Springs.

Enjoy the horizontal house of happiness, the den of iniquity, and believe me when I say you're a perfect pairing match, almost like fleas and whine.

I want this Down Under experience to be something that I can learn and grow from, so thank you for that. You have indeed enabled this learning curve for me. Being with you both has taught me so much about what I do want from all this experience, and not what I don't, and for that very reason, I am grateful to you both. You especially, Ange, have taught me so much about the person I want to be, the traits that I have and love about myself, the energy and the positivity I require and need to work on to develop as a person. I know in my heart of hearts that we want something different from all this and that's fine also.

I worked really hard to get my nursing degree, working two part-time jobs to pay for it all, no family backhanders. That is not a dig, just a fact. It is what it is and I am who I am. I need to follow my passion which is, and has always been, to care for people, therefore I've decided to let go of any self-doubt and negativity that serves me no purpose. I am going to follow my dreams and liberate myself from the pressures of trying to conform and be someone different to who I am.

I chose nursing to be able to give back, unconditionally, with no judgement, complete acceptance of who I am. I sincerely hope that at some stage on your path, you will have the opportunity to explore some of your own unique traits. I do hope so. Someday you will see that everyone is fighting their own internal battle. Regardless of the size of the army, it is theirs and we do best to keep that in mind in our interactions with others. Not necessarily similar or even close to our personal experiences, but part of their own unique journey. And that's okay.

I am passionate about working with genuine people who value my skills, care and guidance. Through good fortune and grace, I know that deep down, and not "six feet deep down" like you have said on at least three occasions Ange, that at my core, the true heart of the matter, I am nurturing, caring, kind and compassionate.

I always try to be and look for the best in everyone and everything. Even when I am sad or feeling down, not listened to, I just smile, put a brave face on and get on with it. Seems an easy choice when it's put like that. Be positive, be kind, just smile. It's that simple and the right direction we all need to be moving in. I felt like a round hole trying to fit into a square peg with you guys, believing I needed to be someone else to be part of your tribe. I really did try to fit in. It just didn't work and I realised that my response to the behaviours, comments, events, etc, was going to determine the outcome for me. I found myself on a number of occasions reacting rather than responding and knew that something in me had to change. It is not and never will be my place to change you, only you can see and do that when the time is right. Hopefully, at the right time, you will also have the opportunity for change. If nothing changes, then nothing changes. You have to continue on your way and I'll continue on mine. Your path is quite simply not my path, that's all. If behaving like social hand-grenades is your idea of fun and growth, then who am I to judge, or stop you for that matter?

Like I said, I applied a while back for the position of nurse in The Outback, but only just got notification. I have accepted the position and plan to be there within a month or so. That gives me time to see Melbourne, Tasmania and Adelaide before starting.

I sincerely wish you both all the very, very best and hope that our paths do cross again someday, somehow, someway, but please don't make it in the liver transplant ward or the drug rehabilitation centre please.

G'day

Lesley, and NOT "Lezzers'"

JULES

Oh, oh, we finally find Nursie's farewell letter as a cork in an empty bottle of fizz. I am shocked as I truly wasn't aware she felt as bad as this. Why hadn't she said something? I thought she took it all in good humour, a joke of sorts. I didn't for one minute think she took it all so seriously. Shame. Shame. I feel so guilty for my part in it all. I truly hadn't thought she'd been so upset with us, that she'd prefer to leave us to work with the aborigines instead. I hope she's ok. Drunk and Disorderly indeed, very amusing. I hope I'm the latter.

ANGE

She might have at least left the note in a full bottle of fizz, not an empty one, that would give us something to toast with while we read her roasting letter. Well, well, well, I resemble, as Lezzers' would say, most of those remarks. We Shirley aren't as bad as all that? Some of those witticisms, repartees and comebacks I have to admit are really very funny though. Perhaps stand-up comedy should be in my future.

In my humble opinion, she didn't even try very hard to fit in and party with us. Her loss…. maybe. We were just having a laugh. She never gave me the impression that she minded being the butt of some of our jokes. I actually thought she liked the attention, making her one of us, part of the tribe. The Cool Gang. Not now though, she's heading to be part of another tribe. Thinks we're Drunk and Disorderly? I hope she thinks of me more like the latter, would hate to think I'm anything remotely like my alky mum. Just wait, though, I can see many disorderly drunks living in

"The Bush" in her future.

JULES

Ange goes outside to make sure she hasn't taken the contents of the garden with her. I decide to finish where Lesley had left off and clean and tidy the place some more. I don't even know where most things belong or where the hoover and cleaning stuff is kept. How have I lived here for this long and not even known there wasn't a dishwasher? She must have done all that stuff by hand, is my guess. Ange's bedroom still looks slightly trashed, in fact the landlord popped by for the rent and was shocked, as he thought we'd been burgled. We tell him we had, and that the police had already been and taken a report.

"Anything of value taken?"

"Only Lesley."

"Wwwhhhaaattt?"

Ange elbows me in the ribs.

"No, nothing of value, just a few dollars that were lying about. The culprits were last seen apparently heading towards Campbell Parade with an armful of clothes."

ANGE

Thankfully she hasn't taken any of Audrey Two with her, or if she has, she's left the rest for us, so I make the executive decision it's time to cut them all down, dry them and bag them for a rainy day. One never knows when they might come in handy.

JULES

It's only been a few days since she left us and I have to admit that I really do miss her, not just because the place looks like a pigsty, but she looked out for me, was always kind, caring and considerate of both of our needs. Ange thinks she's annoying and is enjoying the peace and quiet.

"Perhaps annoying at times but it's only her way of being nurturing, positive and kind. She always has a smile, even when she's sad, it seems. She treated us like her friend and we, well, not my proudest of moments. I miss all her malapropisms, which are hilarious, and I like to think that she knew that and played on it, even if she does have OCD and dyspraxia, she ultimately embraced herself and others in her own unique, quirky fashion."

"Suck it up, she's gone. End of, so no point in crying over spilled milk."

ANGE

It's getting a tad tiresome going out to eat all the time at those all-you-can eat buffets. I reckon I might have taken all those home-cooked meals a bit for granted. It's a beautiful afternoon, so we're going to head out for a nice, long leisurely walk. Clear the cobwebs and hopefully cheer up auld sourpuss Jules.

We pass an event happening at Grace Brothers department store at Bondage Junction and decide we should go in as they will definitely be offering free nibbles and snacks which has to be better than all the to-go shite we've been eating. It's something called "Australian's Next Top Model".

Super, all the more food for us as none of the models will be eating any. The guy on the door tries to stop us as it is a "PRIVATE EVENT".

"Yeah, we know. I'm sure you can tell already, but we're actually working at it, not attending or participating in it as you believe to be the case, although I'm sure you think we could."

And that was all it took, he lifts the red rope and lets us in.

"Take a left at the end of the corridor, go through the door ahead of you as that's where the dressing rooms are."

"Cheers Big Ears"

We enter, turn left and go through the" STAFF ONLY" door. A very stern Victoria- looking, older, bustling, grey-haired woman rocking a black governess dress claps her hands in the air repeatedly at us. Her strong, thick Prime of Miss Jean Brodie accent comes across loud and clear. No mistaking her heritage, and by the look of her, she must have been on one of the first convict ships.

"Hurry, hurry girrrrls, you're late. Quickly get your outfits on and get out there, it's already started?"

Does she actually think we are the models? Ya beauty, eat your heart out Elle Macpherson. We wouldn't be as tall as Elle, even if I stood on Jules's shoulders, but what's a few discrepancies between friends?

She herds us into the changing room where there are three gold bikini-clad, 6 ft skeletal models, legs up to their pussy's bow.

Not one of them looks like they'd had a square meal in at least a decade. These must be Australia's next top models. I personally wouldn't give any of them the time of day, let alone a score of over 2, but who am I to judge? Bloody hell, who do I sound like? Channeling my inner Lezzers' that's what.

"Come on, come on, here are your outfits. You're going to be passing out the appetizers."

Thankfully our outfits are only miniskirts that barely cover our fannies and boob tubes and not the itsy-bitsy-teenie-weenie bits of gold scraps the others are wearing for the first time today. You can only imagine what Jules looks like with her huge knockers in a boob tube. Ain't no mountain high enough, ain't no valley low enough, ain't no river wide enough, to keep me from getting to your boobs babe. She's already having problems trying to balance the tray of horse's d'oeuvres as her mammaries are struggling to stay inside the loose fabric. It does look like she's serving her bosoms on the silver platter we've been given. Aside from knockers, there are vol-au-vents, canapes and flutes of champagne. No one will miss a few if I pop some in my mouth, washed down with a quick swig of rose bubbles.

We go through the double doors leading to the event and to our shock and amazement we see CARS revolving on floor discs, with the gold lame models either spinning round slowly on the bonnets or in the driver's seats. Ahhh, the penny drops, it's actually a model car event. Australia's Next Top Model. Doesn't help Jules though as I'm sure most eyes are ogling her headlights and not the ones belonging to The Holden cars on display.

"HOLDEN" is an acronym for Hope Our Luck Doesn't End Now. Well, I really hope ours doesn't end here too soon either as there's copious amounts of free booze and food going around.

We both manage to tuck in to the offerings, aside from Jules who is still trying to tuck in one mammary at a time to the flimsy garment, while balancing a platter at the same time. All the while, we still manage to work the floor. It isn't too much of a challenge to offer a tray around, munch and swig all at the same time. None of the guys in attendance, and some of the women it has to be said, have eyes for either what's on offer on the platter or behind the flimsy fabric and are not paying the slightest bit of attention to what's going into our gobs. The colourful, exotic smorgasbord spread against the back wall looks amazing. Someone has gone to so much trouble to carve pineapples and other erotic fruit to be shaped like hedgehogs, peacocks, even cars. Very talented indeed. The show stopping ice-carved swan takes pride of place in the centre and is truly spectacular. It all looks too good to eat, but we force ourselves while doing our round of duties. It's really easy to swipe some fizz as well as we fill our trays and pretend to offer it around. Absolutely no one notices or even cares what we're doing. The champagne is quite literally flowing from a tall crystal glass fountain in the corner, its effervescent bubbles trickling from the top to the bottom, spilling out and over the sides, filling the flutes which are stacked delicately and with precision in a 20-tier display. Why would we not?

JULES

We walk round the car showroom, but really all we're doing is drinking the champagne and having the odd horses hoover as Nursie calls them. Eventually I put my tray down and carry on drinking and chatting to some of the rather lovely salesmen. No-one even notices or bothers to stop me. The event itself is fairly dull, so we liven it up by chatting to the predominantly male clients and sales team. Is this why the models are in bikinis and we are half clothed in two pieces of cloth that just cover our tits and bits? Does this add extra appeal to the male clientele? Do they actually sell more cars this way? Am I more likely to buy something if there is a Greek god with a rippling eight-pack, slathered in baby oil in a pair of Australian scrote totes? Yes siree, you're dayam right I am.

A few hours go by and I feel the need to do my stint on the bonnet of one of the cars. I let one of the models go on a much-needed food break and take her place at the helm. I offer her a shrimp in return for her spot on the spinning hood. She declines the shrimp, but gives up her spot. I climb aboard the Holden, initially trying to straddle it, but it has a much wider girth than I think and my legs do not splay that far apart. Believe me, I've tried to perfect that particular skill, but alas, to no avail. However, I'm proud to say that my table tennis groin game is coming on a treat and I'm proud of my pelvic floor suction. I'll leave that for another day though. This is neither the time nor the place to be showing off that particular talent.

I swear the revolving disc starts to speed up so I place my feet against the hood ornament of a lion 'Holden' a stone. I have to grip the wiper blades with each hand so I don't fall off. I've been on a mechanical bull before so I know how to grip my inner thighs tightly against the slightly raised bonnet. I'm getting dizzy very quickly, and as it speeds up, I can feel myself getting dizzier. I begin to slide towards the lion's mouth. I manage to lift my arse up and get to my knees, but can hear the hood begin to buckle under my weight. My knees dig deep into the indentations, the wipers are now horizontal and pointing to the front of the car. My fingers, which have been dipping liberally into the crisp bowl, are sticky, slippy and sliding from their blades. It's really fast, much faster than the waltzers at the fair.

ANGE

Why Jules is straddling the bonnet is beyond me but it tickles me at the same time to think how funny it would be if I speed it up slightly. I find the controls behind some heavy, green velvet curtain. I feel like the Wizard of Oz. Ha ha, the Wizard of OZ.

"You've always had the power my dear, you just had to learn it for yourself."

Well, I now have the power and take it up a notch. Even I couldn't have predicted the carnage that was about to ensue. Give her due, she is good and manages to hold on to the blades, so I up it a bit more. She has been able to get to her knees, great core work girlfriend. Her bahookey is high in the air and her tonsils can practically be seen from her rear end. Her knickers are on full display for all to see on a 360 degrees rotating loop. There might be a full moon or worse any minute if I don't slow it down though. Unfortunately, I press it hard the wrong way which actually takes it to full speed. She is no longer Holden the Holden any longer and flies across the room like a Bat out of a Hell. She'll be gone when the morning comes. But when the day is done and the sun goes down and the mooner's shining through, then like the sinner I am, she'll come crawling back to you.

She is projected feet first, straight towards the Smorgasbord and champagne fountain. The whole buffet folds in on her, and by the time I leave the controls to get to her, she looks like Carmen Miranda with the carved pineapple and fruit platter on her head. The ice swan has a broken neck and is nestled in her lap. Her head is tilted backwards and a steady stream of champagne trickles down into her open mouth which, low and behold, she occasionally swallows. One of her many talents I'm told on good authority. I can only guess where the prickly cheese and pickled onion hedgehog has gone.

Time to make like a tree and leaves methinks. By the time I grab our belongings and get back to her, the management is all over her like white on rice, apologizing profusely. They are well and truly dumbfounded as to how it had happened. They are clearly terrified of a lawsuit, and begin to ply her with alcohol, offering to give her compensation for any damage incurred. To soften the blow, in my opinion, as if the floury baps on the table weren't soft enough. This could absolutely work in our favour.

JULES

Wow, what happened here? One minute I'm modeling on a car bonnet, the next, I'm flying full pelt towards the buffet, feet first. I'm so sure that if we were even employed here, they'd be sacking us. I have totally destroyed their beautiful smorgasbord. Before I can hand in my notice, they offer me some drinks and ask me what I think a reasonable compensation would be? Right there and then, they write me a cheque for $500 and give me three raffle books. I give all the books to Ange to fill in. She is unusually keen and eagerly fills them all out without question. So very unusually placating to all my requests. She's definitely been up to or is about to do something. Far too appeasing for my liking. We eventually get home after convincing them that I'm not going to sue them. Hours later though, I find a troupe of shrimp in my knickers. Ange confesses to her part, the major part, in fact, the sole part of the role she played in my near demise and ensuing lawsuit. They took full responsibility as they thought I was going to sue them. If only they knew the truth, we'd have been locked up in the local jail for fraud, or at least she would have been.

When I wake the next morning, I find half the stolen smorgasbord in my handbag. Sausages, pickled onions and cheese on a cocktail stick, even more shrimp all crammed into every conceivable pocket and behind every zip. There's even an oyster of all things. I don't like the slimy wee feckers but I know Nursie does. They're wrapped perfectly in a napkin and tucked into a zip pocket. I must have subconsciously brought it as a gift for her, forgetting that she is long gone. There's even a slice of Black Forest gateaux, however, that was defo intended for me. The wee cocktail sausages which she also has a penchant for are squished into the seams. Not quite sure why I needed to steal the food as I'm sure they would have gladly given it to me. She once said to me. "You know Jules, you don't have to buy a whole pig, when just a wee sausage will do the trick."

Did she mean it to be funny? It is funny. Yeah, she did, clever. Still makes me laugh anyway. She definitely had her deliberately amusing moments. She always did the cooking, maybe that's why I stocked up as I have no idea where our next meal is coming from. The flat seems very quiet, still and very messy, as there is no Lesley bustling about with her dustpan and brush in hand to clean the place and put it back in order. I do wonder where she is and if she's okay?

Ange is totally nonplussed as I continue to find cockles and other crushed Asians, as Lesley would say, in places that have never seen the light of day or been conquered. A double whammy first on both counts. She reckons that if I dig anymore then I'll likely find Lord Lucan in my search.

I hope that somewhere in that dark soul of hers she is secretly guilty and knows how much we failed Lesley. Tch, tch, shame. Shame on us. She just sings The Peter Rabbit nursery rhyme as she begins to remove some of the mouldy molluscs from her underwear. I wonder how they got in there in the first place as it was me that lay among all the sea creatures, not her. I'm way too scared to ask so I am going to erase that thought and visual from my mind immediately. Perhaps in her drunken stupor she saw me stealing some of the ocean delicacies and decided to join in. No show without Punch.

"Did you fill your gusset with finger food?"

"Why do I do it? What can it be? There's naughtiness in EVERYONE, but twice as much in ME. I'd give the world if only I could, now and then be good. I think a halo would suit me, dangling above my head, then they'd behold me, they wouldn't scold me and now and then I'd be good. Why do I do it? What is the cure? My brothers and my sisters find it easy I am sure. That's how I've been ever since I began. Why do I do it? Why do I do it? Why DO I do it?"

Her singing doesn't really answer my question though. Definitely a case of whose needs were being met there. I begin to feel slightly nostalgic and recall some of Lesley's malaprops. Continental Australia? Easy enough yes? Not for Lesley as she referred to it as congenital Australia. Priceless. When she is corrected, she always says "That's what I said, didn't I?"

Police officers were always "Ociffers" and then would add: "From the heart of my bottom Ange, I think I know what I said."

I wish I'd written them all down now. Maybe she's having the last laugh on us. There's a large part of me that thinks she knows exactly what she's saying. Well, I hope so anyway, softens the blow of her thinking we were bullying her in some way. Good on her, very clever, very sharp.

I notice the time and realize I'm running late for my doctor's appointment. Not sure what the rush is for really as I'm only going to be fitted with yet another diaphragm as the one that landed on the coffee table during tazergate was well and truly fried. Why am I even bothering as a new one will likely exceed its expiry date anyway, given the lack of action I've been having down under of late? Other than the occasional sweep of my own fair hand, that is. Regardless, one can always live in hope. I think the cheeky wee contraceptive buggers must give off a repellent pheromone, far easier to think that for sure rather than believe it's little ole me. Shirley not. I'm beginning to gather dust down there, which is okay, but a regular spring clean wouldn't go amiss.

The clinic is only three blocks away, but I don't want to be late so trot along hastily. It can be very frustrating as if you miss your allotted time, you're kept in the holding pen waiting area which is full of all these sick people, and you have to wait, hence the name I guess, and wait and wait until an opening becomes available. Ange shouts after me that I'm twice as sick as they'll ever be. She has a point. I have time for a quick pee and scrub, making sure there are no signs or odours of any shellfish before my date with Dr. Swartz at my cervix.

I clatter through the doors, heaving and panting, breaking into a slight sweat and stagger up the gauntlet of waiting room shame. The room has a long threadbare clad carpet, like a runway leading to the reception desk at the top. You have to walk the runway, which is lined with voyeurs and would-be doctors who check me out and diagnose me before I get halfway to check in.

They stare at me as I pass, preparing themselves to gossip, dissect and comment as soon as my back is turned. I have to pass each sick-looking face, every cough, splutter, sniff and phlegmy hawkeye as I walk the hall of shame towards the dour-faced receptionist. I pretend to clutch a bouquet of flowers and walk like a bride going up an aisle. I walk down the centre avoiding the small children and table obstacles spilling over with Reader's Digest, Better Homes and golf magazines. I'd go more often if they had a subscription to Hello, but hey ho beggars can't be choosers. It's depressing just being there.

I almost forget why I'm here as the stale, stagnant virus-borne air is sucking the life out of me. I hum the wedding theme tune to my gait. Might as well amuse myself while I'm here. By the time I get to the front, I really have forgotten what I came in for now, but I do feel really miserable all of a sudden for some reason.

As I'm standing with my back to my fellow sorrowful, poorly peers, I lean on the counter, waiting for the receptionist's attention, who holds up her hand to stop me mid-sentence to take a call. I can't help myself, and listen in.

"You need the number for the urology dept? Would you mind holding?"

She puts the phone to her chest: "What can I do for you Miss?"

"Is that a joke? You said can you hold? Now that's funny. You know the urology department?"

Not even a flicker or a crack of a smile. I'm met with a perplexed, frosty look. Ahhh, not deliberate then. As I'm about to give my name I notice a slight jab in my lower back. WTF? As I give my first name, I discreetly put my right hand behind my back searching for the location of the offending jabber. I can feel a hard piece of plastic-like thingamabob material on the waistband of my jeans. I must have forgotten to cut the label off. Hhmm, strange, these aren't even my new ones. I can feel some sticky, gooey substance coating it, so I wipe my fingers cautiously and carefully over and around the offending article, collecting some of the matter on my fingertips. I bring my hand surreptitiously and slowly back around. I lean in nonchalantly over the counter top, resting my elbow on the top and gaze at my fingers. To my absolute horror, I witness some yellow, gummy, tacky, gloopy luminescent stuff dripping from and between my stubby digits. I look horrified and glare at the matter with the wide-mouthed receptionist staring back at me still clutching the phone to her chest. The putrid stuff oozes in a constant lumpy stream down onto the countertop. WTF?

My left hand now joins the exploration. Finding the hard offender, I gently tug at it. It's not giving any leeway, so I yank at it probably harder than is necessary as it quickly yields and dislodges from my jeans, and in doing so, sprays in an arch-like fashion, splashing its contents on the three old ladies who are sitting behind me and to my left in the much sought-after front row. It arches round me like a rainbow until it finally comes to rest on the countertop.

I clutch the irritating perpetrator firmly in my sweaty mitt as the rancid matter resumes its steady plopping on to the sign-in sheet. All eyes are diverted from the magazines, coughing and spluttering at the foreign object I'm holding aloft. I look at it, trying to recognize its familiarity. Then it dawns on me. I am holding a toilet duck…yes…that is correct, a toilet duck. I must have scooped it from the loo as I was rushing to get here, and sure

enough, glancing over my shoulder, I see the trail I have left
behind. A bright yellow, radioactive line of gloopey blobs
highlight the centre of the surgery aisle.

"Looks like I might have leprosy."

The stoney-faced cow doesn't miss a beat, hands me some
tissues at the same time as wiping the gunk from her sweater.

"The doctor will see you immediately, just go through."

"I hope the person on the other end of your phone is still
holding or they'll find themselves with a constant stream behind
them also."

Joke, I think to myself, JOKE. I would have walked out
there and then, but I need the cap, so just look sad and pathetic.
Which I'm beginning to feel I actually am. She does not look in the
slightest bit impressed or amused. Two countries separated by the
same language I guess.

One look at the rather dishy doctor reminds me why I need
a contraceptive. He suggests that instead of the diaphragm, I
should be fitted with a sponge as it offers extra precaution. I don't
tell him that I don't really need it anyway, let alone as any extra
precaution, as I wouldn't want him to think that I don't get any
action. Hmm, the thought of him greasing up and fitting me with it
sends thrills down my spine, they're multiplying and I'm losing
control, cause the sponge that he's supplying is electrifying.

I'm going out tonight with this guy I'd met at the weekend
and fully intend to scratch that itch, if you know what I mean. I'm
going to have to try to remember what he looks like first though as
that particular night is a blur. The love doctor tells me to
undress from the waist down.

"Your wish is my command."

It hits me all of a sudden, he's planning on inserting it NOW. I'm not sure I'm ready for this. What if I have an orgasm?

"Would you mind if I use the little girl's room first?"

I'm sure he gets that often and he smiles knowingly and points to another door at the back of the room. After checking there is no toilet duck, I rummage round in my bag for a wet wipe. I need it to look youthful and moist, only one very careful owner if you get my gist. There's an open packet with one left. Thankfully, it's still wet so the stars are clearly lining up for me here. I clean myself and return to the red room of pain and pleasure. I undress slowly and provocatively and lay on my back while he examines me Down under. He stops suddenly, stands up, puts on a pair of magnifying glasses of all things and picks a pair of tweezers from the tray beside him. He is back between my legs in no time, bending in closer. I feel a slight nip, then see him stand up holding something.

"Let me guess, it's one of those urban myth jokes where you're holding a first-class postage stamp you've found during my examination."

"No, I don't think so."

"Please tell me it's not a prawn."

"I'm not sure I know you well enough to speculate on your extracurricular activities, but no, it's not a prawn."

"Well, don't keep me in suspenders here, well do, but don't if you get my drift. What is it? What have you found? Go gently telling me and prepare me for the worst."

"It looks like, in fact it is, a 100% certified organic banana sticker Made in Indonesia of all places."

Oh, the humiliation. It must have been caught up among all the shite in my bag and got stuck to the wet wipe. Worse still, he maybe thinks my extracurricular activities are with a banana. My modus operandi is to deflect the mortification with humour.

"I have to get my fruit in me somehow if you know what I mean."

Wink, wink. Why the hell am I winking?

"Not really, but do you usually carry bananas in your handbag?"

Thank the lord, he has no clue what I am insinuating.

"I wasn't peeling well, and know how good they are for you."

He nods knowingly. "Well, in that case, we're almost done here, then you can make like a banana and split. I'm almost done here."

"Ha, ha. Thanks a bunch doctor."

He is very professional and even asks me if I want to keep the offending article, which of course I do. I need it to show Ange. He puts it in an envelope and gives it back to me. Then back to business as usual as he fits me with the sponge. It feels very strange, sponge-like, which is a surprise. Not sure what I was expecting, but not a spongey thing. It feels like I'm clamping a double mattress between my labias. I am tickled though as I walk back through the surgery remembering that I had entered this place walking like a virginal bride and am now leaving the love doctor's inner sanctum walking like John Wayne.

I can still see the dried blobs of yellow gunk sticking to the pavement and begin to follow the trail all the way back to the flat. Hansel and Gretel eat your heart out. I wasn't aware that we even had one of those duck products in the toilet. Lesley must have put it there before she left, knowing full well it was likely the only thing that had even a remote chance of cleaning the bowl. These ducks are of an aromatic nature, and I use that term loosely, containing a fair amount of a custard-like product, at least 1LB of the nauseating, gel-like excrement given the evidence I follow from the surgery to the flat. Well, if the doctor ever wants to make his very own certified organic stamp, all he has to do is follow the yellow brick road to find a young, willing and able Scottish recipient.

ANGE

Jules comes through the door walking like she's wet herself and smelling of disinfectant of all things. She's possibly been egged for some reason as there's yellow globules which look like pus running down the back of her white jeans. She holds up a small, misshapen, terribly bijoux white clutch, and waves it in front of my nose. It isn't the tiny purse I originally mistake it for but a toilet duck of all things. I don't quite understand why she even has it in her hand and hasn't left it in the bowl where it belongs. It also looks like it has a variety of pubes still stuck to it. GADZOOKS. What is she on? She shirley hasn't had that monstrosity out in public, has she? Nothing surprises me these days. When she tells me what's happened, I laugh so hard the tears for the umpteenth time run down the inside of my legs. This theme is beginning to become a regular occurrence, but only reporting the facts as they present themselves. Perhaps I should be visiting her Dr. Schwartz at my cervix for a pelvic floor examination. Listening to her describe how the story unfolded, I already feel a tightening of my coccygeus muscle. Can you imagine the miracles he can work when he's off duty, and on his own time, actually in action if you get my drift? I'm going to make an appointment. She's horrified though and isn't able to even sit down properly due to the spongy trampoline that the love doctor has wedged deep inside her. I place a bet that the guy she's meant to be meeting later won't even show, and if he does, then at least she has brought along her own spongy mattress.

"It's so uncomfortable. Perhaps he's fitted me with one of the larger varieties made for someone like you Ange. I'm sure it's doubled in size from the tiny dumpling I originally saw."

"W.W.L.D?"

"Eh?"

"That's what's popped into my head. What Would Lezzers' Do? In this situation anyway? She certainly wouldn't be laughing, unlike me. She'd take charge. So that's what I'm going to do. Listen. Lezzers' would tell you to go and undress, get into a lovely warm, lavender-smelling bubble bath while she removes the stain from your white jeans. That'll ease any tenderness. I'm even going to bring you a cheeky wee glass of fizz and a small doobey to ease the aches and pains. Okay, so Lezzers' may not do the latter, but the thought is there nonetheless. Sorted! See? I do have a caring streak in me somewhere."

JULES

Ange kindly offers to run me a bath and provides me with some medicinal relief while she washes the stain from my jeans. I am suspicious that she won't use itching powder and food coloring in the bath though. I'm such a waddling cynic, of course she wouldn't, especially as she hopefully sees this as my hour of need. There will be no action for me tonight if I don't sort this out.

ANGE

The washing machine has been making unusual clinking noises for a few weeks now, and my motto has always been, don't fix anything until it's broken, or is that one of Lezzers' sayings? No, hers is definitely "Don't break anything until it's fixed".

The machine is heaving, wheezing and groaning under the weight of Jules' few garments and then, just like that, it slows down and comes to a complete halt, still filled with the sloshing murky water pressing on the door. I call our landlord who tells me that he'll call Bruce, his handyman. Everyone needs a handyman on hand methinks, who is actually nearby anyway servicing someone else. Sounds promising.

"Now remember that it's written in your lease agreement that you are responsible for all costs incurred."
"No worries, send Big Bad Bruce on over."

Can't cost that much though, he's only going to be draining a small amount of water and servicing the machine. I imagine Bruce to be one of those rugged, handsome, rough and ready plumbers who goes out of his way to service women in distress and Shirley wouldn't take any liberties from a pair of innocent damsels in distress, without undue authority anyway that is. I have just about enough time to put on some lippy before the doorbell goes. Bruce is not quite the Huge Jackman I'd imagined, more like Huge Jackassman.

G'day Sheila, I believe you have a little problem with your plumbing. Phnarr, phnar."

Seriously??

"Actually, it's always worked. So far so good, that is, never had any complaints. You're here to service the washing machine and not me."

"Righty-oh. Not sure what you think I meant, but I was talking about your washing machine, love. Phnar, phnar."

He's talking in this patronizing, irritating, nasally sort of way as if he has blocked nostrils. Every cell of his sweaty, bloated body seeps testosterone and arrogance, mingled with a smattering of chauvinism.

"So was I Bruce."

I spit his name out like a cannonball and some leftover avocado, which must have been there from lunch, comes hurtling out landing on his oily boiler suit. A touch of green amongst the slime.

"If you know how to mend washing machines then how come you don't use one?"

That wipes the smile off his cheesey, pot-holed, peuce, boozer's face.

Bruce pulls the machine from its cubby and tugs at the big black hose, dislodging it from the back of the machine. He looks me directly in my eyes, puts it straight into his MOUTH, takes an extremely long inhale, then, in quick succession, suck, blow, suck, blow. He goes from a light red to purple, scarlet to violet in the space of 30 seconds and then, just like that, he stops, removes it from his mouth and catches something from the end of its tip in his hand. He then puts the hose back into its hole. Like a magician he uncurls his fingers to expose a massive wad of hair, water and slime. There is also a very recognizable pair of "Hello Kitty" panties. Lezzer looked for them for days and even accused one of us of taking them. Bruce does not seem nearly as disturbed by the contents in his hand as I clearly am. Does he have any of the slimy furballs still in his mouth? He untangles the knot and teases the not-so-pretty kitty panties from the clump. He hands them to me.

"Yours?"

I don't even give him the luxury of a response, I just cast my evil eye at him till he finally breaks my glare.

"$100."

"What?? That's daylight robbery. I can buy a new pack of 12 for half the price with a Batman pair thrown in for free."

"I'm talking about the labour, not the underwear."

"WHAAAT? That's ridiculous, 30 seconds of sucking and blowing into a black pipe is hardly LABOUR! This is pure exploitation, that's what this is. It would have been cheaper and far more pleasant to engage the services of a hooker. In fact I could have stuck the big black hose in MY mouth for thirty seconds and got the same ejaculation results."

"Maybe so Sheila. Perhaps you should set yourself up in business - in fact I have an opening for a talented apprentice."

He smirks his toothless grin. We could stand there all day arguing, but I want him out immediately as I feel dirty all of a sudden and not in a good way either. I pay him and promise myself that I will never do another random act of kindness for anyone ever again. Jules is going to have to wash her own clothes from now on. I can't quite throw Lezzer's knicknack pussywacks out though, so I put them in with the next load to be washed.

Maybe one day I'll get the chance to give them back to her, but I won't tell her the full story until she's wearing them about how they've been in Godzilla's ugly cakehole.

JULES

As I lie in my bath listening to Ange scream (at her reflection I guess), I ponder on where Lesley might be and what she's been doing. Everything seems to be going slightly pear-shaped here but it just might be my imagination. Perhaps it was like this when she was here, but there's definitely something missing, and not just her. I can't quite put my finger on it. Nope, it's definitely different. She most certainly was the glue that held us all together. HUH...who knew?

Oh well, I've got this date with this surfy guy tonight, so no time to waste being nostalgic. The sponge must have taken in water and has swollen to gargantuan proportions, but has come to a rest and is now rather snugly nestled in my birth canal. The doctor mentioned it was an all-natural sponge, vagina-friendly, oh yes, he did, product. Does this mean it has come from the sea? I hope that means it's not living. I don't like the thought of an urchin being inside me, unless he's over 21 of course, then that changes the goal posts somewhat. Or is it more like one of those scobies that make kombucha? If I ponder too much over the scoby mothership being in my uterus, then I might freak out. Have you heard about the new sponge craze? Listen to me, I'm sure you'll be amazed. Big fun to be had by everyone. It's up to you, it Shirley can be done. Young and old are doing it, I'm told. Just one try and you too will be sold. Le Freak. As long as it's 99.99% safe and effective, then it doesn't really matter what it's made of does it? Who was the first person to discover it anyway? I wonder what games they were playing when they came across this new invention.

"EUREKA, I've just found the best all-natural birth control known to mankind."

It does feel a bit strange though, having an involuntary internal intruder of sorts. I wonder what it would feel like having a willy bounce on my inner trampoline? Hopefully time will tell.

ANGE

Not sure what her problem is? She seems very grumpy and for sure has had a whole lot worse in her love canal than an oversized pillow. Besides, if she doesn't get lucky, she could always have a side job cleaning windows with her love sponge.

JULES

I don't even know if I want to have sex with this guy again. I can't remember if our drunken bonk on Bondage Beach was worth it or not, I just remember sand pouring from my honey pot like an hourglass for days and days after. In fact, I could have entered a sandcastle competition with the tonne that left my body. Maybe we didn't even have sex, maybe he just shoveled half the beach in there and plugged it with a condom for good measure.

Now I'm feeling quite repulsed by this porous alien body inside me. What happens when it gets wetter? Do you wait until you smell the foosty, mulchy smell before you extract it? Or worse, what happens if you get used to the smell and other people smell it first, like off-chicken fried rice, or worse still, if you remove it before all the Michael Phelps swimmers are dead, then you run the risk of getting pregnant. There are no winners here, you either smell of a decomposing body or you're pregnant. Do I have to go back to Dr Swartz to have him remove it? Does it just disintegrate? Maybe it shrivels up and dies? I have no idea how to get it out now that it has made its forever home.

I wish Lesley was here, she'd know what to do and how to remove it.

"Go do some yoga moves - that should help it settle."

"Even a downdog is going to have it fire out of me like some spinning pizza dough."

"At least you know how to remove it without too much effort then. You go hole yourself up, s'cuse the pun, in the bathroom and get ready. I'm headed down to the venue and meet you there when you are all shipshape and secure. Have you fully absorbed the plan of events for the evening?"

"Piss off!"

"Alright already, I'm heading out now for a stiff one."

Ange surely thinks she's the original comedienne. Ho Ho, always the jokester, NOT! It does get very wearing, especially when her attention is on you. I bet Lesley was so sick of hearing the constant diatribe of puns, insults and put downs. I get it. So am I.

I continue to wrestle with the internal pop-up cloot. I must look like I have ants in my pants with all the unconventional writhing and erratic involuntary spasms. Perhaps he really has given me the wrong thing and there is an actual air bed in there instead.

It's times like this that I wish I'd done my Duke of Edinburgh and knew how to wrestle and erect a tent in under ten minutes. I should just leave it be and stop trying to remove and reinsert it. Every time I have it in the C-shape that is recommended on the instruction leaflet, the slippy wee blighter springs to life, inflates to monstrous proportions, shoots out of my grip and flies across the bathroom to join the other washcloths on the sink. If you put a couple of google eyes on it, it could easily pass for SpongeBob Square Pants. I give up, it is so not worth my time and energy and no boy is worth this much twubble. I cut it in two, insert one half and leave the other half with all her - it has to be a her, right? (no-one would refer to one of these using a male gender) - new sink-cloth comrades.

ANGE

Jules comes waddling into the pub.

"Get off your hoss and drink your milk."

"Ms. S Ponge at your cervix."

"Deep down, you must know what you want, what you really, really want."

"I'll tell you what I want, what I really, really want. I wanna jiggy-jig jig."

"And to drink?"

"My doctor said I need glasses, so a large glass of wine for me."

"There's also a Victoria sponge cake cocktail if you fancy that, or Sex on the Beach? That worked last time."

JULES

7pm comes and goes, 8pm, 9pm, no show. I'm half cut, SpongeBob is groaning and undulating below, having absorbed most of the alcohol. It clearly knew before me that my date was going to be a no-show. It seems to be dropping slowly inch by inch with each drink I have. It feels like I have an adult space hopper being cradled in my gusset. Lucky for me it's not the whole thing, otherwise it would have been the size of a zeppelin by now. Ange is still entertained by the whole thing and is telling anyone that will listen about my predicament.

"It could be worse I suppose Jules, he might have been your cousin… again. You might want to consider paying the bar bill by putting it to good use by cleaning the bar glasses. Or you could always set up a Punch and Judy puppet show on the beach. Think of all the different foam faces you can make with one sponge? That's the way to do it."

I sit there on my inflated parasitical hemorrhoids and decide that if I can't beat her, then I may as well join her. By the end of the evening we have a feature-length movie panned out starring the one and only half- SpongeBob in the world.

"One Woman and her SpongeBob."

"SpongeBob and the Seven Dwarves."

"True Grot - Clit Eastwood."

"Sean Connery plays 007 SpongeBob in FISH FINGER."

"The Porn Identity, featuring SpongeBob."

"Jurassic Parking of the SpongeBob."

We even come up with a few tracks to go along with the movie.

"Tomorrow Never Lies in your Groin - Pulp."

"Memory Foam- Barbara Streisand."

"Unforgettable- Nat King Hole."

And finally, "Smells like teen Spirit - Nirvana."

We are on great foam, I mean form. On a roll to the very end, squeaky clean that's us.

"It's closing time already, Jules, are you sure you were meant to meet him here at The Tram? It's very unusual for any boy to stand you up, me sometimes, Lezzers' always, but you no."

"Oh, oh, now you mention it I think it might have been Filthy McNasty's at Darling Harbour."

"No wucking furries, after all the manhandling that sponge has received today, it's in for a much-needed rest."

"Sounds like a perfect plan, let's go home before midnight before it turns into a pumpkin."
"Too late for that, it's already 3am."

"Still, an early night. Sounds bliss."

We go back to the flat and get ready for bed. Ange comes through, her face positively glowing.

"Your face looks beautiful and shiny."
"Yeah right. I used that new face cloth on the sink, I hope you don't mind. It really has given me a lovely glow."

"You look radiant, goodnight."
What she doesn't know won't harm her...

BRRRIING BRIING ......BRRRIING BRIING.... BRRRIING BRIING.... BRRRIING BRRING...

Somewhere in my dream I am rudely interrupted by the constant ringing in my ears just before George as in Michael, leans into kiss my ready, pouting, waiting, plump wet lips. It's MY dream and a girl can dream, can't she? As the incessant ringing continues, it dawns on me that it's an external ring and not an internal one. It's actually a phone ringing, maybe it's Lesley. I leap out of bed, catching sight of myself in the mirror as I pass and see my reflection as a lolling, lumbering carthorse dragging a white beanbag, of all things, between my legs and not quite the agile young Giselle I imagine myself to be.

I answer it.

"Lesley?"

"No, it's me."

"Smee who?"

"Not Smee...ME."

"Me who?"

It's beginning to sound like a bad knock-knock joke.

"Mikey."

"Mikey who?"

"MY key doesn't work so help me out here will you? Phnarr, phnarr."

I'm right, a bad knock-knock joke.

"Mikey????........ As in Mikey???.... MIKEY??"

"The one and only, tall, dark and handsome... ha ha...ha." Silence. "Okay, not so handsome, but tall... Lesley's boyfriend, Mikey. Ha ha." Some more silence. The laugh is undeniable, unmistakable.

"Omg, Nursie's, oops, I mean of course, LESLEY'S boyfriend. Sorry.... yes...MIKEY..."

I run through to Ange's room and start to shake her awake.

"MIKEY!" Pointing to the receiver.

"Everything ok Jules? Does my voice sound that different already? You've only been in Sydney a few months. Am I that easily obliterated from your memory?"

"Yes, sorry, I'm still half asleep. Jeez, is it really you? What time is it in Aberdeen? Why are you calling ME? Has something happened?"

"No, no, all good here. It's early evening but I wanted to make sure I caught you before you head out for the day."

"I'm afraid Nursie's, oops I mean Lesley's, not here anymore."

"Anymore?"

"Did I say anymore? I mean, anyway. She's on an early shift and not here."

"That's okay, it's actually you I want to speak to anyway."

"Really??"

Still gesticulating. Ange is feigning boredom, pretending to stifle a yawn and cutting her wrists.

"Yeah, I'm thinking I'm going to take some time off work and come over to surprise Lesley."

"What? Really? You're thinking of coming HERE to surprise her?"

Ange puts her fingers down her throat.

"Is that a problem?"

"Ehh...YES... I mean, what did you just say? It's a bad line, I thought you said you were taking time off work and coming here. Do you mean HERE as in Sydney here?"

This repetition is all for Ange's benefit, who has put the pillow over her head and has gone back to sleep, not in the slightest bit fazed or interested by this turn up for the books.

"YES, I'M THINKING OF TAKING SOME TIME OFF WORK AND COMING OUT TOOOO SURPRISE LESLEY DOWN UNDER. SOUNDS LIKE SOMETHING FROM 'DEBBIE DOES DALLAS'. BUT NOT. Phnar, Phnar."

"NOOOOOO. I'm not deaf you know, you don't need to shout, I hear you just fine."

"Sorry, I was trying to help you out as you said it was a bad line."

"Oh right. Yeah, she'll love that."

Ange's muffled laugh can be heard from under the pillow.

"I'm going to need you and Ange to help me make this secret operation work."

"Suuuure! We'd LOVE to help, wouldn't we Ange?"

Ange comes out from the confines of duck feathers and shakes her head.

"Not me. I'm having nothing to do with it."

"What did Ange just say?"

"She said she can't think of anything better she'd rather be doing."

"It would be a kind of a covert operation of sorts."

"More than you know. I... sure...WHEN?"

"Probably not until December which gives me two months to work my notice and come up with a wicked, cunning plan. She'll be happy, right?"

"Happy? I can't think of any of the other dwarves she'd rather be. She'll be cock-a-hoop. Over the moon. Thrilled. Ecstatic. We just have to locate her."

What do you mean "locate"?"

"Did I say "locate?"

Ange is nodding....

"Yes, I did say LOCATE. We'll need to find the perfect LOCATION is what I meant."

He breathes in relief.

"How exciting Mikey, why wouldn't she be happy?"

"Was Lord Lucan one of the seven dwarves?"

"What did Ange say?"

"Oh, just ignore her, she's as excited as I am and is shaking, oh for feck sake. Nodding. Yes, NODDING her head as we speak. She's overjoyed."

"Everything okay? You sound a bit strange."

"Yeah, I've still got ....eh.... jet lag."

OMG.... why in the hell did I say that? We've been here for months. I do wish Ange would stop rolling all over her bed holding her sides, pretending they're splitting with laughter.

"I know we've been here a while already, but I have a chemical imbalance."

"Is alcohol and marijuana considered a contributory factor towards your 'chemical imbalance' Jules?"

I wish Ange would shut the feck up.

"It takes me longer than the average human bean to get over it."

It's all so cringey. I want to punch the lights out of Ange's smug face.

"I know we promised to give all communications a break until we were reunited, but I'm miserable without her and I'm really going to need you and Ange to help me make this secret squirrel plan work. Will you help?"

"You're happy to break your promise to her? She might be raging."

"I'll take that chance Jules. Being without her is like having a limb chopped off, you know like Tom without Jerry, Laurel without Hardy."

"Lesley without friends."

"What did Ange say?"

"Sonny without Cher, toast without butter, sex without a condom."

Cringe.

"Yes, well, I'm sure we could go on all day Jules, but I need to get some work done here. It won't work without you. You in?

"Suuuure! I'm 110 % in and Ange is too. Whether she likes it or not."

Ange is shaking her head and heads off through to the kitchen.

Kind of a secret though, so no blabbing. It won't work if she knows."

"Rest assured, she won't be able to find out from us"

"Can you keep it to yourself without letting her know?"

"You better believe it. When did you say you're coming out again? I mean out here, not OUT OUT?"

Why did I say that?

"I think that's her coming back though Mikey. Better go before she catches us. I'll mark it in my diary."

"Yeah, right, like that'll be happening Jules. Have you suddenly started to channel Miss Marple?"

"Shhhhhhhh, shut the feck up. NOT you Mikey, I don't want Lesley, yes Lesley to hear us."

"You'd have to have a pretty loud voice for her to hear you Jules. Fat chance of that happening, unless you have a voice like a foghorn."

"Ignore her Mikey."

"I can't make out what Ange keeps saying, but I'll keep in touch through email nearer the time and we can plan the specifics, or pacifics as Lesley calls them. HA HA…...Jules? JULES??? We must have been cut off."

SHIT... SHIT …. SHIT…. SHITTETY SHIT. That's it, we're done for now. Okay, okay, deep breath. What do we do now? Where do we start? How do we start? Should we even start?

Maybe I should call him back and tell him. No, no, that wouldn't be right.

"Hi Mikey, Jules again, I should have mentioned earlier, but Lesley is missing. She's been gone for a week already. No, no, we haven't tried to look for her yet. No idea where she is. Well we kinda think she's heading to The Bush, not her bush you understand, THE Bush, The Outback, Northern Territory. Yeah, no idea why she took off."

Nope that is NOT going to happen. We can't tell him that. Maybe tell him she's travelling.

"Yes, on her own. No we didn't stick together."

That's not going to happen either, and I am definitely, definitely not going to tell him the truth about her disappearance. We'd come out of this looking really, really bad. There's only one thing for it, we're going to have to go find her and bring her back in time for the Bondi Beach reunion date. Yup that's what we'll do, we'll find her and bring her back. Sorted, sounds like the perfect plan. What could possibly go wrong?

ANGE

HA HA HA HA, Jules is having a complete meltdown, a total paddy, maybe even a mild panic attack. She's had a call from Mikey who's supposedly allegedly coming out to surprise Lezzers', well, more like the surprise will be on him. She's NOT here, surprise, surprise, you've travelled 30,000 miles to see your girlfriend who's not actually here. She's disappeared without a trace. The look on his face will be priceless, especially when we tell him that we've not even bovvered to go look for her. She just took off, no idea why. The letter she left was somewhat vague, even though it was as clear as that she wanted to get away from us. And I emphasize the word "US".

Jules is ranting on now about leaving Sydney, buying a car and heading out of town to find her. That all seems a bit of a knee-jerk reaction if you ask me. She'll be fine. Does she really think we'll be able to find her? What are the benefits to calling it a day here, buying a car, going on a road trip, finding her and bringing her back? Hmm, maybe experience some more of Australia, meet some new boys and have some fun escapades. Bob's your uncle, Fanny's your aunt and it's all smelling of roses in the garden of Lezzers' and Mikey. When I put it like that, a road trip does sound like an exciting adventure, it actually doesn't sound like too bad an idea. She's probably got over despising us by now anyway, is lonely and ready for us to come get her, even though her last words to us were,

"You two go together like Drunk and Disorderly. You're positively pitiful. Shame, SHAME on BOTH of you."

Perhaps I misheard her and she really said: "It's been an absolute pleasure travelling with you both this far, but time to move on, you take care now."

Close enough.

If truth be known, I'm bored and so ready to get out of Sydney for a while, maybe being on the road will help my liver deflate. Every cloud and all that.

"I've got the perfect solution Ange. Let's buy a car, follow her trail."

"And how do we follow her trail exactly? This isn't a fairytale story - she's not left us breadcrumbs you know."

"It's Nursie we're talking about here, she's bound to have left one. It's so simple, we follow her trail, find her and bring her back. When we do catch up with her, we'll apologise for any wrongdoings, she'll accept because that's her nature and we'll all travel back to Sydney for a holly jolly Christmas. No wucking furries mate."

"No wucking furries indeed. Do you really believe it's going to be that simple Jules? We're just going to buy a car, set off on a road trip halfway across Australia, find her and bring her back in time for Mikey's big reunion?"

"Look, there is always a solution to everything Ange and this seems to me the perfect one. All we have to do is buy a car, find her and get her back before Christmas Eve."

"Have you heard yourself? BUY a fucking car, find Lezzers' somewhere in The Bush and get back here for Christmas Eve? Have you lost your mind? Don't answer that, I already know the answer. We have absolutely no idea where she is, besides we haven't a scooby doo whether or not she's even made it to the Northern Territory. Besides, it's only, oh let me think, 349,129squillion kilometres away! The only thing we know for sure is that she's got a job on an Aboriginal Reserve."

"It's a start, isn't it? Besides, I miss her. You must miss her on some small level?"

"Yes, about as much as an old man's urine stream misses the toilet."

JULES

It takes me forever to convince her that this is the best plan, buy a car, find Lesley, have her reunited with Mikey for New

Year's Eve. Sorted. I tell her that we really need to redeem ourselves or karma will come back to bite us in the behind and we don't want to come back in the next life as horny toads.

ANGE

Well, I suppose it's doable, not that I mind coming back as horny, without the toad bit though. I only have a provisional licence but that's a minor detail. Jules doesn't really need to know that at this stage. I see myself as Penelope Pittstop, so we can still share the driving. I don't mind in the slightest bit driving, however, the thought of driving under the influence most of the time might be a bit of a challenge though. Having a chauffloosey sounds far more preferable.

JULES

Seriously, no sooner have we made the decision to buy a car, go on a road trip, and find Nursie than the phone rings.

"You get it. I can't speak to Mikey again."

"Okay. Hello?"

" G'day. Is that Angela?"

"Angela?"

Who calls me Angela aside from my mother when I'm in trouble?

"Maybe, who wants to know?"

"It's Bruce. We met at Australia's Next Top Model event, I'm one of the car salesmen that was there."

"Uh huh, I remember you. I never touched that knob behind the curtain and you can't prove a thing. What do you want?"

"Nothing. I know nothing about the guy behind the curtain, but I'm calling to say that you won the first prize in the raffle. Congratulations."

"Really? What did I win? A pack of Tim Tams? An inflatable kangaroo? A cuddly koala bear?"

"No, you won a second-hand used Holden panel van."

"Shut the fuck up. Sorry, I mean, wow, you're kidding?"

"No, we drew the raffle tickets just now, and it's your name and number that was on the winning ticket."

"This has to be the biggest coincidental joke on the planet. You're not trying to buy us off by offering us a bribe because one of your faulty pieces of equipment projected my whiplashed, almost brain-damaged best friend 100mph from one of your cars straight into the display on the fish buffet table? Are you trying to avoid a lawsuit and adverse publicity here? Believing we're that shallow and easily bought?"

"Then it would be her name on the winning ticket and not yours, now, wouldn't it?"

I can't believe our luck.

"And there's that."

"How is she anyway? Any injuries?"

"She is still having migraines that whaley haven't got much better. She's planning to see a sturgeon later and may well be told that the best plaice for her is to leave Sydney and take a road trip. She knows that it was an accident and not done on porpoise."

Yes, it was.

"We don't need any extra time to mullet over, she cod get her lawyer to deal with it, but the panel van seems like a perfect solution to ease all the pain caused. I'm not very koi as you know, and can come to your showroom as soon as to pick up my winning prize. "

"You can look at it, see if it is to your liking and we can even modify it for her special needs. Any fin is possible."

"So exciting, see you tomorrow."

ANGE

Can you believe this? The universe is an incredible, magnificent place and works in truly miraculous ways. Quite odd and spooky really. Maybe not, though, it might have had something to do with the fact that I filled out my name on all 500 raffle tickets they gave to Jules to appease her for all her troubles. Time to pack this shithole up and get on the road.

"How come you won the car? It was me that had the accident and was given the raffle tickets."

"Well, as you were unstable on your pins and still a bit shaky, I filled the stubs in with my name and number. Don't sweat the small stuff. If it makes you feel better, you can use your driving licence and fill in the new owner paperwork."

"That's very generous of you Ange. Thank you. I'm really excited to be heading off and seeing some of Oz. Reminds me of the movie Thelma and Louise."

"Thelma and Louise??? Really? You do know how that turned out right?"

JULES

I'd not been much further than Bondage Beach, so it's all a bit of an adventure going out to Parramatta to pick up the van. It's only 26 km from the centre, but seems much further with all the train stops. We're in the middle of bumfuck nowhere. This could well be The Outback. Maybe Nursie hasn't gone that far and is on our very doorstep after all. How handy would that be? I've been looking forward to seeing kangaroos, but can only see car dealership after car dealership. We're going in the right direction at least. Our friend Steve, a man is not a camel, Colquhoun, is also doubling up as our lawyer and mechanic. Not sure the singlet, shorts and thongs looks like the professional attire that would be worn, but anything goes in Oz is my experience.

Bruce, is every male called Bruce here?, meets us wearing a shiny, silky, but not, two-piece suite, as Nursie calls it. His broad, flashy, pearly white smile almost hides the desperation of getting us out in lickety split time. Barry's eagerness for us to sign the paperwork on the van and have us on our merry way is something only to be seen in The Guinness Book of Records and almost makes me suspicious that we're going to get a clapped-out piece of metal junk, fit for a landfill site only. Boy, they'd really have a lawsuit on their hands if we actually died because of them being negligent and gifting us a dodgy van. Desperation and the resolve that there's going to be no commission on this transaction seeps from every acrylic clad covered pore.

We walk out of the orifice, again, as Nursie calls it. I spot her as soon as I get to the forecourt. She is a piece of engineering beauty. There she lies, nestled in the front row between two large flatbed trucks outshining them both. She almost cries out: "Here's me!"

She is magnificent. I have never seen anything quite like it.
She's cream with a dark brown, sparkly metallic flash up her side
that runs from the front headlights across the two doors all the way
across the side panels, meandering towards and tailing off at the
back headlights. There she is. The wee beauty.

I can tell by the look on Bruce's face that this isn't the van
we'd actually won, but he seems happy enough to pan her off on us
anyway. Steve, a man is not a camel, is also happy to say the least
as it's way past his beer o'clock time and he's itching for his first,
maybe, maybe not, Coopers Brewery Original Pale Ale.

If truth be told, it wouldn't have mattered if she had been
bruised, battered and was a clapped-out old wheelbarrow with an
engine. I know, without a shadow of a doubt, she is mine and the
car I want.

ANGE

Jules squeals with delight, shouts and runs, emphasizing
her knock knees, towards three Holdens. She flays herself across
the bonnet of a cream panel van and not the humongous flatbed
trucks dwarfing it at either side. I think one of those trucks is what
we are meant to win, but as neither of us have our heavy goods
vehicle licence anyway, this old banger will do. She is clearly
taken with it by the way she's drooling and fawning over the hood.
It looks okay, like a regular car if I'm honest - nothing special,
cream with a shitty brown stripe, but what do I know? As long as it
gets us to where we're going and back again, then I'm in. All of a
sudden Bruce seems even more engaged - I'm sure very thankful
to get rid of us even quicker than he'd possibly imagined. I can see
bona-fide, potential customers pulling into the lot and I can see $
commission symbols pop up in front of his eyes. He suddenly goes

into full on sleazy salesman mode, possibly to allow the new arrivals a chance to hear his pitch and sales skills. They're certainly wasted on us, that's for sure.

"Oh, my goodness, you have such great taste. This van is unique, a one of a kind, if I might add.

"Of course, it is."

"No need to be so cynical Ange, she's perfect."

"It only arrived on the lot this morning and will be snapped up in no time had you not bought it."

"Won. By default."

He ignores me.

"It has shiny mag wheels which are so much stronger and more durable than other cheaper ones you see these days."

Of course.

"The interior is to die for."

"I do hope not."

In an overly dramatic, over-the-top flamboyant gesture he opens the double back doors with a

"TARRA". The inside is like a glorified egg box. It has a double mattress that looks like it could be used as an example specimen at the FBI research laboratories to assist newbie agents in identifying foreign bodily fluids donated, and very generously I might add, by either man or beast. He pats the mattress as if to encourage us to hop in.

"Eh no, I'm not up-to-date on my inoculations and haven't been taking a course of antibiotics recently so have no desire to get pissed, stoned or pregnant this afternoon."

JULES

I ignore Ange and clamber inside. The interior roof and sides are lined with a soundproof glitter, yes, that's right, GLITTER foam-like material. It's grey and looks more suited to be a luxurious, and I use that term loosely, egg box rather than lining the inside of a van. I can't help but wonder why it even needs to be soundproofed? Bruce notices the puzzled look on my face, and as if reading my mind, he fills me in.

"The Holden is very popular with surfies and they like to boombox their music when not catching waves."

"Hmm, who knew? Thanks for the information Brucie but it looks like they'll catch more than mere waves, given that I can detect something more of the crustacean variety lurking in the crevices."

"Funny you should say that Ange, but it's known as a surfies fuck truck, a shaggin wagon, a bouncy fun house on wheels. And a car of ill repute."

"I'm sure it is Steve. You will receive no argument or objection with me on that point."

I'm smitten though, and don't care for the big trucks, this is the one I want. Bruce is happy to oblige by informing me that this is the perfect choice for us. I know it is, I feel it in my waters.

ANGE

We go for a test drive with Bruce in the passenger seat and Steve and I in the back bouncing about on the mattress of love or lust. We go round the block a few times and Jules declares it as absolute perfection personified. Drives like a dream. Hmm, let's hope that doesn't turn into a nighthorse at the flick of a switch.

Seriously though, what does it matter, as long as it gets us from A to B and back again. We can always change out the mattress, we'll be fine. It means we can save ourselves some money by sleeping in the back. We can also pick up some poor unsuspecting male hitchhikers to help pay for the petrol and to entertain us on those lonely, dark nights.

JULES

The van is ideal and it seems to drive ok. I just want to sign on the dotted line and get outta Dodgey Dealer City. I am so over this car-winning business even though it is the only one we've looked at. Ange would have taken a golf cart if it gets us from A to Nursie. Steve - a man is not a camel - Colquhoun takes a very quick look under the bonnet while still pretending to be a lawyer with a hobby in mechanical engineering. He knocks a few metal parts, tugs a few wires, strokes a few pipes and gives us the double thumbs-up.

"Can we keep it Bruce?"

"Her, Ange, difinootely a her."

"Come into the office and we'll fill in the paperwork."

"You don't need Steve and I for this Jules. You're a big girl now and I'm sure you can handle this all on your ownio. Coincidentally, I noticed a pub around the corner. Come get us when the deal is done, you can be the designated driver"

Ange and Steve swan off to the pub while Bruce and I go to the office to finish the deal. There is so much paperwork to get through, that I'm sure they'll both be pissed by the time I get back to them. I wonder what we should call the van? She's definitely a girl and must hold a whole lot of dirty little secrets is my guess.

Oooo, if only she could talk? The stories she could tell. Let's hope she'll have a few more exciting tales to tell once we finish with her. I know what I'm going to call her. I'm going to name her Dirty Gertie after the fictional femme fatale who earned the nickname "Dirty Gertie" for the casual nature in which she enticed and then humiliated men. Seems appropriate, especially as Ange is on board. The first thing we're going to do, though, is replace the mattress and hand it back to the FBI.

I collect them both about an hour-and-a-half later. And as predicted, they're practically legless after having had a competition with each other to see who can shoot the most shots before I get back to them. No winners here, well the takings of the establishment, that's all. They hadn't reckoned on me being gone that long I guess.

I make them both ride in the back, at least if they're going to throw up it won't make any difference to the already stained, stinking mattress whose longevity is coming to a swift end.

I drive home in Dirty Gertie with that pair of drunks lolling around in the back of her. I'm really excited to begin this journey. What an adventure we're going to have.

ANGE

I'm going to love this designated driver malarkey, but I can't say that bouncing about from side to side on the sticky, putrid mattress with Steve, a man is not a camel, Colquhoun occasionally landing on top of me is my idea of fun though. I will sue the pants off Bruce if I catch gonorrhea or any other sexually transmitted disease again from this bouncy heap of metal - or Steve for that matter.

"Drop this mountainous cushion of foam-filled love off at the fertility clinic Jules, that might boost their sperm database. I can tell that this mattress is chock-a-block full of live specimens, including Steve's, ready and eager to be harvested."

"Potential world-class surfies right here in this pallet of passion."

JULES

I'm impressed that my stick-shift skills are still razor sharp. You put your right foot in, you put your left foot in, you take your right foot out and you glide it all about. It's also fun seeing that pair of drunken goons rolling around from one side to another. We drop Steve, a man is not a camel, Colquhoun, off at The Tram and tell him we'll be back later. As it turns out, we never do see him again as we get side-tracked with packing all our belongings. He's probably still there at the end of the bar like a barfly staring in the mirror so he can watch how much he's drinking.

We swap the mattress initially with Ange's, but then decide it's probably just as bad, so swap it out with Nursie's which is positively virginal. The only stains coming from it are melted Tim Tam crumbs, the grease from The Flying Pie's sausage rolls and some dark discolour from her nightly cup of Milo. We replace the curtains in the small back windows with one of her flannel nighties that she'd left on the line. We put a plastic tarpaulin sheet over the mattress before making the bed so it won't get wet if we spill our drinks, wet ourselves or add our own bodily fluids. We'll be fine and dandy. Besides, I'm sure Nursie mentioned once before that it is best to expose our bodies to certain bacteria and foods to build up future natural "antibionics". If that is the case, we'll be fine for the rest of our lives.

I walk along Campbell Parade admiring all the other Shaggin Waggins, but none of them even comes close to our Gertie. I'm heading up to Bondi Junction to get some last-minute bits and pieces, including a first aid box. Nursie always says it comes in handy as there are many poisonous things in Australia that can kill you. Not sure if she means the beasties, alcohol, drugs or all three. I want to buy one of those portable wee coolers they call "eskys" here as well. Is that cultural inappropriateness? Possibly not as there are no eskimos in Australia. We can even keep water in it alongside our beer and wine boxes, or goons as they're called. A goon is a cheap drink that tastes good ice-cold or mixed. Hmmm, I use the word "good" here very loosely. It can taste like sour urine, but mixed with orange juice it can be palatable. On the box of one brand, Golden Oak, it says

"Produced with the aid of milk, egg, nut, and fish products, sugar added and trace remains".

What the feck are "trace remains"? After mattressgate, my mind boggles over this one. Well, at least we'll be consuming a whole meal regularly in just one goon by the looks of things. The goon has a silver space bag inside the cardboard box which is filled with wine. It has a plastic tap that can be pulled out of the side to help the wine flow freely. It's so versatile, and whomever thought of this concept has made themselves a squillionaire. A four-litre carton can cost between $9-15, depending on where you go. This is cheap at half the price, I tell you, and they're everywhere; forget the opera house, the koala bear, or Kylie's backside, the goon should be the national emblem of Australia.

When the wine is finished, which doesn't take long when you drink it like it's going out of fashion, you're likely blotto and ready to put the empty bag to good use. You blow it up and play "slappies", where you slap each other around with it, and after the goon fun and games have run their course, you can rest your weary head on it.

Another great idea is to use it when it's still full by hanging it on a clothesline, lying underneath the tap and pouring from it like a Spanish porron. This allows everyone to drink from the same goon without touching anyone's lips, terribly hygienic, which is possibly the downside to the game depending on who's playing. It's not any bog-standard old game, it does require some skill and dexterity to ensure the wine enters one's mouth and does not spill out onto one's clothing. It's like an inflatable watering can of sorts. You have to swallow quickly as there is a constant stream coming from the spout in a fast and furious torrent right towards your gaping gob. I see that as an opportunity to add to my ever-increasing growth of talents. It can also be made into a goon raft for a quick getaway from pirates, nautical patrols or the waterboys. I wish I was a fisherman, tumblin on the seas, far away from dry land and its bitter memories castin' out my sweet line. With abandonment and love no ceiling bearin' down on me save the starry sky above with light in my head.

Ange hasn't come with me on this particular jaunt, preferring to stay behind and hand wash Dirty Gertie. Regardless if she is Gleaming Gertie, she's still always going to be known as Dirty Gertie. After an hour or so I head back towards Bondage beach with my purchases, when I hear a

"WOOOHOOO, here's me".

I recognize her voice, but can't see her either ahead or behind me. Strange, where is she? She must have finished early and decided to come join me. Too late, I've got everything now. I spot her crossing the road from Grace Brothers departmental store. Also strange. Wonder what she's doing in there?

ANGE

I want to surprise Jules with my Jackie Stewart driving skills so I decide to take Dirty Gertie out for a spin and go pick her up. It's been a while since I've sat in a driver's seat, let alone driven a manual, but how hard is it to hold a hard upright rod in your hand and manipulate it anyway you want? I still remember her driving ditty that at the time was very irritating, but it's stuck. I park Dirty Gertie on the top deck of the multi-storey car park attached to Grace Brothers departmental store, far, far away from all the other cars, in her very own parking bay. She is shiny and looking more like the sparkling princess she is. Jules must think we're going to walk home together as she waves, then heads back in the direction of the beach. She's slightly bemused as I guide her back across the road and towards the stairwell at the side of the store. In fact, I have to practically frog march her.

"Come on, come on, there's something up here that you need to see."

"Can't you at least take one of the bags?"

"I'm at least twenty steps ahead of you now, and am not turning back to get a bag. Come on, pick up the pace, why don't you?"

"This better be worth it Ange."

"Jules, it's to die for."

I get up the seven flights of stairs way ahead of her and wedge open the door to the rooftop area. There in all her glory, is Dirty Gertie for all the world to see. She is so bright, shiny and sparkling that I'm sure she can be seen from outer space. I have done an incredible job if I may say so myself. Well, when I say "I", I mean the support workers at The Magic Hand Carwash, who have polished, waxed, buffed and caressed her inside and outside.

"TAAADAAAAA!"

A rather puce and sweaty Jules appears out of breath at the door.

JULES

I see Dirty Gertie straight away and she looks brand spanking new, but I can't quite comprehend how she has not only got here, but how it had only taken Ange a short time to get her to look this good. Who has driven her here? I can tell by the chuffed look on her cheerful phizog exactly who was at the wheel.

"I thought you said you don't have a licence?"
"Pah, minor details. It's like riding a horse, once you can do it, you can always do it."
"You can't ride a horse, besides it's like riding a bicycle Ange. You're beginning to sound like Nursie."

"I resemble that remark."

"So, how did she get here?"

She wouldn't have, would she? Shouldn't have…couldn't have risked it. I look at her beaming face, nodding at me enthusiastically.

"You did not????"

"What's the problemo?"

ANGE

Gertie looks absolutely fabulous and I am chuffed to bits for getting her up here all by my little old self. Besides, licences are so yesterday. What are the chances that some bobby would want to pull over a surfies passion wagon without wearing a hazmat suit? Too much bovver methinks. I wouldn't be caught, besides I can drive, well, sort of, there have only been a couple of kangaroo starts and stalls, I admit, but we are in Australia after all, so it's a given. The manual is a bit tricky, but hey ho, life is meant to deal out some discomforts, right? I do have to drive her in second gear so I can concentrate on the steering without the hassle of constantly changing them. The only gear I have to really worry about is where to stash Lezzer's Audrey Two plants. I'm not going on this road trip without them. She is not nearly as pleased as she ought to be.

"What if you'd been stopped? Hmm, tell me that? Or worse, you'd hit someone."

Blah, blah, blah.

"We haven't even got insurance yet for you."

Yada yada yada.

"Look, this is easy enough to resolve. Give me a chance to show you my Top Gear skills. That'll allay some of your fears when you actually see my competency. We're covered for insurance anyway if you're beside me."

Maybe not, but she doesn't challenge me, so I get into the driver's seat. If she wants me to share the driving, then she needs to let me drive. We set off a little bit faster than I intend and leave some rubber skid marks and a bit of smoke, but on the plus side, I don't lose control and go over the edge. Small mercies. That's for sure a bonus and an admirable skill me thinks. She's overreacting by grasping the edges of the seat which is very off-putting and slightly patronizing if you ask me.

"There's no need to be like that, relax and enjoy the drive."

"Eyes on the road, and both hands on the wheel."

JULES

I think we're going to do the Thelma and Louise final shot after all and finish the journey before we've even started it by careering over the top of the multi-storey car park.

"Slow down. Slow and steady wins the race. Keep your eyes on the road, you won't see the sharp bends coming up while giving me the evil eye. You do know it's not a race, no prizes given out here unless it's for the most reckless. It's beginning to feel like the wacky races with you at the wheel pretending to be Penelope Pitstop."

"Hay- Ulp, Hay -Ulp. Can you Hay - ulp me Mutley? I can drive you know, just because I don't have a full licence doesn't mean I can't drive."

"Oh, you can drive alright. You can drive even a saint to drink!!"

ANGE

It takes me a bit longer to get into the groove as she's barking orders in my ear which is so distracting. As we spiral down the ramp, it begins to feel more like a ride on one of those helter-skelters rather than being in a car park. She should think herself lucky, not only is she being driven home, saving her time and energy carrying all those heavy bags, but I'm also treating her to a free ride at the funfair. We're practically free-wheeling, cruising as we go round and round with very little acceleration being required. When we get to the bottom, I am maybe a tad distracted by the fun that I don't notice the "WRONG WAY" sign directly ahead of me and the "EXIT to the left. I'm going too fast towards the WRONG WAY sign. Jules is not helping either, she's mute now thankfully, flapping her arms about and gesticulating to the left, mouth open, eyes wide. All of a sudden, she shouts: "LEFT, you feckin eejit, LEFT!!!"

I swing Gertie towards the left and hear this almighty scraping, crunching and grazing sound coming from the same direction as Jules's shrieking. Perhaps I have been a bit premature in my manoeuvre. Very in-keeping with the previous occupants in the back of Gertie no doubt. I'll admit, I have taken the angle towards the exit a bit tighter and sharper than I should have, but it's an honest mistake. I use, in my humble opinion, an excellent emergency brake, which surprises and whiplashes both but at the same time. At least it's effective and efficient as the car stops immediately.

I look towards her out of the corner of my eye and notice that the concrete pillar to her left is probably a bit closer to me than it should have been, practically stroking her cheek, almost touching it in fact. The offending article is almost inside the car.

"OOOPS…Sorry, I mean I'm really sorry."

"Get out of the feckin car."

"Surely we can sort it out?"

I drag the car into reverse, taking more of Gertie's stripe off with me, leaving it tattooed on the pillar.

"OUT!"

"Do I have to?"

My bottom lip is wobbling and I'm whimpering slightly. I didn't even know I could do that?

"FECK yeah, I'm not Harry feckin Potter and going to be able to get through this concrete pillar and be magically transported to another multi-storey feckin' car park. I literally and physically can't get out...."

JULES

Ange slinks out of the driver's seat and I scoot across into it. I reverse slowly and gently, eventually extricating my poor destroyed Gertie from the cement post. I get out to survey the damage to our brand-not-so-new van that we've had for less than 24 hours. I caution and advise her to stop apologising and to say nothing as I think I might be on the verge of knocking her teeth out. I'm raging. The last time I remember feeling like this was when she used my razor to trim her pubes, the very same razor I use on my chin for the odd rogue hair.

Our beautiful Gertie now has a lovely dent from the front bumper across the passenger door to the back panel. I'd had my window down and it smashed inside the door frame on impact.

"We're lucky we don't have much to steal, so that shouldn't be too much of a problem."

"It's still a feckin' problem Ange, we can't drive around Australia with an open window. That will need to be fixed and you're paying for it. There is no way we have time to get everything else done."

"I'm quite sure it's going to be the first of many, many battle scars Gertie is going to have to endure."

"Especially if you're at the helm Ange."

We drive home, or should I say, I drive home in complete silence, and for yet another time, I am aware that I really miss Lesley and wish she'd been here for me to offload on. She would know exactly what to say and do in these situations. We leave Gertie outside the flat, put a plastic bag over the window and wait for the repairman to come. It only takes him an hour or so and he's able to panel beat the side of the car enough to replace the window. The only downside is that it has to stay closed at all times now, as if you try to open it, you'll dislodge the bar holding it up and the glass will disappear inside the door frame. It stings Ange's pocket as she is now out of pocket by $200. Not such a free car for her after all. She has plenty of trust-fund money left by her beloved dad, so she doesn't care and is happy to part with it. We have to leave it there for a couple of days until we finish sorting out insurance and road tax. When we finally do get round to opening the door, we both recoil from the stench that permeates our nostrils. I could understand slightly if it had been the original mattress still in there, but it's Nursie's virginal one. It is an unmistakable smell of rotting, dead flesh. Even if we had left the remains of every Thai takeaway or pizza boxes in there for weeks, there was NO way it would have that unmistakable decaying, decomposing smell. We find the culprit under the passenger seat, curled up in a swollen, fetal, rigid state with its wee rodent, are baby possums' rodents? It's wee rigor leggies in the air. How the hell can a wee, cute creature like this give off such an awful smell? It must have been attracted to all Nursie's midnight morsels.

ANGE

Can you believe a possum, I mean a real live, not anymore, very much dead possum is inside Gertie? How can something so small smell so vile? Sydney has its fair share of them and they may well be the state animal for all I know. It may even be illegal for us to albeit innocently transport or kill one in our car. It must have sneaked through the open, smashed window before it was sealed in, incarcerated within the bowels of Gertie. Sure smelled like some exploding bowels. It must have got a whiff of the 20 or so to-go boxes, still full and piled high in the back seat, that I had taken from the fridge, planning to graciously donate them to the homeless shelter, but had forgotten to do it with all the pillar-gate hupladoodle excitement that had ensued. Easy mistake Your Honour. The pesky rodent had died and swollen up to the same size as a small child or my sunburned lips. The van stinks of a mixture of chow mein, pepperoni and rotting marsupial flesh. Now we have a smell of decay permeating the upholstery and foam-carton sides, mingled with animal shit, leftover pizza, Indian pakora, fries, nuts even chicken fried rice, which is the most curious thing as I don't recall having that takeaway.

JULES

We open as many of the doors and windows as we can, spray inside with half-a-dozen cans of fragrant air freshener, adding some more holes to the already hole-punctuated ozone layer here in Australia, and leave it for a few hours.

In the meantime, we take the carcass of the beast and a goon to the back garden to contemplate and plan our route, and to bury the bulging deceased fur vermin. I won't lie, its pelt is silky smooth and pewter in colour that almost looks too good to bury.

Perhaps I could have it made into a merkin instead, but before I can suggest it, Ange grabs it and lobs it into a hole recently vacated by an Audrey Two plant.

"Ashes to ashes, dust to dust, life's a bitch and a spliff's a must."

We don't even notice the slight white haze that's encroaching into our space. At first, I think someone is having a barbie and the snags have caught fire, which is ridiculous when you think about it. As any Australian will tell you, they're the masters of the BBQ and nothing ever, ever burns on their watch. It's quite a dense fog. Too early for the sea haze to be rolling in and carries a familiar aroma though, heady, sweet, tangy, gosh, I'm hungry all of a sudden. I fancy some nibbles.

ANGE

I am naturally inhaling deeply, more from instinct than anything else, and taking in the wonderful elixir of what I initially think might be mosquito repellant. They do that here, they fly over the suburbs spraying the toxic deterrent. Doesn't matter to me one way or another and I take a full deep breath. I fill my lungs to full capacity, allowing my side ribs to expand with the heady substance. Jules interrupts my train of thoughts.

"Fancy some nipples?"

Why would she ask me that?

"Nipples?"

"Nipples? You know with maybe some hummus and carrot sticks?"

" NIPPLES?"

"NIBBLES."

What is wrong with her? That's a rhetorical question you understand, we'd be here all day if we started to answer that. She literally screams that in my face. It's the funniest thing though that I have heard or seen in ages. Her bright red, sweaty bonce looks like a well-slapped baboon's bulging airse. I literally crease myself up laughing, tears are streaming, not just from the thought of her asking me if I want what I thought were her nipples, but also from the thick smoke which we are both now inhaling deeply.

We are belly laughing, trying very hard to tell each other what we have been saying or are trying to say. It dawns on both of us that someone, somewhere is having a marijuana bonfire, but we can't for the life of us even get the words out to share this revelation with each other. If I don't end up with a six-pack after all this laughing, then I don't know what else could give me that chiselled, washboard look. Tears keep streaming down my cheeks and I can't stop. My belly is aching but still I can't stop.

Jules meanwhile has staggered inside, doubled over, giggling the whole way just to get some NIPPLES to share. She comes back out with a large bowl filled with crisps and is literally hoovering them up in constant motion straight into her gob. I can actually see the crisps, hummus and pureed carrots at the top of her gullet, but still she keeps shoveling them in. She has a mouthful of hummus and is trying to tell me something. She leans in closer, I lean in, our faces are almost touching as I wait eagerly to hear what she is so desperate to say. She can hardly breathe now as her mouth is packed to the gunwales. All of a sudden, she coughs, and in an explosion of pureed chickpeas, I end up wearing more than a fair smattering of the contents of her mouth. That is the clincher for both of us to lose all sense of decorum and control. We roll and roll around the grass like weebles for hours it seems like.

"Grass"

The mere mention of that word has us in even further fits of hysteria. I don't know whether to hold my aching tummy or my pelvic floor which is in imminent risk of uncontrollable leaking. I err on the side of caution and hold both for dear life. I rock and roll around the grass inhaling the grass with gay abandon. It's only much, much later that we hear on the news that the local police had set fire to more than three tons, that's three TONS, of confiscated cannabis. The 3.3 tons of marijuana were burned by officers at their sub precinct office in Bondi Beach. Apparently, the haul is valued at $1 million and I reckon Jules and I must have inhaled at least $999,999 of it. The officers wore masks to protect themselves from the fumes but unsuspecting civilians were left unprotected and "high on life".

The police did make a formal statement apologizing for the "green gaffe".

No apologies necessary in this household ocifers. Thanks for a great free, legal afternoon. But, it does remind me of our very own stash.

JULES

Just noooo, it's one thing inhaling the police's accidental green gaffe, but another thing exporting our very own large Audrey stash across states. There's enough of a garden plantation here to give Escobar a run for his money, and personally I don't want to partner with any organized drug cartel in Australia or anywhere else. No doubt my ancestors were sent to Oz on the convict ships for some petty crime, like nicking a loaf of bread, but

I have no intention of upping the ante to drug smuggling and distribution. Funnily enough, when you think about it, I might get deported back to the UK, free of charge. If I run out of money, I know what to do. Worth some consideration then. In the meantime, Ange has yet another wobbly bottom lip, a skill she has learned recently and is using it often and liberally, but it's not going to work on me that's for sure.

"I've never loved or cared for anything as much as Audrey Two and her descendants since my dad died." Quiver lip.

"I believe that to be 100% accurate Ange as I know how much you love those green Marry G Wanna plants like they are your own offspring, have been super excited to see them grow and blossom into fine adults, ready to go out and change the world one toke at a time. But smuggling drugs takes it all to a whole new level."
"How about this? I'll only bag the weed we need to accompany us on our journey and use it only for purely medicinal purposes only."

"No, not happening."

"How about this then? If I can find a place in Gertie so secure that even the best, most highly trained sniffer dogs can only smell dead possum and not one bit of ganja, can I take them? Let me hide some and you try to find them. I promise that if you find any of the weed, then game over, you've won and we'll have to smoke it all before we leave."

"You're on."

"Deal?"

"Deal."

There is no way she can hide anything in Gertie that I cannot find.

ANGE

The challenge has been set, let the fun and games begin by seeing how creative I can be. All that is needed here is for me to come up with a hideyhole to stash the hash. I manage to get all the dried herbs into four extra-large empty goons and seal them securely. These spaced out bags are very futuristic looking and very trendy if I may say so myself. I find the most amazing, highly creative, original place to hide them and challenge Jules to the new game.

"Spot the pot? Like I said, if you find them, I will gladly donate every last leaf to a worthy cause. Mainly us, but a worthy cause nonetheless."

"You're on, if I can't find them, then you get to keep them all for the road trip."

She looks everywhere, well, almost and eventually gives in.

JULES

Damnit, Janet, I can't find any of the sneaky little blighters anywhere and am beginning to think that she's winding me up and that they are in her holdall which is sitting on the pavement in plain sight for everyone to see. I know there are hidden spaces under the driver and passenger seats as Gertie belonged to surfies before us who quite possibly had one or 200 doobies ready rolled in their cache of hash in the van. I look and look and am still convinced that she is tricking me somehow. Eventually, after an hour or maybe a minute or so, I give up. She's won.

"I give up, you can bring your beloved treasure trove on the trip, s'cuse the pun. Just show me where you've hidden them?"

She's like a child in adult clothing who has won a goldfish at the carnival. She sashays here and struts there all the while singing: "Lucy in the sky with diamonds, ah, Lucy in the sky with diamonds".

She settles on the bonnet, lying on her back with her left hand draped over the side. Carefully, she takes a screwdriver out of her pocket, leans over and flips off the hubcap on the passenger side wheel. There, neatly taped in, is one of the spaced-out savers bags full of grass. "One for each wheel."

"It's going to be quite the adventure for sure. If there was any doubt before, it's sealed now. That's if we aren't in jail before we get to Melbourne that is."

"At least we'll be together, that's what good friends are for after all. Now let's make like a prom dress and take off."

ANGE

There is definitely a sense of being a rebel - well, to be fair, smuggling 20lbs of drugs is slightly more rebellious than even I could have imagined, but it's such an adrenaline rush and I am literally buzzing with excitement and anticipation, which may also be due to the fact that I've just finished a rather large joint. We leave the Sydney city limits behind and join the Hume Highway. I am high on life and natural medicinal products and on the way from misery to happiness today. I hope we bump into some spurious highwayman, the likes of Dick Turpin and his merry men who are willing and able to withstand my liver. It's only going to take 10 hours to get to Melbourne, but Jules isn't quite ready to have me drive, so she's doing it all on her onio, which suits me fine. She's cutting off her nose to spite herself which is her problem, so I chill out, relax and watch the non-scenery go by.

"Since I'm driving, you can be the map reader. You can manage that without hitting a concrete pillar, can't you?"

"My map-reading prowess is considerably better than my attention to folding, licking and rolling joint making skills are so we're good to go."

"Well, that is indeed saying something. Let's put it to the test, shall we?"

"Oh yes please, watch the bumps then, I would hate to spill any."

"I'm referring to the former, your superior map-reading skills, not rolling a doobie. Let's see how good you are, shall we? Suppose I ask you to meet me for lunch at 23 degrees, four minutes north latitude and 45 degrees, 15 minutes east longitude, where would we be going?"

"Give me a moment here. Got it. You'd be eating alone in some sleazy diner and I'd be in the library studying up on longitude and latitudes. Relax Jules, as long as I have the map the right way round, I'll manage. Have some faith in me, why don't you? When I woke this morning, I had no idea I was going to be this helpful, but hey, shit happens."

"Speaking of faith, time to put on some sounds."

"Your wish is my command. You have two wishes left, choose wisely. What is your first wish?"

"My first wish is that we play the one and only Winning Hearts and Minds non-stop until we find Nursie."

"Winning Hearts and Minds? Enlighten me, I'm not sure I know that album."

"Oh, not an album, it's an acronym for the one and only most successful pop acts in history."

"Got ya, then it can only be..."

"WHAM."

"Wham bam, thank you mam. Here we go, wake me up before you go, everything she wants, I'm your man. Winning Hearts and Minds eh? Who knew? Not me. Speaking of minds, mine is like an internet browser, 19 tabs are open, 3 of them are frozen and I have no clue where the music is coming from."

"Let's start with Make It Big to get us in the mood."

"I know something else that'll get us in the mood."

"Okay then, but just a cheeky wee one, nothing too monstrous, I know what you're like."

"Trust me I have a degree in English, so I learned from the best."

I'm not going to lie here, but I do get a bit carried away with the scenery, singing and smoking that I completely miss the turn-off for the capital Canberra. We're meant to stop off there, but I realise too late that I've been sitting with the map on my lap, upside down. By the time I notice my faux pas we're in Gunning. No point in turning back now. My finger is getting numb from all the tapping on the window, pointing out the trees, the clouds, the shrubs and the constant beat to the loop of Wham and Club Tropicana, so it's definitely time for a pit stop.

"I hope you don't mind, but we passed Canberra and are now almost in Gunning. I heard that Canberra is overrated anyway and Gunning so much better."

"That's fine, whatever."

She's getting increasingly restless, bored and very grumpy. I notice that her knuckles are gripping the wheel tightly, so tightly, in fact, that I think she might snap it in two.

JULES

It's like having a five-year-old in a confined space. She fidgets here, fidgets there and needs to be constantly entertained. I swear if she says, "Are we there yet?" one more time, I am going to crumple the road map on her lap and throw it out the window, followed closely by her and her tapping, bony, pointy long-nail fingers that are incessantly battering the window.

"Look at that bush?" tap tap tap.

"Look at the tree?" tap tap.

"Look at the clouds?" tappety, tappety feckin tap.

"Look at the sheep?" tap tap.

"Club Tropicana, drinks are free, fun and sunshine, there's enough for everyone. All that's missing is the sea, but don't worry you can suntan!" tappety feckin tap.

She's meant to be reading the directions not pummelling the glass on the window. I'm about ready to ram her whole hand, along with those beating digits, down her throat. We've already missed Canberra. I know Australia is a BIG country, but how can she have lost Canberra? It's only the feckin capital city and she missed it. I'm so ready to pull over, stretch my legs and have something to eat. I'm too tired to argue with her, so we stop in Gunning. Wish we'd been Gunning through it as there doesn't seem to be anything here worth stopping for. There's a roadside cafe up ahead called Merino Cafe - of course it is, considering Ange has been bleating on about sheep for the past few hours and how there are over 150 million of them here, not all here in Gunning you understand, in Oz. I'm hangry enough to eat a whole sheep including its hooves and need to stop and eat now. I am not in the slightest bit interested that it's a billion-dollar business, only how long it will take to make them into a burger and placed between two bits of bread. Seems like the perfect place to stop for a pee, a bite to eat and assess any directional damage. We can decide what the next plan of action should be as I sure as hell am not turning back to Canberra which is a fun place apparently, said no-one ever. It also temporarily saves her from getting broken fingers.

ANGE

Luckily, she's pulled in front of a cafe before noticing that I'd had the map upside down. No wonder I'd missed Canberra. I quickly fold the map and slip it into my pocket before she blames me for getting us lost. Coincidentally we are at Merino Cafe and it reminds me of Little Bo Peep who lost all her sheep. So, I'm not the only one. Little Bo Peep has lost her sheep and doesn't know where to find them, looks like they're being cooked at the Merino Cafe. If Jules finds out that the map was upside down, I'll be cooked also.

JULES

She thinks I don't notice that she's had the map upside down the entire time and has been taking us goodness knows where. I'm too tired and peckish to argue, so I just let it go. We're exactly where we're meant to be as Nursie often reminded us.

ANGE

The cafe is busy, so while I stand in line to order, Jules looks for a table.

"Get me a coffee, a cheeseburger and a packet of those mini, cheese-filled Ritz biscuits. I'll go ask that biker guy over there if we can join him."

"Pretty please and thank you go a long way. Manners maketh the man."

"Pretty pleeease..."

She rolls her eyes and flounces off. I can tell she's on a fine line between holding it together and losing her shit completely. I pity the poor, innocent party that voluntarily crosses that line. I'm going to make it my mission for it not to be me though. When I get to the cashier, there beside the till is a large jar filled with money AND a photo of Lezzers' of all people on it, her arm round some guy on it. WTF? I'm bemused and pick it up.

"What's this?"

"Oh, there was this Scottish nurse in here the other week, came in on the bus and left it here so that a customer could not only buy their coffee, but leave their change here to buy one for a complete stranger. She said it was a random act of kindness, so we took a photo of her and the general manager and started the jar in her honour. Great idea don't you think? Wish more people were as kind as her. Would you like to contribute to it? We give them away randomly during the day. "

"She should get some humanitarian award," I said sarcastically.

"I'm sure she will one day. People like her are natural givers and her kindness will be rewarded someway, somehow, someday. Want to donate?"

"Eh no, it looks like you already have enough in that jar to start a chain of coffee shops. You don't need my contribution."

She grudgingly hands me my change, holding on to the dollar notes a little longer than necessary. I yank them from her and stuff them in my pocket. There are no trays left by the time I order, so I put the cracker biscuits in my pocket and carry the coffees and burgers over to the table, where Jules is sitting with the Wullie Nelson-looking guy.

"I'm off for a pee."

Why do some people feel the need to announce where they're going? Who cares that she is off for a pee, certainly not Wullie beside me. I spread out the map on the table trying to assess the damage. It looks like we were WAAAY off Canberra, in fact, it looks like we're now miles and miles south of it. Oh well, to be honest I never really wanted to go there anyway. Doesn't sound like a barrel of fun, or a huge loss. I sigh, fold the map and wait for Jolly, not Jules to return.

JULES

The guy opposite me, beside Ange reminds me of one of The Potties from Michael Bentine's Potty time. The Potties are bearded puppets whose faces are obscured by facial hair, with only their noses protruding. He takes me by surprise when he blatantly reaches to the centre of the table, opens my packet of my mini cheese Ritz sandwich crackers and begins to eat them. I say nothing, but look from him to Ange, finally settling on his gaze with an icy stare. Although I have only had two bites of my burger, I am not in the mood for his games, so I grab a cracker, tap it on the table and put it in my mouth, whole, not once breaking eye contact with him. He nods slightly, smiles, picks out another one and eats it. What is he playing at? Do I look like someone to be messed with? I glare, dumbfounded by his audacity and snatch another one without even finishing the one I still have in my mouth. They're quite dry, but I can't stop myself, it's now a matter of principle. We lock eyes. He finishes the FIFTH cracker, picks up the packet and has the cheek to offer the last one to me. Completely appalled at his boldness. I rip the cracker from the packet.

"I should think so too!" It comes out as a smattering of crumbs and powdered cheese drops.

He stands up, pushes his chair back.

"G'day, ladies."

I'll g'day him, the cheek of it. He waves at us from the car park as he puts his shades on and mounts his Hardly Dangerous. Revs, then waves back at us again as he leaves the car park and turns towards Sydney. Thankfully not going in the same direction as us, unless Ange continues to feck up and we end up back in Bondage Beach. I hope he sees me flicking the v's at him through the grease-stained window. I'm muttering like Mutley when I notice Ange is howling with laughter.

"What? What's so funny? You saw him steal my crackers."

She slowly reaches into her pocket and takes out MY packet, taps them on the table and hands them over to me.

"Oh no! These are mine?"

"Yup."

"I ate his crackers?"

"Yup."

"How embarrassing. Why the hell did you not stop me? Why did he not say something? Why did you allow me to go through that entire rigmarole? What must he think of me?"

"Let it go Darlene, I wouldn't worry too much about it. What are the chances of ever seeing him again?"

"Yeah, you're right."

"Now, let's make like Usain and Bolt before he changes his mind, comes back and demands you buy him another packet."

There's an old man sitting on his own at the table beside us laughing out loud, amused by my faux pas no doubt. I'm sure I have turned 50 shades of red. At least I'm never going to see the hairy biker again. As we get up to leave, the old man comes over.

"Do you mind if I join you ladies?"

"We were just leaving actually."

"This won't take long."

It does seem rude to dash off immediately. Ange, who does not entertain any male species over the age of 30, is suddenly all over him like white on rice. But she sits back down. She is mouthing at me: "Kingdom ass of rudeness."

"What?"

My lip-reading skills are as bad as her map-reading skills. She sees by the puzzled look that I didn't get it. "Random act of kindness."

"Ah, got ya."

I think her brain has been rattled with all that incessant tapping on the window. This is so out of character for her to show some kindness. He sits beside her, takes my hand across the table.

"I watched the cracker exchange as it unfolded and was ready and able to step in to stop a fight if necessary."

"It must have been pretty funny as the onlooker you understand."

"That guy wouldn't have stood a chance against you missy if it's any consolation."

He winks at me. He doesn't look like he could stop a cold let alone anything else. I smile back politely, not wanting to appear ruder than he already thinks I am, and go along with it.

"My name is Mario Rossi and I was born in Sicily during the First World War."

Golly gosh, he's a whole lot older than he looks.

"I moved to Australia as a young boy though." I can still detect his Italian accent.

"You can take the boy out of Italy, but not Italy out of the boy."

"Exactly, Bella."

Ange has lost interest already and isn't even trying to pretend she's bored. So much for her very fleeting act of kindness.

"I'm trying to make the journey from Sydney to Melbourne as I need to hand deliver a package from my sick brother, Niko, in Naples, Italy, to an associate who owns a restaurant in Little Italy on Lygon Street. The packet is too delicate to post."

ANGE

Not sure where this is all going, but I'm bored of Giuseppe and ready to get back on the road so that I can have a kip. However, he mentions a delicate package which immediately piques my interest.

"That makes two of us, we already have a stash in our van that we are delivering to the hippy masses in Victoria."

JULES

I ignore her and allow Mario, and not Giuseppe, to explain that he is beginning to feel rather poorly and has decided to return to Sydney.

"Ignore her, carry on Mario."

Ange chuckles. I'm not sure where all this is going, but am beginning to feel slightly uncomfortable and not just because he's squeezing my hand tighter and tighter.

"As you're going that way, would you mind delivering the package safely for me. It would be so much appreciated."

"Safely into the hands of…. who exactly??"

"I'm assuming the person's name is Don … Something."

"Ha ha, no his name is Fabio Pugliesi. He owns a restaurant in Little Italy called L'Ultima Cena. You must make sure he gets it, no one else. He will take care of you."

"What exactly do you mean by take care of us? Can you be a tad more specific."

"Och ignore her, we will of course do it, just give it to me and we'll get it to him in lickety-spit time"

"Are you off your head Ange?"

"Where's your sense of adventure Jules?"

ANGE

He hands me the package which is the size of an A4 envelope and gives me a wad of rolled-up cash.

"For your trouble."

Doesn't seem like too big a deal to me.

"Now, make sure you give it personally to Fabio Pugliesi and no-one else and I promise you, he will take care of you. Ciao bellas."

He gets up, heads out the door, leaving us with the package.

"You've really surpassed yourself this time Ange. You have absolutely no idea what's in there."

"Lighten up, how bad can a wee envelope be?"

We see him leaving the car park in his Fiat, and after he waves at us, he puts his thumb to his eye. Does that mean something significant?

JULES

No trouble, not a big deal. TAKE CARE OF US. I'm quite sure he will. We are very likely smugglers and dealers. I might as well turn myself in to the authorities now as they're bound to catch up with us anyway and throw the book at us, lock, stock and smoking barrel. We will never see the light of day again. We're bound to be breaking all kinds of laws here. I'm certainly requesting a single cell, no way I want to be confined in a cell with her for life. The car is bad enough. Her recklessness is going to get us both in trouble and it's beginning to get on my nerves.

"Has it crossed your mind that we may likely be carrying some information from the mafia to the mafia and we might even be mistaken for stool pigeons. We'll wake in the morning in the back of Gertie with a kangaroo head between us."

"It's a horse's head they use, but where's the fun if we never take risks?"

ANGE

Blah, blah, blah, she really needs to lighten up. I'm sure that sweet old Mario isn't involved in anything bigger than a bingo group at his local YMCA. She's so negative, even worse than Lezzers' at times.

JULES

I'm not at all comfortable with this, but what can I do now? Mario has gone and we're still here with the package. I'm too scared to even suggest we open it. We get back on the road to Melbourne and hopefully we'll be there by late evening, drop the package off and get to the backpackers before we get caught red-handed. Ange tells me she'd seen a jar with a photo of Lezzers' encouraging people to leave their change so fellow travellers can be given a random coffee from it, that's why she decided to help Mario out. There's a huge difference between buying a coffee for a stranger and taking a package from a stranger and delivering it to a stranger for money. $500, to be precise. I mean that's a lot of money, bribe money I reckon. Whatever is in this envelope must be pretty bloody important. Perhaps we should open it or take it straight to the police, there might even be a reward. Too late now, I guess, we have the parcel, Ange's asleep within 5 minutes of starting out and I have some peace and quiet for a few hours. I feel pretty chuffed though that Lesley showed a random act of kindness. No doubt with a lovely, unconditional bright smile. I'm sure it will make a difference in someone's day. If we don't deliver this package safely then there's going to be a difference in our day for sure and we'll be dead by dawn. We make it to Melbourne around 7pm, and not only am I exhausted from all that driving, but I am famished again. The two bites of burger and cheese crackers are not enough to satisfy a growing lass.

"How about some delicious pasta? From an authentic Italian, Jules? I happen to know a place that is going to accommodate us. Just what the doctor ordered. I wonder what L'Ultima Cena means in Italian?"

Fabio may very well be a doctor, but not of the medical variety, more like the pharmaceutical variety. I'm too tired to argue, fight her or find our way to the local police station to deliver the contraband, so I drive to Little Italy, in the inner suburbs of Melbourne. We park the car in a nearby multi-storey and I go to the kiosk to validate my parking. The tiny old lady behind the glass-fronted kiosk can barely see over the counter. Her bottle glasses make her look like Sybil Trelawney from Harry Potter.

"Can you validate my parking please?"
"Sure thing. You did a great job, evenly spaced, at nearly a perfect angle."

That makes me laugh out loud, blowing the dark, depressing, heavy cloud that's been hanging over my head since we left Gunning.

"Ah, a part-time comedienne, are we?"

"Well dear, they do say that with age comes wisdom, therefore I don't have any wrinkles, I only have wise cracks."

"Those cracks you mention are few and far between anyway."
"Touche. Parking is on the house."

"Much appreciated. Can you tell us how to get to L'Ultima restaurant?"
"Ah, not only beautiful, but a lady of taste also. It's not far, go out of here, take a right, walk a couple of blocks and it's there on your left. Make sure to say hi to Fabio from me."
"I will, thank you Sybil."

The restaurant is packed, but Ange takes the lead and bulls her way past the queue and goes in anyway.

"Excuse me, pardon me. We're here to see the owner of this fine establishment."

"Aym zorry, but e iz not here."

"Look Sergio, we're not here to complain, so you can stop manhandling us, well her anyway, you can carry on with me if you like. Tell Fabio Pugliesi, neither you or his subordinates will do, that we've been sent here by Mario Rossi and we come bearing gifts."

"Fy did zu not say that in se first place. This way."

We're shown to a large round table against the back wall that commands a view of the entire restaurant and is close enough to the kitchens if a hurried getaway is required. Either for us or for them. There are a few men in suits sitting at the table with napkins tucked into their collars, eating from bowls filled with aromatic spaghetti. The capo cameriere whispers in the Big Yin's ear.

I know I studied psychology at university, but I was also part of the Italian club as it had weekly pasta and wine-tasting nights, so I had picked up a few phrases, which may very well come in handy later. The Godfather-looking bloke, whom I assume is Fabio, snaps his fingers once and his fellow diners get up from the table and stand behind him. He snaps his fingers again, this time towards us, beckoning us closer. Now, ordinarily I'd have an issue with his command, but I can tell that there's no messing with these guys. I only hope Ange gets the same memo.

He removes his napkin, wipes his large handlebar moustache and gestures to the seats at either side of him. His henchmen look menacing and unforgiving, not people to be crossed or toyed with. They stand erect behind their Godfather, hands clasped behind their backs, no doubt within inches of their revolvers which are without a shadow of a doubt tucked into their waistbands. He looks at us and pats the two seats at either side of him. Two other henchmen join the crew and stand behind us, hands crossed in front of them. What have we got ourselves into this time? This is a bit more serious than even I had anticipated. They look like they're ready to draw if they need to. I for one am going to give them any reason to.

ANGE

"Listen up Marlon, Mario Rossi from Sicily has given us a package from his brother Marco and we have it here and have been specifically told to hand deliver it to you and only you."

One of his baboons genuflects as Fabio stares at us in disbelief.

"Non e possibile, e morto."

"Si senor."

I liberally give him the full extent of my Italian. He takes the package from me, opens it, reads the letter a few times as we sit there, tummies rumbling rather loudly as the smell of freshly baked pasta wafts in our direction. I wait patiently, not knowing whether we're going to be taken somewhere to be served as fish food or have our cheeks grabbed, pinched then kissed. After reading it a few times, seemingly satisfied as he's nodding gently, he shows it to the guy behind him, who reads it, then passes it around.

JULES

He gets up from the table, takes it in turn to squeeze our cheeks and kisses us first on the left cheek, then the right. Once was more than enough for me. I'm slightly confused as to which cheek to present first and end up practically winching the old walrus smack on the lips, not once, but twice. Easy tiger. At least we're not going to be fish food. He signals to the waiter, says something in Italian that I don't quite catch, then sits back down at the big round table. One of the rather dishy waiters hands us a menu which is all in Italian. I turn to him.

"My Italian is a tad rusty, can you explain the menu please?"

He straightens up, lifting himself slightly out of his carriage, tilts his head and squints his eyes at me. "I do nit want ti appear rrude heya, but, personally, I do not zink that iz any of your buziness!"

I must look slightly perplexed but Ange and Fabio are laughing so hard they both almost pull a chakra.

"Good one Lorenzo," Fabio says.

He takes the menus from us, pulling mine slightly more forcefully from me than is necessary. Within 30 seconds, plates of all kinds of Sicilian food start to arrive at our table.

The waiters announce what they are as they place them on the table before us.

"Arancini."

"Caponata."

"Pasta alla Norma."

"Sarde a beccafico."

The plates keep coming and coming along with several bottles of wine and beer. The waiters, who are all of the very cute Italian variety, keep asking us if we need anything else. Fabio makes sure we are being well looked after before he leaves us to make an "important" call.

"Please join me for a berretto da notte later."

"I'm not sure what that is exactly, but bien sur Fabio, it would be rude not to."

"I have to chip in here and add that I only drink to make people seem more interesting. He kisses the back of our hands."

"Dopo."

ANGE

Has he stripped Gertie down to within an inch of her metal frame and found all our dope? I do hope not. That might push me over the edge. To finish off our dinner, they bring out two glasses of flaming sambuca with a couple of coffee beans floating on the top. Jules blows hers way too hard and the small blue flame is projected from the top of the glass and lands on my chest. I jump up and begin to pat it furiously out while she looks on with her mouth agape and in disbelief. However, not shocked enough to stop her downing her drink in one and eating the coffee beans on the top. Even though I'm the one on fire, I do think it's odd that she's eating them. At the same time, one of the cute waiters grabs a fire extinguisher from the kitchen and begins to spray me down with the thick white foam. I am covered from head to toe and look like some fluffy white blancmange. Fabio comes back through from a back office when he hears the commotion and is incredibly apologetic.

"There are some private suites upstairs, please go shower and we will have a new set of clothes sent to your room. Please be my guest for the evening and stay the night."

Jules spits the pureed beans onto her side plate.

"Sorry, I thought they were chocolate-covered raisins."

I'm escorted upstairs by the very apologetic waiter who shows me the rather splendid bedroom with en suite. It seems like an opportunity not to miss, so I invite him in. Literally and physically.

JULES

I'm not so sure about sleeping here, but I'm not in any fit state to drive as I've drunk my entire body weight in Chianti. Ange has disappeared upstairs with a waiter who looks like he's straight out of the Fine Young Cannibals. Well, one thing for sure, she drives me crazy, like no one else, and I can't help myself. I can actually. I help myself to another limoncello. I can barely keep my eyes open much longer and accept Fabios kind offer of a bed for the night. Unlike Ange, I prefer to be on my own. I'm too tired to think that it might be some trafficking ring we're involved in. I'm also pretty sure that even if it is, they'd hand us back before you could say "Ritornare al mittente".

ANGE

By the time Fernando and I come back downstairs, the restaurant is empty and closed for the night. Not even the kitchen staff are around. Jules has obviously retired for the night, so no harm done. I'm sure no one noticed or cared about our absence. I go back upstairs solo and find her snoring gently in the room adjacent to the one I had just vacated. I climb back into the very rumpled bed, but keep waking up as I have this constant throbbing in my right middle finger. For some reason not known to man or beast, I had decided I wanted to try on Lorenzo's Bvlgari ring and it has obviously stuck. He must have very small fingers. There is no way it's budging and I am not going to get any sleep with its persistent pulsating. Compounded by the fact I promised I'd give it back to him in the morning and would leave it for him at the reception. I keep tossing and turning and my middle finger keeps throbbing, it's now swollen to the size of a purple aubergine and beating harder and harder, the tight band still secured at the base of my palpitating digit. I suck my finger. Nada. I soap it. Nada. I even use some of the olive oil still on the tables downstairs. Still Nada. I have no choice but to go look for a jeweller who can cut it off, the ring that is, but if I wait much longer, my finger, which is now swollen to the size of a zeppelin and fit to burst at any moment and fall off.

I try to wake Jules, but she rolls over saying:

"I am awake, but please respect my privacy during this difficult time".

I leave her lying there with her eyes wide open, her swollen dry tongue hanging out the side of her mouth and saliva bubbles congregating on the other corner. I scribble a quick note using my left hand and go out seeking a jeweller. I pass through the kitchen first to see if I can prise it off with a skewer or another kitchen utensil, but the only thing I find is tongs and as I grasp the ring, I can feel some of my tendons and ligaments begin to stretch and tear. The chef has left a meat cleaver on the counter, and for a nanosecond I do contemplate it, however the thought of never being able to use my middle finger again as the universal gesture is heartbreaking and unfathomable. There are no jewellers that are actually open, which is strange, and that's when I realize it is only 530am - ah, so that's why I couldn't wake Jules either. There's an emergency department up ahead and it's thankfully open. This is considered an emergency, especially when his wife finds out that he's not wearing his wedding band. Try explaining that one Valentino. I enter through the revolving doors, presenting my swollen digit aloft to the receptionist. It must be a familiar and regular sight as she doesn't even bat a sparkly blue eyelid, let alone crack a smile. I wave my gargantuan, swollen, throbbing, purple middle finger, which resembles an engorged erect penis. Worthy of the top prize at the local horticultural show. Either way, she is not impressed and dismisses me, gesticulating to a bench in the waiting area. I sit there with all the drunks and weirdos of the night. I stick out like a sore thumb or middle finger in my case. When my name is called, I realise I have fallen asleep on some tramp's lap. I awake startled.

"Oh, that's me. Sorry I must have fallen asleep on this tramp's lap."

"Funny that quine[29,] and here's me thinking the same thing - that some tramp had fallen asleep on my lap."

"Ha, touche. Foo's yer doos?[30] Or is that a ridiculous question, given that you're in the emergency department at 530am."

"Och, nithing mair than bein drookit as I spent half the nicht oot on a park bench in the rain as ma missus chucked me oot the hoose after I'd been oot birling maist of the day and came hame stocious. It got ower caul oot yon, so aye came here to sleep it aff."[31]

No matter where you go in this world, there is always a Scot, and usually a drunk one at that to be found.

"Ach, dinna fash yersel, she'll tak ye back in wi open arms the day. A wee bunch o flooers widnae gang amiss though."[32]

The nurse claps her hands to get my attention.

"Sbrigati."

I turn to the old Scottish drunk.

"Och haud yer weesht ye crabbit auld bag."[33]

"Ha ha, yer feil lass, noo, git oan wi it bonnie quine."[34]

"S'later."

I follow Grumpy through to a cubicle in the middle of a cubicle-lined corridor. Most of them have curtains giving the occupants some form of privacy, but I am obviously a thorn in her side and she leaves mine open, exposing my penis digit to anyone and everyone that passes. She is able to cut it off without too much difficulty and hands me back the twisted platinum ring in an envelope.

"La goccia che ha fatto traboccare il vaso."

"Have I been mysteriously transported to Rome, or does everyone speak either Doric or Italian in Little Italy, AUSTRALIA?"

I hope it's a good wish, but I suspect by the stern disapproving, judgemental look on her face that she knows the ring is an Italian wedding band. I race back, leave the envelope with the mangled ring at the front desk and race upstairs to collect Jules. I have to hurry her along as I don't actually know which waiter the ring belongs to as they all have the same swarthy dark complexion, slick, greased-back hair and a moustache, and that's just the women. I don't want to be caught in a compromising situation when the morning shift clocks in. I'm ready to make like a bee and buzz off before all the staff come back for their breakfast duties.

I find a sleepy Jules still in bed and I have to half drag, half carry her back to Gertie in one piece and not the thousand pieces that she had originally thought. I open the back doors, chuck her in where she promptly falls asleep again and I drive off towards the United Backpackers. I'm very cautious of the pillars as I leave the car park. Shame she isn't awake to witness the dexterity with which I take the corners and bends.

JULES

Well, that shows me, I am totally cynical and had expected to wake up with Ange's finger lying on a lace hanky beside me and Kanga's head. I see the note on the pillow, which I initially assume is a ransom demand laying out the financial details for her safe return. Tensions have been building between us after spending so much time in the confined van space and I'm contemplating how much I'd pay for her safe return. I would pay a maximum of $100, make that $50, okay, realistically $10 to get her back. I unfold the note and see the scribble from the kidnappers saying they are taking her to the jewellers. I think that's what it says, but I am still so tired and my eyes are stuck together with sleepys so I'm not able to read it properly, besides it looks like it's been written by a child who may have been using the pen wedged between their toes to write it. I'm able to read that she's going to be returning soon, which is good news as I haven't quite finished sleeping and am ready to go back to dreaming about romping in the surf with Leo DiCaprio, laughing with gay abandon, clad in very little attire. Sexy man. It does cross my mind to call the cops and report her missing, but she pales into insignificance as Leo's form takes over. I'm all of a sudden shaken awake and she appears beside me with her middle finger aloft, all strapped up like a bandaged helium balloon. She's somewhat frantic and in a rush for sure, but I am truly unable to keep my eyes open. She heaves me up and out of the bed, grabs our belongings and drags me back to Gertie, who is thankfully, like us, still in one piece. I'm aware of being thrown in the back and must have fallen asleep again, either that or I am rendered unconscious somehow, as I sleep the whole way to our next destination. Thank goodness, I am comatose though, not sure I'm ready for another experience with her behind the wheel.

We had originally booked into a Backpacker's, before Mafia-gate, as it is one of the only ones in the city that actually has a bar in its premises, The Quiet Woman, a great name for a pub incidentally. Oh, the irony of having us there. It's a unique hidden bar, right in the heart of Melbourne, adjacent to Flinders Street station and has a secret side entrance via the historic Campbell

Parade. What is it with that? Bondage Beach also has a Campbell Parade.

I only recently found out that "Bondi" or "Boondi" is an Aboriginal word meaning water breaking over rocks. I much prefer that to our version of Bondage which is more like water breaking over cocks. The hostel claims that throwing parties is their business. They clearly haven't met us yet.

We sign in, leave our stuff in the room and go mingle with fellow travellers having their breakfast in the kitchen.

ANGE

When we arrive, it seems like a lively enough place, even at 9am. Right up my street. It's only been open a matter of weeks, so everything is brand spanking new, even down to the fresh-faced, innocent, naive-looking warden. Like a lamb to the slaughter, I say. Quel dommage. I can already sense a twinkle in my eyes and a mischievous stirring in my gut when he tells us: "I've not been here that long and it's my first ever job as a warden, so I'd really, really appreciate any thoughts, suggestions and/or opinions you have that will help the running of the place."

"How fortuitous for you as I have plenty of experience and am more than happy to share with you a few ideas that I already have and can run by you later."

"That would be wonderful. Your expertise, time and knowledge Ange is so very much appreciated."
"You're welcome, happy to be of service."

Dear, sweet innocent, unsuspecting Russell has no idea what he is letting himself in for.

"I've had so much experience with bars and hostels and can impart my knowledge of ice breakers I have gleaned from other places. They are actually very trendy at the moment, in fact they're the new black. In my opinion, it's great you're getting ahead of the pack. The most popular nights are taking place on Friday and Saturday evenings."

"I'm not aware of this, so thank you for bringing it to my attention."

He hasn't the foggiest idea I have made it all up, and is none the wiser, but he doesn't really need to know that miniscule attention to detail, now does he?

"Tell me more. How can we get onboard with all the other hostels?"

"The first thing to know is that the hostel supplies wine and horses d'oeuvres, allowing the inmates or fellow hostilers to get the chance to mingle, get to know each other, partake in a few games and drink copious amounts of free beverage."

"It does sound like a spiffing idea."

"Absolutely spliffing. Coincidentally, it's Friday today."

Oh, quel surprise. "It is indeed. Righty ho, I'll get the wine and snacks and you pair think of some jolly games for tonight's soiree."

It doesn't even cross his mind that every night in a hostel is a night for drinking, games and debauchery. However, it's not usually funded by the manager of the hostel. The "hostilers", as we called them, will love it. True to his word, he comes up trumps later in the afternoon and begins to set up the upstairs common room with some soft drinks, Tim Tams and three casks of wine.

"This may not be enough to draw in the crowds as we, I mean you, really want it to go on longer than 15 minutes Russell."

"Oh, you think? What will we do? I have to stay here now."

"I tell you what, out of the goodness of my heart, I'll add my contribution to the event. Jules and I can go to one of those drive- thru liquor stores we passed on the way here, one of those Brew-thrus, party barns, bootleggers, bottle shops."

"Wow, that is incredibly kind of you, thank you."

These places make it stupid easy to pick up drinks without getting out of your car. Kinda like a click and collect with your fingers. We are able to get plenty of goons packed in the back, besides what isn't used is ours anyway. We arrive back in time for the meet and greet and to really get things going. I add some extra special dried herbs to the hummus. To liven up the festivities, you understand. A bash without hash is just a lash. Seems like a perfect combination to me. There are a handful of Japanese girls giggling in the corner with their Tim Tams and cokes, but when they see us arrive back, laden down with casks, they take off to fill in their daily journals. Steadily more and more people arrive as word gets out there is a free wine double happy hour upstairs. Russell claps his hands in excitement.

"What a super turn out this evening and for those of you who haven't met me yet, I'm Russell, your hostel manager. Please take the time to introduce yourself to some new people. Mingle and help yourself to some food and drink."

It all seems to be taking far too long as I have already spotted some rather cute Irish boys mingling with some leggy, blonde attractive Swedish-looking bints. Not good enough.

"I think everyone is ready for some icebreakers Russell."

"You know what Ange, you might be right. Have you got any game suggestions?"

"Oh boy, do I? Let's start with the cask circuits. It's a drinking game that involves having a wine cask at each station. See it as yet another one of my personal contributions to the hostel."

"How kind Ange."

"You're very welcome Russell."

"Would you care to explain to the group the rules of the game?"

"I'd be happy to Russell. There are six stations in total, so we need to divide ourselves into teams. There's probably about 20 here, so teams of four work. I'll begin by taking Jules and the two Irish boys over there, chatting to the blonde girls. The rest of you find your own teams of four. Each station has a drinking game to be completed. Russell will mind the time and ask everyone to move on after 10 minutes. The six fun drinking games are: Kings Cup, Never Have I Ever, Drunk Jenga, Thumper, Straight Face, Flip Cup. Any questions? No? Good. Then let's get started."

At 11pm, Russell appears back upstairs.

"It's way past the initial planned happy hour, so before things get totally out of hand and completely out of control, let's draw it to a close. Besides it's now quiet time as there are hostellers downstairs who want to go to their beds and this rumpus is preventing them from doing so."

Have I suddenly been transported back to kindergarten? All the goons are almost finished anyway.

"Can we play one more game, Russy? I promise to make sure everyone will retire to their quarters after? Besides, our room is the closest to the rumpus and is right here off the common room, so we would be the ones most affected by the noise."

"Okay Ange, I'm going to head downstairs now, but I trust you to make sure this stops after one more round."

"Scout's honor."

JULES

Not sure how she does it, but she manages to convince Russell that, A) he should foot the bill for some of wine night and B) That she was a scout. He actually buys into her devious plan and buys some wine, cheese, nibbles and Tim Tams. Clearly that is nowhere near enough for her as she persuades me to drive to one of those booze barns to add to the already adequate selection. Everything starts out completely civilized and then it just kinda evolves into buoyant fun and nonsense. It starts off with a cask circuit. After Russell retires for the night, it naturally leads to our favourite pastime of tangles. Bodies are piling up everywhere, some due to the game, some due to over-imbibing during the circuits and some seeing it as an opportunity to winch a fellow hostiler. I think I'm a bit of both, but Ange is definitely part of the latter group, having identified her victim of choice from the outset. She has honed her pouncing skills to perfection and goes in for the kill.
No one will come out of her attention alive.

"Will you walk into my parlour? " said the spider to the fly. Poor lad won't even see you coming until it's too late."

"Oh, he'll see me coming alright."

At one stage I think we're all going to come through the kitchen ceiling just like the pussies in The Aristocats playing

Everybody Wants to be a Cat. The night has been one boozy success in my opinion. The lovely Russell tells us it is getting way too loud and lairy and that we all need to pipe down a bit, retire or go out. He is persuaded by the hardcore dozen or so of us left that we'll take it down a notch, but as soon as his back is turned and he heads downstairs, Ange says as we only have one more game allowed, we might as well make it a good one.

"Let's forget tangles and play pile-ups instead? It's much less complicated. I'll begin by pointing to a person or a place at the same time as shouting GO! All you guys have to do is race as fast as you can to the designated spot or person and pile on.

"I LOVE rugby and this sounds right up my street, like a glorious scrum."

"Exactly, the last person there has to drink the dregs of any drink nearby. Ready, steady, GO."

She points directly at Declan and we run and pounce on him, but as Ange has a head start she is on top of him in lickety-split time. There are boozy bodies piling high, the last remnants of beer and wine spill, legs and arms are twisted and buried. I have someone's finger in my mouth, well, at least I hope it's a finger. It's a big finger and I hope that it's Ange's penis-shaped digit, but I can't quite see as I have someone's voluminous breasts cupping my eyes, I hope it's breasts though and not some bot's full testicles, those for sure do not belong to her. No sooner have we started it, maybe four pile-ups total, than we hear from downstairs.

"That's it. Enough. People are trying to sleep down here. Time for y'all to retire."

Good timing in my opinion as it is getting slightly out of hand and is becoming more of a cross between a game of Aussie rules and an orgy. He has to speak to us like a bunch of naughty schoolchildren to get our attention. He reprimands us like a school counsellor in a forced authoritative voice that is actually quite surprising, and somewhat attractive I might add. We all know, though, that he wouldn't say boo to a goose. "All of you, bed NOW!"

Funnily enough, Ange and her victim, Declan, are nowhere to be seen and have managed to disappear from the last pile-up melee, the dressing down and clean-up duty.

ANGE

Hurrah, my cunning plan goes exceedingly well, Mr Kipling - beyond even my wildest expectations - and this week's hot totty is well and truly trapped, tangled and ensnared in my web of pure unadulterated rumpy pumpy. Who needs a dating service like munch.com, or minge.com, or whatever it's called when you can just host a mass voluntary pile-up. Declan and I end up in the pantry downstairs, not sure how we got here, but here we are. My back must have been resting on a rather large bag of flour as with every thrust a massive puff of the stuff engulfs us both. It's somewhat fortuitous though as his face is sweaty and kinda red looking, even under all the white powder, and I'm glad to see it fade and disappear behind each puff. We both must have passed out on the floor as I suddenly come to and we're lying on a fine film of flour all around us. We look really funny, tought, and it gives me an idea. I grab the bag of flour and head back to the kitchen.

JULES

I wake with Heath Ledger's Joker looming over me in the dark, but then realize it's only Ange, covered in feck knows what.

She's lugging a large half-empty sack of flour of all things behind her. Her face is snow-white, with smears and streaks of red goop all over it. I recognize the shade of red immediately, it looks very like the lipstick she wears. In fact it IS the lipstick she wears, just snog-smeared all over her face. She looks incredibly freaky, with dough ball clumps of goodness knows what else, and lipstick on her cheeks, chin and even her forehead. She is excited about something and feels the need to wake me up to tell me what has happened and is, in her words, "really, really funny".

Before she actually tells me, though, some boy comes in behind her, so to speak, equally powdered and face smeared. They both collapse in a playdough blob on her bed and promptly fall asleep.

ANGE

We wake the next day to a very loud scream from Russell. "ANGE? JULES?"

Russell, disguised as Santa Claus, appears at our door, his ginger beard speckled with white powder, his hair and clothes finely dusted. Ah, yes, I remember. I remember doing something funny, was eager to tell Jules, but had fallen asleep so had forgotten what it was, until now that is. I'm thinking that perhaps his over-the-top overreaction has something to do with it. His voice is very firm, unexpectedly I might add, quite masterful in fact. In its own way, it's surprising, yet attractive and commanding: "BOTH OF YOU. DOWNSTAIRS TO THE KITCHEN ......NOW!"

We shuffle down to the kitchen and through the double doors where we are met with a snow blizzard that appears to be slowly, gently, drifting down from the ceiling and settling on the counter tops, the floor and a few early risers who are sitting at the table, not moving, frozen, it looks, to their seats. Possible shock. The couple of early birds are still mid-breakfast, their powdered eggs in front of them. Ooops, it all comes back to me in perfect colour motion. Russell must have come through earlier and switched on the ceiling fan. Ah, yes, it's as clear as day - or should I say in a flash of powdered dust - what I had done last night. A windmill of flour sprinkled on top of the ceiling fan blades had seemed like an amusing prank at the time. There is a tall floury boy standing in the centre of the room with his hands on his hips. Good ol' Russell.

"Explain all this please and you'd better make it good."

"Well, after we'd tidied upstairs, I came down to the kitchen as I was feeling peckish after only eating hummus. I went to the larder to find something to nibble on and found a tin of shortbread beside a bag of flour and, well, one thing led to another and I thought it would be funny to sprinkle mounds of flour on the ceiling blades. Honestly, your hostile honor, I hadn't quite expected this full flour tornado!"

The white hostile blobs just sat there in the whiff of flour, their cereal still coated in a fine film of smeddum. I'm sure that's a dish that's a delicacy somewhere in Southeast Asia anyway, so no harm done there.

"It's winter back home, Rudolph, and I was feeling rather homesick so I wanted to make the place more like home. If you squint your eyes, it almost looks like a beautiful winter wonderland. Wouldn't you agree?"

"No Ange, not in the slightest"

Mr. G. Rumpy has definitely got out of the wrong side of the bed this morning. I bat my eyelashes and try to eye-fuck him, but to no avail. He must bat for the other team I guess.

"I'll pay someone to clean it up before everyone else gets up. There are plenty of hostilers looking to earn some extra cash."

"Absolutely no way, if you want another theme party tonight, then you pair have to clean every inch of this kitchen. Every dust particle has to be removed and this place needs to be spik and span, so clean that I can eat off the floor."

"No need for that Russell, I'll give you a plate."

"Stop being a sook Jules."

"I'm serious, there really will be no theme party tonight if this place isn't immaculate. There are consequences for every action and cleaning this kitchen from top to bottom is yours. Capire."

I widen my eyes to the size of saucers and pretend to look slightly spooked, very much in keeping with the kitchen backdrop. He is far more forgiving and lenient than I think I would have been if someone had done it to my kitchen. He flounces off out of the kitchen.

"Does everyone speak Italian in Australia? But more importantly, and correct me if I'm wrong, but did he just say there will be a theme party tonight if this place is sorted?"

JULES

WE? Eh, no…. YOU. I keep quiet as Russell is raging and insists on both of us cleaning up the mess or there would be no wine theme night for us tonight. In fact, it would be" Silent Night" for us since we miss winter back home so much. There's even a

"Ho ho ho" that slips from his lips as he departs the kitchen followed by the early riser ghouls. Did he really just say that? Hmmm, so he isn't totally banning us from another wine night party - IF we clean up that is. Ange can be such a fanny at times and even manages to look a little shocked, mixed with fake remorse. Neither of which she is. I have seen her acting skills on way too many occasions now to know her genuine insincerity. A wine night is incentive enough for me to don my marigolds and help her out here, even though I was firmly in the land of nod during the alleged crime. I'm sure she would have done the same for me. Or would she? He comes back to the kitchen.

"And another thing, not only do you need to replace the flour, but you also need to BAKE and replace the shortbread that has been eaten. There was a Scottish girl here recently who made an entire batch of shortbread for the homesick hostellers."

ANGE

Oh, for FUCK sake, surely NOT!! Nigella fucking Lezzer Lawson has been and done it again.

"Do you happen to remember her name perchance?"

"Sure do, who could forget a random act of kindness that absolutely changed some difficult times for some homesick travellers? Her name is Lesley, a nurse from Ardrossan."

Of course, he remembers her fucking name. I stare at him, mouth open, in total disbelief.

"She also spent her time helping me clean and get this place ready for our grand opening. She's an angel in disguise."

More like a fucking angel in my disgust. A real thorn in my side. My guardian angel has a drink and drug problem, is a sex addict and hers happens to be holier than thou. Go figure. How did I get landed with that particular short straw? I think I'm going to throw up, but he's not quite finished.

"She literally rolled up her sleeves and helped me clean this place from top to bottom, without wanting or expecting anything in return. Did it from the goodness of her very big heart."

"Of course, she did. I'd have been surprised if she hadn't, that's her to a tee, a natural giver. An exemplary example of conduct and virtue."

"Ah, you know her then?"

"Know her? Know her? Every tall good-looking chick needs a short, dumpy best friend and Jules doesn't fit the bill yet."

"I resemble that remark Ange."

There is only one person I know in the whole wide world that would even contemplate cleaning a hostel, not expecting anything in return, have it spik and span, bake a shitload of shortbread AND still offer to pay her keep. Of course, he remembers her bloody name.

"I'm off for a shower girls. I'll be back in a few hours, see how you're coming along."

"Better make it quick, wouldn't want you turning into a doughboy, unlike our wee Nursie pal, now would we?"

He leaves us to our cleaning.

"That's so unnecessary Ange."

"Can't help myself, of course he couldn't forget such a gracious gift to humanity? Had to be none other than our very own dearly beloved Lezzers', nurse to the ill, coffee giver to the weary driver, cleaner of hostels and master baker to the homesick. Little friend to all the fucking world."

JULES

Are you kidding me? Lesley has been here, cleaned this place till it was spotless, not only had it ready for opening, but baked shortbread of all things for everyone else. Only she could and would do that. Good on her.

"What is wrong with you Ange? You seem particularly irritated by her good intentions and deeds."

"Eh, no shit Sherlock. Is it only me that finds her sympathetic pity and concern towards the sufferings and misfortunes of others extremely infuriating?"

"Mm, yes, actually it is Ange. I believe it's called compassion. She has, and has always, gone out of her way to help and guide the physical, mental or emotional pains of another before herself. A trait that perhaps we both need to recognize and learn from."

"This is all psychobabble shite and quite frankly gets on my tits."

"This is an opportunity for us BOTH to reflect on our behaviours and see its effect on others."

"Oh, don't you start."

"I'm going to bake the shortbread, as I think you're the better scrubber between us."

"Now, I resemble that remark."

She never ever thinks through the consequences of her actions. Almost everything she does has to be for her amusement and her own gain. She doesn't realise, or in fact care, that there is a ripple effect to her behaviour and not in a good positive way either. It's all about her needs being met. All I can do is sigh and get on with the baking, thankfully in a completely different part of the kitchen. Boy, is it going to be a long day. I find myself saying for the umpteenth time.

"What Would Lesley Do?"

She wouldn't be happy, that's for sure. There would be plenty of tutting and headshaking, but she would just get on with it until the task was done. Then she'd put it all behind her and get on with life. Which is precisely what I am going to do. Before I go through to bake, I hoover the entire room first, emptying four FULL bags. I start dusting, wiping and polishing. Do you know how long it takes to get mounds of flour off of surfaces, tables, nooks and crannies? No? Then let me tell you, fuckin hours. Why hadn't she put wrapped Quality Street chocolates on each blade instead? A shower of chocolate, nuts and strawberry fondant, even the coffee cream ones would be better than this. I wouldn't mind tidying that up. Wouldn't have helped my waistline though. I still can't get my head around what she'd been thinking when she poured the entire bag of flour on top of each blade. Beyond me, let me tell you. Precisely 5 hours, 14 minutes and 12 seconds later, it finally looks like the kitchen we'd first seen on our arrival. We didn't do it entirely on our own either, some of the other hostellers from last night come in and help out, which is really kind. Someone pops their head round the door, laughs and retreats pretty pronto, followed by the dustpan and brush I lob at them. The two Irish boys are great, really helpful, I mistake all their hard work for goodwill, but it's actually pure unadulterated guilt that encourages at least one of them to help us. Declan happened to be the one in the bed with her when Russell shouted us down this morning. Very likely he was her partner-in-crime for flour-gate. I should know better as she only behaves in this atrocious fashion when she's out to impress, and I use that term loosely, some nubile young boy.

Ange disappears for a couple of hours, only to be found sound asleep in her bed. Selfish cow. I scream in her ear and shake her violently, perhaps more than is necessary, but it does feel good. Not only does it get her attention, it is immensely satisfactory. She claims to have a headache. A headache? I'll give her a feckin headache. In a way, I'm better off leaving her there because all she does is scuff around, moaning loudly, sighing heavily, professing how boring it all is. She should have thought about that before she did what she did.

"Just because you're in pain Ange, doesn't mean you have to be one. Didn't you say that to someone recently? What goes around, comes around."

I mean that from the bottom of my heart, or the heart of my bottom, as Lesley would say. She takes complete umbridge, or the opportunity to feign indignation, and sulks off to the showers with her tight, puckered duck lips. At 5pm, it's all done satisfactorily. Russell is impressed that we've actually done it, well some of us had anyway. Does he really think we are that shallow not to have done it? Again, one of us isn't. If it had been left to Ange, then it wouldn't have been done at all.

"Do you happen to know where Lezzers' went after she left the Golden Palace of Gleaming Hosiles?"

"Lezzers'?"

"That's our pet name for her. You call her by her Sunday name, Lesley."

"I call her Lesley, Ange."

"Actually Jules, you refer to her as Nursie."

"From now on, I'm going to use her given name. The one she prefers to be called, Lesley."

"Whatever."

"I do remember where she went. She left here to go to Hobart in Tasmania."

"Tasmania eh? The land of the devil."

"You'll fit in there fine then Ange."

"Thanks for those words of encouragement Jules."

"You need no encouragement Ange. You can do it all by your wretched self!"

"You leaving me? Happy if you want to go find her yourself."

"As tempting as that sounds Ange, we're in this together. At least till we find her."

"No skin off my nose either way. Tomorrow, we can make like the devil and get the hell out of here, but first there's a party to be had."

ANGE

Silly cow. She must be on her period. I'm the one here with PMS. Positive Menstrual Suffering. She needs to come off her high horse and stop criticising me with her self-righteous, smug, superior reaction to all this. I know exactly how to help her dismount. I add some extra sprinkling of special magic to her shortbread I have removed from the hubcap of Gertie. That should liven up The Happy, Hippy Homesick Hostilers considerably. Shame she won't see the benefits of her baked goods as we'll be well and truly on our way to Hobart.

JULES

Ange can definitely be charming when she wants to be, or is it mass manipulator? She plays with her auburn curls and bats her hazel eyes when she wants something. Seems to always work though, many, many unsuspecting victims fall for her allure. While I have been cleaning and baking, Ange has not only researched ferries, hostels and routes, she has booked us and Gertie on the ferry for 7am the next day. We're headed to the Nook hostel in Launceston. She's paid for it all as well. I suppose everyone has their own unique skills. Hers is buying her way out of wrongdoings. Suits me though as we're getting closer to Lesley. I can feel it in my waters.

"Why, The Nook?"

"Not sure, but I like the name. Here's hoping we get some nookie into the bargain."

"Haven't you had enough? I'm exhausted trying to keep up with you."

"Some people collect stamps. I like to see it as my travelling trophies."

"You'll need one helluva big cabinet to display those then."

"You can count on that. Actually, Russell told me he'd recommended it to Lezzers' as his friend Patsy is the manager there."

"With a name like that, she's bound to be a party Patsy animal."

"Oh, I do hope so."

Ange has the audacity to suggest to Russell that Boozy Bingo should be the theme for the evening's entertainment. He must be off his head, but he thinks it's a terrific idea. There she goes again with her trout pout, twiddling her luscious locks and fluttering her eyelashes. Credit where credit is due, it works a treat. He must be stark raving mad to trust her ever again, even a brightly coloured pink dobber could end up being lethal in her hands.

ANGE

We almost miss the ferry the next day as we drank far too much at boozy bingo. In fact, I didn't even get to bed. Too busy playing rolling around the common room carpet with the lovely Irish boy Declan to even consider it. How lucky is he to have my lovely legs 11 around him at bingo? I see it as his parting gift.

Jules drives Gertie into the belly of The Spirit of Tasmania, a giant car ferry that is going to take us across ya Bass Strait. We park below deck and go for a wander. We have 10 hours to kill and I am hoping the name of the ferry is a reflection of an opportunity to buy some voddy for my body. It'll certainly make the ten hours to Devenport pass more quickly, but the bar doesn't open for another five hours. My cunning plan to get rat-arsed is completely foiled. At the very least, I'll get five hours later to catch up. I haven't slept a wink for days, it seems, so I can snooze for a few hours before it opens. We find a cozy, and I use that term loosely, four-seater with a table on the top deck. There aren't too many screaming brats up here and I can lay my weary head down to rest. We manage to ward people off by saying we've saved the extra two seats for our friends. I'm asleep before we leave the port.

JULES

Ange sleeps through the squall, as no sooner do we leave the harbour when it starts to get choppy, and I do mean CHOPPY. The huge vessel is listing this way, that way, forwards and backwards, up, down, up, down and over the deep blue sea. Well, actually it's over the Bass Strait, but I can't get the nursery rhyme out of my head for some reason. People are literally sliding from port to starboard side, and just as they regain their balance, they head forward to the bow and then back to the starboard. I'm so glad we got this table at the top. I'm imagining Gertie and all the other cars below deck to be underwater by now. Ange continues to sleep soundly. Captain Pugwash, or whatever his name is, apologises over the tannoy.

"We are experiencing some rough seas and high winds and it's too dangerous to go outside currently, so please stay indoors."

No shit. I don't plan on going out there Captain Pug, I've seen The Perfect Storm. We are in a floating tin can with a gale force storm raging outside. No sign of George, unfortunately. Inside is not much better as there's coffee, food, puke and small children involuntarily flying about. Call me selfish, but thankfully neither of us get motion sickness. I watch the eye of the storm unfold from the inside, from the comfort of my seat. Ange flops about like a fish out of water, her head lolling forward and backwards like a prostitute on a Saturday night. Still she doesn't stir. Finally, after what seems like an interminable time, the ferry comes to a gentle roll and the sea outside looks still and calm. People begin to breathe normally again, stop gripping the furniture, strangers, their loved ones and children in that order. It must be a regular occurrence as no sooner has the ferry come to a stable sway than the cleaning crew comes out. Hence why the bar isn't open is my guess. Captain Pugwash stays at the helm while the rest of the crew, including Master Bates, Roger the Cabin Boy and Seaman Stains, tidy the debris on the decks. My bad, the latter is nowhere in sight other than on the jumper that Ange is still wearing from the night before.

ANGE

That has to be one of the best dreams ever. I dreamed I was dancing with Patrick Swayze for hours and hours, he literally took me in his arms and moved me forward and backwards, up and down, then, just as we were about to lay down, I was rudely awakened by Jules.

"We've docked. Time to return to Gertie. Hope she's not taken in water and is waterlogged."

"Have I slept for ten hours? Must have done. How fabulous. How come I don't feel refreshed, renewed and raring to go though? I feel slightly groggy and out of it. If this is what sea air does to me, remind me never to go on a cruise."

JULES

Those sleeping tablets in her morning coffee have worked an absolute bloody treat and it's done her and her fellow passengers a favour and no harm done whatsoever. See it as my public service duty. You're welcome. I had an entertaining, quiet, peaceful, wonderful crossing across the Strait, ya bass.

The customs ociffer stops us as we leave the ferry in Gertie. He's checking to make sure we're not travelling with any contraband. Apparently, you're not allowed to bring fruit, vegetables, plant products or fish into Tassie. He's curious as he says he can smell fish, which is one of the products on the banned list. He's at Ange's side sniffing away.

"We don't have anything on the banned list in our car as we're both vegetarian. And if it helps explain the smell, Ange here hasn't changed her clothing from last night, if you get my gist, or jizm."

I even manage a wee wink and a nod. He looks perplexed, then, as it dawns on him what I have said, he looks appalled and inhales through his nostrils so hard so that he can confirm my claim. The familiar smell is instantly recognizable to him. He seems totally repulsed, which is my main goal and waves us through. Launceston here we come, only a couple of hours. As soon as we hit Highway 1, Ange reminds me of the stash stowed safely away in our hub caps and what a clever idea of mine it had been to distract him from them. It's amazing how convincing and believable you can be to a customs officer when you totally FORGET that you are a drug mule. She's always been an ass in my mind though. We've now crossed three different states now, NSW, Victoria and now Tasmania, so we are now boner fide felons. Narco traffickers for sure.

ANGE

We arrive in Launceston just in time for a "Happy Travels" night. Whatever that involves, I'm in, very happy, still groggy, but happy.

JULES

It's very tempting to continue to drug her, but I only have a few left, so I need to pace myself, pick my battles and use them when really, really required. We manage to sneak a wee dooby in and smoke it out of our window before going downstairs to the exceptionally clean and tidy common room. Has Lesley been here also? Maybe she's still here, having changed her vocation to a domestic support worker. I look around, but other than Ange, there are no familiar faces among the pack of packers who have congregated with their booze. It's not uncommon to see the same usual suspects that traipse around the world.

ANGE

The first game of the night is about to be introduced and explained. Patsy, the manager, has asked us all to sit in a circle as we're about to play a game.

"We're going to play Hi Harry."

"Do you know that in the good ol' U S of A, Harry, Hurry and Hairy all sound the same?"
There's a brief pause then the group, which covers at least seven different nations, including a lone Uhmerikan, try it out. Only the latter has a problem.

"You're yanking my chain here as they are all the same sound to me."

"Exactly my point. Better to remain silent and listen than be considered a fool, or worse, an American, than to speak out and remove all doubt don't you think?"

"Ange!"

"I'm sure he's happy for me to yank his chain so to speak. Yes?"
"Ah, one of these games, is it? Ange, is it? I'm Brad and I hear the trash gets picked up first thing in the morning, be ready."

"Touche John Boy, a game of insult tennis, which just so happens to be one of my favourites."

"If that is the case then please know it isn't my intention to push your buttons, I was actually looking for mute Ange."

I do believe John Boy is flirting with me. Bring it on Big Boy.

"Being Uhmerikan must feel like you're in a cemetery, there's many people around you, but absolutely no one is listening."

"Your verbal flexibility amazes me Ange. How do you manage to get your mouth and your head up your own ass all at the same time?"

He is flirting with me, the cheeky, handsome-looking stallion.

"Okay, okay, alright already. Enough the pair of you. I'd like to put an end to all this now before it gets out of hand and someone says something that can't be taken back. We can resolve this simply enough and I can help you both out of this retort/insult rally. Which way did the pair of you come in?"

"Ha ha, good one Patsy."

"Let's hurry back to the hairy game of Hi Harry, shall we?"

We all laugh, aside from John Boy, who still thinks we're all now taking the piss. I do like a man that stands up to me. I smile over at him and wink. He smiles back. Whether he knows it or not, his bed card has already been marked.

"Here we go then. We begin with, let's say you Jules, saying to the person on your left 'Hi Harry, I'm Harry, tell Harry'."

Sounds easy enough. Wonder what the catch is?

"The next person does the same to the person to their left and so on."

"Until?"

"Until someone makes a mistake. When someone makes a mistake, a spot is drawn on their face with lipstick. It just so happens that I have a fabulous red lipstick in my possession called 'Pervette'."

"Our friend Lezzers' would call it pervert."

"This then signifies that they are no longer 'Harry', but are now 'one spot'. Do you follow?"

"I will follow. I was on the outside when you said you said you needed me. I was looking at myself, I was blind, I could not see. A boy tries hard to be a man, his mother takes him by his hand, if he stops to think he starts to cry. Oh, why If you walk away, walk away I walk away, walk away, I will follow, If you walk away, walk away, I walk away, walk away, I will follow, I will follow."

" U2? At least we have you pair playing. Now, the person who has become 'one spot' is going to say to the person to their left "Hi Harry, I'm ONE SPOT, tell Harry.""

"When do we get to drink?"

"Any time you or anyone else gets a spot."

"This could get messy."

"That's the idea. Assuming no one else messes up, the game returns to the person who made the mistake. They then say

"Hi Harry, I'm one spot, tell Harry. And so forth. The game commences with each person gaining another spot each time they make a mistake and believe me, this happens rapidly and has been the inspiration behind many of the greatest nights I've ever seen in this place."

"Until we arrived."

"Yes, Russell forewarned me, so your cards are already marked. Two mistakes will make you two spots and you will have two drawn on your face, three mistakes makes you three spots and so forth. When you reach 5 spots you are OUT."

"It seems to me that before this happens, everyone will already be fucked up and have forgotten that there's even a game being played."

"That's the intention."

For a moment, I think we've changed games and are now playing charades as a tiny Asian-looking girl who doesn't speak much English begins to mime. Her English is better than John Boy's though. Again, yet another example of two countries separated by the same language. However, I'm not planning on having a deep conversation with him later. She keeps taking her right hand to her mouth and waving it. At first, I think she's offering to give out blow jobs, but apparently she's telling us she doesn't drink. No harm there. There are plenty of willing volunteers to step in for her and take one for the team. That way everyone continues to swig when she will inevitably make a mistake. No one remains Harry for long, including Ping Pong. No surprise there really. True to Patsy's prediction, everyone is soon completely bladdered. We all look like red Indians so it's hard to tell how many spots each one of us have. Doesn't really matter though, the aim of the game has been achieved. Ahhh!

"Happy, hiccup travellers."

Indeed.

JULES

Very, very happy red-faced travellers. Night night. Hic.

ANGE

That was a fun night, but I was aware that I hadn't been firing on full cylinders. I didn't even pursue John Boy. I must have still been slightly motion sick as I kept losing my balance. Jules said I was probably still queasy from the ferry and trying to find my sea legs. She's probably right, but it has been a full day since we'd come off. I am feeling much better today, much more tippy toppy and ready to head off to find the Hobbit, in Hobart. I crack myself up. As we're leaving, Patsy stops us.

"Girls, take a look in the lost, found and giving box before you leave will you."

"What's the lost, found and giving box Patsy?"

"It was started by a Scottish nurse a number of weeks ago who felt that we carry around more than we need, so she started the lost, found and giving box, which was her idea of giving to others less fortunate than ourselves. Simple enough really. You add to the box what no longer serves you and take something that either you need or you can gift to someone else on your travels."

"Wow, that's a lovely, selfless act. Do you happen to remember her name Patsy?"

"Yeah, how could I forget? Her name is Lesley."

"Awww, I'm chuffed to bits to say that she is our dear friend and we're heading to join her, well, when we can catch up with her, wherever that might be. My heart is filling with pride and I feel very grateful to call her a chum."

"Yeah Jules, she is a very special lady that's for sure. They broke the mould when they made her."

ANGE

Not my heart, but my mouth is filling with something resembling a bout of seasickness. I'm close to throwing up all over Patsy's Jesus sandals. Those niceties that Jules is spewing out makes me want to throw up even more.

"What a spliffing idea. I'll grab a bundle of bits and bobs from the box and make sure to deliver it exactly where it is best suited. Straight into the hands of a deserving receiver. Anyway, we're a bit pressed for time here and although we could spend all day shitting the breeze with you Patsy, we'd best get on the road or we may miss catching up with our very own angel of the destitute in Hobart. Come on Jules, let's make like sheep and get the flock out of here."

Back in Gertie, I have a few pressing questions.

"Am I missing something here Jules? Tell me in basic, simple terms how all these random acts of goodness work?"

"I can try to explain it so that your monkey-like brain can absorb it. It's random, non-premeditated, consistent actions designed to offer acts of goodness and kindness to the outside world."

"I hear you, but I still don't get it. How does it work? What's in it for me?"

"Nothing, that's the whole point. It's a senseless act of beauty. You can be like owl from Winnie the Pooh sometimes Ange."

"This stuff is well above my pay grade I'm afraid. Surely I'm more like Tigger than Owl."

"You are a blend of all of them my friend, with Snow Not-so-White added to the mix."

"You're my Grumpy wingman for sure."

JULES

I try to explain the effect on your inner world when you do something for someone else without any expectations in return. Being kind shows compassion, empathy and sympathy for someone else.

"Possibly, but there is no such thing as a selfless act. Everyone doing something for someone gets something out of it."

"If you say so Eeyore."

"It's true. Lezzers' gets her positive strokes by giving, and her recipients of her senseless acts of beauty and kindness get theirs by receiving. It's the natural way of the world. The ebb and flow, the yin and yang. And I recognize this in my case, I am happy to be the receiver of all the Giver's good deeds."

"Indeed, but there has to be some balance between all life's sweet gifts and all the bitter human experience we have to consume during our life. You can't be totally alive without facing both extremes. It's only then that you can grow and learn."

"Hmm, I know you have a psychology degree Jules, but it all sounds like a crock of Freudian psychobabble bullshit to me.

I've even heard Lezzers' say something similar, but as always, not quite."

"Each to their own, you need to focus on your own experience and experiences without judging, criticising or imposing your will on others' experience. It's all about timing also, and when the time's right, you will hear exactly what you are meant to hear."

"The time is right for me to show you my natural kindness by giving away some of these cheap, tasteless, threadbare clothes from the lost, found and giving box, that absolutely no one else wanted. They were left in the box in order to placate their egos and give them their positive strokes, knowing they were giving to others they considered to be less fortunate than themselves. Really kind and selfless ... not! In fact, the arrogance and audacity they think just because they're giving a piece of tat that no one wants, is not, in my EXPERIENCE, a random act of kindness but more like a kick in the teeth."

ANGE

I now see it as my mission in life to make sure that the shit from the box I'd grabbed goes to someone deemed more deserving of this crap than I. It's roughly 2 ½ hours to Hobart and we pass through Corona, or something like that, Campbell Town (who the fuck is this Campbell bloke that keeps popping up everywhere?) and York Plains. We see plenty of hobos, but they never seem to be in an optimum place for me to chuck something out the window at them. Besides, my window doesn't open, so I'll have to have the door ajar and chuck it as we drive by. I'm not going to lie, I become obsessed, scanning the streets, alleys and pavements in search of the perfect down-and-out of luck poor beggar. It's me that's having no luck stalking the residents of the road. Jules is right though, it is all about timing and there never seems to be the right time.

My head is pressing against the closed window, my new car game, Hobo Hunting, scanning the streets, checking the gutters as we drive by. I'm ready, willing and able at any second to pounce on my prey. Where are all the fuckers? Finally, finally, as we drive into Hobart, hours of stalking later, a series of unexpected events begin to unfold before me. I see the traffic lights ahead have turned to red, it isn't raining, it is slightly chilly and there is a homeless guy standing at the corner. Ya beauty. Talk about timing. This is the right time now to show Jules how fucking considerate and giving I am. All the stars line up for me.

"Pull over Jules. There's one."

I dig deep in the bag behind me and pull out the first thing that comes to hand, it's a rather nice Baja poncho. He's not getting that, I can use that for sure. Next, I pull out a rather nasty-looking bright yellow acrylic sweater that probably belonged to John Boy which I'd want to lose if it were mine. It's perfect. Jules pulls over, alongside the tramp and I open my door slightly waving the offending article towards him. I would have preferred to wind the window down and chuck it at his feet, but as it's broken, the crack in the door will have to do.

"Here you go, Sir, I think you'll find this to your liking."

Succinct, polite, COMPASSIONATE without being condescending, me thinks. He looks at me slightly puzzled, but beggars can't be choosers. Picky bugger.

"TAKE IT. take it, you need it."

With some reservation, he finally takes it. And rightly so. He's being far too persnickety here for my liking. Rather ungrateful if you ask me. Unappreciative dirty wee fuck. I add.

"I refuse to give you money as you'll immediately spend it on drink and drugs."

A number of things happen in quick succession that take me by surprise. He takes the unflattering rag, the lights turn to green, he looks behind Gertie at the same time as I do. I slam the door.

"DRIVE!"

We screech through the lights as the bus pulls up behind us and the not-so-homeless perplexed chap boards, clutching the flimsy gaudy garment. No doubt considering his attire at the same time as he has just been mistaken for a tramp. Easy mistake.

JULES

"OMG!! Have you just tried to give something to a poor unsuspecting bloke waiting for a bus?"

"It was a case of mistaken identity on my part."

"No kidding Miss Marple."

"Yeah, very funny. Glad it amused you."

"I wonder what he's thinking now Ange?"

The tears are streaming down my face and I can hardly see to drive. I have to pull over to get it out of my system, but then the bus overtakes us and we both start all over again.

"You know what, Jules, I always take life as it comes, usually with a grain of salt. And a slice of lemon. And a shot of tequila. Hands down 6.30 is the best time on the clock as it means HAPPY HOUR."

"Should we drink tonight? A) Yes B) A or C) B."

"Let's do it Clyde."

Unfortunately, we'd left it too late to check in to the Backpackers, which means we have to go to Hobart Central YHA, which is fine, but it comes with RULES. Neither of us are very good at those kinds of things, but tonight we don't have a choice. We have to do chores and be back by a certain time or they lock the doors. There is a late pass until 11pm, and if you exceed that time, you have to wake the matron up and then you get extra tasks the next day. The trick is to leave a downstairs toilet window ajar and sneak in. After checking in and dumping our backpacks in our room, we head to the common room and ask if anyone wants to come to Wrest Point, Australia's first legal casino with us. Around 10 of us head out for the night. Everyone is drinking much faster than me. They're already on their second round and I'm still trying to finish my first. My gin and tonic doesn't taste of anything. Bastards behind the bar are giving me half measures it seems. I'm sucking through the straw like an escort on a Friday night hoping for a tip of the financial kind. Why do they call it blow jobs, when there's no blowing involved? Beats me. I'm sucking so hard, in fact, that the inside of my cheeks are touching one another. Everyone else is managing theirs just fine and I don't want to seem like the odd man out, so I continue to try and drink. Eventually, I lean across the bar counter and quietly complain to the bartender that I've been given a faulty straw and a watered-down beverage.

"I've been sucking like a lady of the night yet have yielded none of the delights. There's not even a soupcon of gin getting anywhere near my taste buds."

The bartender reaches across the counter, removes the straw from my glass, hands me another one and gives me a wink.

"Not surprised really as you've been sucking on the cocktail stirrer."

He could have said it a bit quieter so that everyone didn't hear. I become the butt of their jokes. No surprise, but Ange leads the volleys.

"What's the difference between Jules and a mosquito?"

"A mosquito stops sucking when you slap it."

"You're like a hoover Jules, you never suck hard enough."

I'm learning to let her roll with it. Get it all off her ample chest and just like that, she gets bored, gives in and moves on to her next victim for the evening. I don't need to be a fortune teller to know that she's so predictable.

ANGE

Enough of this malarkey, it's so boring. Who has taken the original Jules and replaced her with some serious bint? She used to be a better crack than this. Think I'm going to go play the pokies instead. I'm sure I'll get a better reaction from them than I do from her. She needs to lighten up a bit. We know these machines better as one-armed bandits, with the arm or lever on the side that you pull down. I've never actually played one before, but surely it can't be too hard. I sit down at a slot machine, put a handful of 50 cent pieces in, grip the handle, gently at first, but then harder and pull it firmly up then down. The four drums spin fast initially and then come to a slow stop with four peaches in a perfect line. Suddenly, lights start flashing and bells ring. There's a commotion that ensues all over the place. I haven't a clue what I've done, but there's no mistake that the alarm and lights are coming from my pokie machine. People are coming towards me from all directions and strangers are clapping. WTF? Initially I think perhaps I've broken something. Perhaps I've used a rather firm pull after all, as is my want. I sit there, not knowing what to do, which is so out of character for me. A couple of big, beefy, muscular bouncers in black suits and ear pieces show up beside me. Now usually when I have the misfortune to see a bouncer up this close it's because I'm intoxicated, stoned, belligerent, cheeky and they're here to escort me out of the premises. I now have the opportunity to express my natural kind self by being kind and respectful towards them.

"I'm terribly sorry boyz. I believe there may have been a misunderstanding here. I only pulled the lever gently. What have I done exactly?".

"Oh, good one Darl, you've only gone and got a hit."

"Darl? That's a new one on me. Far be it for me to correct you here, but I haven't taken a hit all night. I've been sitting here all on my ownio minding my own business."

"Well, you've done it this time Darl."

"Are you trying to hit on me here? Is this what it's all about?"

JULES

Now what has she gone and done? Lights and bells are going off like Blackpool fair or a raid at a Bordello. I step over to see what's going on.

"What has the lovely Ange done this time to attract Butch and Cassidy?"

"She's only gone and won the night's jackpot."

"Jackpot?

"Jackpot?"

"Yis, it's a whopping $6,500 and we're here to see that she gets it safely."

"Shut the fuck up. $6,500? Don't spare the horses lads, take me to your leader."

This is where the best of Ange comes out. When she gets her winnings, she buys everyone from the hostel a drink.

"Champagne sweeties, champagne all around."

She keeps us in bubbles for the remainder of the night. Next time we see Not so Little and Large, it's to tell us that the casino is closed as it's 2 am and time to leave.

ANGE

Go figure. I won the jackpot. Fair chuffed with myself. I recognise that playing these pokie machines does indeed take skill, talent and that je n'ais ce quoi. No problemo. We head back to the hostel but know that there's no way in hell that the stuffy rules-are-rules matron is going to let us in. Luckily for us, I have left the downstairs toilet window open. We can all sneak in as quiet as mice and be in our beds faster than a toupee in a hurricane. Now that's all very well, if you're trained like a ninja warrior and sober, not boozed up and foo of alcohol and blow. We are behaving more like the herd of elephants from Jungle Book and not a superfluity of nuns' penguin-marching to a nunnery. We unanimously decide that Jules, who is the smallest package amongst us, will go through the window, sneak around and open the door for us. The idea is to quietly launch her through the open window. She insists on going in feet first. We all lift her overhead, with a beautiful, and in my humble opinion, rendition of "Hup two three four, keep her up, two three four, hup two three four, keep her up, two three four, push her through, two three, four, push her through, two three four."

It's almost akin to putting a sausage filling into its casing. Perhaps we're a bit louder than we think we're being as all of a sudden, all the outside lights come on. We give Jules one final heave ho and push her through the gap. We then leg it round the corner.

JULES

Without any warning, I am propelled through the window like a human cannon ball. I land feet first....in the toilet bowl. Lucky, I hadn't gone in head first. My legs are completely trapped. I manage to swivel slightly and sit on the cistern., and wait, the others will be here soon to set me free. I wait and wait and wait in the darkness for someone to come to my rescue and release me from my porcelain chamber. I must have fallen asleep, as when I come to, my feet are for sure still asleep and stuck deep inside the bowl. I have lost all feeling from my knees down. The sun is up and the bushman's alarm clock is the only background noise I hear. The family of kookaburras continues its variety of trills, chortles, belly laughs and hoots. The calling starts and ends with a low chuckle and has a shrieking laugh in the middle. I think it's kookaburras, it could be Ange and her tribe playing outside, totally unaware of my predicament. I strain to listen to the sounds beyond the birds, trying to identify anything from inside the hostel. I can vaguely hear banging and clattering from the kitchen upstairs, breakfast time no doubt. How long have I been here? Am I going to have to have my feet amputated? Why has Ange not come to my rescue? Where is she?

ANGE

We're not able to get back to Jules as the matron never turns the lights off. Best-case scenario she has snuck up to her bed with the stealth of The Pink Panther without being noticed. Worst-case scenario, she's been caught and has some extra chores to do later. Myself and the remaining six other one-armed bandit hostellers manage to squeeze into the back of Gertie, three lying with their heads behind the back seat, two with their heads at the back door, and one in the passenger seat, all packed in like little sardines. It's tight, but comfy enough. At first light, when we know the hostel is open, we walk in nonchalantly and go upstairs to the dorm. No sign of Jules anywhere. She's maybe already doing her daily chores. Where the hell is she? We march downstairs to the basement where we know we last saw her being catapulted through the window. What if she's cracked her head? What if she's lying there slowly bleeding to death? We burst through the door only to find her sitting on the cistern with her feet firmly stuck down the drain.

"That's another fine mess you've got me into Ange."

After much pulling, pushing, twisting and manipulating, we manage to pull her free. She can hardly walk, though, as her feet are swollen, she has trench foot and they are completely drained of colour due to the three hours plus stuck in a very small pot. The old cistern in the basement toilet has come away from the wall and water is pissing everywhere. The room needs mopped and cleaned up before Matron Hattie Jacques catches us. We do the best we can, and as a parting gesture, I wrap cling film over the bowl, closing the lid and hoping against all hope that Hattie has the pleasure of my gift. I think we've learned a lesson here though, never climb through a window that's over a toilet cistern under the affluence of incohol. We go back upstairs to pack. Onwards and upwards my faithless mare. How can I change the world if I can't even change myself? I cannot change the way I am, can I? I don't know, I don't know. I take a good, long hard look at the world behind my eyes, every nook, every cranny, every space. Perhaps there is room for a reorganisation. It makes me feel quite sad as my behaviours aren't actually a true reflection of me. I miss my dad.

"Hey Ange, do you know that Lesley has already been and gone from this very hostel? What are the chances of that?"

"How do you know?"

"Guess?"

"Let me think, there's a surplus of shortbread? A Lost and found Giving Box? A coffee jar?"

"Nope."

"I give up, pray tell me how you know how Florence Fucking Nightingale has been here?"

"She's written in the hostile's guest book."

She hands me the leatherbound book

"Joined-up writing? Who knew? A woman of many, many talents. How terribly impressive."

"No need to be like that. Give it here."

"What does she say? Any clue as to where she's heading next?"

"I'm not sure you want to see what she's written."

"Give it back."

It says: "Be the change you want to see in the world - Gandhi."

"Oh for fuck sake. I'm going to throw up. Actually, I really think I am going to be sick."

I can feel the warm bile, red wine, tequila mixed with effervescent champagne bubbles rising and I race to the nearest loo.

JULES

Too late. I hope she remembers her earlier prank. She soon appears smelling of parmesan and carrots clutching her wet, newly cleaned obligatory backpacker's cotton-soled Kung Fu shoes. Ah, definitely too late then. She had forgotten the cling film prank. Serves her right really.

"Confucius he say, don't do unto others what you don't want done unto you."

"Fuck off Jules. Let's get Gertie packed, make like lesbians and lickety split."

While Ange showers and cleans herself and the toilet again, I try to pack the car, but my lily-white chicken nugget-shaped flippers are only good for noodle slapping the ground one slap at a time. Like it or lump it, Ange has to drive to Devenport. Courage is being scared to death and saddling up anyway. So I put my big girl pants on and bite the bullet. I have no choice in the matter though and hope that we don't come across too many multi-storey car parks on our way back north. If we leave now, we'll have plenty of time to see the scenery and catch the overnight ferry back to Melbourne.

"On a positive note, with you driving, there won't be that incessant tapping on the windows as you'll have BOTH hands on the wheel."

"Look, I almost passed my driving test. I got 8 out of 10."

"Did the other two manage to jump clear then?"

"I'll try my best to avoid the potholes so I don't spill my beer."

ANGE

She tries to take a swing at me, but can't actually run in any form to make contact with me whatsoever. She looks like one of those headless chickens as she flails around the common room, her feet slapping like a pair of fish against the wooden floor. At least I now have the chance to show off my driving skills. She had banned me from driving since the car park escapade, but now she doesn't have a choice, does she? I'll show her. Other than the guest book, I am so relieved to be leaving the hostel without some kind of reminder that Mother Teresa, in the shape of a Lezzers', nurse extraordinaire, hasn't been here and done yet another random, more carefully considered, humanitarian act of charity. A rather rotund girl approaches us as I'm packing Gertie. Jules is sitting in the passenger seat trying to bring some life back to her lifeless flippers.

"Hi there, I saw your notice on the message board offering a lift to Devonport in exchange for a share of petrol. I'm English and I've got plenty of snacks if that helps. A huge stack of crisps and chocolate."

"We were thinking of balancing the car with three or four young Swedish guys, but I suppose you might do instead. Is it Cadbury's chocolate?"

"Ignore her, she got out of the wrong side of the van this morning. The snacks sound great, but you sound even better. Sorry if I don't get up, but my feet are somewhat useless at the moment, hence why you have to take your chances with Dick Dastardly here behind the wheel."

"I'll take my chances. I did say I'm English, didn't I? Believe me, they all drive like Looney Tunes there."

"Of course, you are. English, you say? I personally promise not to hold that against you, but I can't vouch for Jules here." "Pipe down will you Ange, I'm Jules and the one with the mouthy gob is Ange. Her bark is equally as bad as her bite, so come prepared. Be warned though, she's a member of a magic circle and before you know it, your crisps and chocolate will disappear."

"I'll take my chances. I'm Mary, Mary Hinge."

"Of course, you are. You do know there are beauty salons that can take care of that, so you shouldn't worry too much."

"Don't even make eye contact with her Mary, that way she'll get bored quickly and move on, besides she'll be concentrating on the driving so much that she won't have time to eat a chocolate-covered raisin."

JULES

It's settled there and then, she's in. Truth be told, she seems like a really sweet, innocent young country girl and I feel bad about inflicting Ange on her or anyone else. We decide that, as the back of the van only has a double mattress, we can only take her.

It's also reckless and positively dangerous taking any more passengers with Ange at the helm.

"You need to be extra careful driving as we have a passenger that you are responsible for, so ca' canny with the speed."

"Ye of big boobs and little faith"

ANGE

The bloody cheek of it. We stand there for a few more minutes volleying insults at my apparent lack of driving skills. The Butterball from Birmingham keeps interrupting. Eventually, I stop bickering and turn towards her. "YES??"

"I'm sure your driving is just fine, but I totally understand if it's too much trouble."

"No trouble at all Mary Hinge, it's sorted, you're coming with us."

I smile ever so sweetly.

"There are no seats in the back, only a mattress which will give you the space to spread out. It's a double mattress, so you should be fine. Just make sure to leave the blue light off."

"She's joking Mary, ignore her."

"There were six people sleeping in here last night and goodness knows what bugs, viruses, plagues and sexually transmitted diseases they carry."

"And that's just her she's talking about."

"Ho de ho, there goes another pulled chakra."

The broad Brummy broad laughs as if it's all a big joke.

"You're in safe hands Mary Hinge, I drive like Niki Lauda."

"I do hope not, he's dead, isn't he?"

"He is, but not related to his expert driving skills. Now, let's make like a dog in a car and head out."

Too early in our relationship to say, "another dog that is" as she needs a little warming up and stamina to appreciate my unique humour. No sooner have we left the hostel when Buddha in the back starts twittering on about how she's heading to the Outback to work.

"I met this really inspiring Scottish nurse recently."

"NOOOOOOOOOOOOO!"

I scare the bejesus out of her and Jules.

"I'm sure it's a fascinating story, but I really need to concentrate here and can't have such stimulating stories distracting me from the task at hand. I find it easier to listen to music while driving."

There is no way I'm going to listen to any more acts of fucking charity about Saint Lezzers', Patron Saint of Lost Causes. Twenty minutes later, under the expert skills of yours truly, we leave the city limits, heading to the A5, then Jules starts.

"Slow the feck down will you, you raving lunatic."

"I'm not going fast, everything else is moving slowly."

JULES

She's going far too fast. I tell her countless times to slow down. She's driving worse than a blind child at the wheel. She says she's only doing 50, but when I try to look at the speedometer, she slaps my hand and blocks me with her left elbow. She's adamant she's only doing 50, but it feels more like we're going faster than the speed of light. We're weaving all over the shop and I try to grab the wheel to straighten us out.

"I know you mentioned keeping the blue light off, but there's one behind me, coming from outside the back window."

I look in the wing mirror and see the blue lights and when I turn Wham! down, belting out I'm your man, I hear the sirens.

"Waaaaaahhhh, waaaaahhhh"

ANGE

I suddenly notice the flashing blue light, but ignore it as it surely isn't for me. It doesn't give up though, or try to overtake which is strange as I have my hand out the window, flagging him ahead.

Out of the back, Lardy in her whiney voice starts up.

"I think you need to pull over."

"Look, take a breath, slow down and pull the feck over. He's not tailgating you."

"I can't."

"Why not?"

"I'm not sure they take too kindly to someone driving with no licence."

"No licence?"

"Keep out of this Hairy!"

"You still have to stop. What do you mean anyway? You don't have it? What with you? Or not at all? You at least have a provisional, don't you?"

"Nope."

"FFS. You told me you had your provisional. You still have to stop."

"I'm not lying, I do have my provisional, just not here with me in Australia."

"What's going on? I want to get out."

"You still have to pull over Ange. Listen, here's what we'll do, you'll stop the car, I'll jump out and get my driving licence from the back. Hopefully with our dark hair, we might get away with it. Say you're me. Now pull the feck over…. Hold on…keep going…What about the drugs?"

"DRUGS?"

"Shit yeah, that's it, we could end up going to jail."

"I did not sign up for being a drug carrier. Let me out NOW."

In unison: "SHUT THE FUCK UP!"

"Okay, stop the car. I'll go round to the back, get my licence and NO mention of drugs. That applies to you too Brummie, or we'll all be done for."

JULES

WHAAAAT??? she doesn't even have a licence, a provisional or otherwise on her, silly cow. Not much time to think here as the blue lights and siren are very persistent. We both shout at Brummie to shut up so we can come up with a cunning plan. I'm going to jump out when she FINALLY decides to stop, and grab my licence. He might not even notice the difference, you can't see in the wee pictures that she is tall and I am vertically challenged, i have blue eyes, she has hazel, my hair is straight, hers curly. Shirley the pictures are too small to notice these minor variabilities. Suddenly Ange gives it the emergency brake, and Brummie, her family-sized bag of Cheetos and most of our belongings, including the police bike, almost come hurtling towards the front of the car. I immediately hop out of the car to go rummage in the back for my licence. Brummie passes me as I open the back doors which are within a baw hair of the popo's car. He looks rather familiar, but no time to ponder on him as I rummage through all the debris for my licence.

ANGE

Perfect idea. Tonight Matthew, I'm going to be Jules. The Brummie girl in the back, can play her larger-than-life self. For some reason she's in hysterics, a complete shambling mass of tears and lard. What is her problem? I'm the one driving after all, not her. It's not as if we're deliberately smuggling drugs intentionally. Oh, but wait, now that I think about it, drug smugglers...oh...shit we are.

I do my very best emergency brake all of a sudden, spraying up some of the loose scree from the semi-unsealed road, catapulting the fat English rose into the front between us. Her head is in the well at my feet, large arse in the air. First time I'm sure she's been down on anything, other than a family-size bag of crisps that is. Jules doesn't miss a beat, she jumps out, dashes to the back, opens the doors and ransacks her bag looking for her licence.

Chips gets off his bike, but I'm already out and leaning on the bonnet of Gertie.

"That was a close shave officer. You almost rammed me in the rear end. Good driving though, any closer and you'd have been inside me."

He's very familiar.

"Do you know why I stopped you?"

"Search me...please."

"You were weaving all over the place."

"I can explain that. I was trying to swerve the trees, but it turns out it was my air freshener all along."

"And you were speeding. I can give you a ticket for that you know."

"What am I supposed to do with that?"

"Well, when you collect four of them, you can get yourself a bicycle."

"I was trying to keep up with the traffic."

"There isn't any."

"I know, that's how far behind I am."

"Funny little lady. Papers?"

"Scissors. I win."

"Have you been drinking?"

"Only water."

"I smell wine."

"Oh my gawd, it's a miracle, he's only gone and bloody done it again. Do I know you? Maybe in the biblical sense?"

"We met last night."

"We did? I mean, we did. You're one half of the security team from the casino. My guess, by your incredible driving skills, you're Pace. Did you leave Hale at home? The way you handle that large throbbing machine between your legs is pure expertise by the way, really quite impressive and masterful. I'm lucky to be alive though, as my flip flop caught under the pedal and I was struggling to free it."

I bend over, booty towards him and rub my lower leg up and down with BOTH hands.

"Is there anything I can do to get me out of this pickle officer? We can maybe conduct an internal investigation later? Over a beer or two?"

"I'm off at 5pm."

Is bribery always this easy? Note to self, use it more often when caught in compromising situations.

"How about The Brewdog pub at 8pm? Does that wet your appetite?"

"You mean whet?"

"I know exactly what I meant."

"That sounds like a plan. In the meantime, change your shoes. I'd hate to have to pull you over again."

"I've never been on a date with a police officer before. I've come close to a few truncheons in my time though. Would you mind if I have a quick straddle of your bike before you go?"

"Better make it quick."

"I can be as quick as you like."

I straddled his big machine as he holds the handlebars.

"VROOM! VROOM!"

I slip off and sidle back to Gertie's driver's side

"Thank you, officer. See you tonight."

"Brew Dog. 8pm it is. Drive carefully."

"90% of accidents are caused by not being careful. I'm careful. Boys like you are bad through and through. Still, girls like me, always seem to be with you. We can't help but worry, you're in such a hurry, mixing with the wrong boys, playing with the wrong toys. Easy girls, and late nights, cigarettes, and love bites."

I swear he sashays back to his bike like cock o' the north. The cat before he gets creampied. He attentively mounts his steed, adjusts his mirror shades, flexes his bulging biceps, gives a small wave, then U-turns and heads back to town. Slam dunk.

JULES

By the time I find my licence, Chips is heading back to his bike. Ange is back behind the wheel and has not only got off with a speeding ticket, but has arranged a date with him.

"He's cute."

"A feckin date? We're leaving town, not going on a day jaunt."

"By the time he realises I've stood him up, we'll be on the ferry. No harm done. Let's make like a game of Monopoly and use the Get Out Of Jail card. Put Wham back on will you? Call me

good, call me bad, call me anything you want to baby, but I know
that you're sad, and I know I'll make you happy with the one thing
that you never had. Baby, I'm your man, don't you know that?
Baby, I'm your man. You bet! If you're gonna do it, do it right."

"Right,"

"Do it with me. If you're gonna do it, do it right,"

"Right,"

"Do it with me, If you're gonna do it, do it right,"

"Right,"

"Do it with me, if you're gonna do it, do it right."

"You have no morals, no scruples and your judgment on
how to behave is severely lacking. You do know that there is an
actual living, breathing human being behind your complete lack of
consideration and disregard to his feelings here."

"Life is too short to worry about what others say or think
about me. It's none of my business what he thinks at the end of the
day. I'm having fun and it gives him something to talk about."

"Did it cross your mind that the next person he stops is
going to be on the receiving end of your lack of judgement?"

"Not my problem. Besides, I left him a gift on the seat of
his bike after I had a wee shotty sitting on it."

"What was that?"

"I left him a groin snail trail on his seat from my sweaty
groin. It is very hot after all. Not my fault I'm sweating dow
nunder in this heat. I'm sure that will take the edge off me not
showing up tonight. See it as a release of sorts. That and that alone
will stay in his memory for a very, very long time and possibly the

gift that keeps on giving and giving. Much better than the real deal.
"

"You are incorrigible."

"Oh, I do hope so"

We get to Devenport with George and Andy belting out
their songs accompanied by us, who sound more like Matt and
Luke from Dross rather than Pepsi and Shirlie. We have just
enough time to catch the ferry, driving straight on. When we go to
get out and take a stroll up to the top deck, we realise with horror,
well me anyway, Ange isn't the slightest bit perturbed, and
actually finds it mildly amusing that Brummie isn't in the back. I
remembered her passing me when Chips stopped us, her stuff is
not in the back, so we reckon she must have decided that spending
any more time with Thelma and Louise would not be in her best
interest. GOOD judgment call, but where is she? We, actually I,
don't even see her on the ferry. I hope she makes it okay and that
Chips doesn't wait too long in the pub.

My godmother lives in Melbourne and I had promised her
I'd call when I was in town, but to be honest, I'm not sure it's fair
to inflict Ange on them as they're good, sweet, innocent folk.

However, sitting on the ferry watching Ange's head lolling
with each crest of the waves, snoring as the boat rises and falls in
sync with the dips, helps me make my decision. A change of
scenery and a familiar face is exactly what I need for my mental
wellbeing.

The first thing I do when we disembark in the morning is
call them. She is so kind and hospitable and insists we come to her
straight away for breakfast and stay for the night. She won't take
no for an answer, not that I have tried too hard to persuade her

otherwise. I can't even remember the last time we'd eaten properly other than Brummie's bag of snacks she'd inadvertently left behind in her haste that we ate on the ferry. It was a real delicacy which consisted of cheese and onion Golden Wonder crisps, Cheetos, Mars Bars, a couple of Cadbury's Flakes and a Creme Egg which we split. No harm done, we put them all to good use and saved her demolishing 6,000 calories to herself. I take down the address and off we go. If Ange's map-reading skills have improved, which she says they have, it won't take us too long to get to their house in Toorak. However, the morning traffic is heavy and picking up by the minute.

ANGE

Reluctantly, I agree to go to Hyacinth and Richard's place, but only for ONE night. The thought of staying with the aged pensioners from Keeping up Appearances for any longer might drive me to drink more. Maybe I can sneak in a wee dooby, that should take the edge off any fuddy duddy, dull behaviour. As we approach a really large intersection where all the cars are yielding to one another, taking turns, first come, first severed, right of way to the car that arrived at the junction first. Like an honesty box of sorts. I'd be shite at this as I wouldn't know who arrived where first. I spot a fluffy wee dog curled up smack bang in the centre. The cars are whizzing by it, paying not a jot of notice to the tiny canine. I can see from here that the poor wee fur baby is shaking with fear.

"STOPPPPPP!"

Jules slams on the brakes.

"I can't sit here and wait till some fucking lunatic driver makes road kill of Toto."

I get out of the van among all the harried drivers and begin to whistle on the tiny pupalup. With one hand aloft, I hold up the traffic and call the dog towards me with an inviting tone. Some drivers hold their hands up in despair, some toot their horns, others watch me as the live rescue unfolds. I keep walking amidst the screech of brakes, honking and shouting. A woman on a mission. I try to play charades with the onlookers, pointing to the hairy hound, cradling my arms, gesticulating that my throat is being slashed and then using my thumbs up to show everyone that everything is okay once it is saved, then I can take it back to Jules and Gertie. I stop the cars from moving any closer to the tiny dog which must be terrified as it hasn't moved an inch since I got out of the car. Sitting there curled up in a minute ball. I hope it hasn't already been hit and had its innards displayed on the tarmac underneath its fragile-looking body. I get closer and closer and I can sense something isn't quite right. The irate drivers are still blasting their horns and shouting at me. As I stand over the furry shape, I see it isn't actually a Yorkshire Terrier, a cat or even a wee moose, but is, in fact, a coyote-fur aviator hat. FUCK!!! Now what? I've only held up the morning rush-hour traffic to save a hairy headpiece. I have to keep up the pretence that it is actually an animal of some description and not straight outta Marks and Spencers accessory department. I lift it up carefully, cradling it gently in my arms and quickly tuck it into my jacket. I kiss its oil-streaked, dirt-spotted, tyre-imprinted 'head'. I coo, stroke it, giving it more pecks than is necessary. I give thumbs up to all the other drivers, some of whom clap, some cheer and I signal to them to continue on their merry way. I trot back to Gertie before my ruse is spotted by some beady-eyed canine lover.

"What are we going to do with a four-legged hairy mutt? We can barely take care of ourselves for feck sake."

I put Toto on my head and growl.

"Let's not hang around shall we, let's go on a head."

"OMG, it's a feckin hat. You just stopped rush hour traffic to rescue a Tibetan Terrier trapper hat? That is so funny, or should I say furry?"

"Now let's make like a tampon and get out of this bloody mess I've got us in."

"Again."

"Again."

Now, that's funny. Toto the trilby rests pride of place on our dashboard to fight another day. We drive towards the suburb of Toorak, but I'm pretty sure we have the wrong address as the streets are full of mansions, consulates and very swanky houses which line the tree-infested boulevards.

"What exactly do they do Jules?"

"I'm not 100% sure, but he may have worked in the diplomatic service at some time."

"I think we should make like Tom and Cruise for a bit more."

"Not sure that's a good idea, we're being followed by the neighbourhood golf cart security."

"Speed up then, there's no way he can keep up."

Surprisingly, he does keep up, which is a revelation. He must have some souped-up horsepower in that engine of his. We stop at a gated entry.

"This can't be it."

"This is the address she gave me."

Paul Blart sits in his cart revving, well I use that term loosely, waiting in all hope that we are not granted to whatever lies behind the forged-iron security gates."

With trepidation, Jules presses the intercom.

"Hello?"

"Is that you Jules?"

"Yes."

"How exciting, come on up."

Up? What does that mean? Where are we heading now? I think of waving at Paul with my middle finger, but think better of it as we might need him if we're heading to Hell and not The Stairway to Heaven I am hoping for. I lean out the window and blow him a kiss instead as the gates to Heaven, hopefully, close behind us. It takes us at least five minutes to get to the actual house. The drive is lined with rhododendrons at either side which are magnificent and in full bloom. It takes my breath away. We pass landscaped gardens, a stable, tennis courts and a pool, all of which leads to a circular drive that sweeps in front of a spectacular tudor mansion. It even has a fucking turret.

JULES

This can't be it. Shirley not. However, there is no mistaking the elderly white-haired, plump lady waving at us in a gentle, appealing, welcoming manner. My auntie Nora, my godmother, standing there in her twin set, tweed skirt, pearls and sensible brown brogues. I don't usually notice flowerbeds and colours, but the ones that frame the house are breathtaking. A myriad of colours, shapes and sizes frame the magnificent building. We've made a good call for sure coming here, maybe one night isn't going to be enough. She strides towards us, grabs me in a massive bear hug that renders my upper arms immobile. There is something incredibly nurturing and comfortable about the cuddle and I find myself nestling snuggly into her ample bosom.

"How perfectly wonderful to see you Jules. We had your fabulous friend Lesley here a month ago, and now you. Truly spectacular. It's tremendously spiffing that we now have the extra-special bonus of you and your friend."

"Wait. What?? Lesley was here? Here? How do you know her?"

"Remember? We met her that summer, when we were visiting you and your mum. It was our winter here and we were touring Scotland. Do you not remember? We all went for dinner at the restaurant you worked in and she was our waitress."

"I had totally forgotten that."

"Well, bless her, she has always kept in touch, written regular postcards and letters, so when she told me she was coming to Victoria, we invited her to stay. She was an absolute godsend really as John had done his back in doing the garden when Monty, our gardener, was away on vacation. She didn't bat an eye, rolled up her sleeves and got stuck in, helping me prune, mulch and plant all the flowerbeds. She definitely has the magic touch. The garden looks beautiful, wouldn't you agree? I couldn't have got through those first few nights without her either as she helped John shower and settled him comfortably in bed for the night."

"How wonderful. Did she happen to mention me and my friend Ange here?"

"Nice to meet you Ange, I'm Nora. She did speak of you and her time in Sydney, but said not too much more than that, only that she was ready to move on, be independent and do some nursing in the Northern Territory on a reserve somewhere outside Alice Springs. Giving back is really important to her."

"That's a relief auntie, I mean that she's well, safe and happy and not been saying anything bad about us, if you know what I mean."

"Why would she?"

"No particular reason, it's really good to hear she's all right and continuing her good deeds, and not talking ill of us."

"Ill of you? Oh no, she said only wonderful things."

"How admirable of her. You can call me Ange."

ANGE

Well, knock me over with a Ken Dodd feather duster. I'm glad she clarified the mulch smell though, I thought it was the musty odour that accompanies older people. How in the hell has Lezzers' not only managed to get to Downton Abbey, but play nurse AND the green-fingered Jolly Green Giant gardener? I sincerely hope this is where her skills end and that Lady Nora Crawley here doesn't continue with the diatribe of any more good fucking deeds she done. Maybe I should show her Lezzers'' magic touch by producing the stash she grew in Sydney. That'll wipe the smile clean off her face. Let's see if she still waxes lyrical about her then. I hate to admit it though; the flowerbeds do look like the prizewinner at the Chelsea Flower show. She's certainly managed to work her charm here and win the heart of Queen Nora.

JULES

At least we know she's safe, happy and healthy, we now have another piece of the puzzle and we are getting closer and closer to being reunited with her and bringing her back to Sydney. I commend her for not only doing all the weeding, but planting all the flowers in the ground and planters, then, if that wasn't enough, she goes feeding, showering and bedding John. I couldn't/wouldn't have even done the flowers, let alone clean his nooks and crannies. That does take a certain skill and certain person who is not only willing, but able to do all of that.

Nora shows us around their beautiful home, finally ending the tour at the extensive wine cellar which is full of top quality, EXPENSIVE, collectors' wine. "If I were to do any planting Nora, it would be to plant myself down here and empty, polish and clean up this area."

"Ha ha, that sounds like a perfect plan. I think I might join you."

"Let's do it Nora."

What's she like? All she does is talk about polishing off the wine bottles. It amuses Nora though and she does laugh. I'm not sure she knows just how serious Ange is, I know from experience that she's not joking either, she means every word of what she's saying, right down to the last drop. If we're all lucky, maybe she'll get alcohol poisoning. That way, I can go find Lesley in the peace and quiet of my own space. She just doesn't get it and keeps asking me what's in it for "Lezzers'".

I wish she'd stop calling her that as well, it's so patronizing and condescending.

"Every time she smiles or does something nice for someone, it causes a ripple effect of kindness, hope and compassion that affects everyone who happens to be fortunate enough to cross her path. Perhaps you should consider the ripple effect some?"

"Complete bullshit. The only ripple effect I'm interested in is the Galaxy chocolate one."

I can only shak' ma heid. Nora is so lovely and welcoming that I find myself offering to make dinner for everyone. She welcomes the idea as she has been only making soup or a salad for her and John.

"That, my dear, would be lovely as we've been eating soup and salad day-in-day-out and it's getting terribly boring as you can well imagine. I thank you and take you up on your kind offer. Lesley is a superb cook and made us dinner when she was here."

"Really? Well, I can cook also, in fact I could give good ole Nursie Nigella a run for her money. I insist that you, John and Jules take the time to catch up while I produce some delicacy or delisaky as she would say."

ANGE

I've had enough of our very own beloved Lezzers', nurse to the ill, coffee giver to the weary, donor to the homeless, cleaner of hostels, master baker to the homesick, carer to the infirm, gardener to landscapes and now chef to culinary clients. Little friend to all the fucking world. Is there anything that she can't/won't do? This meal is going to be hands down better than the mince and tatties or whatever she made for them. I pass Paul, the security golf cart fart, at breakneck speed as I head to the local store for the provisions.

He tries, but can't keep up with me on his toy go-cart. See ya sucker. I give him my best Queenie wave and blow him another kiss. That's bound to make his day. I see him waiting in the bushes when I return with the groceries, but he's sound asleep and doesn't see me as I drive through the gates. He'll be there a long time is my guess. I am tempted to honk my horn, but he must be weary from saving the hood from dangerous criminals ..not! How boring his job must be. The biggest excitement he's had in years is trying to chase me and Gertie down.

JULES

John is certainly on the mend, which he puts down to the care he received not only from his carers, but from Nora and Lesley also. Lesley apparently not only nursed him, but she read to him and kept him company while Nora took a much-needed, deserved break. I'd better keep that to myself as it seems to rile Ange up so much, and she's already trying to gain a one-upmanship over her. Who am I to tell her it has to come from a place of authenticity and not forced? Hell mend her.

"Tada, dinner is served."

The dining room is a dark heritage green with heavy, luxurious velvet Jacquard panels, the valance is held back with weighted, gold antique tassel tiebacks. The room is sumptuous, inviting and hospitable, well proportioned, book-lined with a roaring fire beneath a magnificent mahogany mantelpiece. The family's forefathers are encapsulated in large, 19th-Century gold leaf, ornate gilt frames that look easily down on the diners. It's a warm, old-fashioned opulent upper-class space. Four place settings have been set at the 16-seater mahogany table, two at the top, and two opposite each other in the centre at the sides. Each place setting has a plate, two large knives, three large forks, a soup spoon, a water goblet and, optimistically a wine glass to the right of the plate. The linen napkins have been folded into a bird of paradise. It looks beautiful.

"Where on earth did you learn how to do all this Ange? It was Lesley and I that worked as silver service waitresses while we were students, not you. I never thought you'd worked a day in your life."

"I haven't Jules, but my observation skills are highly honed, and I watched the staff on numerous occasions set our table."

"Woah, I had no idea."

"It's irrelevant, surely"

"You're so right Ange, it's how you treat yourself and others that truly matters. It looks resplendent and requires a wine that is in keeping with it. John, will you please do the honours?"

"Delighted to oblige my dear."

Well, blow me, I never thought I'd say this, but Ange has done herself proud, she's made vichyssoise, coq au vin, using of course some of the wine from the cellar, and to top it off, she's baked a sticky toffee pudding for dessert. John insists on pairing each course with something special from his collection and the soiree evolves into buoyant banter. We fondly share tales of Lesley's malaprops which we all find endearing, even Ange, and have us laughing out loud. I burst into tears all of a sudden.

"I have to tell you both something. We, or should I say I, as I need to take responsibility for my own actions here, I haven't been too kind and thoughtful towards Lesley of late and feel guilty about that. I hope to redeem myself somehow, find her wherever she is and can only hope that she forgives me."

Nora gets up from her seat and hugs me.

"We all have to consume bitter human experience some time in our lives and the trick is to recognize, accept, learn and grow from it. Lesley has a good heart and only has kind words and blessings for you."

This makes me cry even more and I sit there in her bosom and let it all pour out.

"Everyone has the privilege of their own unique path and experiences to be part of this great thing we call life. It's up to the individual to learn what is important to them. Those wise words, by the way, are straight from the horse's mouth, so to speak. Lesley knows without doubt that you're on different paths, and makes no judgment or comparisons as to your experiences. She believes that your paths will cross again and you will hopefully be in alignment."

I keep crying.

ANGE

Gosh the fact that she has no hard feelings towards us is surprising, but Nora never actually includes me in her words and I'm too scared to ask. It has kinda knocked the wind out of me - or is that the wine taking effect. I'm not so sure I'd be quite so forgiving and generous towards her if the foot was on the other boot, as she would say. The truth be told I don't really have anything negative to say. She cared for us, you know, looked after us, made us breakfast, lunch, dinner, nurtured and made us laugh. Constantly. She could be quite annoying though, straightening our clothes, removing fluff balls from our shorts, even chasing us to brush our hair. Does that, or even should that cancel out all the rest? Eh no it doesn't. When it's put like that, it does seem unfair and unkind. All she has ever shown us is friendliness and loving kindness. We must sound and be awful human beings. I'd hate to have a friend like me. What's happening to me? Am I becoming soft? Being broken open and vulnerable scares me. Shite, this has to be the wine talking. I feel my eyes begin to well up. Right that's enough. Better keep this all to myself for the time being.

"I'm off for a walk in the gardens before dessert if that's okay. Nothing like the smell of fresh grass under the stars."

JULES

Lesley gave up her valuable time, with no hidden agenda, to make an elderly couple more comfortable. How many people would do that, and if it did create a ripple effect, then I wanted to be in its slipstream. Ange has pissed off to the garden for a smoke and her comment about smelling fresh grass did not go unnoticed by me.

ANGE

I end up walking further down the drive than I plan and see that Paul is still there in his Tonka toy.

"Hey? Fancy some company?"

"Well, look who's here. It's Edwina herself, did you leave Patsy back at the manor?"

"That's so funny. Is your real job a comedian?"

"Come and have a seat. Is that a joint you have there?"

"Yeah, I need it. Want a toot?"

"Sure, why not, I'm off duty now."

"I'm pretty sure you can't be held responsible anyway for being stoned while driving a toy car anyway."

"It's battery operated so I'm pretty positive that I can't be charged."

"Definitely a comedian."

Not sure why or how, but I end up telling him all about my family.

"My mother is an alcoholic, I'm estranged from my older brother and my dad died three years ago. My dad and I were very close and he protected me from my mother's vitriol. I was a real daddy's girl. No man has or ever will come close to him. I guess it's easier for me to live a shallow life, not considering others' feelings because I can't even begin to feel or even want to sense my own shortcomings.

"It hurts too much to love, then lose it. I deliberately lost touch with mum and Roderick years ago, too painful I guess."

I wish I'd stopped there and shut up, but I carry on telling him all the vile things that I've said and done to Lesley. He doesn't bat an eyelid, takes an extra long draw, looks at me and smiles.

"There are two friends backpacking together and they're staying in a hostel near an enchanted forest. One of them is particularly mean and unkind to her so-called pal. She would tease, ridicule and put her down at every opportunity in order for everyone to see that she is funnier, more clever and brighter than her basic boring friend. One day the mean friend goes into the forest and stumbles upon a magical tree. She begins snapping the branches of a tree. She always seems so angry with the world. The tree says, 'Oh kind lady, please do not snap my branches off. If you spare me, I will give you golden apples'.

She agrees, but is disappointed with the numbers of apples the tree gives her. As anger overcomes her, she threatens to break the entire trunk if it doesn't give her more apples. The magical tree, instead, showers hundreds and hundreds of tiny needles upon her. Literally pinning her to the ground. She lays there, crying in pain, as the sun sets. The caring friend is worried when she doesn't appear back at the hostel so she goes in search of her friend. She finds her lying in pain near the tree, with hundreds of needles on her body. She rushes to her and laboriously removes each needle, lovingly and gently. After she finishes, the mean girl apologises for treating her so badly and promises to be better. The tree sees and believes the change in the mean girl's heart and gives them all the golden apples they would ever need. Do you know the moral?"

"Yes, if at first you don't succeed... skydiving is not for you?"

"Ah, you're the real comedienne here."

"Go on then Paul, indulge me, then I have to get back to Downton before they send out a search party and find me being needled by you."

"Friendships, my dear girl, are as important as books, you don't need to read them all, just pick the best ones. It is important to be and to recognize kindness and graciousness as it is the ultimate reward. And how did you know my name's Paul?"

"It's on your badge. Goodnight and thank you."

"I'm trying not to be negative here, but remember I'm battery-operated. Feel free to charge me."

As I smile and walk back up the drive he shouts: "I'm positive, charge me anytime. I think we'd make a great power couple."

I can't resist it and holler back down the driveway. "By the way, see that story of yours? I think it's a crock of shite."

I smile and skip back up the drive. Sticky toffee pudding awaits.

They're all still sitting in the dining room chewing the fat. I come in, hug John, hug Jules, hug Nora and sit down beside her.

"Where have you been? We were beginning to get worried."

"I've been chatting to Paul the Hall Cart Cop."

"Have you been drinking with him?"

"No."

"Have you been drinking out there at all?"

"No, why do you ask Nora?"

"It's just that you have your elbow in my sticky toffee pudding."

"Bloody Nora, I have, I mean bloody hell, not you Nora, I'm surprised that I didn't even notice the toffee sauce seeping through my sweater."

I wipe the dripping ice cream and sauce from my elbow and wipe it on my jeans. I hope it isn't too obvious that I'm stoned out of my head.

"Let me take a stab in the dark here. Your eyes are pink, bloodshot and half shut, your behaviour, although amusing, is somewhat bizarre and you have a fixed smile on your face. Now, I am no Ms. Marple, but this eccentric old broad and her wingman husband here have been around the block many, many times and we are both familiar with the effects of marijuana and when someone is completely off their face."

"I am so, so sorry Nora, I can only apologise for my behaviour. You see, I have a chemical imbalance of sorts and need the medicinal benefits of marijuana to keep me normal. I can pack my things and leave immediately."

"What do you think John?"

"I believe you know my answer Nora."

"Indeed. On the contrary to you leaving my dear, we would like for you and Jules to stay here for as long as you care to. It's also been many years since John and I partook in the substance and I believe tonight is the perfect occasion to do it again. John?"

"Bloody Nora, I was hoping that's where this conversation was going."

"Wow, just wow. Okay. Let me go to the car and get a bag."

"Dear lord, how many bags do you have?"

"You don't want to know the answer, trust me on that."

JULES

I can't believe what just happened. I was waiting for Nora and John to blow a gasket. Instead, their inner Cheech and Chong made an appearance and the rest of the evening evolved into a rolling, smoking, laughing soiree where the mood soared with buoyant banter, fun and frivolity, a melody of music and uncontrollable giggling ensued. It was a timeless occasion where past and present memories and relationships intertwined to create the narrative. It's the best night ever. I love my godparents and Ange I suppose. Of course, we stayed longer than we intended, actually a week over our "only one night" self-imposed limit. We help in the garden, the kitchen, doing odd jobs and general maintenance around the place, even getting Paul, the Hall Cop to help out. I manage to clean the pool without falling in, well, only once, but to be fair, it was almost deliberate. Nora and John even include Paul for dinner. It turns out he's a retired cop, widowed recently, kids all grown and flown the coop and loves the company and is more than happy to muck in and help them out. Everyone gels well. Ange continues to shine in the kitchen producing a Michelin-worthy meal every night, which is always accompanied by John's select wine and an illegal 'herb' shaker on the table for those that want the extra spice in their life. One night, John shares the origin of Nora's name.

"Bloody Norah is an urban myth that was coined after a servant of the wealthy Duke Wodingtonshire in the 17th Century. She earned the name Bloody Nora after she killed a servant of the duke with a stick of celery."

Ange loses it at this stage and can't help but spray her lemon posset across the table. We all belly laugh and poor John can hardly continue with his story.

"When the Duke caught her repeatedly slapping the bloody corpse with the stick of celery, he shouted "Oh dear god you're all bloody, Nora....and after beating her, he banished her to a basement cell for three years."

I'm not sure any of us can take any more of this - I am now in so much pain from laughing that I think I've burst my appendix. Nora tries to cover his mouth with her hand to stop him continuing.

"When the three years was up, the Duke set her free, but Nora insisted on working for the Duke. Reluctantly he gave her the job of cleaning the stables only to find four days later she had killed another servant, this time with a kettle."

"No more."

"When he found her once again maiming her victim with the dented kettle, he cried: "Oh, bloody Norah" and grabbed a horseshoe and attempted to kill Nora. After a long struggle Nora escaped and left the Battered Duke cussing to himself.

"Bloody Norah!"

"Please stop!"

"The expression came from the Duke himself as he would tell the story of Nora to all he knew and would always refer to her as 'Bloody Nora'. As the Duke aged he grew senile and would be heard talking to himself and shouting '.... BLOODY NORA!!!!......'

"As people around saw him still as a respected figure in the community, they all started saying Bloody Nora as they all thought the Duke had invented a new cuss word. It stuck and people continue to use it to the present day."

The preposterousness of it all keeps us in stitches for at least an hour. Ange teases them both by using stalks of celery as a centrepiece the next night as a reminder to John what could happen if he pushes his luck too far. John continues his generosity by pairing every dish, including the celery, with another stupendous wine from his stock. The company is enlightening, scintillating and easy. We laugh until our sides hurt, and the shaker has been refilled three times.

ANGE

On our very last night, we tell them of Mikey's Mission to reunite with Lesley.

"We've undertaken the mission to go get her and bring her back to Sydney."

"Mikey isn't actually aware that she left us, has gone walkabout and is in The Bush somewhere."

They listen in silence for a few moments, with no judgements, criticism or opinions as we share our exploits from our point of view. When we have regaled most of the tales that are relevant to Lesley, Nora nods her head.

"That is super, very exciting to hear. Lesley is very clear that she loves and misses Mikey. She is incredibly grateful what travelling and relationships have shown her and feels very blessed to have someone like him in her life. That's the way I felt and feel about John. When you know, you know. It is such an honour to share this incredible journey we call life with your soulmate. Each moment in life holds such power, so it would be a shame to miss the opportunity by being upset about the past and anxious for the future, as all we have is the ability to ground ourselves in this glorious earth in the here and now - only then have we won. Is it a mere coincidence that NOW and WON, EARTH and HEART contain the same letters? I believe not. I'm excited for you both, this is a unique opportunity to grow and learn and see what is important."

"Nora, that is some intense profound shit. I think my head is about to explode."

"ANGE!!"

"No worries Jules, when the student is ready, the teacher appears and vice versa. Isn't that right Ange?"

"If you say so. I believe I'd take anything that you say in like soup Nora."

"Changing the subject and moving swiftly on here, why do you keep peacocks here? Granted they're beautiful, but oh boy do they screech and squawk a fair bit."

"I am so glad you ask that Jules, they are a reminder."

"Reminder? To buy ear plugs next time you're in town?"

"You're funny, very quick off the mark Ange. I like that in you. Humour at the right time, in the right place, with the right intention, definitely allows you to embrace the joy of being. Which ultimately is our J.O.B in life. To embrace, accept, be excited and enthusiastic about the joy of being."

"My job right now is to finish this wine, that will give me joy."

"Ignore her. What about the peacocks Nora?"

"Do you know that peacocks eat poisonous plants?"

"Why?"

"Well, they eat hard, pointed razorlike thorns which are processed in their gut and contribute to their plumage and feathers having the most magnificent colours, shapes and textures, unmatched throughout nature for their extraordinary beauty."

"Seriously?"

"Yes. And so it is with us, Jules, Ange, me, John, Paul, Lesley, Mikey and everyone else. We all get the opportunity to stumble, to fall and make mistakes. Often that which is the hardest to digest, to process, to integrate into our life experiences is what ultimately transforms us in a positive way. We become who we are meant to be sometimes by having to consume some hard-edged, bitter thorns of human experience."

"OMG, this is heavy. How much have you had to smoke Nora?"

"Just listen Ange."

"Thank you, Jules, who among us hasn't stumbled? We have failed at relationships, and then those failures have propelled us to more deeply understand what relationships are for and how to master the art of loving."

"I hope you're paying attention here Ange."

"I think that's for you also Jules."

"It's for everyone to hear when they're ready. We have grieved the loss of a loved one and then come through the experience with more appreciation of every day for nature, the small things that give us pleasure and those we love."

"Here's a small thing that gives me pleasure. I'll spark it up shall I?"

"You find it easier to deflect rather than feel uncomfortable Ange, which is fine, and when the time is right, you will hear the message. We have lost business and work opportunities, but then on reflection, see that loss and failure was exactly what we required at that time. We have even been betrayed, then experienced the incredible power of acceptance and forgiveness. We make mistakes then experience the heart of the matter where we acknowledge, atone for and make amends for them all. Anything and everything can be a platform for growth or a lesson to be learned. Sometimes it is our suffering that mysteriously delivers us to the true essence within ourselves. Having tasted that which is most bitter, we often taste that which is most sweet."

"Here Nora, take a toke on this before you go on."

"Ha, okay, pass it here. Our hearts have been broken, leaving us broken open and vulnerable. The tiny light of hope that we glimpse in the midst of our suffering can become a light so bright that the immensity of its power seems second only to the depth of its tenderness. Having entered the regions of our personal hopelessness, we find at last where true hope lies. We come to understand more clearly who we are and why we are on the earth."

"So, remind me what this has to do with peacocks? I'm lost."

"The peacock's plumage is a living example and reminder of turning poison into beauty. This amazing animal is a symbol of how suffering and pain can yield strength and beauty. Every event, experience and occasion is an opportunity to learn and grow from or not…or not…"

"So happy I didn't ask about the Grinny pigs you keep in the cage in the kitchen."

"We breed them for our dinner guests."

"Phew, that's a relief as I used one in the stew tonight?"

"What!??"

"Joke!"

We collapse laughing. My head's like mince right now. So I slope off to bed, one hand holding my aching laughing belly, the other between my legs as I'm afraid I'm going to pee on their

Persian rugs. That night I have nightmares about peacocks pecking out my eyes and I wake up in a cold sweat. What am I meant to learn, if anything, from all this? Maybe we have been a tad harsh on Lesley? Who's that? What did I just call her? That's interesting. Maybe all the expensive wine, good food and copious amounts of drugs have softened my brain. Better keep that to myself for the time being, I wouldn't want anyone to think I've gone mushy. Like in Great Expectations though, I need to find a way to perhaps redeem myself, even if slightly. It's not easy for me to be broken open and expose the ugly truth of who I really am. A lonely, sad, selfish, egotistical individual. That's quite the resume right there. I do have great hair, teeth, boobs, figure and my eyes are like pure liquid gold. Those, however, all make up my external being, not my inner one. I cry myself back to sleep. I wake later with a spring in my step and a resolve to be compassionate, more aware, more boring and intense probably, but nicer. Who knew that old people could be so informative and so much fun?

"I'm genuinely sad to leave and promise I'll be back sometime, if for no other reason than to help polish off your wine cellar and to put those noisy iridescent blue noisy fuckers in a cast iron pot."

"I feel overcome with emulsion Aunt Nora, Uncle John. I'm not sure where all this crying and nonsense is coming from?"

"Well girls, John and I have loved having you here and from the heart of my bottom, as Lesley would say, it's been an absolute delight."

We finally manage to get into Gertie after lots of hugging, kissing, crying and waving. Even Paul is at the gates to give us a jolly send off, much to his relief I'm sure. He can now start behaving like a real security guard and not a drug-taking, booze-swilling interloper. That actually may well continue as John and Nora have offered him a position of general manager, which I'm sure he'll take.

JULES

We drive out the gates and head towards the Great Ocean Highway. It's roughly 12.5 hours to drive to Adelaide, so we'll stop in Horsham for the night.

"Okay Jules, let's make like a couple of hippies and blow this joint."

"I'm on it Bud."

"I hope they like the leaving present I left them, aside from a couple of herb 'shakers' that is Costello."

"What was that?"

"I left a plaque on their lawn near the peacocks that says: 'Please keep off the grass'."

"The stakes have never been higher."

"A friend with weed, is a friend indeed."

"In weed, we trust."

"Can I be 'blunt' here Jules, I think I've had a difficult but positive and powerful realisation about my behaviour. A shift of sorts."

"A shit?"

"A SHIFT, you know a change."

"A shit or a shift, same thing really, it's all still spewing out of your mouth like diarrhea."

"Very funny, you're dope."

"I hear you though, but actions do speak louder than words you know. Now turn that map the correct way and don't feck this up. I don't want to be driving into the sea with your amateur directional skills. Speaking of shift, Thelma and Louise ain't happening today, well, at least not on my shift anyway. Do you see the hitchhiker ahead, up there? Do you think we should stop? Or have we decided those days of picking up complete strangers to ride with are behind us?"

"Hitchhiker you say? I think she's complimenting you on your driving. We have a long road ahead of us, I say keep the clutch out and drive."

"She could have been a serial killer anyway."

"Not sure on that. The chances of having two serial killers in the same van are astronomical."

"Ha, you know Ange, the best therapy sometimes is a drive and music."

"It gives us the freedom."

"I don't want your freedom. I don't want to play around. I don't want no hitchhiker."

"Jules, all I want right now is you."

"But you know that I'll forgive you, just this once, twice, forever, cause Ange, you could drag me to hell and back, just as long as we're together."

"Freedom."

Aside from the occasional glass tap, singing, munching and crunching, gentle passenger snoring, we get to Mount Gambier in relative silence. I think we are both in deep contemplation about the past week to make conversation. Not only was the week magnificent, we have learned so much from it all. No matter how many degrees one has, or how many textbooks one has read, or what type of education one received, there are some things that only life can teach. Lessons that can only be learned from the knocks, the connections and people that one meets in the biggest school we have the good fortune to grace and attend. The School of Life and Strife.

After checking in to Brambuk Backpackers, we head to the food court in the local mall for something to eat. We've enjoyed rich, delicious, fresh food for a week and are secretly excited about having some fast food crap. I get some chicken/peacock/guinea/grinny pig nuggets with a coke and Ange gets a double cheeseburger, fries and strawberry milkshake. We sit down in the common area surrounded by the counters of multiple food vendors, having a Captain Cook at the hustle and bustle of their fellow diners.

"Don't look now, but there's an absolutely gorgeous-looking Adonis at the table over there giving me the sexy eye."

"What? The handsome guy with the George Michael beard eating the ice cream cone?"

"The very one. Try not to make it so obvious though. He's definitely noticed that I've clocked him, clocking me."

"Well check him out. He's not half making his intentions obvious Ange. I won't crick my neck ogling this sensual exchange, however, I'd like a blow by blow, so to speak, running commentary on what he's doing?"

"Mmmmmm, have him washed, scrubbed, prepared and sent to my boudoir Prissy."

"By the tilt of your head and the twinkle in your eyes, I can feel the sexual tension pulsating between the two of you. What's he doing now?"

"He's licking his cone in a very seductive manner, it's dripping down the length of the wafer. His very long tongue is gliding, full span from the base to the tip. He hasn't broken eye contact with me yet."

"Bloody hell, this is so hot. Press your breasts out a bit and pretend they're two scoops of vanilla ice-cream with two bright red maraschino cherries on top. That's right, rim your chipples"

"Chipples?"

"A combination of cherries and nipples. Now carry on rimming them slowly with your middle finger."

"Mmmhmmm. He can have both scoops with the cherry on the top."

"I can barely contain myself, it's all very arousing being picked up by an incredibly sexy stranger in the middle of a food court."

"There's a throbbing heat coursing its way through my tingling vagina."

"Mine too. If I'm not careful here, I'm going to come and I've got my back to him."

"He has a twinkle in his eye and a provocative smile on his full, creamy lips. Ahhhh, I'm anticipating some hot, sweaty, active desires and games being played out here later. Full steam ahead captain."

"Can I come? Again!"

"It's all very tantalizing."

"Eat your heart out Jilly Cooper."

"Well, eat something out, that's for sure."

"I can see the swell in your voluptuous breasts heaving from across the table. Your pupils are the size of a 12-inch black vinyl record."

Let's hope it's not the only 12-inch record to be seen today."

"I'm pickin' up good vibrations, he's giving me the excitations, oom bop bop, I'm pickin' up good vibrations, good vibrations, oom bop bop. He's giving me the excitations. Now what? I can hardly stand it."

"He's lashing the cream slowly, gently, deliberately, all the way round and round to the very tip."

"OMG, blow him a seductive kiss."

"I'd certainly like to be blowing something."

"We're in the middle of a food court for feck sake, a kiss will do for now."

"His lips, and mine, are glistening with the Italian-looking spumoni he's toying with. My entire body is vibrating, pulsing, throbbing with excitement and anticipation. Somebody try to stop me."

"How can you stop a pocket rocket?"

"Sounds like rocket man has his bags all packed and ready to blast off."

"Lick it till ice-cream."

"Never mind his ice-cream. He's definitely making you and me both melt."

"Mmmmhmmm. Here goes. He's pushing his chair back. He's putting on some really dark round shades."

"Huh? That's a tad bizarre. We're inside."

"He certainly will be soon. He's getting up."

"By the sounds of it, he already is."

"He's picked up a stack of thick white poles that are each about 20cm long from the floor. They seem attached. He's holding the rubber grip handle and giving them a shake. They've unfolded out in about five sections. Oh, for fuck sake!"

"What? WHAT?"

"It's only a fucking folding white walking stick."

"No! You're not saying..."

"Yes, I am. He's visually impaired"

"Bwah ha ha. You mean to say, you almost went on a blind date?"

"Oh, my giddy aunt. I'm mortified."

"Haaaa haaa ha. Do you know for curtain he's blind?"

Ange brings her wrist to her mouth and whispers into it.

"Take the shot. Take the fucking shot."

"Well, I for one didn't see that coming."

"Neither did he."

"From now on we have to be super alert and keep an eye on things."

"I could call him back, tell him I'm open to him reading the braille bumps around my nipples with his finger lickin', ice-cream lapping tongue."

"I just called to say I love you, I just called to say how much I care. I just called to say I see you stare, and I mean it from the heart of my bottom."

"I think I'm the one as blind as a bat here."

"You got blindsided on that one for sure, Ange. It is almost like the blind leading the blind here."

"They do say love is blind..."

"Love? Spoiler alert here, it's more like lust."

"Yup. Let's make like a guillotine and head off before anyone catches on that I have just made a complete and utter tit of myself."

It's a relaxing evening playing backgammon, and as it's only five hours to Adelaide, we even manage a long lie. We decide that, aside from pee stops, we can do it in one go. We stop at a service station in Keith, fill Gertie up, stretch our legs, buy some water and I buy a bag of dough rings for the remainder of the journey. I try to hide them from her as I know what she's like and will eat the majority, probably leaving just one for me. I have to wait until she's sleeping before I sneak one, but she hears the rustling of the paper bag and is all of a sudden awake and alert, like a dog in heat. I'm forced to put the entire thing in my mouth so as not to raise suspicion.

"What was that?"

I can't speak as my mouth is full of very dry powdered dough. I shrug my shoulders.

"Do you smell that?? It's a sweet, sugary smell?"

Another shrug. I take a side glance at her.

"What the fuck is that on your face?"

Another shrug. It's really hard to swallow as it feels like hard, dried playdough sprinkled with sugar granules.

"Your face is moving."

As she says that I notice a tingling sensation in and around my mouth. I smatter the windscreen and dashboard with the remainder of the pureed batter. I watch in horror as a saliva trail mixed with sugar, batter and feckin real-live ants trickle down the glass, console and wheel. I turn to look at Ange.

"Jesus, you look like you have a live designer beard going on there. Your face is positively mobile. Fuck, it's covered in ants!"

As she says that, I feel the army of little ants marching in and around my entire face. I brake hard and jump out at the side of the road.

"Arrrgghhh!"

I dance around spitting, wiping and killing the mass colony off my body. The pesky black critters are everywhere. Up my nostrils, on my arms and on the powdered sugar on my top lip. I can feel them swimming around inside my mouth lodging themselves between my teeth. Ange stands on the verge before me, one hand on her hip, the other pinching a white paper bag between her thumb and pointer finger. She drops it to the ground. It is swarming with ants. My bag of doughrings is totally infested.

"Are you being ANTisocial here? Being sneaky and trying to avoid sharing with me?"

"Oh gawd, I can feel their dead carcases between the enamel tombstones inside my mouth. You'll have to drive, I've got the heebie jeebies now."

"Serves you right for being so selfish and I'm AdamANT about that."

"They're biting me and I can feel where their pincers have left their spotty, stubble marks."
"Come on Captain Kirk, let's make like the Starship Enterprise and have them beam us up Spotty."

By the time we get to Adelaide my tongue and the inside of my cheeks are red raw from all the internal rubbing, sucking, squashing, poking and swallowing. My fault for not inspecting the bag of fried round balls with sugar sprinkled ants on top more closely.

"I'm so glad you're letting me drive Jules, I feel positively BuoyANT."

I take it all on my blistered ant-bitten chin. But she is persistANT and carries on ridiculing me for the rest of the journey.

We arrive in Adelaide just after teatime and check in to the local Y. Again, we would have stayed at the backpackers, but yet again, they say they're full. Is it a mere coincidence or do they have a hotline between backpackers alerting them to trouble ahead? I'm sure not, but…..anyway, it's becoming more than a mere coincidence. Backpackers don't have the same rules and regulations as the Y which is so much more appealing and better suited to us. We still have to do chores, which enrages Ange. That in itself is quite bizarre as she bent over backwards to help John and Bloody Nora with cooking, cleaning, even feeding the screaming peacocks. She didn't even need to be asked, she just did it.

There must be some kind of rule-breaking gene in her body. I noticed on our drive here that there is some rattling coming from Gertie which needs to be checked out in the morning before any long-distance driving is done. We're heading into The Outback soon and we don't want to be caught short and break down there as it could be days, if not weeks, before someone comes to our rescue. I wouldn't be in the slightest bit surprised if there isn't an ant mound in the engine that's been built by the doughring escapees.

ANGE

I tell Jules I'll do the chores at the hostel in exchange for the late key. See it as an act of random kindness from yours truly. Actually, I still feel guilty about her buckled feet. The manager tells me to clean the showers and sweep the patio before getting the key. What is wrong with me? That's a rhetorical question. But seriously, what is wrong with me? It's not like cleaning a shower or sweeping the patio is a big deal, but I hate it when I'm told I have to do something. Like I have no choice in the matter. Well I do have a choice and that's not doing it at all. Put that in your pipe and smoke it.

There seems to be some fun people at the hostel, so I suggest an Adelaide pub crawl effective immediately. There is a reason for my madness asking some of these people as one or two of them look like goody-two-shoes and suck-ups so are bound to have done their jobs, therefore they will have the late key. Upstairs for thinking, downstairs for dancing. There's a lovely lad, Jamie from Essex, who I have my beady little eye set on, a boy child called Justin Savory. He's not an actual child, but he looks it - went to La Di Da Eton, speaks like he has plums in his mouth and is on a gap year before heading to Cambridge or Oxford. Same thing really. And Jacob, a larger-than-life, chubby chap from Belfast. This special occasion deserves some extra special attention, I think.

"What the hell are you doing?"

"These are my magnetic nipple clamps"

"What the hell are you doing with those?"

"Well, in the unlikely event that I am going to get no action tonight, these little spherical beauties will have to do."

"Can't we go out and have a normal drink with normal people without adding some S & M?"

"Clearly you've never tried them. They will bring some intense sensations to what might turn out to be a rather mundane night. Do you know how many nerve endings are in your nipples?"

"Never mind endings, would it not be easier to end the evening and leave rather than diverting your attention to your tits?"

"My attention may very well be their attention."

"You are seriously unbelievable and so EXTRA."

"What exactly do you mean by that?"

"You take it so far, where most people would stop, you continue with a little bit extra. You're completely over the top."

"With any luck, I will be over the top... over the top of some nubile young chap from Essex. Given the magnetic nipple rings, he won't be able to help himself from being totally attracted to me."

"Ha, well, if having magnetic clamps on your erogenous zones helps you pull, then I'll be signing up for some."

"You're a bloke magnet without them."

"Sometimes I'm repelled by the ones they attract."

"Stick with me kid, not too close though or they may never be able to pull us apart."

Roll on many, many hours, copious amounts of adult beverage and here we all are, stumbling back through Elder park singing "Born to Be Alive".

Not sure how that song pops into my head, but I love it and think it should be my mantra song. "Born, born to be alive, born to be alive, yes we were born, born, born, born to be alive. People ask me why I never find a place to stop and settle down, down, down. Down Under." I remember seeing the video somewhere years ago and try to choreograph everyone in pairs to reenact it. Not everyone knows the song, let alone the video, so it ends up as a massive pile up instead. Grass stains on knees, elbows, chins and backs. How does it get much better than this? I totally blindside Jamie with a side tackle, he doesn't even see me coming, but he will. However, it doesn't all go according to plan as my magnetic nipple balls clamp themselves to his spaver. At least I'm hoping that it's his spaver and not a Prince Albert he's had pierced to his genitals.

"Can someone please help here? We're kinda stuck."

"I knew you were attracted to him Ange, it beggars belief."

"Never mind beggars belief, how about beggar's relief. PLLLLEEEASE?"

"Those magnets are strong, it's not going to be easy to pull you apart. It is, however, entertaining watching his spaver going up in perfect synchronicity with your heavy breathing."

"Shame someone hasn't invented face recognition underwear yet, that would have liberated me faster than you can."

JULES

Silly cow, she's gone and got herself stuck to Jamie's zip and they're stuck together tightly. Not that he's complaining, mind. Our quiet game of tangles becomes a Tug o' War. This isn't the tug that she had in mind I'm sure. I take hold of Ange's waist, Justin holds mine and Big Jacob grabs Jamie. All the others take sides and we pull against the force of the world's strongest magnet. It suddenly gives up and we all fly in opposite directions creating two pile-ups. I look at Ange.

"Lose the magnets or your breasts will be picking up all the 'Men at Work' road signs."
"Who can it be now? Who can it be now? I'll be trapped, and here I'll have to stay, I've done no harm, I keep to myself, there's nothing wrong with my mental state."

"I beg to differ."

After dancing, tangles and an impromptu tug o' war in the park until very, very late, we womble our way back to the hostel, only to find the door is unsurprisingly locked and lights are out. It is 3 am, so no shocker there. Thankfully Ange has done her chores in exchange for the late key.

"You do the honours Ange."

"Ah, well, therein lies the problem."

I stare her down.

"Did you do your chores?"

"I meant to, but never actually got round to it."
Oh no, not again. My feet start throbbing from the memory of the
Tasmanian U-bend. She was given a list of chores to do. How hard
can it be to carry that out?

"Shirley someone has a late key."

Turns out that no, no one has a late key. Bunch of feckin
slackers. We decide it's easier to wake the manager, rather than
trying to break in, and there is no way I'm sleeping in Gertie with
eight relative strangers. The manager eventually opens the door
and informs us we get extra duties as punishment.

"You'll be doing mine in addition to your own, Ange. Your
reluctance to conform has come back to bite you in the bahookey."

"What a pain in the ass you can be also Jules."

"Here's the thing, Ange, you should never trust your
tongue when your heart is bitter."

"Calm the fuck down will you. It'll get done."

"Never in the history of calming down has anyone ever
calmed down by being told to calm down."

"You're a real piece of work."

"A masterpiece obviously."

"I'm going to bed."

ANGE

What is she like? It's not a big deal. I'll do her chores, my chores and everyone else's if that makes her happy. I'll do so many fucking jobs that I'll accumulate enough late fucking keys for an entire hostile army. There's construction going on in the place so it hardly seems fair to ask us to sweep a constant stream of sawdust from the floor anyway.

I do all my chores and hers the next day and Mr Bumble, the warden, gives me the key glorious late key. I won't lose this in a hurry and slip it into my bra and make sure it is holding fast to my nipple accessory. There is no way I'm losing these spherical balls of pleasure in a hurry. Aside from Jules, I'm not sure I've ever seen someone as Grumpy as him. Why be a warden of a YOUTH hostel if you clearly don't care for the YOOF. Due to the fact I'm not very good at following rules and regulations, I decide that I shouldn't in fact hold the key, and give the prized possession to Jules to look after.

It's a glorious day so we buy a few goons, liberate a bag of hubcap stash and head off to the River Torrens. We collect all the ample supplies of empty goons from Gertie and peg the bladders along with a few full ones between two trees with a long piece of rope. By lying on the ground underneath our homemade clothesline and opening the spigot, we extract the last remnants of wine from the empty bladders and begin on the full ones. When the goons are well and truly dry, we are the ones that are utterly and completely bladdered. We blow up each goon and decide to have a competition between three teams to see who can make the best goon raft, then sail it on the river. Seems like a great idea, what could possibly go wrong? After designing, blowing, tying, sticking, pegging and constructing our fabulous shiny, silver, inflatable rafts, they are ready to be launched. Jules's team raft looks almost passable, held together with black sticky-backed plastic and Val's knicker elastic. Not sure it's as watertight as a duck's backside though. The hearty crew on team three are not as enthusiastic or as competitive as us and their float looks more like a puffed-up aluminium rug.

I'm beginning to feel light-headed and faint from all the huffing and puffing. I have another hit of hashish to settle myself before we christen Bluebottle and Eccles in a ceremonial sack-slap across their bow before launching them on their maiden voyage. Team three and their Moet et Chandon mat are a complete non-starter, so they sit on it on the embankment and watch the The Goon Show as it commences. The very brazen goon tub-mariners toss their floats, and I use that term loosely, off the jetty. Some jump, some clamber, some miss their raft completely. Jules, being the lightest in her crew, lands square in the centre without even a ripple, but when Big Billy tries to land beside her, he propels her skyward and in a very unlady-like cartwheel fashion. She flies far and high into the deep blue yonder, arms windmilling uncontrollably through the air only to about turn mid-flight and come racing back down to earth, belly flopping into the centre of the murky water. Her arms and legs are flying every direction. What goes up must come down. From the middle of the river, she's whooping.

"Mayday, mayday. Taking in water."

She can swim just fine, so I take her squeals to be a mere distraction and a cunning plan on her part to prevent us from winning the race. Man overboard before they even begin. The goon voyage has been launched. We paddle ours out from the shore before we climb aboard. No flies on us. We're only a short way out when Jules appears at the helm asking permission to climb aboard. We drag her up and over, but her bra catches on a spigot and off it comes. However, all is not lost, she has managed to grab the oars from her craft as she took flight and is able to use them to stand on the bow. She ties her ample bra top between two of the oars and we now have a sail with which to catch wind. The hope of being the first modern-day Guinness Book of Records goon entrants is in our midst, we are set to change history forever. However, the dream of the floating goon is soon quashed as my trio of dickheads, oops I meant deckhands, can't keep their balance and fall off the edge into the wild brown yonder.

Myself and Jamie settle into coxswain position, while Roger takes up the position of Cabin Boy at the rear. Roger the cabin boy? And why the hell not. Jules stands perfectly balanced at the front like a mermaid figurehead. It takes us 15 minutes to paddle from one side of the jetty to the other, I'm knackered from all that "heave ho".

There's plenty of shouting coming from the cheap seats on the safety of the dry embankment. The boys are doing an amazing job and have flexed their muscles and paddled within sight of the shore.

"Land ahoy Captain!"

We jeer at the other team who are catching up rapidly. It's going to be a very close finish. Team three are the perfect cheerleaders for the final stretch. Their rooting, encouragement, jumping, screaming, whistling and chanting gives us that final push.

"Let it run, let it glide, just make sure there's no wine inside."

They do look a little winey, though. They win by a baw-hair, but we notice they aren't actually aboard their deflated raft, but are in actual fact waist-high in the water, dragging their sorry, punctured silver sinking blanket asses through the water. We are the true winners, rejoicing the fact by cracking open another goon and sparking up another dooby. Someone has brought a boombox and we dance on the dock of the bay until the sun sets. Sittin when the evenin' comes, watchin the goons cruise in, then watchin' me roll another spliff again. I grab the boombox, my wine in one hand, my joint in the other and head to sit at the end of the jetty so I can sit like Otis at The Dock of the Bay.

JULES

We're all chillaxing when Ange seizes the boombox, hoists it on to her shoulder and starts prancing, bordering on sprinting, backwards to the end of the pier. One hand clutches a full cup of wine, the other a joint. Between alternating mouthfuls of wine, and taking a few drags, she shouts.

"Let's go sit on our docks at the end of the day."

Clearly too much alcohol has been consumed and for sure too much marry J wanna smoked. It's funny though. I know she means sitting ducks on the bay. We can all see the edge of the pier coming far too close to her but she doesn't stop. Suddenly she disappears off the end. We all run up the jetty and peer over. Thankfully the tide has gone out and the river is low. There she is, sitting like Shrek in his swamp, river gunk on her head, full glass of wine in hand, what a pro, boombox still on her shoulder, joint in her mouth like Fag Ash Lil. She's singing out of the side of her mouth like Popeye, "Here I am sitting on my dock IN the bay".

We pull her out, saving her wine, dooby and box first, then hoist and drag her sodden body up and over the edge. I'm surprised she doesn't end up with an undercarriage full of splinters. It cracks us up and we laugh all the way back to the hostel. The moody manager doesn't see the funny side as we come in wet, sunburned, pissed and stoned from our day trip. He hauls his lardy ass from his grubby armchair in reception and comes through to the common room, where we are all dancing to Super Trouper.

"You may well all be backpackers, but it may have escaped your notice here that this establishment is a youth hostel, and there are certain expectations as to how you behave while staying here."

"You say backpackers like it's a dirty word."

"Carry on like this and you will leave me with no option other than to report your inappropriate behaviour to my superior."

"Inappropriate? Is twerking an offence here? Shirley the festival state of South Australia is trendy and open-minded enough to accept a dance in a sexually provocative manner which involves thrusting movements of the derriere and hips while in a low, how low can you go, squatting stance?"

"I have to say, Ange, I'm in complete agreement with the warden here as, in many cases, just watching some twerking participants is very offensive."

"Hardly worth getting your knickers in a twist over unless you're doing it incorrectly that is."

"Take this as your only and final warning - carry on like this and I'll be writing you up for disorderly behaviour."

"Disorderly? This ain't nothing."

"Two negatives make a positive Ange. Which means it is disorderly I think."

"You've been warned."

He is almost back to the safety of his grubby little office when he spots the gash on Ange's elbow.

Ange does have a rather nasty cut on her elbow and her makeshift bandage made from some sanitary fairy hammock has come unstuck and is flapping about. She's been spraying the room like a crimson rainbow from the bloody gash. The warden suddenly goes into duty doctor mode when he sees the blood pissing from the laceration and goes to fetch his first aid kit from his office.

"You, little lady, are really lucky I have this to hand as it was only recently restocked."

"Gosh, how fortuitous for me. Serendipity clutched right there in your sweaty little mitts."

"A nurse stayed here recently and was shocked at the basic kit, so replenished it with new supplies and put it in my office."

"Do you happen to remember her name? Or did she say orifice instead of office?"

"You must be a white witch as I do remember her referring to my office that way. I'd have to look up her name though."

"Oh, don't bother yourself. I'm pretty sure I can fill in that detail for myself."

"Let me tell you this, if she hadn't replenished the first aid supplies, it would have meant a hospital visit for you as that cut requires steri-strips and she added them to this kit."

"Whoop de fucking doo."

ANGE

Probably not. I mean, what are the odds? I can't help myself though and ask if he remembers her name perchance. As I'm asking, I look at the replenished full first aid box and immediately recognize her handwriting, itemizing every piece along with notes saying how to apply, use and what they're intended for. FFS!!! Is this some horrible kind of farce I'm in - you know, where the guy Jeremy Beagle comes out and tells me I've Been Framed or is it some twisted nightmare? Crikey, here we are again, our very own Lezzers', nurse to the ill, coffee giver to the weary, donor of all tat to the homeless, cleaner of hostels, master baker to the homesick, carer of the infirm, Alan Titmarch of all things garden and landscapes, Jammy Oliver to culinary clients, Nurse Nightingale to first aid kits. Little friend to all the fucking world. Is there anything that she can't/won't do? Aside from being on Queenie's New Year's Honor list that is. She'll be up for a sainthood next. Hmmm, do I detect some jealousy creeping into my thoughts and voice? I do hope not. I tear off the stained sanitary pad, drop it to the ground and kick it under the sofa. Someone doing their tour of duty chores is in for a right bloody surprise. I wonder how long it's going to fester under there before being found? I hope it's the overweight bumbling, buffoon of a warden that comes across it first. Unlikely though, as that would mean him actually putting his lardy arse into some kind of housekeeping gear.

JULES

Oh, my goodness, Lesley has put a kit together, and of all people, Ange is the receiver of her well-considered generosity. The tension in the air is palpable and she's silent for a change, stewing in her own juices it seems. I can practically see the fumes oozing from her as Mr. Bumble cleans and dresses the wound, using everything Lesley has personally put in. I contemplate telling him that she's our friend, but one glance at the look on Ange's face persuades me otherwise. He continues waxing lyrical about how fabulous Lesley is and how sorry he was to see her leave, but she had a mission in The Outback that she needed to pursue. Ange is giving him that look, you know the one I mean, if looks could kill look. Staring at him with unwavering focus, no doubt imagining him and Lesley to be the effigy recipients of the daggers she's pinning on him. He returns her stare.

"Most backpackers are forgettable, but she is one in a million and is remembered here for her kindness, generosity and compassion."

"Indeed. She has the heart of a lioness and a lifetime ban from Taronga zoo. I would love to repay her with an axe of kindness myself."

ANGE

As soon as I'm all cleaned up, I tell Jules I want to leave in the morning. Time to get back on the road. The sooner we find Florence Fucking Nightingale, get her back to Sydney and be done with it all, the better. I'm sick of the constant reminder of goody-two-shoes. Perhaps, as unlikely as it seems, I'm missing something in all this.

"Is it just me that finds all this altruistic behaviour all a bit nauseating?"

"Why do you take all this so personally? This speaks so much more about you than it does about her Ange."

"What on earth does that even mean?"

"Look Ange, did you hear nothing that Nora said? It's about timing, when you're ready you will hear, reflect and respond in that order. When the teacher is ready, the student appears and vice versa. Look, all I can suggest is that you stay open-minded, like a parachute, it works best when open, stay heart-centred and speak to your own experience. On a different note, we're going to drive Gertie around the block, see if we can't work out where all the knocking is coming from."

"We?"

"Yeah, Jamie's going to take a look, says he's used to tinkering with cars."

"What? MY Jamie?"

"Settle petal. He's going to be under Gertie, not me. You really need to be pressing that verbal pause button of yours and spend more time listening and leaving any expectations of yourself and others at the door. I'll see you outside."

"Have you been digesting The Dummy Rule Book for Youth Hostellers?"

When did she swallow Buddha's book of psychobabble shite? I'm not taking anything personally. Or am I? I sulk for a bit more and hear some of what Jules said. Maybe Lesley's deeds highlight my lack and insecurities in some way. I

haven't been aware as to how lonely and sad I really am. It's easy for me to behave in a certain way without scratching beneath the surface as that only opens up a very dark, cluttered basement full of stuff. I know it no longer serves me but I'm not sure I'm ready to go down there with a torch and shine on what needs to be let go of.

I know Lesley is so much better than me in almost every way. Makes me feel quite sad actually. I miss my dad. I wish he was here to help guide me to be a better person. I sit all alone in the toilet allowing the tears to come. The years of sadness, anger, guilt and self-loathing flow from me like a burst dam. When my emotions eventually calm, I wash my face and go outside to find Jules. Jamie is underneath Gertie's carriage. Jules, Justin and Jacob are standing watching the mechanic at work. I notice that Jamie's tackle, which I recognize immediately as I have had my gums around those plums, are hanging out the side of his jersey shorts. I bend down to gently tuck them in.

"Himmen, yer giblets are hingin oot"

There's an almighty clatter and a few knocks from under the van.

"What the hell are you doing Ange?"

As I stand up, a spanner fastens to my breast. Oops I had forgotten to remove my nipple magnets, and I slowly turn towards Jules, Justin, Jacob and now Jamie, who has suddenly appeared from nowhere, with a big ol' spanner hanging from my nip. It slowly dawns on me.
"Oh no. Who's that under there?"

As if in slow motion the warden appears from underneath Gertie, nursing the bump on his head from under her carriage with a completely shocked, disbelieving look on his face.

"I am so sorry sir. I was totally going with my hormones and ovaryacted. I thought you were someone else."

"No worries, I take it as a compliment. A 55-year-old rather rotund man being taken as a young nubile boy isn't in the slightest bit insulting. Perhaps you may want to consider wearing glasses in the future though."

"Indeed, then I won't make such a spectacle of myself."

"What about Gertie?"

"It's not a big deal, all she needs is brake fluid."

"Great, then we can stop anytime we like. Wouldn't you agree Ange?"

He takes it in good faith and everyone enjoys the giggle at my expense, but I race inside to wash and disinfect my hand, the spanner still dangling from my breast goes unnoticed and is hardly even mentioned. For the time being, that is - I know, without a shadow of a doubt, they're going to get some mileage out of this one for sure. When it comes to life's bitter pills, the hardest one to swallow is the taste of your own medicine. Happy to take it…. this time. I go back inside and finish off my chores, making damn sure that the bloody, crimson, jammy rag is still under the chair. For shuwa the well-endowed warden won't forget me either for my injuries or my testicle-tickling talent. He hands me the late key, holding on to it marginally longer than he necessarily needs to in my opinion. We look like we're competing in some crazy Christmas cracker competition that I ultimately win. Time to grab The 3 J's, a goon and a joint in that order. We sit on the pavement in front of the hostile, drinking, smoking and chatting under the watchful eye of King Dong from the office window.

JULES

I'm not in the mood to drink as I know I'm going to drive tomorrow, but I do partake in a wee toot. The joint seems much stronger than usual, no doubt due to the fact it has been in the hubcap for so long, it has been exposed to carbon monoxide, petrol emissions and roadkill. It's certainly having an effect. I am well and truly wasted and need to go to the loo immediately. I get the late key from Ange and head back towards the hostel. I'm not sure why, but the late key isn't fitting in the lock. I keep trying, every which way but loose. I can hear all this laughter coming from the pavement behind me which I duly ignore and concentrate on opening the feckin door. I'm seriously on the verge of peeing myself, so use a little more brute force on the door than is possibly necessary using my shoulder as a battering ram, and give it an extra hard shove. As I'm doing this, the door suddenly yields and springs open. I end up involuntarily spilling in, doing a commando roll across the carpet. I didn't remember there ever being a carpet in the reception area of the hostile in the first place. After rolling a couple of times, I come to a complete stop and look up. I see a pair of black patent shoes standing beside me. They're attached to black trousers, a long apron, a white shirt and black tie. That's odd, he looks very much like a waiter. I can still hear the screams, the guffaws and the hilarity from the pavement outside which is reverberating around the room. I sit up and see a number of people at tables staring at me, some with a fork halfway to their mouths, some with a glass of wine, but almost every one of them with dumbfounded, flabbergasted and quizzical looks on their faces. Does the hostel have a restaurant theme night that we've missed, or worse, weren't invited to? The waiter offers me his hand and pulls me up off the ground. It dawns on me that I have thrust my way into the Mexican restaurant NEXT DOOR to the hostel. The clock on the wall reads 730pm. I thought it was way after midnight, hence the need for the late key. Shit. Quick, think on your feet.

"Table for one please."

"I yam afraid zer iz no tablez left for ziz evening."

Must be a French restaurant.

"Okey, zank you. I'll try for anozer night."

I'm not deliberately trying to take the piss out of his accent, it just comes out that way. Speaking of piss. "Can I use the toilet?"

ANGE

Jules has just tried to break into a French restaurant in full daylight. She is off her tits and I think it's safer if I get her back into the safety of the hostile environment. How can I smuggle an almost full goon of wine into the Y? Another fucking rule. No alcohol on the premises. How stupid is that? Everyone knows a party without booze is just a meeting. Anyone who thinks drinking is bad for them should give it up thinking in my opinion, but since when has that ever stopped anyone? It's getting rather cold outside and we may all get piles if we sit here for much longer.

"Come on chaps and chapesses, let's take the show off the road and into the cozy, warmth of the hostile."

Where did that caring mentality sneak in from? Who knew I was capable of that? I tuck the spigot down the inside of my jeans so it pokes out from behind my spaver, and gather the top end of the bag, securing it under my bra. I have a large jumper on so I look either fat or pregnant. The duty hostile guard doesn't even bat an eye.

JULES

It seems like a good idea at the time. Ange is wearing the four-litre wine cask under her sweater, and tries not to look nine months pregnant as we'd only paid for a twin room. It's hysterical seeing her pulling down the zip on her jeans, pulling out the spigot, opening her legs, squatting slightly and filling up everyone's glasses. It looks like she's using a shewee. The less wine, the bigger the bend and squat. And guess what? It works, people are soon flocking round us and the warden is none the wiser, thinking we're just incredibly engaging, funny and popular. Four litres doesn't go a long way though, so we have to keep restocking the pregnant goon belly until the entire hostel is inebriated. We top it off with yet another one of our prized possessions. We flip off the last hubcap containing the very much treasured last bag of grass. The bag itself is black with soot, emissions and what looks like splatterings of animal carcass. That must have been my driving, even though I have no recollection of killing some furry mammal. I know without a shadow of a doubt it had to be me, as if Ange had done it, she would have freaked out as she loves animals, even the dead ones apparently are worth more than life itself. See? She does have a soft side to her, well, especially where fur babies, or actually any scaly, hairy creature is concerned. The contents of the baggy look fine…. ISH.

ANGE

All this pouring makes me desperate for a pee myself, and on top of that, I'm completely wrecked. Jules tells me to slip out the side door, up the backstairs and not by reception as the warden is on high alert. Actually, it's us that's high, he's on alert, still looking for any misdemeanour to chuck us out no doubt. If he gets close enough, he might catch on to my weaving and bloodshot eyes. There's construction going on in the back building where new showers are being put in and some of the builders are still there as they're putting in overtime. I walk through the construction site holding the semi-full goon under my sweater. I see them almost wolf whistle at me until they spot my pregnant belly. They wouldn't dare. I head up the stairs. At the top, there's a sign with an arrow pointing further along a corridor.

"TOILETS."

There's a flimsy piece of rope across the top and bottom of the stairs. I tentatively step over the bottom rope and under the top one. No way I'm going back to run the gauntlet of construction workers. I'm sure I have a joke about them, but I'm still working on it. There's another sign. "Out of Order."

The message is not written in a proper formal request way, but in some five-year-old learning to write scribble. Not really valid then. I step over, but catch my toe on another rope and come crashing down on my inflatable belly. Thankfully it cushions my landing somewhat, but the spigot presses into my bladder, making me pee a little with the shock of it all. I seal the flow using my super tight kegel muscles that I've exercised and honed to a fine skill, but am very briefly taken off guard. You're welcome boys, my hard work is your gain. I waddle to the loo, making sure my thighs are firmly pressed together.

The door ahead of me to my left says "WOMEN". It has a yellow piece of tape across it for some reason, but I manage to limbo under it without any more leakage. I head straight to the first single cubicle. The toilet lid is down with some cling film wrapped over it. Yeah, yeah, I've seen this old trick before. No flies on me. I tear off the wrapper, sit down and let loose.

"I'm singing in the rain, just singing in the rain, what a glorious feeling..."

When suddenly from between my legs comes a male, Australian voice.

"Hey Sheila, so am I. Would you be a doll and nip it in the bud as I'm still working on the pipes down here."

NOooooooooo…. Oh, my gawd. I am actually giving a plumber a golden shower. I am indeed able to nip it in the bud and head back through the site to join everyone. The jungle drums have obviously reached the hard hat brigade as this time they don't hold back on their wolf whistles and I embrace the challenge of doing the walk of shame with my head held high. I can't believe I actually showered a plumber with some watered-down filtered Riesling. I should feel mortified, but my foof is now covered up, and that is the only identifying thing he saw. There will be no identity parade held here. I tell Jules what happened.

JULES

"It would be very easy to take the piss here, but my guess is urine enough trouble as it is."

"Well, urine luck, I can take the joke. But, I'm only telling you and no one else."
"Huh, if it had been anyone else, you'd have been faster than a girl untagging herself of an unflattering photo on social media. You'd have relished to dish that dirt out, to publicize and ridicule the victim. I'm sure that's why Lesley left."

"That's completely unfair Jules. She left because she couldn't hack the pace and her good deeds were like her wetting herself in a dark pair of trousers - it gave her a warm feeling, but no one else noticed, so she had to take them on the road to be appreciated."

"Exactly my point. We didn't appreciate her. All we did was mock her with our jokes, jibes and blatant innuendos. Can you even begin to imagine how it feels to have that relentless barrage from people who are her so-called friends? I, for one, feel ashamed of my behaviour and regret not being more accepting and kinder. How could I have been so cruel? When we find her, I'm going to apologise and hopefully make up for it."

"You do you and I'll be unapologetically me."

"Therein lies the problem. It's all very well being unapologetically you, but there's no need to snuff out someone else's candle in order for yours to glow brighter."

"I do hear you, but sometimes, more often than not these days, you get on my wick."

"There's a time and place for jokes, Ange, gauge your audience, gauge your audience."

"What the hell's got into you all of a sudden? Have you been smacked with a guilt stick?"

"Maybe. Everything coming to us, the good, the bad and the ugly, are all opportunities to grow and learn from."

"Are we talking about Brummie here?"

"Perhaps. She's probably a decent person also, but we never gave her a chance, just dismissed and discarded her. Never even bothered to consider what happened to her after she disappeared."

She also said some other shite like: "Deep down Lesley is one incredibly special person and we blew it. Plain and simple."

"There's only one incredible special blow I'm interested in and deep down I do know she's a good person."

Aye, 6ft, make that 12 ft deep down.

JULES

There is no point in arguing or discussing any of this with a brick wall. Someone coming into this argument wouldn't know which one of us is the fool. I walk away as this is one performance I choose not to attend. There may well have been a time I found all this amusing, but not anymore. They're cheap shots and always at the expense of someone else. Lesley is a better person than both of us put together.

ANGE

Oh me, Jules has become holier than thou and is probably hormonal and in need of a good rogering or something. She warbles on about the connections we make with others that make all the difference to our lives … yada, yada, yada, blah, blah, blah. Jeez, when did she take a swig from the super-sensitive intensity bottle?

"I'm only joking Jules. I don't really mean it."

But she's gone.

JULES

As I walk out the door, I hear her parting remark. As tempting as it is to turn round and tell her if she doesn't mean it and it's only a joke, she has to be more aware of where her wisecracks land. I'm not going to be dragged in, so continue on. One day she's going to have to be truly broken open to learn this difficult human experience we call life and living. In some ways, I hope I am there to see it. I am so ready to find Lesley sooner rather than later. Not sure how much more of Ange I can take.

ANGE

Quite glad we're moving on again, I want to find Lesley, take her back to Sydney, leave her and Jules with Mikey and then enjoy the rest of my time here without any reminders as to how unkind, selfish and inconsiderate I am. Not that anyone has said that to my face, you understand, well, not in so many words.

It's mid-morning when we finally get our act together and leave.

"Let's make like a portopotty and leave this shit hole Jules."

"I'm so ready. Only one more stop between here and her hopefully."

"Let's stay in Port Augusta, that's only 306 KM on the Princess Highway."

"Super. You get me out of the city and it's a straight Golden Path all the way."

"Do me a favour will you? Pull over and let me ask which is the quickest way there as there are so many."

"Wait. Are you trying to test my starting and stopping, gear and blinker control?"

"If you think I'm that shallow, then yes, if you think I'm only concerned about getting us there quicker rather than later, then yes. Just pull over, there's an old lady, she'll tell us."

I use my best cruising control and glide alongside granny, slightly ahead, giving her ample time to have her catch up with us. Jules opens her door and shouts at her.

"Excuse me, would you be kind enough to tell me which is the quickest way to Port Augusta?"

"Of course. Are you driving or walking?"

"Eh, driving."

"That's the quickest way then."

She walks on, giving us those precious few seconds to realise what she said. We crack up laughing and I tell Jules to take her pick, they're all six and half-a-dozen. The Three J's are coming with us to Alice Springs and are happily bouncing around the back smoking the remainder of the blow. I'm not really paying too much attention as I'm trying to inhale as much smoke as I can so that I can unselfishly take the lion's share to prevent Jules's from inhaling it as she's driving. Call me unselfish or what.

At Gepps Cross, I accidentally direct us on a minor detour to the Barossa Valley, an honest mistake your Honor. We stop at Langmeil Winery as it seems such a shame to miss out on some of the best wine in the world. We take a short tour and do some tasting, not Jules you understand, being the responsible, grumpy, secondhand toker driver that she is. We replenish our stocks, replace our depleted goon shortage with some rather tasty bottles of white, rose, red and fizz. That'll surely be enough for the night. As we're heading back to the car park, from the top of the hill, I notice two suspicious-looking characters checking Gerie out. They have low foreheads, beady eyes, jeans semi-belted at the lowest part of their Calvin Klein clad backsides. Bloody criminals trying to nick our stuff from the van. It makes my blood boil, the audacity of it all, and in broad daylight as well. I quicken my step. The creep on the passenger side clearly breaks in as he gets in, and leans over to let the other guy into the driver's side. This makes me mad. How fucking dare they? I channel my inner Flo-Jo and head towards them like a speeding bullet. I grab the driver by the scruff of his scrawny neck and yank him out, giving him a slap about the head and a swift boot to the groin.

"You pair better get out of my fucking sight or I'll really start in on you."

I must sound really scary and serious as they both start running in the direction of the gift shop.

"Don't even think of nicking anything from there either or I'll call the cops you lowdown lazy scumbags."

I feel totally chuffed with the ferociousness of my confidence. No one messes with me.

"What the hell are you doing?"

"Oh well, thank you very much Jules, but I have just saved Gertie from being carjacked."

"That's not Gertie."

"What?"

I look inside and see some McDonald's wrappers, a basketball and a pair of Nike trainers the size of a small boat. None of which belong to us. It dawns on me then that I have assaulted two unsuspecting innocent young chaps from getting into their own car. Jules is pointing to Gertie who is parked undisturbed a few rows back and down from where we stand.

"Fuck, let's make like the Red Sea and split before they call the cops."

We take off like Greased Lightning. The Three J's are flying around in the back like they're in some kind of inflatable bouncy castle as Jules takes off spraying the car park with chuckies and leaving a well-earned skid mark. No sooner do we leave the city limits than we hear the familiar sound of a siren.

"Oh, for fuck's sake, here we go again."

"Thankfully I'm driving this time and have a clean, legal licence."

JULES

Thank goodness, I'm driving and pull over to the side like the responsible driver I am. I'm not speeding and there are no red lights to run, so I'm not quite sure why we've been stopped. The child copper approaches the car.

"We've had a complaint about an attempted abduction."

"What? There was nothing tempting about those two gallahs officers."

"Ange? Be quiet, let the officer speak."

"Someone, well namely your passenger, meets the description of someone that attempted to kidnap two boys at a winery."

"Boys?? They were men and it was an innocent mistake."

"I'll need you all to calmly get out of the van and show your ID."

Kidnapping? No way I'm going down for this besides it really was an accident.

ANGE

I try to channel my inner Lesley, see if her charm works here.

"What are you trying to inseminate here? It's an honest case of mistaken identity occifer. I thought they were wolves in cheap clothing trying to steal Gertie. I have extra-century perception when it comes to these things you know, but it wasn't until after I'd removed them from the car that I realised the carjacking was actually a pigment of my imagination."

"Hold on here little lady, I'm getting confused. Who was trying to inseminate Gertie?"

Perfect.

"I said insinuate and Gertie is our van. I thought they were trying to carjack her, but I got it wrong, they were actually getting into their own car. It really was an accident."

"They were both quite shaken up."

"What are they? Men or mice?"

"Pardon?"

"I said that's not nice. I had just left the conception when I saw them trying to break in. Do you prostitute trespassers here?"

"What are you saying?"

"You seem like a great cop and I'm sure it's easy for you to dissolve the mystery here?"

"Dissolve?"

"I said resolve."

Thank you, thank you, thank you Lesley. It's working.

"Can you all please show your ID?"

We rummage through our backpacks and bring out our passports, aside from Justin that is. He looks at the copper somewhat surprised.

"I'm terribly, terribly sorry sir, but I'm afraid I don't believe I have my passport on me as I left it in Sydney with my Aunt Matilda."

The rest of us start to fidget and giggle somewhat.

"Fair dinkum, the rest of you wrap your laughing gear up, sit down at the side of the road while I have a Captain Cook at this bloke here."

Hmmm, I bet. He looks straight out of Village People and I'm sure he would be more than happy to wrap his laughing gear around something of Justin's.

"Never mind him occifer, he's a few stubbies short of a six-pack."

The road is scorchio and scarring our backsides with a fine red dust tattoo.

"Can you bunch of galahs keep it down a bit, you're scaring the wildlife out here. Now you, young man, what is your name?"

"Justin, Justin Savory."

More laughter.

"Can you find anything with your name on it, so I know you are who you say you are?"
Justin spills the contents of his belongings all over the red road and is sweating, becoming increasingly more distraught and frantic in his search. Manky t-shirts, holey boxers and stained shorts are flying out of his backpack in every direction. After ferreting about

for a good five minutes, we are all beginning to lose the will to live, and the bobby especially is becoming increasingly exasperated, when Justin suddenly throws his hands up in the air as if surrendering.

"I'm really not trying to pull the wool over your eyes here, but I have nothing for you. You'll need to take me in, I have nothing, nada, rien, NEE-chee-vo. Fair dinky old cobber, you have me fair and square."

He turns his back, leans on Gertie and spreads his legs, offering his wrists for cuffing.

"Okay no worries, You are right mate."
We are all now creasing ourselves, rolling in the dust disregarding the heat, the temperature coming off the ground and the red ants who are getting mighty close. We all must have third-degree burns by now, but that doesn't stop us. Justin, on the other hand, is clearly not joking as his face has turned the same bright red of the desert sand. The police officer is about to say something else, when Justin starts to jump up and down like a kangaroo on steroids, at the same time as shouting: "I do, I do, I do."

At the same time, he's trying to take off his left boot. He's hopping all over the place. He finally falls over, but manages to pull his boot and sock off. He's doing the Aussie salute, brushing and batting away the flies with one hand at the same time while proudly presenting the cop with his crusty looking sock, pronouncing

"Crikey Sir, here's my name".

We all stand up to take a closer look and crowd round the dangling object he holds tightly in his sweaty mitt. Sure enough, there embroidered in blue on his schoolboy sock is his name: "JUSTIN SAVORY".

Only a 19-year-old public schoolboy would have his socks with his name stitched on it. We all crack up, even the bobby smirks.

"Blimey? I've never seen the likes. Right, you bunch of pommy bastards, put a sock in it and hit the frog and toad. I sincerely hope not to see you again. I will, however, let my colleagues further north know you're heading in their direction."

Warning noted.

"Ok Jules, let's make like a guillotine and head off."

JULES

He leaves us all rolling around and Justin looking very perplexed as to what had just happened.

"Whaat?"

He keeps repeating.

"What on earth is quite so funny?"

The road is unsealed and bumpy as feck and fine red dust manages to come through the vents, the windows, the undercarriage and gets everywhere - and I mean everywhere. Ange and I have to make masks out of our bras just so we could breathe. Jacob makes do with a scarf from our homeless box, while Jamie chooses a bra from the box which he must think belongs to Ange, but each cup alone can cover his entire skull, must be mine then. Justin prefers a makeshift contraption using a pair of his socks which haven't been washed in months. However, he's the one inhaling the rancid hard cheese, not us, his emblazoned name sitting snugly across the bridge of his nose. We really are heading to the middle of bum-fuck nowhere, the bowels of the universe. My teeth are rattling in my head from going up and down over all the divots and potholes in the road. We all look like extras from the Last of the Mohicans film set. I'm sure Gertie's suspension is going to give up the ghost any minute and leave us stranded in the middle of The Bush. I'm thinking of Priscilla Queen of the Desert without the drag. Well, actually it's becoming a drag, miles and miles and miles of straight, and I do mean straight, unsealed road. However, the thought of getting to Alice Springs sooner rather than later gives me a pep to the pedal and I drive straight through Port Augusta, leaving any form of traffic light and temporary relief with the occasional sealed road behind. Who knew how happy that would make me? I head towards Pimba Road signs warn us we are arriving in The Outback. What the feck? Where have we just come from if this is The Outback we're only now entering?

The first part of the drive takes us through low, undulating hills with lots of scrub. Ange starts her nonsense again and begins to tap the window, pointing out all the emus, kangaroos and camels for the umpteenth feckin time.

"One more feckin tap on the window and I swear I'm going to snap every one of your fingers off."

"No need to take the hump."

She suddenly screams: "STOP THE CAR!"

I give it the emergency break; the three J's end up in the front with us and we are engulfed in a cloud of red dust from the skid.

"Photo opportunity!"

She jumps out and stands below a road sign that says.

"SHIT road. Careful driving techniques are advised"

We take our obligatory photos and no sooner are we back on the road when: "STOP THE CAR!"

Another emergency brake, it's like deja vu.

"Photo opportunity!"

We all clamber out, again. This time the sign says:

"ELEVATION ...150m

CAMELS.... 2,000

SHEEP...22,500

FLIES...3,000,000 (approx.)

HUMANS...3000"

"Okay that's the last time we stop for a photo, I want to get there before dark."

"Hey, don't shoot, the messenger, you'll regret the photos you never took when you're a crusty, crabby, incontinent old lady, possibly even as early as next year."

"Ho dee feckin ho."

JULES

We are slightly later than intended, given the detour to the winery, the police stop, the fact that we didn't stay in Port Augusta and all the photo ops Ange insisted on. The remains of Nurrungar, a joint US-Australian spy base, is on the left as we enter the dilapidated pretty ugly place. Who stays in a town like this? At the mere mention of joint, Ange rolls one to welcome us.

"Let's keep going? There's a place further down the road called Woomera where there was a cold- war project between the British and Australian governments. Seems fitting."

"I read about that somewhere. It was developed to fire lots of rockets into the middle of nowhere and is considered to be unpopulated, but truthfully the Aboriginal people were moved out of their traditional lands and displaced. It has taken them decades to move back to their lands. New settlements have been created, many tribes have died and all for the sake of creating weapons of mass destruction. I cried bittersweet tears when I watched 'Benny and the dreamers'. If you haven't seen it already, I highly recommend it. I can absolutely see why Lesley wanted to be here and share her gifts in this part of the world."

We check into the Eldo Hotel and find the place completely EMPTY - and I mean EMPTY. Not one single other traveller, not one swagman in the bar, I don't even see any flies. It's very eerie. Perhaps they should rename it to Bates Motel. Or not. Now, this is either a good sign or a bad omen. There are only six of us, including the very old manager who could be anywhere from 55 to 112 . She has a deep gravelly voice like she smokes Capstan full strength without the filter and has done since she was two.

"It's very quiet at this time of year as most people are out on the ranches on a Tuesday night, but by Friday the place is jumping. Relax after your long day's drive and enjoy yourselves. There's an honesty box through in the bar, so help yourself, but make sure you pay for it."

"We'll get our stuff, no need to get the staff to help."

"I am the staff. The chef, housekeeper, barmaid, kitchen porter, bouncer and gardener. Not that there's much of a garden around here though, some tumbleweed blows through regularly, but other than that, it's pretty desolate."

Grandma Walton is stone deaf also it seems and hasn't heard a word we say.

"No shit."

"I'm heading to bed as I've been up since 4am shearing sheep out the back and there's some quilting I need to finish."

"As you do."

"If you'd kindly lock up when you retire that would be much appreciated."

Thankfully she hasn't got wind of us yet. Even if the copper had called to warn her, she wouldn't have heard the phone, let alone his warning. By the smell of the place she clearly has enough wind to start her own tumbleweed tsunami. We have free range, carte blanche over the entire place.

"Yippee, where do we start?"

"Caw canny Ange, I don't fancy being chucked out of this place as it may have escaped your notice here, but we're in the middle of nowhere."

"Och behave, besides granny won't hear us, she's deaf as a post. We'll be as quiet as church mice. I promise."

As the sky darkens to a deep indigo and the last rays of sun slip beyond the horizon, the night sky is lit by thousands of stars. The land and its iconic rocks, so dominant during the day, disappear into the dark and the sky takes centre stage. We are transfixed by the extraordinary sight. I have never quite fully grasped the concept of Australia's indigenous peoples' relationship to the land until this very moment. It's breathtaking. Aborigines know they do not own the land, but are part of it and see it as their duty, as we all should, to look after the earth and our heart, and again, is it a mere coincidence that they contain the same letters? I believe not. Everything in that natural world leaves its mark on both. In Aborginal stories, every meaningful activity, event, word we use, thought, intention or life's process carries a vibrational residue that connects everything and everyone along its energetic current. Our very own unique vibration. They know the past is still alive and breathing today, as it will be in the future, so we need to relax and lean into every experience and take an appreciative breath. A full, deep breath that fills and expands our body, merging our form to the energetic field around us. A lesson we should all take from them.

"This is magical and spine-tingling. I'm sure I can even hear a didgeridoo somewhere in the distance. Look. There's the Southern Cross."

We crane our necks towards the brilliant mass of stars that begin to transform into shapes as our eyes focus and adapt to the voluminous twinkling above and around us, literally enveloping and bathing us in its magnificent light, each with its own story and meaning.

"I wouldn't mind if we get barred from here, sleeping out under this twinkling canopy sounds perfect.

You can literally get lost in the stars"

"Great idea Jules"

"Eh?"

"Let's do exactly that. Let's play hide and seek out here in the desert."

"I'm not sure that's a good idea. What if someone gets lost?"

"Look, there is absolutely nothing and no-one within miles and the combination of the clear night sky and stars gives us the perfect full-lit stage. Besides if someone does get lost, we'll find them pretty soon."

"Maybe."

"Done deal. Here's the rules. We can use the downstairs of the hostile and only out to the sheep paddock and back. I'll count to ten. Go!"

We haven't even had the chance to disagree, but the moment she shouts, we all scurry off like field mice. I'm too feart to stay outside as some of those stars have slipped to the horizon and look more like dingo eyes. I head to the kitchen and hide under the table. I've suddenly remembered why I hate this game so much. My heart is racing, my palms are sweating. I'm terrified, not just because I begin to think of the Overlook Hotel but because I'm being hunted down by Ange. That alone is petrifying, I think I'd rather take my chances with Jack Torrance. I can hear steps coming down the corridor and a whisper: "Light, of my life. I'm not gonna hurt ya. You don't let me finish. I said, I'm not gonna hurt ya."

Feck this, there's too much tension rising in my body and I'm going to give up before being caught. But before I can, this stream of sticky white foam is propelled like a jet right up my jacksy. I'm launched across the floor and pressed up against the fridge. This constant stream keeps coming and coming. I can't see my way out of or through the foam wall that has me well and truly pinned. I try a body roll, but the next spray hits my back and has me travelling again across the floor and practically stapled to the corner. I'm on my back with my legs over my shoulders. The surge continues and there is a significant amount of spume pressure directed right at and in my bottom. I'm not able to move as it's too powerful and has complete control over me. The white surf keeps expanding and expanding. Now, I've never had colonic irrigation but after this experience, I can say from the heart of my bottom, quite literally. that I never want ANOTHER one in my entire life. Everything slowly settles and I can see a large, red cylindrical canister being held by fireman Ange. If there had been a fire I am quite sure it hadn't originated from my rear end. It gives a few more spurts as it empties its final contents in my hair. It all settles around me in an entire white foam pool. How can one wee container hold so much?

ANGE

I give them all an additional 10 and count to 20. Everyone scampers off in all directions. I know without a doubt that Jules has gone inside, she's far too scared to be out in The Bush on her own. I head for her first. I notice a fire extinguisher attached to the wall in the kitchen at the same time as I see the tablecloth twitching. I know who's under there.

"Light, of my life. I'm not gonna hurt ya. You don't let me finish. I said, I'm not gonna hurt ya."

I have an idea. Why not seek everyone out with a blast of foam? I move like a ninja around the table and see Jules's arse sticking out. I slowly, steadily, stealthily approach, like a predator to its prey. I unhinge the cap and let her have it. Fuck me, I'm blown across the room and I struggle to hold the tiny canister, let alone the black hose which is snaking its contents out at 50mph. It eventually comes to a less forceful expulsion and is soon down to its last dribble.

"Now that's what I call fun. How the hell is there so much stuff in a wee space? Story of my life, and even though I'm behind it, it's in my hair and eyes, again the story of my life. Through the foam I spot another fire extinguisher beside the stove. Why should the game be over? Not everyone has been found. The others must be outside, so I go outside to get them with the other extinguisher. Not so much mess to be made in the desert.

"Come on Jules, this is fun. Check the larder for another one and we'll go get the boys."

"We're like The Lone Ranger and Tonto."

The desert soon becomes a sea of foam under our careful guidance and like many things it has premature ejaculation and doesn't last long after the contents are expelled. No need to clean up after it though as we're all pretty sure it evaporates. Jamie and I decide to sleep, and I use that term loosely, under the stars and only wake at the crack of dawn to a cockerel crowing, however, on closer inspection, it's Grandma Walton shouting us all to the kitchen. Now we're in for it. It's like deja vu all over again.

We congregate sheepishly in front of her, however, we're all pleasantly surprised to find the kitchen with not a trace of foam. The floor and chairs are slightly sticky though, and as I cross the floor, one flip flop sticks after another, making a sucking noise as I pull each foot off the floor. It must have evaporated after all, however, I can see a few mounds of white stuff through the window, plopped around the red ground, giving it a striking colour contrast. We all have hair like Phyllis Dillar, Johnny Rotten and Cameron Diaz... and Grandma Walton. So now we know her trick.

JULES

I sit with my sticky head between my hands and wait for the worst. What punishment is worthy and going to be bestowed upon us now? GW sits at the end of the table, her half-glasses perched on her boney bridge, held up by a few wrinkles. She has her quilt in her hands and is eyeing us all up. I think she's doing that, but she may be blind also.

"I want to attract more people to this 'dessert' hostel. I like to call it that as there was a Scottish nurse passing through recently who kept calling the desert, dessert. It was her idea that we came up with dessert Friday."

"OH FFS!! No, just NO! Please stop right there. No need to tell us any more. We get it. Actually, I don't get it. Dessert Friday?"

She completely ignores me as if I haven't even spoken and carries on.

"As a matter of fact, in her honour, we have a different dessert every Friday in the desert. I hope that when you leave you spread the news, as opposed to the foam, to every other hostel. We're already getting people coming here because of our very own special Queen of the Dessert."

ANGE

Here we go again, Lezzers' to the fucking rescue, Nurse Nightingale to the ill, coffee giver to the weary, donor of all things tat to the homeless, cleaner of hostels, master baker to the homesick, carer to the infirm, gardener of magnificent landscapes, chef extraordinaire, replenisher of all things first aid and now Queen, of all things, desserts. Little friend to the fucking world.

All that's missing is a fucking shiny halo over her immaculately brushed shiny blonde head of hair. Queen of the fucking DESSERT?? I mean, seriously? I nearly threw up. Someone is definitely taking the piss here. If I hadn't promised to go get the Queen of the DESSERT, I would have thrown the pavlova in and headed to the second star to the right and straight on to Darwin. Unfortunately, I have no choice but to go through Alice Springs to get there, so might as well finish this task off.

Thankfully, Grandma Walton says no more, leaving us to have our breakfast in peace as she continues her quilting. This is all becoming a complete and utter joke and I'm not sure which one of us is beginning to look like the fool. I hate to say it but it's beginning to look more like me. Surely not, c'est non possible. I know that as soon as we find her, I'm going to pay Jules to take her back to Sydney and I'm going to part ways with them both and head north. Anywhere really that I know the Queen of Desserts hasn't already been. She can see how it feels to be in my wake for a change.

"Are you going to stay till Friday? Our dessert this week is Cake a Diem. Lesley came up with that name all by herself."

"Hmmm, you sure? Not like her to have a considered play on words, they're usually malaprops. I think raspberry fools would be more fitting."

"Sadly not, we have to leave after breakfast."

The three J's mutter something about wanting to get to know the Queen of Desserts as she sounds special. I'll show them fucking special. I ask them politely if they've done their chores as I want them out of my sight. They head outside to sweep the barn.

"Yeah, as much as we'd love to stay around for this pure delicacy, we need to make like our very own dessert and beat it."

"I understand, but perhaps you'd be kind enough to ask the boys to stay on. They can help me inseminate the sheep. I pay good money."

"Not sure you want to be inseminating your sheep with anything that comes from those three. Gosh knows what ewed end up with!"

"Very funny, you know I didn't mean that, but the shepherd is gone and I need some jam boys while I use the basting technique."

"Jam Boys?"

"Yes, I'll slather them in a jam, that way the flies will be attracted to them and not me. Gives me the chance to get through 500 sheep without having to worry about flies."

"I'm sure they'd be delighted, let me ask."

The three J's do decide to stay on the sheep station and help Grandma Walton. I omit to tell them about the jam, but just desserts really as I'm fed up with them anyway. After a brief goodbye, we need to get out of Dodge before GW cracks open the jam jar. We make like Tigger and bounce out of town literally and physically to Wham for the 3,877 time. Two hours on and plenty of jigging later, I spy Ayers Rock in the distance and practically knock the glass out of the window with my head. She had said she'd break my fingers, so giving her a break here by using my head for a change, but she doesn't even bat an eyelid, says nothing, slows down and stops. It doesn't look too far.

"Come on, you won't regret it - a minor sidetrack is all it is and we can take some compulsory touristy photos so we can claim to have been there, done that, bought the t-shirt kinda thing."

"Okay."

The road, if you can call it that, is even more unsealed, bumpy, dusty and full of mammoth craters. It's much further than it looks, so after 40 mins driving, we have probably only covered one mile as we have to go really slow. It's almost like playing Buckaroo, we lose a piece of Gertie with each dip in the road. Fuck this, it still doesn't look any closer, so we stop to take photos with the rock in the background. Much easier from here, any closer and we may be under some obligation to climb the sandstone mountain. A quick photo is enough. We get out of the car and pose from a safe distance in all types of positions. We pretend to kick it, lie under it, kiss it, straddle it, lick it, you get the gist. Far more fun from here I'm sure. Eventually, we get back on the road and make like my ex and move on. We're all completely chuffed that we've ticked another Aussie icon off of our list. No sooner have we got back on to the main road than we see a sign.

"Ayers Rock (Uluru) 100km."

"WTF?"

"If Ayers Rock is 100 clicks, what the fuck was that termite pile of sand we wasted our time on?"

"Maybe this takes us around the other side."

"Looking at it, even from here, it's a different shape."

"There's a sign behind us."

"Erldunda 55KM."

"Well, that may have saved us almost a whole day if they'd had that sign on the other side of the road for us to see."

"Surely once you've seen one pile of red dirt, you've seen them all. Let's forget it, make like horseshit and hit the trail."

The outback isn't as flat, boring and dusty as I had imagined, it has mountains and lots of trees. Who knew? There are birds of prey, or some other type of prehistoric animals, bigger than the size of Gertie. They swoop down at us like we're some kind of mobile prey on wheels. It would not have surprised me one bit if we had been clutched in its massive talons and taken to a nest at the top of a mountain in the middle of nowhere. We're playing I Spy, which is getting a bit monotonous as we're running out of diversity. The road ahead begins to play tricks on our vision and begins to look like a mirage, like a body of water or an oasis, or maybe a pub, but it's not until we get closer that we realise it's sadly only an optical illusion.

"I'm pretty sure I'm not delusional, but it appears there is definitely some prey or something on the road further ahead."

"I see it. It might be a tree trunk."

"Big fucking tree, it spans the whole road."

"We have to stop and move whatever it is, because I can't go round it."

We stop, get out of the car and venture closer.

"OMG, it's only a Perentie lizard. I LOVE lizards, couldn't eat a whole one mind, but I do love them nonetheless."

"Holy shit Ange, don't go too close, it looks like it could eat you whole, it has to be about three metres long."

"It's magnificent. Is it dead do you think?"

"If that thing had been hit, there'd be a wrecked car nearby. It looks like it could take out an entire fleet of road trains if it had been hit."

The prehistoric bird continues to circle above us, waiting for its breakfast, lunch and dinner, which could have been either of us plus the reptile as a chaser.

"Well...... NOT on my watch Hawkeye."

I venture closer as Jules is too scared.

"You're pathetic. It's really harmless. Trust me. Do I not exude the epitome of sincerity? Okay, maybe that's too much of a stretch even for me."

I can see the gentle roll of its breath.

"YIPPEE, it's alive!"

I gently nudge it with my Chinese slipper-clad foot.

"Oh gawd, don't touch it with those shoes, you'll kill it with the stench."

"You're not wrong. They haven't been washed for months, I think they're actually superglued on now. We are one. On the plus side we're not being bothered by bush flies, are we?

If you'd prefer I wear some strawberry jam, I will."

"Speak for yourself, my bush never ever attracts flies and at this stage, strawberry jam, even revolving papaya jam sounds much more appealing than the rotten aroma and foot jam of your feet. Just keep those shoes on forever and you'll be fine. I hate to think what the smell will be like if you take them off. I wonder how the Three J's are taking to their new job? I'm sure it's preferable to inseminating sheep."

"Hmm, not sure about that. I feel for the sheep. I saw the boys polishing their gumboots as we left."

The lizard finally gets a downward wind of my chicken fried rice feet, and rather than biting me, decides it's easier to meander into the scrub area at the side of the road than tackle this Asian fayre.

"Yippee, I am now officially the saver of reptiles and furry hats, at least until the next time it chooses to sunbathe in a very exposed, dangerous spot. I'm quite sure they're on the endangered list, so it can now be free, go forth and breed. Eat your heart out Lesley, I can also do good deeds."

JULES

Ange is so excited to see the scaly monster lying across the road, but there is no way I'm getting any closer than Gertie's bonnet. It's like a scene from Jurassic Park. I'm waiting for Big Bird in the sky to swoop down and take them both. The muckle beast on the road, which is more like a crocodile on steroids, actually it could very well be, but Ange is adamant it's a harmless lizard and takes her chances as she escorts it to the side. My money is on the hangry, snappy croc beating Big Bird, but I wouldn't put any money on Snappy or Hawkeye in a grappling ground fight with Ange, her bite is even worse than her bark. Once Lizard Dundee finally gets back in the car, we take off in pursuit of the real Ayers Rock. I'm knackered and ready to stop for the night, so we check in at Ayers Rock Campground which must be close to where Lesley is. If we get up nice and early then we can climb the mound in the morning before heading to Alice. We stay in Gertie to save money and are pleasantly surprised that there are plenty of other travellers camping right beside us. We join a group around a bonfire where s'mores and snags on sticks are being cooked. Ange picks up something and sits down on her esky. At first glance, I think it's a camp puppy, but on closer squinting, I see it's a feckin dingo. I get up slowly

"Ange? No need to panic here, but get up slowly and put that thing down."

"What? Chewbarka here?"

"Chewbarka there happens to be a feral dingo dog, not some cutsie lap dog."

"Don't get your knickers in a twist. Does she look like she's going to rip my throat out?"

"Maybe not her, but see all those sets of eyes watching you from the scrub? They might. Besides it wasn't that long ago a baby went missing from this very campsite, never to be found again and they think it was a pack of dingos that took her."

"It would take more than a pack of these mangy mongrels to drag me off."

"You have a point there, but let's not put it to the test shall we?"

"Pawty pooper!"

She gets up slowly, walks to the scrub and puts the pup down. No sooner has she turned her back than the wee thing is enveloped by a sea of eyes and disappears into the black of night. We sit round the fire for hours drinking, smoking, eating snags under the watchful eyes of thousands of fireflies who light up the night sky. Or maybe it's Chewbarka and her family waiting patiently for someone to go out in the bush for a pee.

ANGE

At sunrise, we get up and begin to climb the real Big Yin. It's huge. It's official Aboriginal name is Uluru which it should really be called always and not after the guy who named it after himself. Like the dude who calls everything after himself, Trump Towers, Trump International Golf Course, so egotistical and arrogant. It blows my mind that this rock was formed 600 million years ago, again, that's 600 million years ago, and previously sat on the sea bed. Crazy. It's 6km long, 1.9km wide, with a circumference of 9.4kms. They reckon it's only 1.6kms to climb, but there's at least 2.5kilometres beneath the ground. Thank gawd it's not the other way around. The steep angle to get to the supposedly flat summit is already taking its toll. Halfway up, Jules starts to moan and complain about the heat, the flies, the height, the steps. She's already lagging behind.

"I'm thirsty and my head is throbbing."

"You're not wrong there, you look like a well-slapped Queen of Hearts."

"Feels like my head is about to explode. I'm going back down."

"Look, it's not far, besides there's a coke vending machine at the top."

"Really? That'll make it worth it."

Her wee leggies get a second wind at hearing that and she legs it to the top, only to be disappointed when she gets there to find a bare rock.

"Where's the machine?"

"Seriously? It's beside the hammock?"

"Where? I can't see it."

"I was pulling your stumpy, quivering leg."

"Whaaat?? Actually, I'm glad you did. This is one of the most dramatic, panoramic views I've ever seen in my entire 23 years I've been on this planet. I'm actually overcome with emulsion. It takes my breath away, well, what I have left of it after that strenuous hike."

"Let's make like Kool and The Gang and Get on Down."

JULES

My legs are like jelly, and against my better judgment I ask Ange to drive, which I know is risky, but my legs aren't working having gone into temporary atrophy. I must have nodded off as I suddenly wake to find a train at my window moving at breakneck speed. What the feck? She's racing a feckin train of all things. Why is she so close to it? I feel sick and faint at the same time and I can't even speak. I just tap the window pointing at it.

"See, I'm not the only one that gets a thrill tapping on the glass window."

Then I see the wheels and realise it's one of those road trains and a feckin long one at that.

"Speed up."

So she does, and I mean she really does, she completely plants her Chinese slipper and is soon doing a ton and we're still overtaking.

"Holy shit, it must be 1,000 metres long. Slow down!"

"Make up your mind, do you want me to speed up and leave it in the stream of our red dust trail, or leave us in its?"

"SPEED UP!"

"You sound like a manic screech preacher. Here we go. Hold onto your britches, Darl, and think of all the benefits this ride is doing to your pelvic floor."

"We haven't seen any traffic, oncoming or otherwise in days, so what are the odds that there's going to be something coming towards us?"

Gertie is rattling more than usual.

"Come on girl, you can do it."

"Anything coming towards us is more likely to swerve before you do as you're a dead ringer for Cruella Deville, down to the white knuckles, bloodshot eyes and two-centimetre distance to the windscreen."

"Rather that, than being dead."

Ten minutes later, we finally overtake the trucking beast and both breathe a huge sigh of relief. The driver blows his airhorn and waves at us in our wing mirrors before disappearing in the wake of our red dust tornado. I have never ever been so happy to see a sign before.

"WELCOME TO ALICE SPRINGS."

It's etched in a red piece of rock. We must look slightly worse for wear if Gertie is anything to go by. She is now a pale shade of pink and her side flash is flapping. She's missing a hubcap, thankfully from an empty stash wheel. Her windscreen is smattered with the innards of flies, bugs, the occasional small bird on the outside, spittle, pureed crisps, ants, chocolate, coke from all our singing and shouting on the inside. We have dried sweat on our brows, red dust packed tight in almost every orifice, heads are thumping, but we're here and alive which is almost a miracle in itself.

"Stop the car!"

I get out, go down on my hands and knees and kiss the first sealed bit of road we have seen in days. Thank goodness for no bends, lights or much traffic, we'd never have survived if she'd been driving much more than she has already. It's bad enough having to grab the wheel on a number of occasions when she was distracted by all the animals in this wondrous country. She'd have face-planted us through the windscreen to save a snail crossing our path. There is fine red dust everywhere, and I mean EVERYWHERE. We've cleaned flour from a kitchen, foam from the dessert but there is no way we can get rid of all this. Coughing and spluttering seems to be the new black. It doesn't help that when we arrive at the first hostel, we're told it's full. We try two more before the penny drops that some sneaky, grassing bastard must have called ahead and ratted us in. Ange thinks that along with her quilt, Grandma Walton stitched us up, but my guess is there's probably a line of complainants. And not just from the Northern Territory either, stretching all the way back through South Australia, Victoria, Tasmania, even NSW. Tomorrow we will find Lesley, but first we need to get a place to stay, one that will actually take us. The last place, The Haemo Globe Inn, has the audacity to say:

"Your reputation precedes you. No room at this Inn for you."

"We'll be good I promise, we won't party like we aorta."

"Try Nobody Inn."

It seems we have quite the reputation and we begin to accumulate a following of sorts as we move from one place to another. A backpacker's convoy, our very own Gertie Road Train.

ANGE

By the time we arrive at the very last campground left in Alice Springs, we have quite the procession. Bit of a shocker really that we are this notorious and have built up quite the fan base. Not everyone recognizes us, but they sure do know Gertie. We hadn't realised we'd met so many people on our way but they all know Gertie as she rolls up, even before we've even got out of the car. We are now a road train of five vehicles, and you'd think that they should know better, especially if they'd come across us before, but apparently not. Like lambs to the slaughter. They still decide to follow along regardless. FINALLY, someone says, "YES" and lets all of us into the campground. Instead of renting and pitching a tent, we park Gertie into our designated space and get the wine out while the others put their tents up. We are the only ones to have a mattress in the back, well I say that, but it looks more like another sacred sandstone that has appeared from all the driving in The Outback. It has risen at least a metre with all the sand and dust from the roads. We sit on the roof of Gertie watching everyone else working hard while we're hard at work scoofing wine and smoking yet another joint. When all the hard work is done, everyone else joins us in relaxing on the roof of the cars to watch the dessert sunset. After the sun's well and truly gone, we use the light from the sky to release some of the tightness and tension from all the driving by playing the compulsory, obligatory game of tangles, which is exactly what one needs after days of being thrown around inside a car on an unsealed road. We come to this conclusion after the first, or maybe the second six-litre cask of wine. Eh, no judgment here. There is a senior group of travellers from Mike Rotch Tours - which I don't know and don't really care about the place in Australia. The pensioners have already started to compete music wise with our boombox music that is blasting out Midnight Oil and our Wham anthem. They're not too happy that they can't quite hear the devotionals and lyrics of kumbaya and some other shite they're playing. Time is marching on and we continue to celebrate sunset well and truly after it's dawning at the other side of the world by disco dancing on the roof of our car, which turns out makes an excellent dance floor. The campsite commandant has to reprimand us a couple of times, but has skulked off after being informed that the damage being done is to our own property, and we take full responsibility for it.

"On your own head be it."

"Or roof."

Eventually, however, he threatens to call the polis if we don't pipe down as others are beginning to retire and can't hear their evening prayers for the "racket."We promise to take it down a level, but the holy wullies have the audacity to shout out their prayers far too loud in my opinion, over the sacred, dulcet tones of George and Pete. It becomes a game of verbal, melodic table tennis. A battle of the bams. Nature has a better idea to deal with all us interlopers and drowns us out by the extremely loud and constant cacophony of crickets, cicadas, dingos and eventually old folks' snoring. It starts off as an accident, Jules and I have to leave our rooftop dance floor to use the loos which are somewhere out there in the pitch dark. As we stumble away, not really knowing where we're headed, she accidentally trips over one of the far-too-taut tent strings of the highly disciplined, ancient prayer group. Their entire flock of tents are uniformed and precision placed in

the shape of the Southern Cross, which I can see from the top
of The Gertie. Surely, it's a divine mistake, who would deliberately
do that? It's as if a lightbulb goes off in my head as the noise the
twanging makes is such a unique sound. We try to see if the other
strings can make the same vibrational tone. We actually make it
sound like Kumbaya as we pluck each string easily from the
ground. We get quite the rhythm and style going on, like a
beautiful symphony of sorts. By the time we reach our second
rendition, we hear choral cries accompanying us from deep
beneath the depths of the green canvas. The Holy Rollers have
risen. Hallelujah. Needless to say, the campground warden doesn't
take too kindly to being interrupted from his slumber at all the
catcalling. We scurry back to the safety of Gertie, close the doors
and windows and stay as quiet as if we're lying on bubble wrap.
Doesn't work though and soon someone appears at Gertie's back
doors, knocking furiously.

"We're trying to sleep here; can you take it down a notch
out there please."

"It's the manager here. Open up immediately."

"Manners maketh the man. Open up sesame, pretty please
will suffice."

"You'd better not knock quite so hard out there, you'll put
a few dents into Gertie."

"She won't be the only one who gets a few dents if you
don't open up and get out here now."

"Alright already. Keep your striped pyjamas on."

We clamber out and the man in striped pyjamas stands in
bare feet, shaking from anger is my guess over cold or fear.

"Get out."

"We are out."

I mean out of here. Out of the campsite."

"What?? It's not even sunrise."

"I don't care. I want to see the back of this car leaving that exit in under five minutes."

The cowardly others that have been partying with us have disappeared into the bowels of their tarpaulin at the first sign of twubble. The campsite christians are reassembling their tents and muttering prayers deliberately directed in our direction. It's not legally safe for Jules to be driving as she's still wearing an empty inflated wine goon under the back of her sweatpants. She's been entertaining the troops twerking her large inflated, silver bootie.

"It's highly irresponsible of you to ask us to leave as the chauffeur has a chemical imbalance and is blabbering and bladdered."

"I'll take my chances."

"It's a long shot, but how about asking the bible bashers to leave instead? They're up and about already and most of their tents are already down?"

"I can always call the local constabulary if you'd prefer."

"Alright already, come on Jules, let's make like nuns and cross this dump off our list."

"This is becoming a bad habit Ange."

Since when has letting a tent down been a crime? It's not worth trying to persuade him otherwise. We get back in the car and drive out. Jules's head is bent over and reaches the top of the roof because she forgets to take it off the bootie wine extension. She gets in the driver's seat and leaves the site driving while involuntarily staring at her crotch. We weave through the streets of Alice until we find the perfect parking place and crash…OUT thankfully.

JULES

Not even sure what time it is, but we're rudely awakened again with more bloody hammering on the back door. This time though there are blue flashing strobe-like lights rotating around Gertie's grey, glitter foam interior. Not a good sign. The sunlight is marginally poking through Lesley's flimsy garment drapes covering the back windows. I push open the doors with my head and realise I still have a balled-up tissue pressed to my tongue which I had placed there to stop the drooling. It's dry and firmly stuck. It feels like a lump of papier mache has been placed there. It's still attached to the roll of loo paper and it keeps unravelling like I'm playing wheel of fortune. I fall out and blink towards the sun. I can see the silhouette of two angels standing before me. Have I died and gone straight to Hell's Angels? I blink rapidly, trying to take it all in and also to get the sleep matter from my sticky eyes. Not angels or bikers, more like two aliens before me, they have massive round heads, reflective, shiny eyes.

"Run for your lives. ALIENS."

This in itself is quite a talent to say clearly with a wad of paper balled in my mouth. Ange finally stirs, sits up and squints to the extraterrestrial beings.

"Check out their helmets?"

"What kind of girl do you think I am Ange? I barely know them."

"Their helmets on their head stupid - they're not aliens, they're bikers."

 "Ladies, when you're quite finished discussing our helmets, we'd like to introduce ourselves. I am Sergeant Eric Shun"

"I'm not in the slightest bit surprised to hear this Sergeant given that you're seeing us in all our natural beauty first thing in the morning"

"And this here is PC Chris Peacock"

"Again, not in the slightest bit surprised as having your nether regions as close to the scorchio bike tank in this searing heat will do that to a man"

"We're Alice Springs Highway Patrol, or A Hip as we're more commonly known. We've had one or a hundred complaints about you ladies."

"Of course, you have. Firstly, I feel I must apologise profusely for directing my pal Jules's gaze to your private parts boys, but I seriously meant the helmets that you're wearing...on your heads...on top of your shoulders. Whatever the complaints are, it's all a complete misunderstanding and easily explained. You see, we were going for a pee in the middle of the night and it was pitch dark. Jules here has rather large feet for her rather small stature and accidentally tripped over a guy-rope string which then became a domino effect as when one fell, they all came tumbling down. Everybody ran and screamed at the sound when the walls came tumbling down. A blinding light, the sun had died, a new moon took its place, tidal waves and open graves the fate of this particular human race."

"You've got Style I'll give you that. Let me check with my fellow counsel here."

That fell on deaf ears, but I thought it was clever.

"We've come to the conclusion that you've outstayed your welcome here in Alice Springs. It's likely to be bringin On the Heartbreak though."

"Ahhhh, a glimpse at some humour."

"It ends here ladies."

"That's another fine mess you've got me into Jules."

"If you must make a noise in the future, make it quietly."

"Look Sargeant Eric Shun, I'm not as dumb as she looks and I promise to keep her in check and be good from now on."

"Sorry, not this time. And to prove that we're not as heartless as we believe you think we are, we're going to escort you to the city limits."

"Och well, it was worth a try. Lead on Macduff, let's get this show on the road."

The Chips Brigade, or A shits unit, lead the convoy of one and drive through the deserted streets to the city limits. They get off their bikes and flag us over.

"Now what?"

"We want to warn you not to pick up any hitchhikers around these parts as it's not always safe."

"We're big girls Sergeant Eric Shun and can take care of ourselves"

"You say that, but we recently had to rescue a girl from your part of the world, who obviously thought the same."

"Please stop there, no need to go into any more details. We have to continue our journey."

"Wheesht Ange, I for one am dying to hear all about this Scottish girl you speak of. Is she a nurse per chance?"

"She is, how on earth did you know that?"

"Please just drive Jules."

"We're actually looking for her. Do you happen to know where she is?"

"Tell us only that ociffers, no need to tell us any good deeds, random acts of kindness or exemplary behaviours that she displayed. We really don't have the time or the inclination to hear any of it."

"I beg to differ. This is for sure worth hearing. Especially for you two to hear, some of it might rub off."

"Don't worry about me PC Chris Peacock, I've been rubbed so many times I am practically luminous."

"That may well be the case Missy, but she really showed her heart of gold. She'd been out here trying to hitch for a few hours when we picked her up and told her it wasn't safe, but she said she needed to get to her new position in an outpost a few hours from here, but there was no transport heading there for at least another few weeks.

"We brought her back to the local jail until we could get her a safe lift. For a few days she came in to the jail at the crack of dawn, read to some of the illiterate juvenile delinquents, even teaching them a few basic writing skills, and at night she would entertain the inmates at the local prison, reading some Famous Five mysteries, so when me and Rob here next got the day off, we drove her out to Utopia, an Aboriginal homeland, in my Ute. She is a very special lady. Now there's a lady, right there."

"Speaking of special, we're actually a very specialised unique unit in the forces and she's a very much wanted person of interest in Aberdeen."

"Nooo, I can't believe that. What did she allegedly do?"

"We're not at liberty to say, but she's a danger to herself."

"We have to be quick here or she might be in danger of committing another crime by dropping another bomb."

"Bomb?"

"Yes, we must dash now that we know where she is. Thank you for that."

As we drive off, we leave them in the slipstream of our red dust trail scratching their heads, looking bemused and perplexed, Ange shouts out her window.

"The F bomb that is. We don't allow that type of unruly behaviour in Aberdeen. And what the fuck is a Ute?"

We're well on our way to hear or care about any response from them.

ANGE

It turns out she's been volunteering at the holding cells reading The Famous Five, of all things, to the detainees and then to some reprobates at night, so as reciprocation, Sergeant Eric Shun and PC Rob Banks had escorted her in a Ute, which turns out to be a flatbed utility truck and not the side car from the Aristocats I had imagined, and secretly hoped it to be, to a settlement three hours north.

We're that close, that close, I can feel it in my weary red dust-filled bone marrow. I'm soon going to have my "come to Jesus" moment with Lesley, nurse to the ill, coffee giver to the weary, donor of all things tat to the homeless, cleaner of hostels, master baker to the homesick, carer to the infirm, gardener to landscapes, chef to culinary geriatrics, replenisher of all things First Aid, teacher to illiterate delinquents, reader to the happy inmate masses. Little friend to all the fucking world. I can't wait to flush out all of her insincere, annoying ways. Never mind being a nurse extraordinaire, she could be a professional do-gooder instead. A real live Good fucking Samaritan in the flesh. No one, no one is that nice and unselfishly worthy and giving. NO ONE

JULES

Ange is raging and muttering about all Lesley's so-called altruist traits. I can't quite get my head around why she is so angry.

"Why does this make you so cross?"
"I'll tell you why Jules, because she goes about consciously doing good deeds with a side order of self-righteousness."

"I disagree, she actually does what she does from the goodness of her heart - a trait we should both learn from."

"Whateva."

We drive in silence and continue to bob along on the unsealed road, watching the red dust coming and going on the windscreen with our all-but-knackered wipers. It's like Groundhog Day, draining, repetitive and very, very boring. Aside from the silence that is, which is an absolute blessing just to listen to her being silent is a gift in itself. Again, making the mundane all the more pleasant. Hopefully, it gives her food for thought. The landscape hasn't changed for miles and miles and miles. Thankfully Ange's repetitive finger tapping has stopped also, so I don't feel the urge to turn into a homicidal, steering wheel wielding maniac. I'm actually enjoying this part of the journey. I'm so tired though and on the verge of pulling to the side, curling up into a wee ball and sleeping when I see the sign for "UTOPIA."

It's actually a handmade piece of wood:

"URAPUNTJA HEALTH UTOPIA."

It has a big red arrow pointing to the right. Maybe we can stop at a cafe first, get some refreshing freshly squeezed lemonade and a salad, but as we drive into town we glean pretty quickly that's not going to be the case. Littered on either side of the road are carcasses of animals, not all dead either. We drive by, gobsmacked at what we see, the almost living cadavers move and bark at us. Abandoned cars, corrugated shacks line the sides and a Lutheran church dominates the horizon ahead of us. This is it we realise, taking in the full extent of what we are witnessing in a very different stunned silence. This is how the residents of Utopia live and I'm assuming Lesley also. Families are actually here, in this shithole, in the most adverse poverty one can imagine in one of the wealthiest countries in the world. It blows my mind. How can such a travesty be allowed? Who takes responsibility for this, I wonder?

We pull over, both of us slightly in shock at what we see and begin to walk through the reservation. There appears to be no ventilation whatsoever in the accommodation, certainly no air conditioning, no electricity, no anything, only dank concrete, rusted corrugated iron, decrepit and filthy. No escape from the intense sun, the grime and fly infestation. Men, women, children and dogs are lying on the concrete, swatting flies, only the latter barely aware of our presence. The makeshift shanty church, its red earth floor swept clean, is in complete contrast to everything else. Ange and I walk in a dwam, mouths agape until we catch a shitload of incessant, buzzing flies. We get temporary relief from them when we tie bandanas around our faces. I guess this is how the Akubra with corks dangling from the rim originated. Slightly stunned, traumatized and shocked by what we are witnessing, we head towards the health clinic, and I use that term loosely, in the centre of the community. There are scores of sick, infirm, old, young, indifferent, sad, abandoned, hopeless Aborigines waiting their turn patiently at the doors. We pass them all, taking each step slowly and deliberately, making eye contact with each and everyone. Yes, we can see you. I inhale deeply and realise I've been holding my breath. The desperation etched on the faces on the outside and no doubt the inside is palpable. I want to cry. The sun is beginning to set behind us in the shrublands, the silhouette of three kangaroos jumping towards a watering hole. The contrast of the inhabitants of Utopia, the smell of the desert, the magnificent light, the energy of the sun as it sets and draws a veil over the settlement does not escape me. I begin to cry, soft, gentle, heartfelt tears. I look at Ange, expecting to see her hard face set in stone, but see silent tears slowly, gently, escaping and then quickly absorbed by her dusty face mask. We can still hear the dogs barking and milling around, scavenging for morsels on the red earth. Families emerge from the shacks and take up positions in the cooler shade of their doorways and porches. There is definitely something surreal and magical at the same time. We walk through the door and into the waiting room of sorts, full of coughing, spluttering, sick indigenous individuals. We go up to the desk. I can't even speak, so Ange takes the reins.

"We're looking for our friend Lezz, Lesley, she's a nurse from Scotland and we believe she's working here."

"Yes, yes, Nurse Lesley is here, but not right now she isn't as she's the flight nurse today and with The Royal Flying Doctor Service at one of the outposts in The Bush. My name is Marg, what can I do for you girls? Here to work?"

"Oh, hell no, seems like purgatory."

"Ha, ha, it does seem like a sentence at times, although it does get under your skin after a while and the benefits outweigh our overworked, underpaid, isolated, frustrating, fly-infested existence."

Another wink or a fly in her eye.

"I'll take your word for it, but not for me. I'd rather poke my eye out with a sharpened boomerang."

"Ignore her Marg. You mentioned outposts, plural in The Bush? There's more places...like this?"

"Oh yes dear, there is. Plenty more. We're kept busy, very busy."

"I can only imagine. It seems very grim."

"On the contrary dear, it's terribly rewarding, challenging faw shuwa, but enriching."

"If you say so. Is there somewhere we can wait for her? We're her friends, Jules and Ange, she may have mentioned us."

"Yes, she does speak of you. Welcome to Utopia, she's due back in a few hours or so. You can wait for her in her donga."

"Donga?"

"Yes dear, it's our luxury temporary staff accommodation."

More winking or stigma perhaps, I can't tell.

"The staff accommodation is out back and down the track, second star on the right and straight on till morning?"

Does everyone say that? And most definitely a wink.

"You'll see it. It's the only decent place out there. Relax and chill until she gets back."

"Thank you. We're exhausted."

"Take this kerosene lamp, there are no street lights out here, so we're dependent on the stars, moon and fireflies."

Another wink, fly or stigma. She turns her back and hollers over the counter.

"Next!"

It never even crosses my mind that we've skipped the queue and no one has said a word. Who do we think we are? Seriously, who do we think we are? Luxury dongas indeed, definitely a wink from her as basically they're glorified individual corrugated containers with a camp bed, a desk, a chair, and that's about it. There are communal showers in the centre of the long row and another container at the end has a central sitting area with a basic kitchen of sorts. I can't believe this is where Lesley has been living. The toilets are in an outhouse at the back of the premises. We sit on the so-called porch which is a concrete step and take it all in. We are completely silent, much too stunned to talk.

ANGE

This is a complete eye opener. I never in a million years expected this. I'm finding it hard to breathe as the air is dense and stifling and I've only been here a minute, nowhere near as long as Lesley or the other volunteers, let alone the local residents. Credit where credit is due, she's been here for over a month now, bless her. Speaks volumes. Good on her for volunteering in a part of the world where it is very much needed. It does change my opinion of her, only slightly I might add, nothing too extreme, but certainly a shift. Not everyone is willing or able to do this kind of work. I know I wouldn't. Having said that, though, if there's a volunteer needed to start a dog shelter, I'm first in line.

"I'm not sure I'm quite ready for this."

"What do you mean?"

"Well, this all ends."

"End?"

"It's been an incredible journey to get this far and we're here now. Once we take Lesley back to Sydney, then what?"

"It doesn't end here Ange, it begins here. We only have to relax and be, let it all unfold the way it's intended."

"I know, but we've had so much fun, a few scrapes along the way for sure, but more fun and laughter than anything else."

"It can still be that way, but we need to let go of the shackles that drag and lure us back to the past or pull us into the future before our time. This, this moment right here, is all we have with any certainty. Let's take a breath, relax and just be, enjoying the peace and calm from the inside out."

"You know, you make so much sense sometimes, psychobable shite the rest of the time though. I'm not looking forward to seeing Lesley."

"Why not? That's why we're here isn't it?"

"I've been such a bitch Jules."

"Yes, you have. We both have. Our past behaviours don't define us, we have every opportunity to choose our experience in every given moment. Choose your response carefully as opposed to a reaction."

"Easier said than done. How exactly do you pay that much attention to yourself and your actions?"

"You can start by focusing on your breath and the aliveness inside your body. There are senses, signals, and energy constantly. All you need is to pay attention. It's 90% hard work, you have to be aware as to whether it's your ego or your awareness taking the reins of your being. The latter is the right direction I believe. When you awake to each moment, you will feel the energy of being alive, and I mean really alive, a constant tingling, vibrating that tops you up with a spectacular light and unwavering energy."

"Steady Pooh, don't get too carried away with yourself, it's still me here remember."

"Ha, one breath at a time Ange, start there."

We must have fallen asleep, curled up on the dirt, resting our heads on our backpacks, waiting for Lesley to return. We are woken up by the stupendous light rising from the horizon. Yellow, orange, red, gold beams of light radiate out along the rust-coloured earth, inching its way up and over our sleeping bodies. As we blink towards the rising desert sun, the silhouette of an angel with a beautiful halo is clearly seen set against the core of the sun coming up the track towards us.

"Can you see the angel Ange?"

"There's no such thing as angels, besides it doesn't have wings."

"Not all angels have wings though."

"I do see a ring of bright light around its head though."

"A halo?"

"Yes, a halo. It's beautiful. Looks so incredibly magical against the backdrop of the rising sun."

It moves gracefully in our direction. I am mesmerised. As it does, it begins to expand, the form taking shape. The halo transforming before my eyes into what I can now clearly see as a nurse's cap with a red cross on the front.... OMG... LEZZERS'.... She continues towards us.

"LESLEY?"

"LEZZ... LESLEY?"

She stops dead in her tracks as soon as she hears our voices. She shields her eyes from the sun, blinking from the glorious light, adjusting her vision to the blazing brilliance. She centres her attention on us, a pair of muckle dusty, red-coated galahs sitting on her doorstep. I can see the smile melt from her wee cherubic, shiny face and I can see, even from this distance, the disbelief as she stops dead in her tracks and stares at us both. Jules gets up and runs to her like a clucky hen in floods of tears, gives her a huge hug and spins her off her wee Minnie Mouse white-clad feet. She only then smiles at the same time as trying to take it all in. Jules is garbling on, faster than a speeding train and I can tell Lesley is trying to keep up. Jules is going on and on.

"We've been following you all the way from Sydney, to Melbourne, Tasmania, South Australia and finally here, in The Bush, we've found you."

"What do you mean following my trail? Why? I don't understand."

"It's a long story, but we're here now. Come in out of the sun and we'll explain, or at least try to."

"I think I may need to lie down to take all this in. Are you a pigment of my imagination? Pinch me."

So, I did.

"Ouch, not that hard Ange. You really are here, but why?"

"We'll get to that, sit down and we'll explain. It was a huge mistake letting you leave us to go off on your own. We are so, so incredibly sorry for all our awful, selfish, hedonistic behaviour."

"Let me get this straight? You have come all this way to apologise?"

"Well, yes, kind of."

"Kind of?"

"We are genuinely, sincerely sorry for what we put you through and we're here to make amends and we want you to come back to Sydney with us so we can prove and show you how much we've changed."

LESLEY

I can't believe my eyes or my ears as I hear my name cut through the morning cacophony of cicadas, dogs, clicking sounds of bush kangaroos and cockortwos. The high-pitched screams are blood-curdling, and rip through the daily animal rituals. I can make out my donger and one, no two forms, sitting on the step. The next thing I know I'm being picked up off my feet and spun round....

"Jules?"

I can't believe what I'm seeing. Anastasia and Godzilla are here on my porch in UTOPIA. I'm more confused than usual.

"Why are you here? How?"

My Piglet brain is having difficulty taking it all in, it's all so strange and very, very surreal. Jules puts me down, takes my hand and leads me to the donger where Ange is still sitting, waiting. Jules continues to hug me.

"I've really, really missed you Lesley, you're a complete star. We've followed all your good deeds for months."
"Good deeds? What are you talking about?"

Ange is a little more reserved, staying back for a while before getting up and approaching me with a high five. Typical. She's not getting away with that. It's good to see her, so I wrap my arms around her and squeeze tight.

"Come here you big oaf and give me a proper welcome."
"Good to see you, Lesley, finally. It's been quite the intrepid journey to get here to you."

"This is a whole lot to take in."

"Can you ever forgive Ange and I?"

"Forgive you for what exactly?"

"We'll have plenty of time on the way back to Sydney to discuss it."

"Sydney? Look, I'm not going back there yet, why would I? I have everything I need and have been looking for right here."

"What about Mikey? He's not here is he, or have you changed your mind about him?"

"Heavens no, aside from him, of course, everything I've been wanting from this trip is right here. I feel very much needed and wanted."

"Mikey needs you. We need you."

"Perhaps, but he's not here, is he? Look, as much as I'd like to discuss this further, I can't think straight, I haven't slept in over 20 hours. I need to sit down, take my shoes off, have something to eat and rest a while, then we can chat."

ANGE

I can tell from the get-go, that Nurse Nightingale isn't going to be the pushover we naively thought she'd be. It hadn't even crossed our narrow minds when we took off from Sydney that she might refuse to return with us. Jules continues to snivel.

"We're really sorry Lesley, Ange and I just want us all to return to Sydney together and begin again."

Lesley completely ignores her

"I hear you Jules, please come in and make yourself at home. It's not much to look at, a bit basic, but it's cleanish, warm and safe. I'm better off here than most locals of Utopia, and for that I am eternally thankful and grateful. Now, let me rest awhile, then like I said, we can chat."

LESLEY

I can see by the expression on their faces that they aren't as taken with Drogheda, as the locals lovingly call it, as I am. Shame there isn't a Richard Chamberlain-type character to cast my eyes on. I would settle just seeing Mikey actually. Boy how I'm missing him at the moment, more than anything else in the world right now. We can't have everything though, now can we? However, I know he's been waiting on me patiently for the past few months, giving me the space and time to find out what I'm seeking from life. I'm at a place now where I know exactly who I am and what my passions and purpose are meant to be. I can't wait to tell him. Before I know it, I'm sound asleep thinking of my Love.

ANGE

Lesley falls asleep as soon as she lies down on the uncomfy, unsealed bumpy-looking camp bed. I take off her shoes and tuck her up under the insubstantial, sheer, nylon so-called blanket. We can wait until she wakes to discuss our return to Sydney. Jules and I go for a walkabout in The Bush to explore and experience the red outback. We talk to the locals and hear stories of their incredulous Aboriginal culture. The town itself is very basic, rustic, punctuated by the big, beaming, pearly white smiles of the residents. The children seem very taken with us and hold our hands, leading us a short way out of town, followed by a few mangy looking dogs and their puppies.

They take us on a well-trodden path through the brush and scrub, that eventually opens up to expose an incredible watering hole, a rare gem in the red centre, flanked and surrounded by

towering red quartzite cliffs that provide the backdrop
of breathtaking views of Mother Nature's design that transform in
colour before our eyes as the sun does its thing. I have never been
in such a magical place. We are both blown away. The wild
swimming wonderland is quite remarkable and an easy escape
from the dry, arid, dusty heat. What a fabulous place to wallow and
do some hardcore chilling.

   We share the serene space with a throng of birds, reptiles,
marsupials, dogs and laughing children. How much better does it
get than this? There's a cheeky rope swing and a secret beach if
you swim through the waterfall to the right. Jules and I spend
almost the entire day at the watering hole with the local children,
playing, telling stories, swimming and laughing loads. From
absolutely nowhere, or so it seems, a picnic appears and we are
invited to share the fresh fruit and water with our fellow watering
hole inhabitants. I cannot remember the last time I enjoyed myself
quite as much as this. Not an adult beverage or an illegal joint in
sight either. As the sun begins to set, we make our way back to
town and to Lesley, who is hopefully feeling more refreshed and
able to chat. We hug and kiss the happy children goodbye and head
down to Lesley's donga. She has found three rocking chairs from
somewhere and is sitting patiently outside her donga anticipating
our return.

   "Pull up a chair ladies and let's enjoy the sunset together."

   The sun slips gradually towards the horizon, naturally
shifting easily, gradually and majestically from our day into a new
one for somebody else. No setting here, rising there, a continuous
energetic ball of light moving through its cycle. It's spherical
brilliance beaming rich colours over The Bush, casting its
constantly changing palette of rose, purple, orange and gold in

glorious hues, drawing a rich veil over the rocks, the desert, the creatures and the town of Utopia, taking centre stage and putting everything else into the dark shadows of the wings.

It disappears from our world only to appear in all its glory somewhere else, to be welcomed as a new dawn on another's horizon. As it departs behind the desert setting, it radiates it's final spray over The Outback's full stage. We continue to sit, taking it all in. As one set slips, fades and vanishes, it is replaced to reveal the crystal-clear sky spotlighting the famous constellations in all their greatness in a stunning galaxy above our heads.

I sense the direct pulse of the sacred red earth as it courses its way to join the incessant rhythm of my beating heart where it takes repose, sealing this moment in my memory. I feel grounded and am in awe of the twinkling stars that litter the sky. We have the best view of The Milky Way on Earth from our rocking chairs in front of the corrugated shack in the middle of The Outback.

"Do you know that the Aboriginal people have been reading skies for over 65,00 years, making them the first astrologers?"

"Astrono…really?"

"They used the night sky to find food, to teach their culture about their land, to direct themselves at night and so much more. It's fascinating, this ancient science that has been passed from generation to generation, woven into Dreamtime stories."

"There must be so much knowledge in those stories."

"There are. I hope you get the chance to hear some of them. They are integral to their lives. One of my favourite stories is Gugurmin the Celestial Emu."

"Already sounds better than Rod Hull's Grotesque Emu!"

"Quite. When they see this emu in the sky, it lets them know when the time is right to look for their eggs solely based on its position in the sky. It's like a seasonal menu."

"Bloody hell Lesley, you're right. Can you see the Southern Cross up there? Look to the left of it and down a bit and you can see the shape of a big fat doobie, which means the time is right to spark one up, wouldn't you agree?"

"Not really Ange, but you be you."

"Good idea, besides everyone else is taken."

"Let's get back to the nitty gritty - what's the story, morning glory? Tell me what this is really all about? You haven't travelled all this way to apologise, sit out here with me and watch the night sky while smoking a joint."

"I can't speak for Jules here, but that sounds about right to me. Oh, you forgot that we're here to take you back to Sydney also."

"And why exactly would I do that? Tell me, I'm curious, one good reason is more than enough."

JULES

What can we say without actually telling her the truth? We promised and I sure as hell am not going to be the one to blow the secret. I'm aware that I'm rocking a bit faster than necessary and I'm sure I look like Danny DeVito's character, Martini, in One Flew Over the Cuckoo's Nest.

LESLEY

Something is up and I can definitely smell a fish. Jules is rocking fast enough to make two scores in the dirt with the rocker rails. Any faster and we'll see sparks fly.

"Look Lesley, we've learned our lesson and recognize the good, kind person you are."

"Was there ever a doubt about that Jules?"

"No, no, not from me. We BOTH feel we treated you unfairly and want to make amends."

"And this needs to be done back in Sydney?"

"Yes, in Sydney."

"Can it not be here?"

"No, not really. We need to go back to where it all began and start over."

Ange continues to rock slowly and gently, sipping her beer and smoking a joint. Saying nothing, not adding to the conversation one bit. Staring out into the big bad yonder.

"You seem very insistent and Adam Ant. Is it that important to you?"

"Yes, yes, it is."

"Look, you have nothing to apologise for really. Being stuck in past events won't serve any of us any purpose. Life is too short to hold on to regrets or seek revenge for possible wrongdoings. But if it means something to you, I accept your apology."

"Great, thank you Lesley, you won't regret it. When do you want to leave?"

"Oh, I'm the one that is sorry now, perhaps I didn't make myself clear. I accept your apologies, but I'm not going back to Sydney with you."

"What??"

Ange suddenly stands up and stands in front of Lesley.

"Look here, we came here specially to collect you, it's no skin off my nose if you decide to stay in this godforsaken place, but it may be something you will come to regret."

"Really, Ange? It's magical here, and not the god-foreskin place you think it is."

"It's already beginning to get under my skin, that's for sure. Now where's the shithole dunny in this shithole place? It'll give you some more time to rethink your decision."

"Make sure to check under the toilet seat as black widow spiders love living in dark, dank spaces."

"Look Ms. B Ossy Britches. I've had it up to my pussy's bow with you telling me and everyone else what to do and not do. I'm big enough and ugly enough to look after myself and make my own decisions and mistakes. I certainly don't need Nurse Nightingale, I don't need a charitable cup of coffee, I don't need yours or anyone else's secondhand tat, I can clean my own hostel, thank you very much, I can bake my own fucking cakes, I don't need a carer to brush my hair, smooth any wayward clothing wrinkles or clean my arse. I can landscape my own garden, cook my own Michelin star worthy dishes. I have my own First Aid box and I can teach those who can't even do joined-up speaking, let alone writing. I can read to the Holy Wullies and I can be friend to all the fucking world, so no, I don't need you, of all people, to tell me what I should and shouldn't do. Now, if you don't mind me,

I'm going to read the fucking stars and find the direction to the toilet."

ANGE

Too much? Possibly, but once it started, the caustic lava continued to spew. I didn't intend to be quite so brutal, but maybe if she bunches that with all my other misdemeanours I've done, then we can tidy all this up, put a big red bow around it then make like diarrhea and run out of here. The dunny is like a wooden porta potty in the back garden.

"Blah, blah, black widow spiders, yada fuckin yada, toilet seat. Seriously, though, who gave her the righteous stick?"

She must think me some fucking idiot. The place is a hole, literally. A big hole with a cracked unfixed toilet covering it, with a gnarled seat trying to keep some of the flies in or out, not quite sure. The single bulb being held by a greasy piece of coil dangles overhead. I unzip my jeans, am about to lift the lid, turn around and squat when I hear this squeaky voice in my head. "Better check for black widow spiders under the seat."

I tentatively lift the lid with my pointer finger. Nothing but dubious-looking stains, chips and cracks on the seat. I keep hearing Lesley's warnings about spiders and I carefully lift the seat up also. I squint enough in the dim light and adjust my vision to the gloom. My face is an inch from the rim and I can make out a tiny wee spec on the bowl. Closer. As I come closer the wee spec becomes two, then four. FUCK ME. My heart is beating through my singlet and I can see the red dots and the wiggling legs. I gasp and stagger back through the door. Phew, that really was a close shave. There, before my beady wee eyes, is a colony of the fuckers. Lesley is right. I go back in and ever so gently close the seat and lid, no need to kill Mummy Charlotte and all her babies. They probably got an even bigger fright than I did and are heading off to pastures new anyway. Every life, in my opinion, is sacred, even the poisonous ones. I retreat with my shorts and knickers sagging below my waist, tight across my upper thighs like some angry youth disrespecting the system. My large white derriere leaves the latrine first. The fresh air, in contrast to the shitty, clatty, musky inside, hits my arse like a slap with a didgeridoo. Using the light from the gazillion stars, I penguin my way over to a dilapidated shed in the bush adjacent to the dongas. I check the ground and surrounding area before directing my behind at the back wall. I aim at a 45-degree angle and spray the rotting wooden slats. I come back to the front of the donga to find Jules still trying to persuade Lesley to come back with us.

"Look here, we could go on all day and night discussing the pros and cons, but the bottom line is this. It's actually very simple, it's either a yes or no, that way we can plan to get back in our van and head north towards Darwin and leave Nurse Nightingale to her bog standard charitable work in this bog-standard shithole."

LESLEY

There is no doubt that going back to Sydney is very appealing as I do miss my everyday comforts, the basics like my hairdryer, a shower that comes out with more than one drip at a time, a flushing toilet and sausage rolls. I miss them so much. Most of all Mikey, I really miss him. But I'm also adamant that I'm not going to let Ange see or know just how homesick and tempted I am to return with them, not just to Sydney, but back home. I've seen and done enough here to know where I need to be and that is back in Aberdeen with Mikey working as a "bog standard" nurse and loving every minute of it. She's really worn me out though with this vitriol and diatribe directed straight at me. I had no idea how it might come across to someone with as little self-worth as she clearly has. However, it's no way to speak to anyone and I can feel all this pent-up energy simmering somewhere deep within me ready to boil over to the surface. I think the mention of "bog standard" and "shit hole" is the final straw that breaks the caramel's back. I'm not proud of myself here, but I let her have it, both barrels blazing. I pride myself in my patience, but I feel myself losing control and reacting to her constant jibes, it's been a very long time in coming in my opinion.

"Life is all about love and connections Ange. Our first relationship needs to be with oneself, first and foremost. One tends to forget this and we look outside ourselves for validation, happiness, companionship, love or whatever it is we deem to be missing from our lives. The truth, and nothing but the truth is that we are whole, complete and perfect just as we are, where we are and who we are.

We need to really prioritize this deep connection with the self, become aware of it, nurture it, allow it to grow, develop and flourish into the full expression of our true essence. We need to lean in, accept that every experience, event, behaviour and person we come across has a purpose for us to grow and learn from. People, including so-called friends, come and go from our lives Ange, whether by choice or circumstance. Initially my time with you was upsetting, caused considerable heartache and I shed copious amounts of silent tears. Believe me when I tell you that I tried, I really tried to fit in, to be one of the cool kids. I thought it was me. I took it all so personally. I tried to analyse the cause, the disregard, the indifference to what I was doing wrong? I completely blamed myself. I tried to change myself, but all I felt was stress. I tried to get you to like me. Desperate and happy to take even a little bit of attention, like being thrown a scrap of rancid meat.

Finally, I gave up the fight. I lost sleep, confidence, sadly no weight, but plenty of self-worth in the battle. You wore me down until there wasn't much left of my old self. It eventually came to the point where I needed to come to terms with all that had happened and process it. I came to the conclusion that by travelling, I'd get the space, perspective, insight and ultimately the peace that I needed. I learned my strengths, my weaknesses and ultimately, I came to the conclusion that I'm okay with the person that is here before you tonight, warts, malaprops and all. It's been challenging for sure, but I'm in a place where I'm awake to awareness and fully accept all that I am. Everyone wants to be seen, heard, valued, happy and loved but it has to come from believing that they already are in their inner world. No amount of seeking any of those traits in the outer world will be able to do that, it will only be temporary until they look inside themselves. I know I am not everyone's cup of coffee, but for those that choose to sit with me, they will not be betrayed, they will feel the ripple effect of my smile, my compassion, my hope, my love and joy for this precious life which hopefully lights me up from the inside out, radiates and beams out on everyone, everything and anything.

"For whatever reason, our friendship has never served you any purpose. I'm not funny enough, pretty enough or clever enough, but I have learned that life is full of transferences, reflections and projections and it speaks more of your feeling of self-worth or lack of it than mine. I no longer take any of it personally and set you free to find the person you're meant to be. It's there and there are glimpses of it, certainly when animals are involved. Your sarcasm, put downs and vitriol do not, in my opinion, allow your light to shine any brighter. I wish you no harm, I thank you from the heart of my bottom for being my teacher, guiding me to the lessons that I needed to learn. One day, when you're ready, your teacher and guide will appear, hopefully you'll be ready to recognize and appreciate it. Now, I'm going to make like Michael Jackson and beat it. I need a few moments on my own."

I get up slowly, a bit shaky and go behind the donger.

"Wow, and wow. Tell me how you really feel Lesley? That was brutal. Did she just regurgitate one of Deepthroat Chopra's books?"

"More like, make like Michael Jackson on fire and get roasted."

"It feels like a constant spray of paintball pellets have been shot into my chest, a direct bullseye to the centre of my heart, precisely and accurately fired. I had no idea that's how she sees me. Am I that bad?"

"You're bad, you're bad, you know you're bad, you know you're bad, you know, and the world has to answer right now, just to tell you once again, who's bad?"

"Me apparently."

ANGE

At that very second, a blood-curdling scream comes from behind the donga. We look at each other and take off racing round to the back to find Lesley lying face down in the scrub, rotating like a succulent piglet on a spit. Her eyes disappearing to the back of her head, her jeans, Minnie Mouse panties round her ankles and a red ring of squashed black widows on her bottom. She looks up at me with blank eyes and I realise that she must have sat on the toilet without looking under the lid first. She must have assumed that I'd checked and it was clear for her.

"OH NO!!!"

"WTF?"

"She's been bitten."

"What? How? Did you not check before you went?"

"Never mind that, go get Gertie, we'll need to take her immediately to the clinic. She needs antivenom and she needs it now."

I kneel down beside her and take her head in my arms, brush the spiders from her backside. Fuck, fuck, what do I do? Lesley sure as hell can't tell me.

"I'm sorry Lesley, I'm sorry."

I know I'm beginning to panic and am trying to frantically remember what I can do to relieve a spider bite.

"I'm sorry Lesley"

I gently turn her over, in an emergency one has to do what one has to do and this, after all, is an emergency. I pull my shorts and pants down, squat over her backside and try to pee. I've just been, so can only squeeze out a few drops at a time. Thankfully Jules comes rattling round in Gertie in no time at all. She'll have to do it.

"What the feck are you doing?"

"Urinating on her sting. I read somewhere that it can reduce the pain and swelling."

"That's a feckin jellyfish, not a spider bite. Get off her and grab her legs, I'll take her head and we'll get her in the back of Gertie."

JULES

I reverse up the side just in time to see Ange about to piss on Lesley. Between the two of us we pull her shorts up somewhat, but leave the angry, engorged swelling site exposed. Ange is crying and repeating:

"I'm so sorry, please be alright, please be alright, I'm so sorry. I promise to change, just be alright."

It isn't her fault, so I'm not sure why the big remorse now. Lesley appears unconscious, so I take off like a bat out of hell down the dirt road.

"Ange, you need to get some of that poison out."

"How?"

"Suck it for feck sake."

"But it's on her backside."

"I don't care if it's on her poonanny, suck it up Darlene and spit it out. I know you can do that well enough as you've had plenty of practice."

Ange carefully turns her over and begins to suck Lesley's arse, it sounds like little kissing noises.

"Watch the bumps, for fuck sake. I keep losing suction."

"Latch on as if your life depends on it as hers does for sure."

I pull up in front of the clinic and see that all the lights are off, they're closed. I need to drive to The Royal Flying Doctor Service about five miles down the dirt road.

"Hold on there Ange, just a wee bit further."

"Come on Lesley, hang in there."

ANGE

I'm not sure how much she can hear me, or is even aware as to what I'm doing, but she suddenly takes my hand and squeezes it tight. My tears stream down my face almost as fast and furious as Jules's driving. I'm truly, truly sorry, not just for not killing the spiders when I had the chance, but for everything else I have done to her. What a horrible, selfish cow I am. She doesn't deserve this. She could die right here, right now, and it's all because of me. I continue to suck and spit, suck and spit until we come to a stop at the small airstrip.

JULES

It's like something out of a horror movie or a hideous nightmare at the very least. As I approach the RFDS strip, I start honking my horn, coming to an abrupt halt in front of the hanger and stumble out of Gertie, running towards the main building. I burst through the doors.

"SPIDER!!!!!!"

Everyone just sits around a small table and looks at me.

"No shit Sheila, they're ten a penny here in The Outback."

Is this the kind of thing that happens on a regular basis? Time seems to be suspended and I half expect to see tumbleweed tumbling and blowing across the floor.

"It's Lesley. In the van, outside, she's been bitten by a redback. She works here with you."

That gets their attention, they all jump into action and the on-duty doctor, having heard all the hupladoodle, comes out of a back office, grabs her bag and races out the door I'd just crashed through.

"Why didn't you say that in the first place?"

We all run to where Lesley lies motionless in the back of Gertie. Ange is still sucking furiously at the same time as holding her hand.

"You can stop that now, we got this. Lesley? Lesley? It's Dr Bonar here. Can you open your eyes?"

She is calm, in complete control and in a commanding, confident tone, she gives her orders out.

"We've got Nurse Lesley here, go check her file, find out what blood group she is and see what antivenom and blood we have in stock. You get whatever antivenom units we have, she may need it on the flight."

"Flight?"

"Yes, we need to evacuate her immediately. She has taken the worst reaction to the poison one can take. Her vitals are dropping and it's imperative we get her to the nearest hospital."

The doctor is taking all her vitals, shaking her head.

"What happened here? Do you know? She's having a severe reaction to a bite."

"She's been bitten by at least a dozen black widows."

"A dozen? That explains it. How?"

"She was in the toilet."

"That's strange, she knows better than that not to check before using. A dozen you say?

That's not good. I'm afraid she's going to need more than the few units of antivenom we have here. She requires urgent aeromedical evacuation to a major hospital if she's going to survive this."

"Survive?? Oh please, please, please."

The doctor completely ignores me and continues barking out orders, now to the flight crew.

"Get the plane ready for immediate take off."

The nurse returns as Lesley is being stretchered into the belly of the cessna.

"She's B Rhus positive and we don't have any."

"We'll have to fly without it and take our chances then."

"Did you say B Rhesus positive?"

"Yes."

"That's my blood group."

"Are you sure? It's very uncommon, less than 10% of the population."

"I'm 100% sure."

"Then you're coming with us. She's one very lucky lady to have you on board if needed. We probably have enough antivenom here to inject into your lips also, you may have been slightly poisoned with all that sucking. What did you say your name was?"

"Ange. No, give it all to her, I can live with my trout pout, but she needs all you can give her."

"I promise you, one unit is not going to make a difference to her. She's critically ill and her life is hanging on a thread as it is."

As we prepare for take off, they tell Jules they will let her know where they've taken us and she can follow in the van.

JULES

Ange looks grotesque, like some demented, scary clown. She's still crying, her lips are red, engorged and inflated to the size of an adult rubber ring. She's still making those involuntary sucking noises that babies make when there's no nipple, even though she's nowhere near the bite site. She refuses to let go of Lesley's hand. I'm telling you, I couldn't make this stuff up.

ANGE

I know she's in a really bad way, her backside is already swollen to twice its usual size, as apparently are my lips, but I don't care as long as she is alright. I'll never forgive myself if she dies because of me. It's all my fault. She has a number of smaller bites on her buttocks, but thankfully the pressure of her weight sitting on the nest had killed most of them.

She's slipped into a coma, and even with all the units they have in stock injected into her, she does not come round OR loosen her grip on my hand. This is not good.

"You know Ange, if you hadn't been so quick off the mark and sucked the majority of poison out of her before you got here, then we'd be looking at a very different story. She's very lucky to have you as a friend."

"That's not how it feels doctor."

They don't even try to prise us apart, not that I would have let them. We take off into the rising sun. I can see Jules standing in the dust vortex, looking up at us, hands in prayer position over her mouth.

"We'll meet you at the hospital."

I'm not sure she can hear me over the propellers. I have this horrible feeling in my gut and know how serious this life or death situation is. I feel sick.

"Come on Lesley, you got this. I love you."

She's one tough cookie, if anyone can pull this miracle off, she can. My tears continue to spill over her still, sweet, angelic, face.

JULES

I'm in shock as I watch the plane take off and leave me on the airstrip in a cloud of red dust and debris. What the feck just happened? I'd best pack Gertie and wait here until I hear where they're taking her and go and join them later. Whether Ange knows it or not, she managed to stay calm in an emergency and quite literally saved Lesley's life. It doesn't bear thinking what might have happened had she not been there and acted so fast. Well, aside from taking a piss on her that is, not sure that was necessary. Whose needs were being met there I wonder? I hope Lesley pulls through.

ANGE

We take off as the sun is beginning to rise, and if I hadn't been a tad occupied, I may have enjoyed it better. We seem to fly for hours and hours, finally landing at the hospital where a team is already there to meet us. Lesley is whisked off in one direction and I am taken to a cubicle where I'm asked to lie on the bed and give more blood. It's exhausting. I'm not sure how much they take, but I do feel shaky, light-headed and dizzy. They give me a cup of tea and some buttered toast and eventually someone comes through and tells me there's a family room beside the intensive care unit where I can wait for news on my sister. I don't correct him.

"Intensive care unit?? How is she?"

"We'll let you know as soon as we have something to tell you. We're making her comfortable right now and I'm sure you'll get in to see her soon."

I curl up into a wee ball on the two-seater love seat and close my eyes. I'm gently shaken awake by a doctor and nurse standing at my side.

"Where am I? How is she?"

"It was touch and go for a while as she took a really bad, adverse reaction to the venom. I heard what you did."

"I know, I know, I feel dreadful, I should have got rid of them."

"Thankfully, you must have got rid of most of the poison from her, as her system wouldn't have been able to take much more poison and was already beginning to shut down when you got to her. Much more and we'd be having a very different conversation right now. She's one very, very lucky lady to have a sister like you who was not only on hand, but able and willing to do what you did, at the risk of poisoning herself at the same time."

"You gave five units of your blood in four hours and that's considered a massive transfusion. So be easy and kind on yourself. The swelling on your lips seems to have gone down a bit, but I'll get the nurse here to take a look and give you some cream and pills for the pain."

I hadn't even noticed my lips, but as soon as he mentions them, I can see my top lip almost touching the tip of my nose. I gingerly touch them, they're stretched to their limits. In fact I'm surprised they haven't begun to split and are hot, pulsing and throbbing. Fuck it hurts.

"I'll take whatever you got. Bring the medication trolley in, pour the entire lot down my gullet, inject it directly into my heart, do what it takes to make me look Like Jennifer Anniston"

"Not sure I have enough here for that. Joke"

"Very funny, but I wouldn't give up your day job just yet. Do I look like one of those proboscis monkeys chattering away here?"

"I wouldn't say that. Maybe a saiga antelope. You can get in to see your sister as soon as we get you sorted."

I'm sure he winks at me as he leaves the room. What is it with Australians and winking? After being given some pain medication, cream, more tea and toast. I am taken through to see Lesley. My excitement soon disappears when I see this tiny wee frail soul in the bed, hooked up to blinking, beeping machines.

"Oh no, look at her? Are you sure she'll be okay?"

"She's had a rough few hours, but she's stable right now. We've sedated her for the time being. Your sister's quite the fighter."

"Yes, she is."

"She is so lucky that you're family and have the same blood group. So very, very lucky, it's not a common blood group. Sit with her and talk to her, she can hopefully hear you. I'll leave you to it and come back shortly to check on you both. I'm outside at the station if you need me."

"Thank you."

I pull a seat up beside her bed, take her hand, kiss the back of it and begin to chat to her. She's a captivated audience and a great listener, so I tell her everything. How my dad died, how I miss him, how my mum is an alcoholic, how my brother and I are estranged. I lay it all out before her. My hopes, my dreams, my visions, my insecurities, my fears, everything. No stone uncovered. No holds barred. Eventually, completely drained, I rest my head on her chest and close my eyes. I'm not sure how long I sleep for, but as I begin to stir, I can feel my arm and hand have cramped and my back is throbbing due to the buckled position I'm in. Before I lift my head I feel a tightening of sorts, a squeeze through my aching right hand. I look up to see one of the most beautiful things in the world, Lesley is looking down at me, blinking, a faint smile on her face. I jump up, almost yanking all the drip lines out of her arm. I lean over and kiss her forehead.

LESLEY

I blink my eyes against the light and try to focus on where I am. Machines, bright lights, beeping and humming sounds, a green robe. I know this picture well enough, a hospital. Wait, what?? It all comes back to me in moving snapshots. Me giving it to Ange both barrels then going to the toilet where I must have forgotten to check under the toilet seat before sitting. Why did I not check? Rookie mistake. I can only think that I'd assumed Ange had done it when she'd gone and it was all clear. To my peril, I might add. I remember feeling a searing pain on my backside and knew I had made one of the biggest mistakes of my life. I must have fallen out of the cubicle and screamed for help. Now, only flashbacks, seeing Ange over the top of me. Did she really try to pee on me? Funny. Jules, Gertie careering round the side of the donger. Hoisted into the back. Did she really suck my backside? Doctor, plane and now here. I can just about make out the top of Ange's curly auburn hair resting on my chest. She is definitely a sight for sore eyes, maybe I have been a bit too tough on her. I squeeze her hand and she awakes.

"That's another fine mess you got me into."

"I'm so sorry. I'm so, so sorry. I saw the spiders under the seat Lesley, but didn't want to kill them, so I left them there. It didn't even cross my mind that's where you were going when you flounced off. I was too busy licking my own wounds after your lecture."

"I know, I'm sorry"

"Don't be, I deserve it. I was trying to absorb the sting in my tail from your words, never expecting you were about to get a sting in your tail, when I heard you scream."
She smiled.

"Look it doesn't matter. What matters is that you risked your life to save mine and I am and will always be eternally thankful and grateful for that."

"Naw, anyone would have done it."

My tears fall in a constant stream on her blonde locks that I have combed lovingly since I took up position at her bedside. She'd have been mortified if I hadn't. I held a straw to her dry lips while she drank some water from a cup. She looks at me and continues in a dry, croaky voice.

"No, not everyone. You saved my life Ange, and it makes me smile to think that you kissed my ass to do it."

"Yup, I've never been much of a big suck-up till then."

We both laugh and I climb into the bed, untangling and moving wires to lie down beside her. I feel so relieved and grateful she is alive.

"If I can change, I will."

"Naw, don't do that. That would be too cheesy at this stage. Being yourself in a world that is constantly trying to mould you into something you're not is an accomplishment in itself. You be you."

"That's quite profound. Did you just make that up?"

"No, Ralph Waldo Emmerson did."

"I'm impressed you got it right. If you did that is."

Och, shut up you!"

I notice a huge swelling through my left sock, a giant tennis ball-sized carbuncle on the top of my foot. I reach down to stroke it and notice that it's soft and squishy. I put my hand inside my sock and remove a pair of Hello Kitty knickers that must have got entangled in the wash and got inside my sock.

"Yours, I believe."

"Please tell me you didn't travel all this way to return these."

"It's not easy being purr-fect, but you have to do what you have to do and I think now is the right time to return them."

"They look like they've been through the mill."

"There is a story attached to them, but I'll save that for when you're feline stronger."

"I'm not sure I'm ever going to be ready for that."

"Perhaps not."

We both must have dozed off as when I wake the light is streaming in through the blinds. Lesley is lying beside me still sleeping gently, her Hello Kitty knickers balled up in her wee fist. I gently wipe her brow, kiss her again on the forehead and tuck her in. She begins to stir.

"Hey sleepy head, fancy something to eat that's not tea and toast?"

"Oh yes, please, I'm ravished."

"Ha, I'm fam… ravished too."

I leap off the bed, bound out of the room, a spring in my step, a smile on my face and a twinkle in my eye. She's alive and going to pull through. All is good in the world today. Ahh, what a life. Thank you for a brand new, never lived before day.

JULES

After days of driving practically non-stop, I finally arrive at the hospital they'd told me she'd been taken to. I'm told that Lesley is out of intensive care and recovering nicely. Her sister hasn't left her side since they arrived.

"Wait? What? Intensive care. Sister??"

She doesn't have a sister. Do they mean the nurse on duty?

"Yeah, if it hadn't been for her sister having the same blood group, then it would have been more serious than it already is. She needed a blood transfusion and pints of it."

The nurse ushers me to a private room off the general ward. I know without even asking that Ange must have paid for this. I gingerly open the door, not knowing what the hell I'm going to see. Nothing could have prepared me though for what I witness before my eyes. Ange and Lesley are lying in the same bed, together, yes, you heard it right, in bed together. At first, I think that maybe I've drunk too much coffee on the road, as I haven't slept in days and could quite easily be in a delusional state. Maybe it's a hallucination. They both sit up when I walk in, still holding each other and, dare I say, laughing together.

"Jules?"

"What the hell is going on?"

"You look like a bag of shite. What took you so long? You clearly haven't stopped at a spa before you got here."

"Ho di ho Ange. Never mind me, how are you Lesley?"

"I'm on the mend, thanks to Ange here. She saved my life."

"Let's not exaggerate things. Okey, let's. I saved her life."

"I've been worried sick. I've been driving for days, only stopping for petrol and pees. I've hardly slept. You can tell by the Gucci bags under my eyes."

"Don't flatter yourself, more like Primark bags. Wait? Days?"

"Yes, days and days."

"Where are we? I've never even thought to ask."

"What do you mean, where are you? There's only a few hospitals that carry the amount of antivenom that Lesley needed, so you were flown here."

"Where?"

"Where?"

We say in unison.

"Sydney of course. You're in Sydney. This hospital here in Sydney was the closest and the only one that had the 12 vials you needed. That's a huge amount of antivenom apparently. Where did you think you were?"

"Yahooo, we've done it. High five all round."

"Done what exactly?"

"Got you back to Sydney."

"Why is it so important I ask myself?"

"Eh, cos it's Christmas and apparently the decorations on Bondage Beach are to die for. When you're up for it, we'll wheel you down to see them."

"Eh, okay, but not sure we needed to come all this way to see some Christmas tat. You seem overly excited, Ange. You didn't plant those spiders, did you?"
"How could you think such a thing? Mind you, good idea though, if I'd known in advance they were going to fly you here though I might have."

"Oh, shut up!"

"I can't believe our luck. We're back in Sydney, we've done it and you're here. In relatively good shape as well, only a few minor scrapes, bruises and scars to show for it."

LESLEY

Not sure why Ange and Jules are quite so excited we're back in Sydney. I smell a possum, but am happy to go along with it, like I have a choice in the matter. For the time being that is.

ANGE

Although Lesley is out of the woods, she has a long road of recovery ahead of her.

"You're still really weak and need care which I'm happy to provide, at a price you understand. Joke!! It's free of charge, all done out of the goodness of my very kind heart."

LESLEY

"Steady Ange, all this kindness, generosity and niceness is beginning to unnerve me."

"Look at it this way, because you have more of my blood in you than I have in me at the moment, we are practically related, almost twins in fact. That bond can never ever, ever be broken."

"Double trouble."

"Speak for yourself. We can be triplets though, we can let the ugly one go get Gertie to take us out for a spin. We'll keep her around in case we need spare parts."

"The three amigos, a male fantasy right here in the making."

"Perhaps not always living up to the male fantasy."

"You're on thin ground, Ange."

"It's Ic ground, it is."

ANGE

Christmas Eve rolls round fairly quickly and the big reveal is imminent. Jules is off to get Gertie while I get Lesley in her wheelchair. She's coming on leaps and bounds, well not quite leaps or bounds, but you get my gist. Seriously, Jules and I have worked so hard to keep all this a secret and today's the day. We're heading to Bondage Beach to see the decorations, get some fresh air, sun and sea breeze on our skin. It's all planned to the minutest detail. What can possibly go wrong?

JULES

I get Gertie while Ange puts Lesley in a wheelchair. We manage to get her straight into the back and bungee strap the chair down on either side. She has the perfect seat, right in the middle in the back of the van.

"Not quite so fast Jules, we have some precious cargo in the back."

"Don't teach your granny how to suck eggs."

"Hey, listen, if there's any sucking to be done, it's got to come from Ange."

"Yeah Lesley, I'm The Queen of Sucks."

The bungee cords are not great, and by the time we get to the beach, Lesley has tipped out and is splayed out on the mattress. No matter what they say, my driving is not to blame. Ange hadn't secured her in properly enough.

"Girls, girls, no need to fight, I'm fine, seriously, I'm fine. Smells divine down here. Not! What the hell has this mattress been through? On second thoughts, don't answer that."

Regardless, we are exactly where we need to be, and it's perfect timing. It's a beautiful evening, the sky is clear and the sun is about to set. It's going to be like a scene from a movie. Let's go with Titanic without the wreck. We just have to get her over the sand and down to the water's edge.

"Fuck, pushing a wheelchair through the sand is not as easy as it looks."

"I'm fine here girls. I can watch the sunset from the comfort of my very own personal chair up here on the pommade. Leave me here, you go down to the water's edge."

"NO!!"

"NO!!"

Ange and I are pushing her at a 45-degree angle through the sand and we seem to be getting deeper and deeper. Soon Lesley is going to be buried neck-deep in Bondi's finest grit.

"One final push. After three. One, two..."

Ange doesn't wait for my command and launches all her weight into the back of the chair, projecting Lesley out and head first into a sandcastle. We pull her head from the turret and brush off most of the sand and shells from her hair and face.

"Nice shell suit Lesley, glad you're making the effort."

Her nostrils are clogged with it though.

ANGE

FUCK, I can see the boat coming from the west across the horizon and know I only have minutes to get her down there.

"Grab her head and shoulders Jules."

I grab her legs, leave the wheelchair where it is and start to run, stumbling, half-dragging, half-carrying Lesley down to the shore.

"You're not pulling your weight here Jules."

"You take the head end then, it's heavier than the legs."

Not quite the romantic reunion we had envisioned or planned.

"Leave me here girls, I can see the sunset fine from here."

"We leave no man, woman, child or nurses behind, only wheelchairs."

"But, I'm slowing you down, go on without me."

I can see the boat circling just offshore.

"Fuck that!"

I heave her over my shoulder in a fireman's lift and start for the water's edge. The sand is so bloody hot that I have to jump from towel to towel, not even caring if anyone is on it.

"Cause something ain't right, you gotta do it right, come on, if you make sure you're connected, the writings on the wall, but if your mind's neglected, stumble you might fall, stumble you might fall."

Jules is bringing up the rear, dragging the wheelchair in my wake.

"Made it!"

"Here, you can get back in your chair."

"It's beautiful, thank you."

"Check that boat out Lesley. Can you see it?"

"Yes, the one with the people on it? Must be a party boat."

"Looks like some kind of celebration, don't you think?"

"Someone has just belly flopped into the water and is swimming in this direction."

"Hmm, kinda reminds me of that movie where the silhouette of Daniel Craig wearing a skintight pair of sky blue swimmers, his tanned, toned six-pack glistening in the sun, his pecs and muscular arms wet, sea salt stained, emerges from the surf."

"You have a vivid imagination Ange, the vision I behold isn't quite as glamorous."

"Perhaps you need a leap of faith here Lesley."

"Big leap Jules, all I see is a pasty, flabby smonstrosity, far less defined than the image you describe."

Unfortunately, my eyes do not deceive me. He is wearing sky blue trunks however. Look, look, he's carrying something under his arm. Don't look now, but he's coming this way."

"All because the lady loves Milk Tray."

LESLEY

I can hardly believe my ears. Mikey? My Mikey, here?

"No!"

I get up, run towards him, meeting him halfway and launch myself at him, actually throw myself at him without gay abandon. He grabs me, picks me up in his safe, strong muscular arms and spins me round. At the same time, a breaking wave lifts us both off our feet and unceremoniously dumps us at Jules's and Ange's feet.

"I thought you were Daniel Craig, but this is so much better."

We both lie in the water, being swept by the continuous ebb and flow of the waves. I don't care. My Mikey, here, now, with me. I could cry. Actually, I am crying. I can't stop kissing him.

"My real-life Shite in Nineing Order. My love, my hero."

"Daniel Craig?? After all…This is the end, hold your breath and count to ten…."

THE BEGINNING OF THE END

The problem and/or relief at finishing "One In The Bush" is that you'll never really know what happens to them after they all go to New Zealand together. …Or will you?

K G Cooper

DIRTY GERTIE - In The Bush

GLOSSARY

I have included a partial glossary for the non-Scot / non-Doric / non-Australian readers amongst us.

Doric is a Scottish dialect spoken in the North East of Scotland commonly heard around Aberdeen city, Aberdeenshire and Moray. The term 'Doric' is thought to come from the Greek for 'rural' or 'rustic' perhaps due to its strong associations with the farming and fishing communities of the region. There is an extensive body of literature, poetry, ballads and songs from the North East. In the Disney animation 'Brave', a character speaks Doric and there's a running joke that nobody can understand him. Visitors to this part of the world will be hard pushed to glean what's being heard. Although Doric is the traditional dialect of the North East, don't worry, we do all speak English…. of a fashion

1. Irn Bru - Scottish carbonated soft drink, often described as "Scotland's other national drink".
2. Foof - A much less vulgar, more acceptable alternate word for the female genital area.
3. Fizzog - A person's face or expression.
4. Ca' canny - To go carefully or slowly; to take care.
5. Fa's looking at you onyway quine - Who's looking at you anyway girl/lass.
6. Stappit - Scots for "stuffed full
7. Fa's clocking- Who's looking
8. Wee - Small, tiny
9. Barf – Vomit
10. Loos - Toilet, restrooms
11. Foosty - Smelling moldy or stale, Decaying
12. Cattywampus- Crooked; awry

13. Wee jobby - Small poop, Faeces ; a piece of excrement.

14. Bung - An advance of money

15. Chook - Australian slang for chicken

16. Weegie - A native or inhabitant of Glasgow. Often used as a contemptuous form of address

17. Quaffing - drink (something, especially an alcoholic drink) heartily

18. Dunnys - (Australia, New Zealand, slang) A toilet, often outside and rudimentary. ... (Scottish and northern English, slang, dated) An outside toilet, or the passageway leading to it; (by extension) a passageway or cellar.

19. Arse - A person's buttocks or anus; a stupid, irritating, or contemptible person.

20. Donger – Penis

21. Numptie - A fool or idiot

22. Dag - Australian - an entertainingly eccentric person; a character.

23. Fair dinkum - Australian - used to emphasize or seek confirmation of the genuineness or truth of something

24. Barbie – BBQ

25. Banshee - A female spirit whose wailing warns of an impending death in a house.

26. Ragin - Angry(mainly used in Scotland)

27. Bawbag - Scots word meaning scrotum

28. Fair chuffed - To be very excited and/or impressed

29. Quine - Girl/lass

30. Foo's yer doo's? - How are you?

31. Och, nithing mair than bein drookit as I spent half the nicht oot on a park bench in the rain as ma missus chucked me oot the hoose after I'd been oot birling maist of the day and came hame stocious. It got ower caul oot yon, so aye came here to

sleep it aff. - Nothing more than being wet-through as I spent most of the night on a park bench in the rain as my wife threw me out of the house after i'd been out drinking most of the day and came home drunk. It got very cold out there, so I came here to sleep it off.

32. Ach, dinna fash yersel, she'll tak ye back in wi open arms the day. A wee bunch o flooers widnae gang amiss though. Don't worry, she'll take you back with open arms. A small bunch of flowers wouldn't go amiss though.

33. Och haud yer weesht ye crabbit auld bag. - Be quiet you grumpy, old man

34. Ha ha, yer feil lass, noo, git oan wi it bonnie quine. - You're crazy girl, now, off you go, you beautiful girl.

https://media.scotslanguage.com/library/document/RGU_Doric_Dictionary.pdf

www.oneinthebush.com (Under Construction)

Audiobook (Coming soon)

Audiobook with a 'live' audience, also known as a Podcast, (In the works)

Other people's misfortunes are and have always been my gain, so if you have a funny, laugh out loud story that you'd like to share, then please email it to;

OneInTheBushDownunder@gmail.com